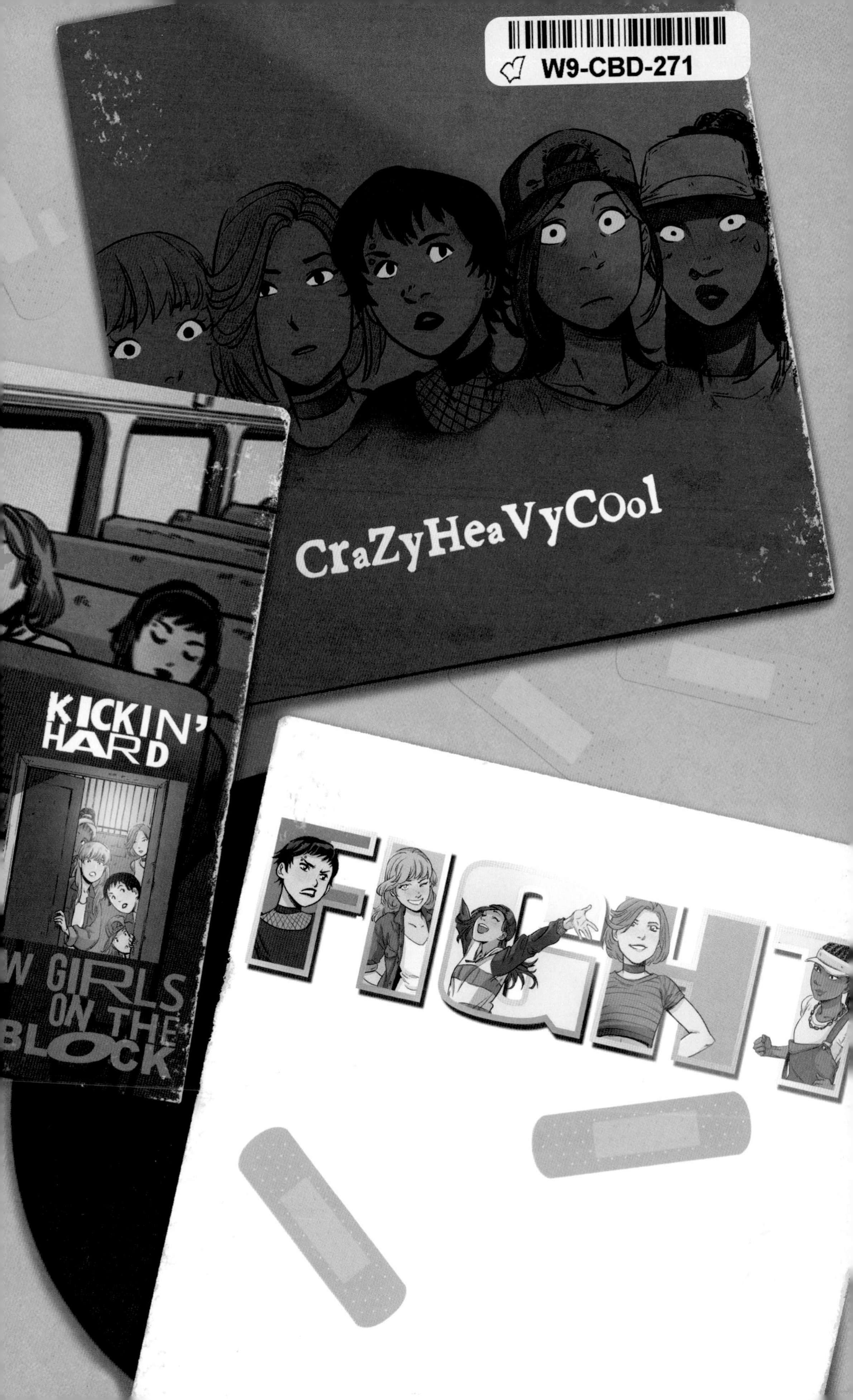
CraZyHeaVyCOol
KICKIN' HARD
W GIRLS ON THE BLOCK
FIGHT

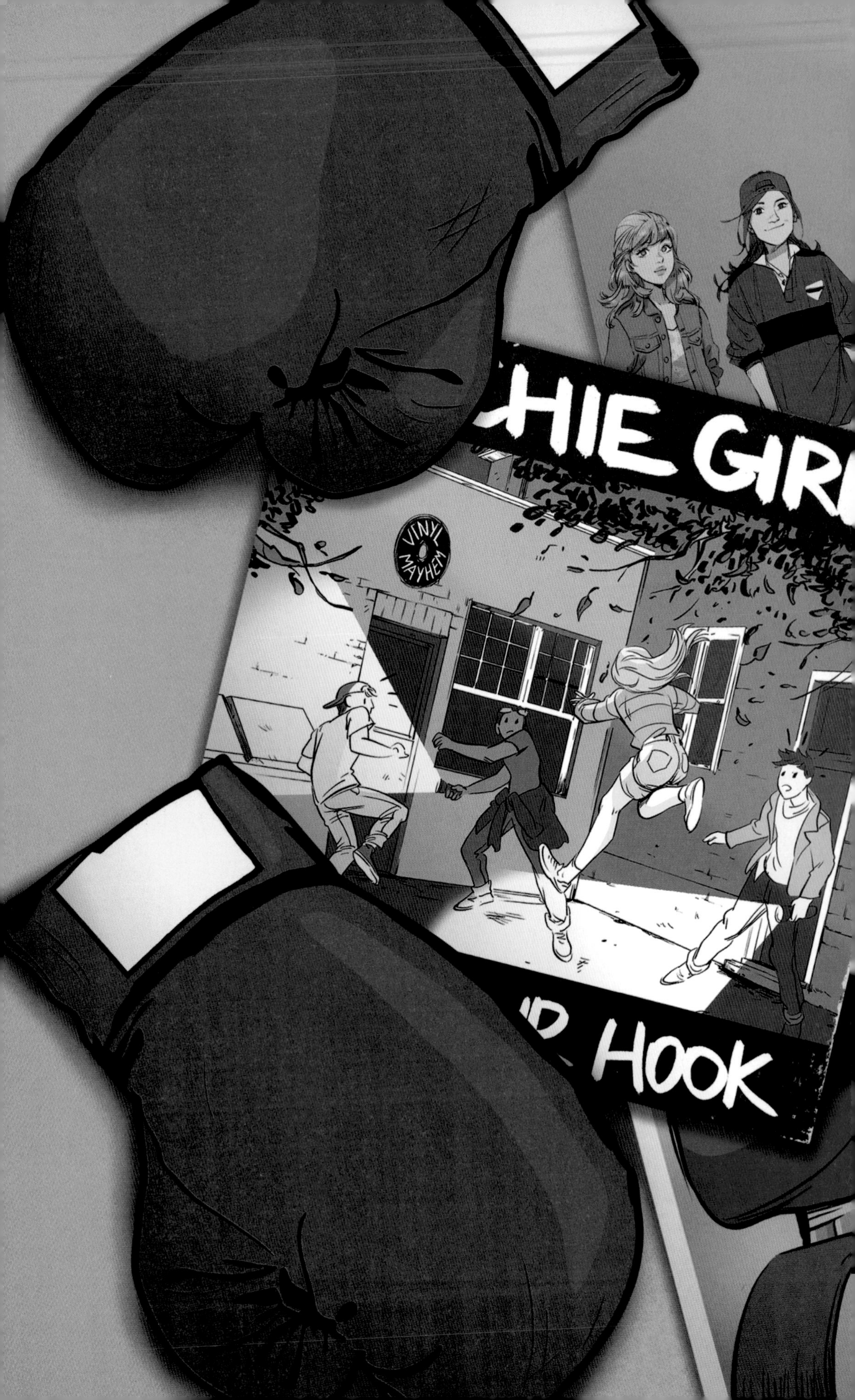
HIE GIR
VINYL MAYHEM
HOOK

SWAMPSCOTT PUBLIC LIBRARY

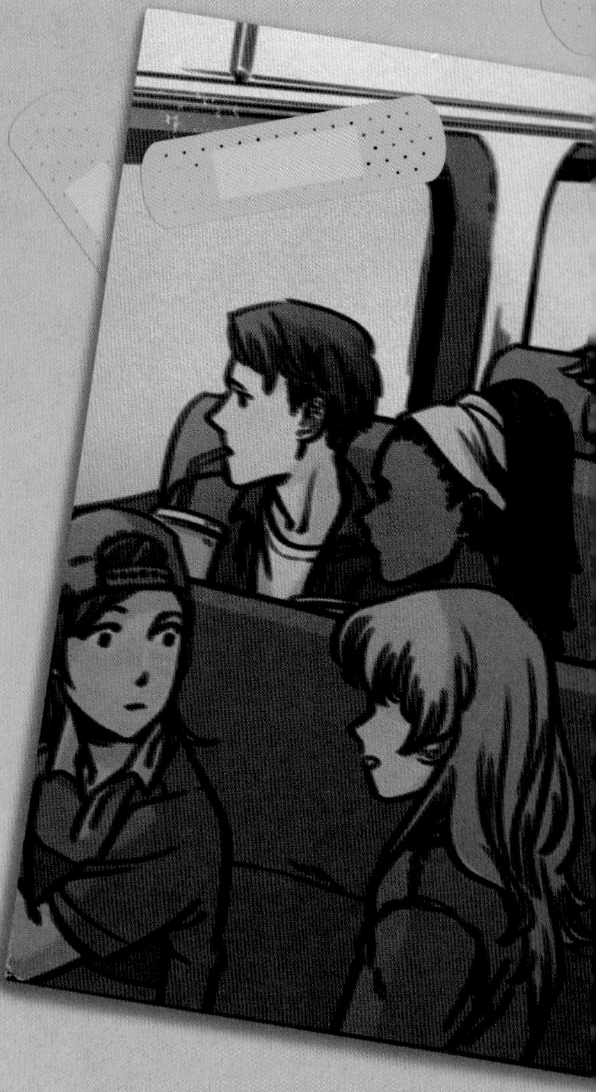

BOOM! BOX™

HEAVY VINYL: RIOT ON THE RADIO, September 2018. Published by BOOM! Box, a division of Boom Entertainment, Inc. Heavy Vinyl is ™ and © 2018 Scheme Machine Studios, LLC. Originally published in single magazine form as HI-FI FIGHT CLUB No. 1-3, HEAVY VINYL No. 4. ™ and © 2017 Scheme Machine Studios, LLC. All rights reserved. BOOM! Box™ and the BOOM! Box logo are trademarks of Boom Entertainment, Inc., registered in various countries and categories. All characters, events and institutions depicted herein are fictional. Any similarity between the names, characters, persons, events and/or institutions in this publication to actual names, characters, and persons whether living or dead, events, and/or institutions is unintentional and purely coincidental. BOOM! Box does not read or accept unsolicited submissions of ideas, stories, or artwork.

For information regarding the CPSIA on this printed material, call: (203) 595-3636 and provide reference #RICH - 813554.

BOOM! Studios, 5670 Wilshire Boulevard, Suite 400, Los Angeles, CA 90036-5679. Printed in USA. Second Printing.

ISBN: 978-1-68415-141-7, eISBN: 978-1-61398-880-0

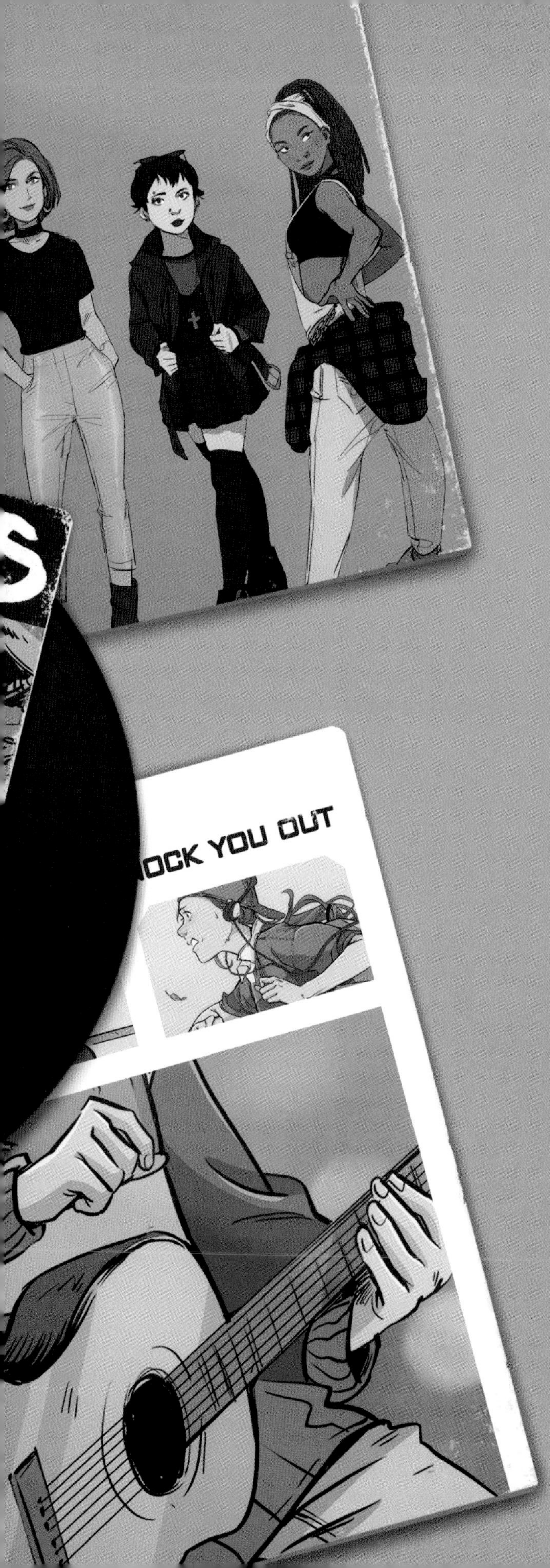
OCK YOU OUT

Created & Written by
Carly Usdin

Penciled by
Nina Vakueva

Inked by
Irene Flores

Colored by
Rebecca Nalty
with **Kieran Quigley**
& Walter Baiamonte
(chapter 4)

Lettered by
Jim Campbell

Cover by
Nina Vakueva

Design by
Marie Krupina

Logo design by
Marie Krupina
& Kelsey Dieterich

Assistant Editor
Sophie Philips-Roberts

Editor
Shannon Watters

CHAPTER ONE

...nds,
...there for
...our guidance.
...olved in Jurassic
...s and Tilt for letting us join
... the best label, Imaginary Selves!!
...ve our I.S. family!!

ROSIE RIOT would like to thank her idols:
Cinder, Shirley, Gwen, Poe, Joan, Kay, Skin,
Kathleen, Carrie and Corin, for showing her
the way.

CHARLIE would like to thank pizza for
always getting him through the day.

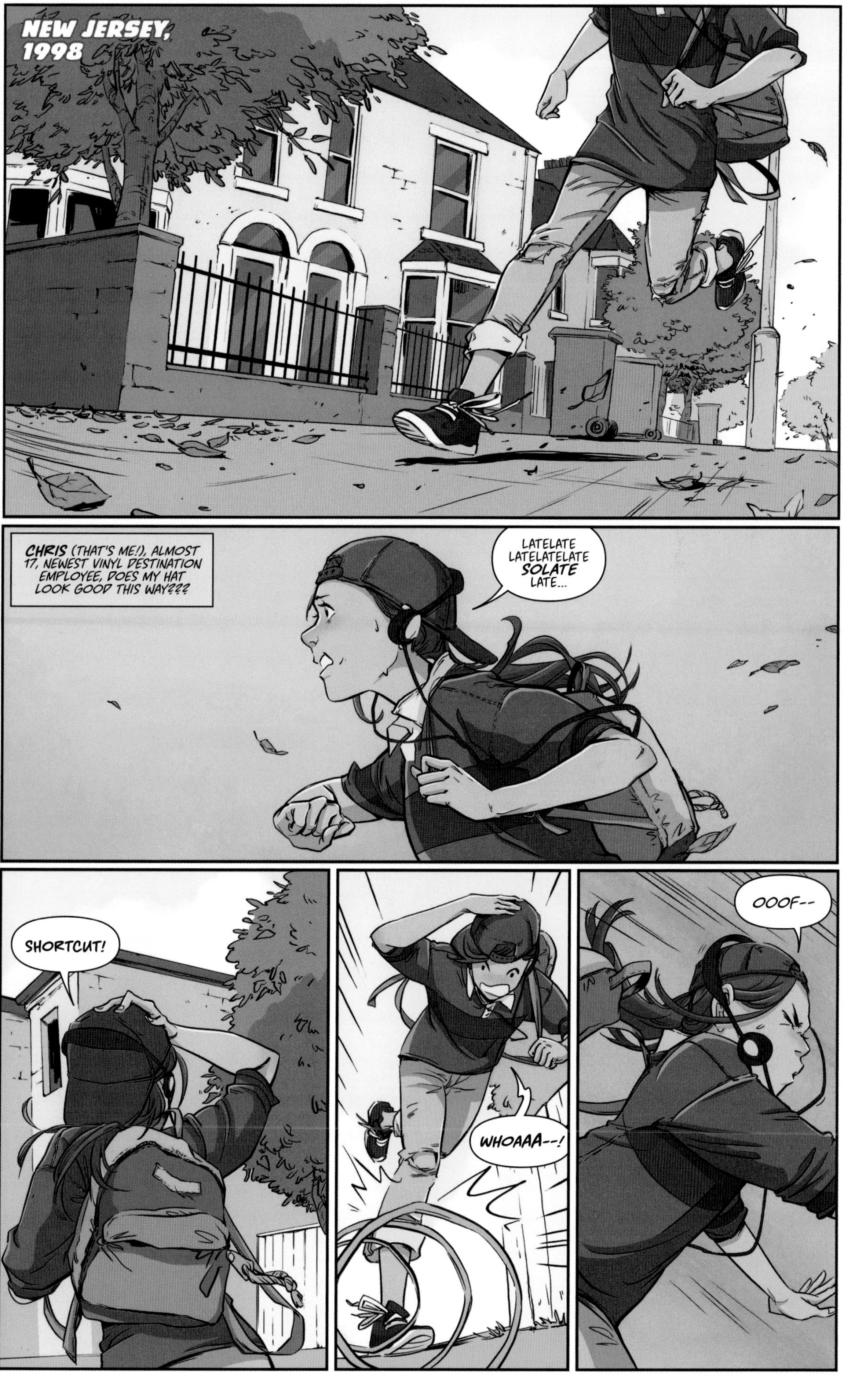
NEW JERSEY, 1998
CHRIS (THAT'S ME!), ALMOST 17, NEWEST VINYL DESTINATION EMPLOYEE, DOES MY HAT LOOK GOOD THIS WAY???
LATELATE LATELATELATE SOLATE LATE...
SHORTCUT!
WHOAAA--!
OOOF--

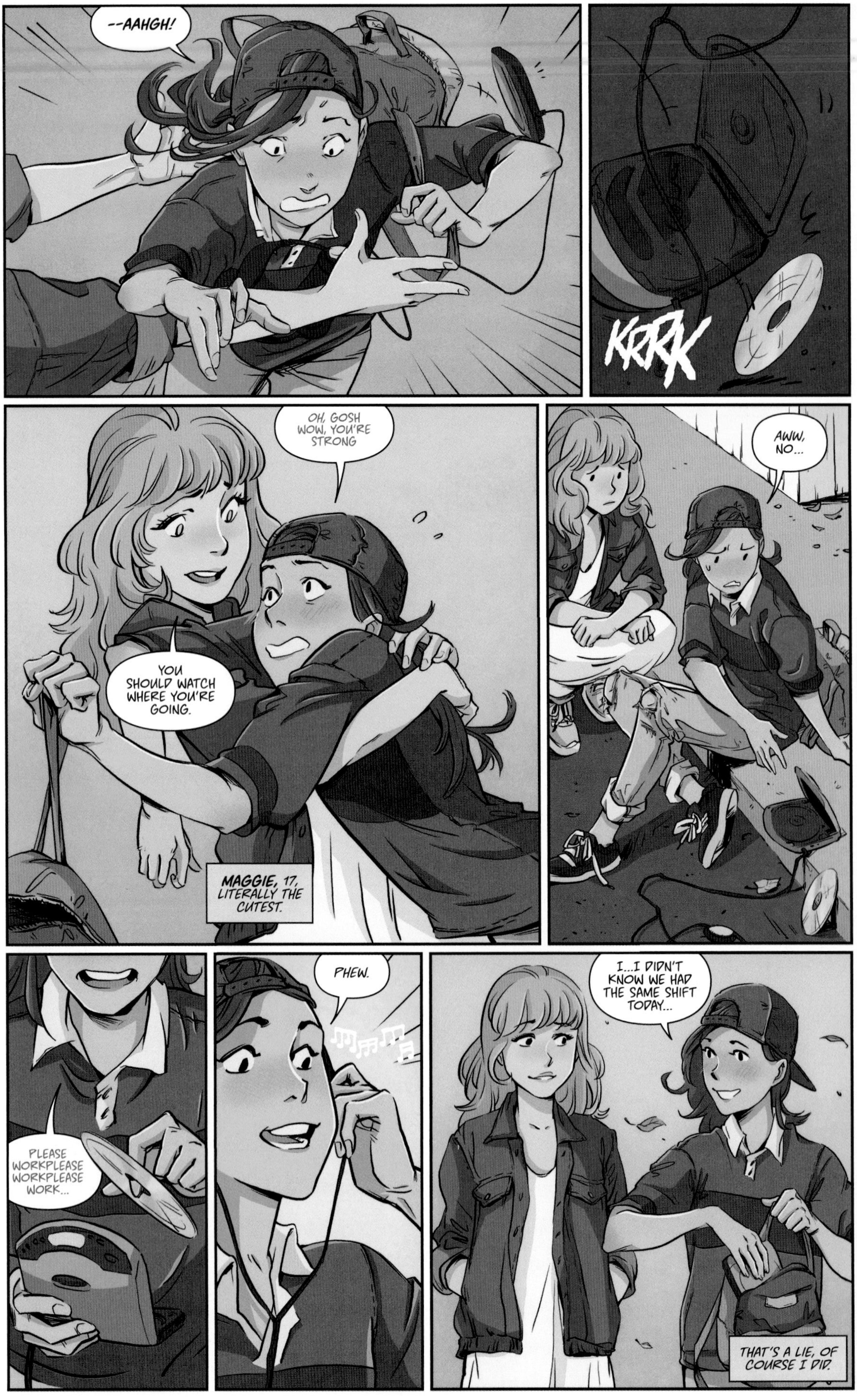
--AAHGH!
KRRK
OH, GOSH WOW, YOU'RE STRONG
YOU SHOULD WATCH WHERE YOU'RE GOING.
MAGGIE, 17, LITERALLY THE CUTEST.
AWW, NO...
PLEASE WORKPLEASE WORKPLEASE WORK...
PHEW.
I...I DIDN'T KNOW WE HAD THE SAME SHIFT TODAY...
THAT'S A LIE, OF COURSE I DID.

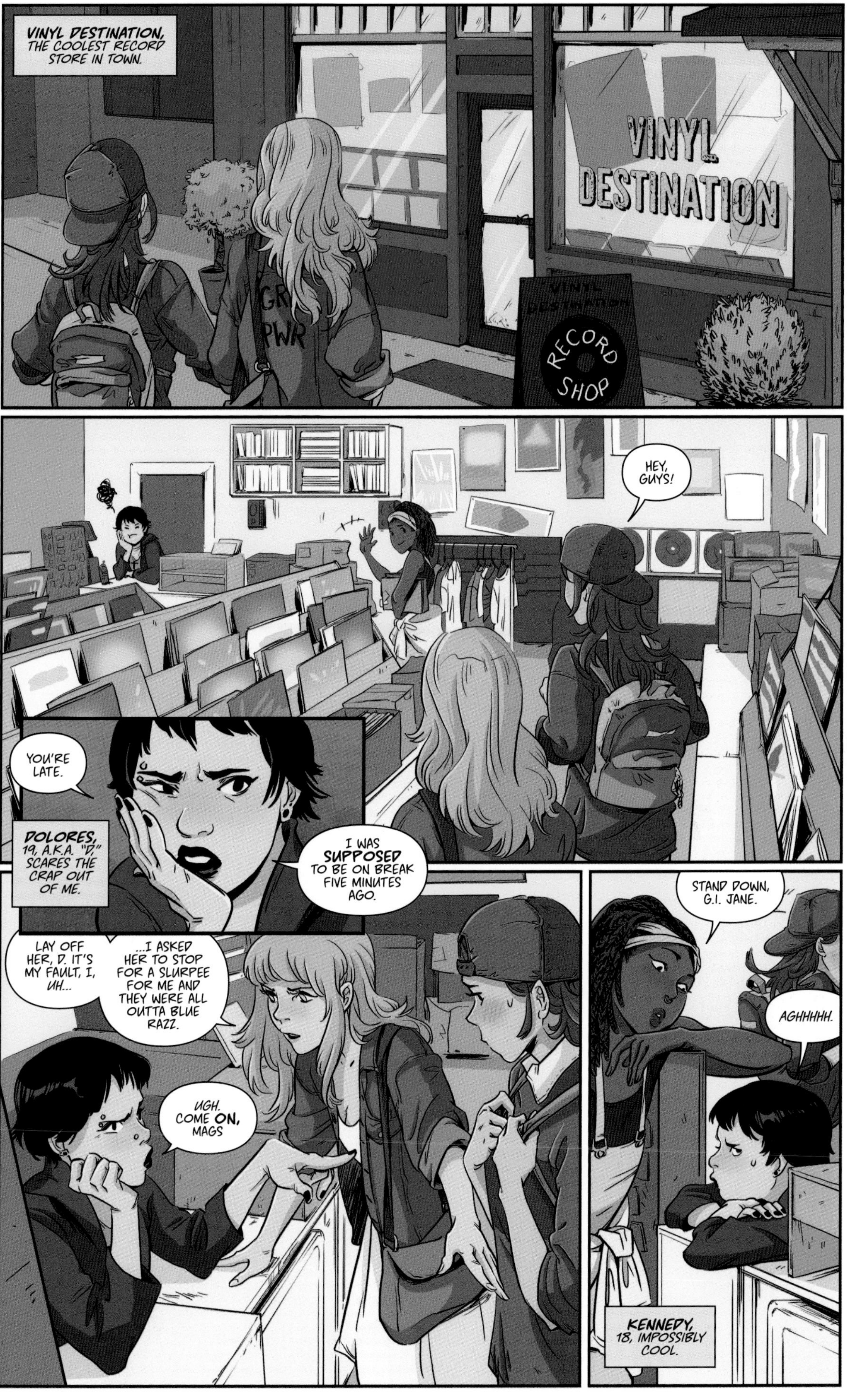
VINYL DESTINATION, THE COOLEST RECORD STORE IN TOWN.
VINYL DESTINATION
GRL PWR
VINYL DESTINATION
RECORD SHOP
HEY, GUYS!
YOU'RE LATE.
DOLORES, 19, A.K.A. "D" SCARES THE CRAP OUT OF ME.
I WAS SUPPOSED TO BE ON BREAK FIVE MINUTES AGO.
LAY OFF HER, D. IT'S MY FAULT, I, UH...
...I ASKED HER TO STOP FOR A SLURPEE FOR ME AND THEY WERE ALL OUTTA BLUE RAZZ.
UGH. COME ON, MAGS
STAND DOWN, G.I. JANE.
AGHHHHH.
KENNEDY, 18, IMPOSSIBLY COOL.

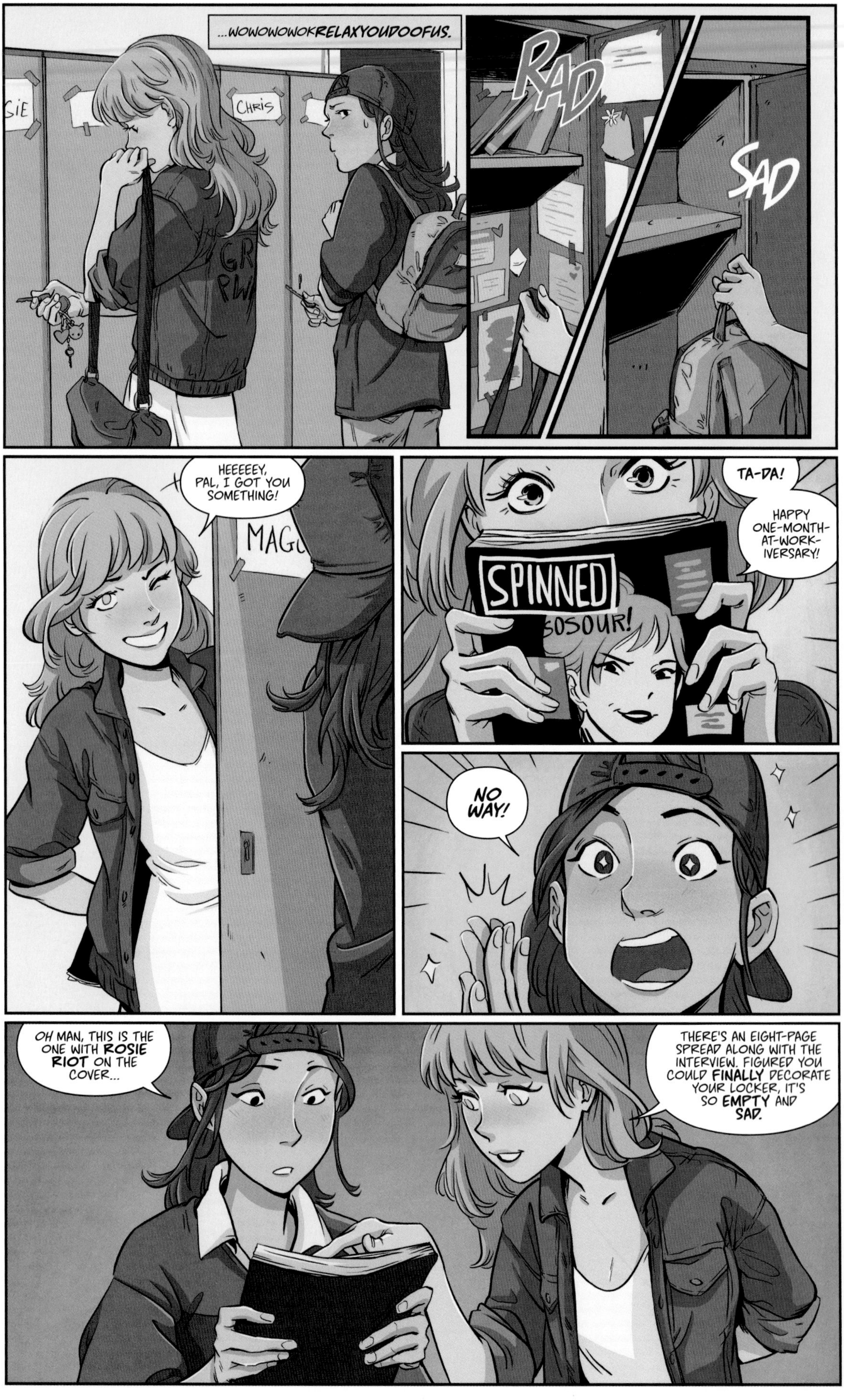

...WOWOWOWOKRELAXYOUDOOFUS.
GIE
CHRIS
RAD
SAD
HEEEEEY, PAL, I GOT YOU SOMETHING!
MAG
TA-DA!
HAPPY ONE-MONTH-AT-WORK-IVERSARY!
SPINNED
SOSOUR!
NO WAY!
OH MAN, THIS IS THE ONE WITH ROSIE RIOT ON THE COVER...
THERE'S AN EIGHT-PAGE SPREAD ALONG WITH THE INTERVIEW. FIGURED YOU COULD FINALLY DECORATE YOUR LOCKER, IT'S SO EMPTY AND SAD.

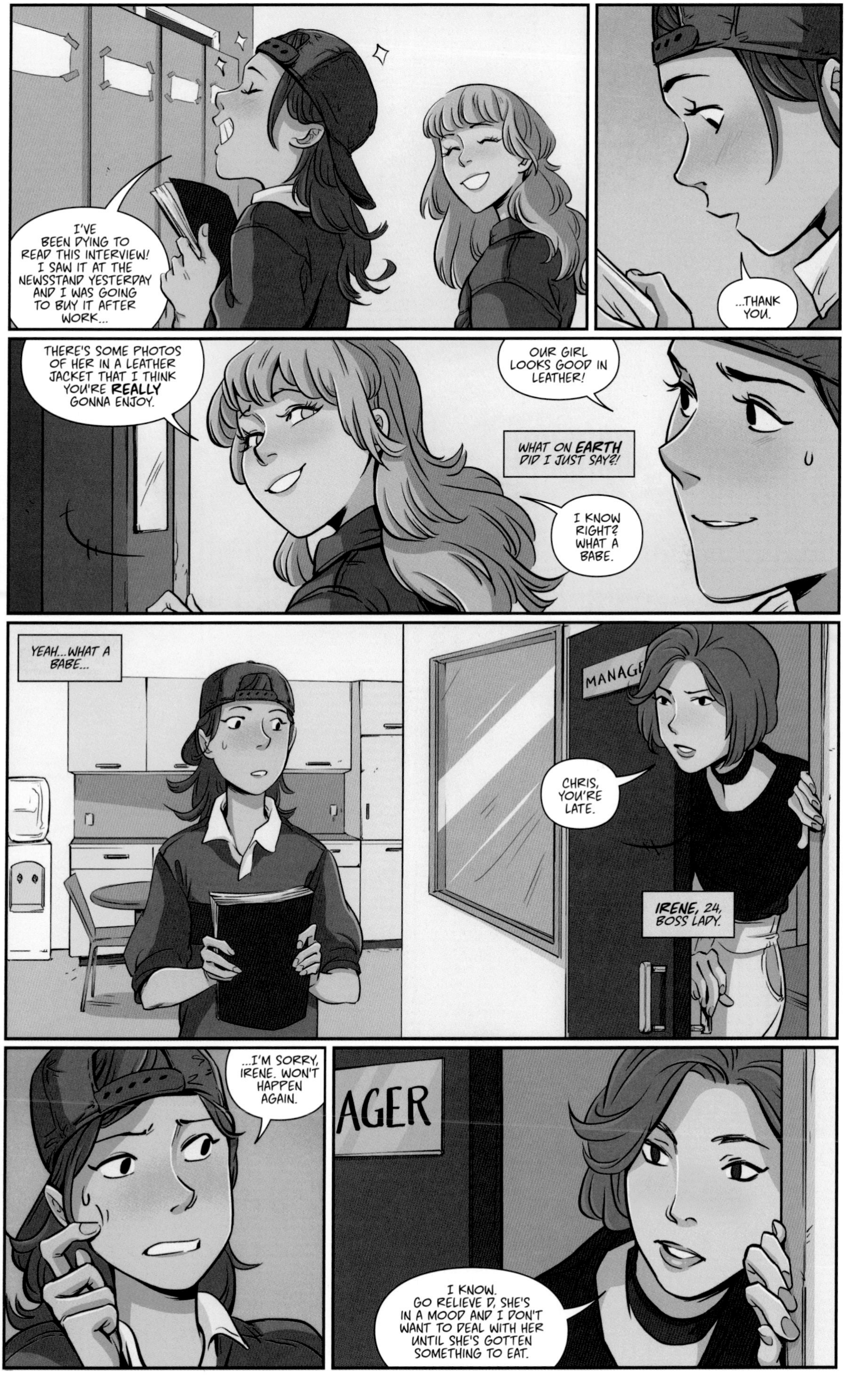
I'VE BEEN DYING TO READ THIS INTERVIEW! I SAW IT AT THE NEWSSTAND YESTERDAY AND I WAS GOING TO BUY IT AFTER WORK...
...THANK YOU.
THERE'S SOME PHOTOS OF HER IN A LEATHER JACKET THAT I THINK YOU'RE **REALLY** GONNA ENJOY.
OUR GIRL LOOKS GOOD IN LEATHER!
WHAT ON **EARTH** DID I JUST SAY?!
I KNOW RIGHT? WHAT A BABE.
YEAH...WHAT A BABE...
MANAGE
CHRIS, YOU'RE LATE.
IRENE, 24, BOSS LADY.
...I'M SORRY, IRENE. WON'T HAPPEN AGAIN.
AGER
I KNOW. GO RELIEVE D, SHE'S IN A MOOD AND I DON'T WANT TO DEAL WITH HER UNTIL SHE'S GOTTEN SOMETHING TO EAT.

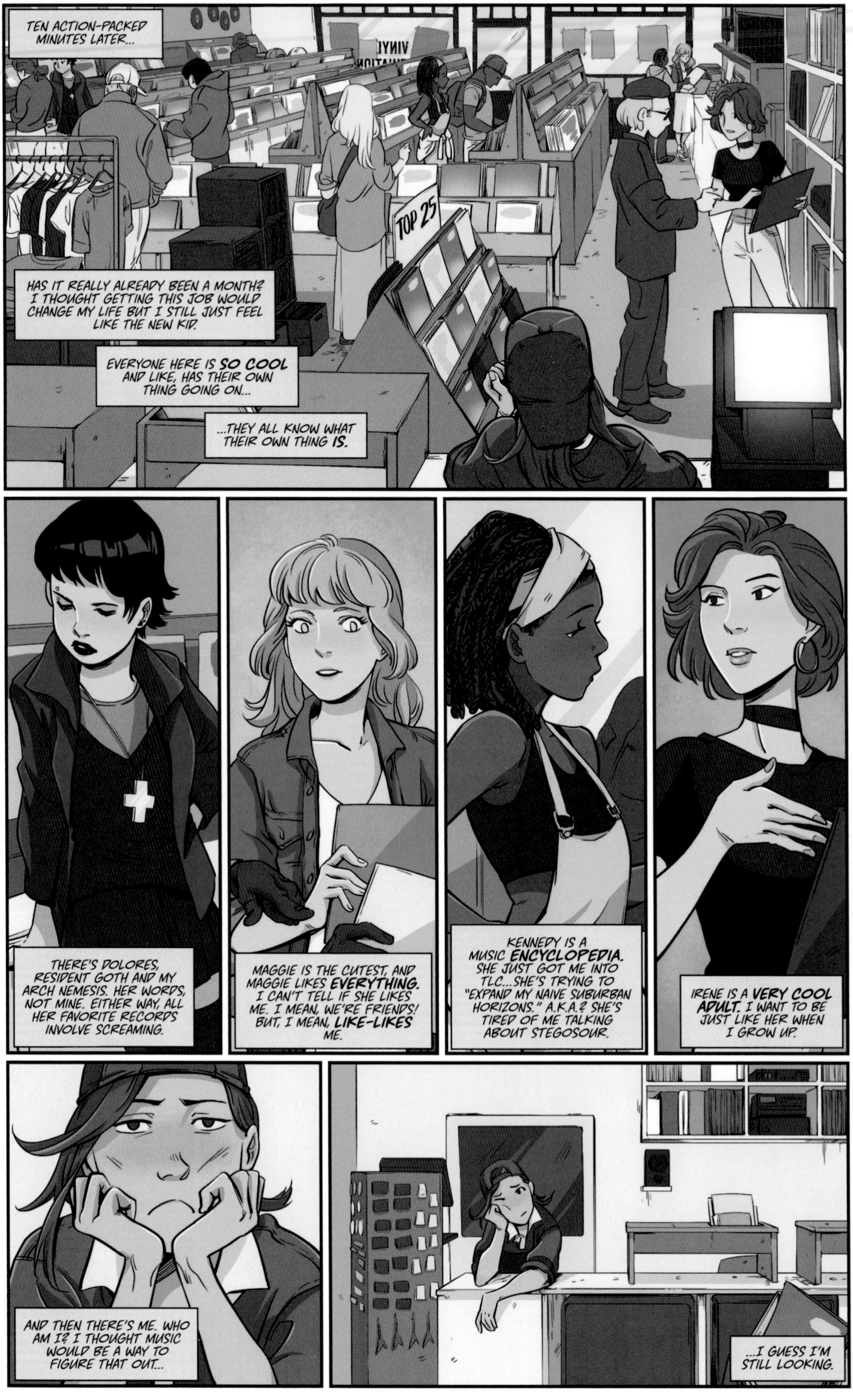
TEN ACTION-PACKED MINUTES LATER...
VINYL
TOP 25
HAS IT REALLY ALREADY BEEN A MONTH? I THOUGHT GETTING THIS JOB WOULD CHANGE MY LIFE BUT I STILL JUST FEEL LIKE THE NEW KID.
EVERYONE HERE IS SO COOL AND LIKE, HAS THEIR OWN THING GOING ON...
...THEY ALL KNOW WHAT THEIR OWN THING IS.
THERE'S DOLORES, RESIDENT GOTH AND MY ARCH NEMESIS. HER WORDS, NOT MINE. EITHER WAY, ALL HER FAVORITE RECORDS INVOLVE SCREAMING.
MAGGIE IS THE CUTEST, AND MAGGIE LIKES EVERYTHING. I CAN'T TELL IF SHE LIKES ME. I MEAN, WE'RE FRIENDS! BUT, I MEAN, LIKE-LIKES ME.
KENNEDY IS A MUSIC ENCYCLOPEDIA. SHE JUST GOT ME INTO TLC...SHE'S TRYING TO "EXPAND MY NAIVE SUBURBAN HORIZONS." A.K.A.? SHE'S TIRED OF ME TALKING ABOUT STEGOSOUR.
IRENE IS A VERY COOL ADULT. I WANT TO BE JUST LIKE HER WHEN I GROW UP.
AND THEN THERE'S ME. WHO AM I? I THOUGHT MUSIC WOULD BE A WAY TO FIGURE THAT OUT...
...I GUESS I'M STILL LOOKING.

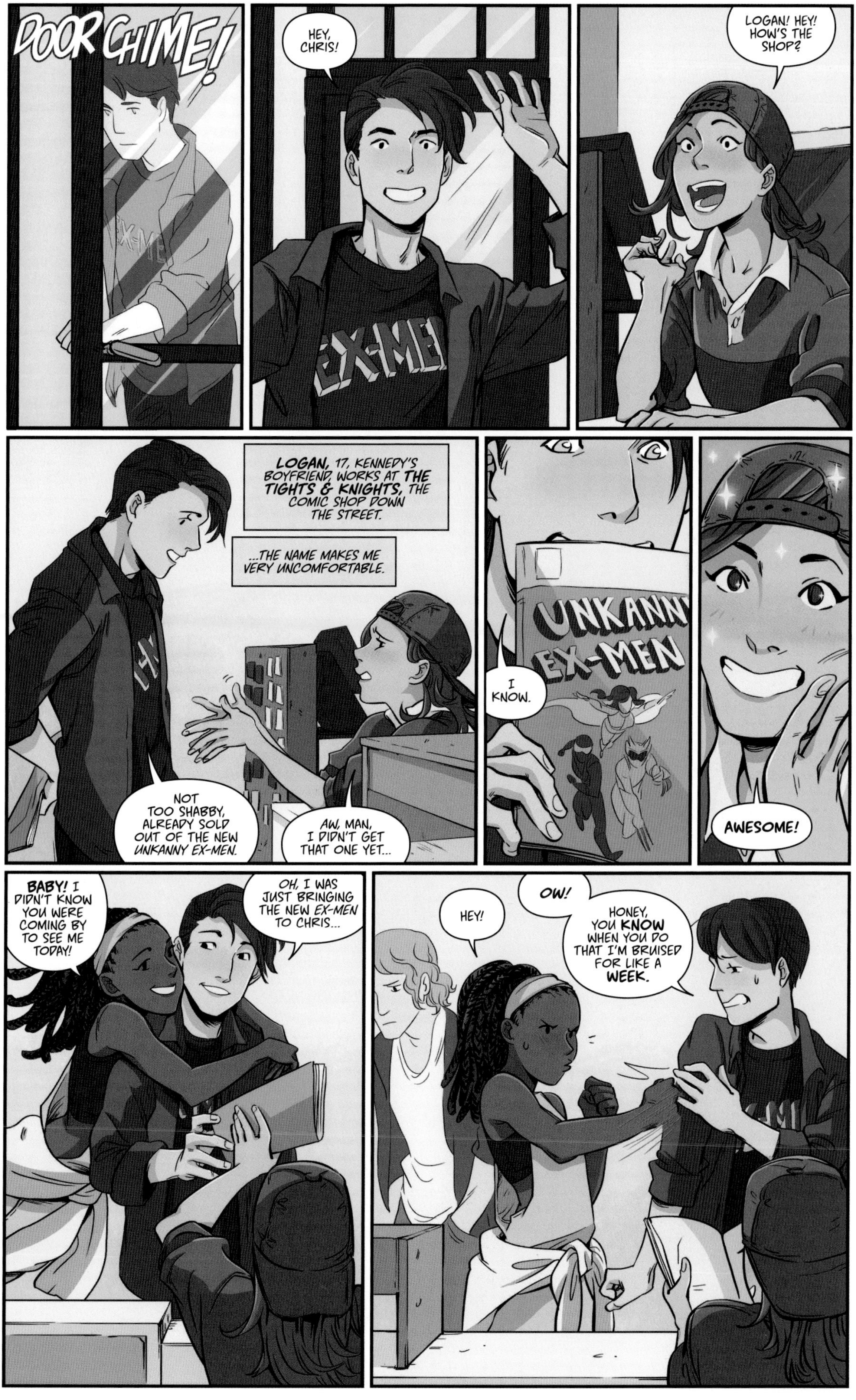
DOOR CHIME!
HEY, CHRIS!
LOGAN! HEY! HOW'S THE SHOP?
LOGAN, 17, KENNEDY'S BOYFRIEND, WORKS AT THE TIGHTS & KNIGHTS, THE COMIC SHOP DOWN THE STREET.
...THE NAME MAKES ME VERY UNCOMFORTABLE.
NOT TOO SHABBY, ALREADY SOLD OUT OF THE NEW UNKANNY EX-MEN.
AW, MAN, I DIDN'T GET THAT ONE YET...
UNKANNY EX-MEN
I KNOW.
AWESOME!
BABY! I DIDN'T KNOW YOU WERE COMING BY TO SEE ME TODAY!
OH, I WAS JUST BRINGING THE NEW EX-MEN TO CHRIS...
HEY!
OW!
HONEY, YOU KNOW WHEN YOU DO THAT I'M BRUISED FOR LIKE A WEEK.

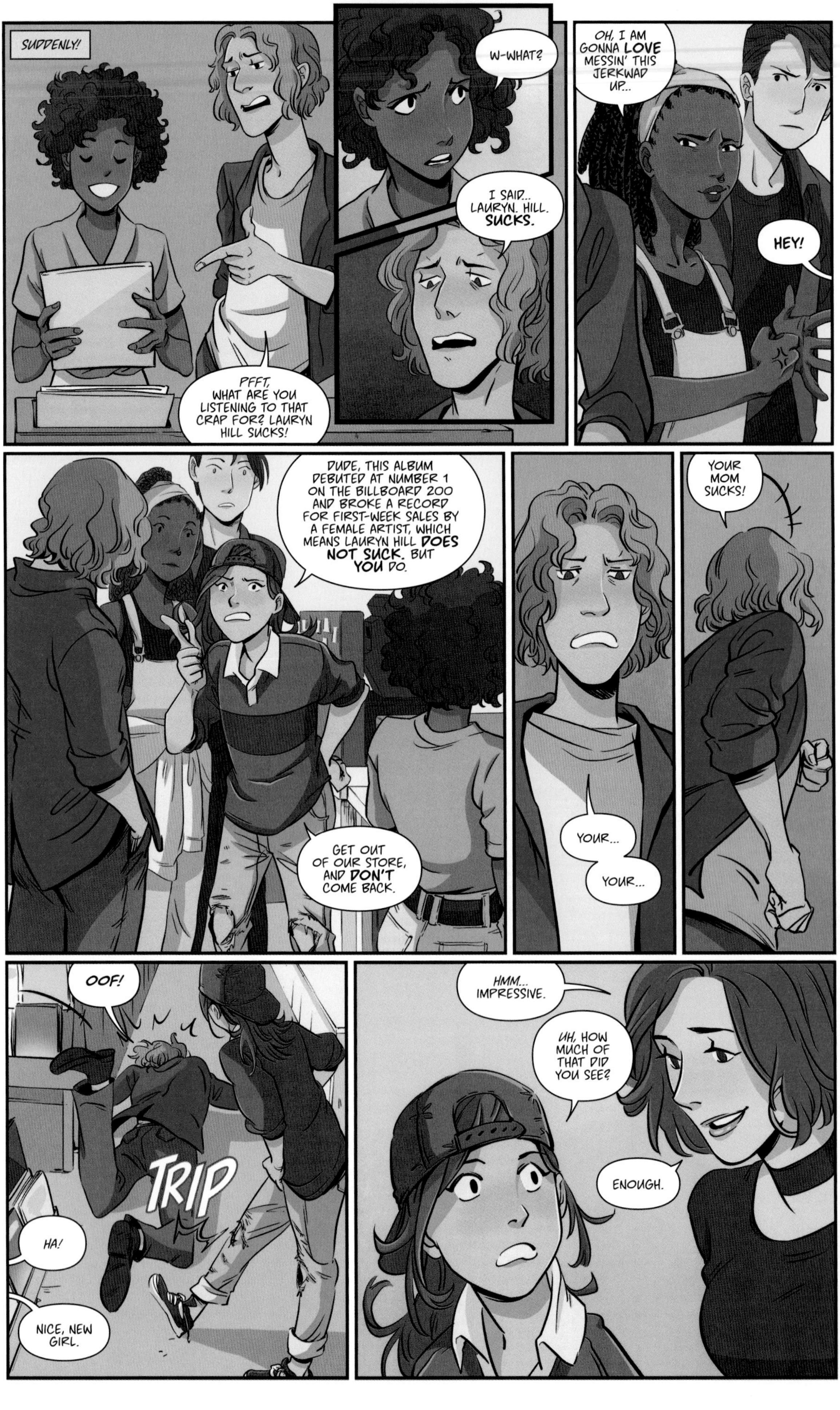
SUDDENLY!
PFFT, WHAT ARE YOU LISTENING TO THAT CRAP FOR? LAURYN HILL SUCKS!
W-WHAT?
I SAID... LAURYN. HILL. SUCKS.
OH, I AM GONNA LOVE MESSIN' THIS JERKWAD UP...
HEY!
DUDE, THIS ALBUM DEBUTED AT NUMBER 1 ON THE BILLBOARD 200 AND BROKE A RECORD FOR FIRST-WEEK SALES BY A FEMALE ARTIST, WHICH MEANS LAURYN HILL DOES NOT SUCK. BUT YOU DO.
GET OUT OF OUR STORE, AND DON'T COME BACK.
YOUR...
YOUR...
YOUR MOM SUCKS!
OOF!
TRIP
HA!
NICE, NEW GIRL.
HMM... IMPRESSIVE.
UH, HOW MUCH OF THAT DID YOU SEE?
ENOUGH.

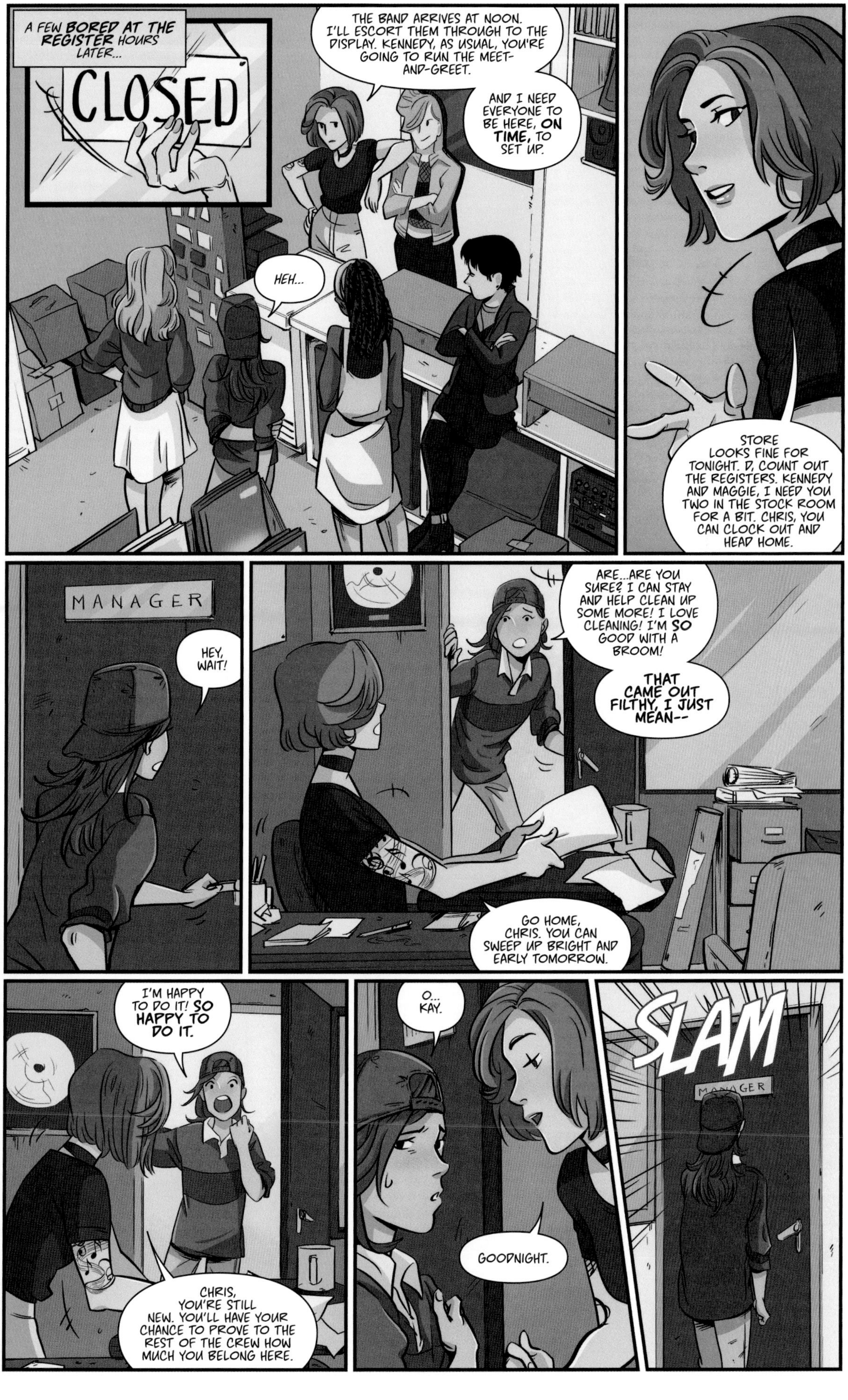
A FEW BORED AT THE REGISTER HOURS LATER...
CLOSED
THE BAND ARRIVES AT NOON. I'LL ESCORT THEM THROUGH TO THE DISPLAY. KENNEDY, AS USUAL, YOU'RE GOING TO RUN THE MEET-AND-GREET.
AND I NEED EVERYONE TO BE HERE, ON TIME, TO SET UP.
HEH...
STORE LOOKS FINE FOR TONIGHT. D, COUNT OUT THE REGISTERS. KENNEDY AND MAGGIE, I NEED YOU TWO IN THE STOCK ROOM FOR A BIT. CHRIS, YOU CAN CLOCK OUT AND HEAD HOME.
MANAGER
HEY, WAIT!
ARE...ARE YOU SURE? I CAN STAY AND HELP CLEAN UP SOME MORE! I LOVE CLEANING! I'M SO GOOD WITH A BROOM!
THAT CAME OUT FILTHY, I JUST MEAN--
GO HOME, CHRIS. YOU CAN SWEEP UP BRIGHT AND EARLY TOMORROW.
I'M HAPPY TO DO IT! SO HAPPY TO DO IT.
CHRIS, YOU'RE STILL NEW. YOU'LL HAVE YOUR CHANCE TO PROVE TO THE REST OF THE CREW HOW MUCH YOU BELONG HERE.
O... KAY.
GOODNIGHT.
SLAM

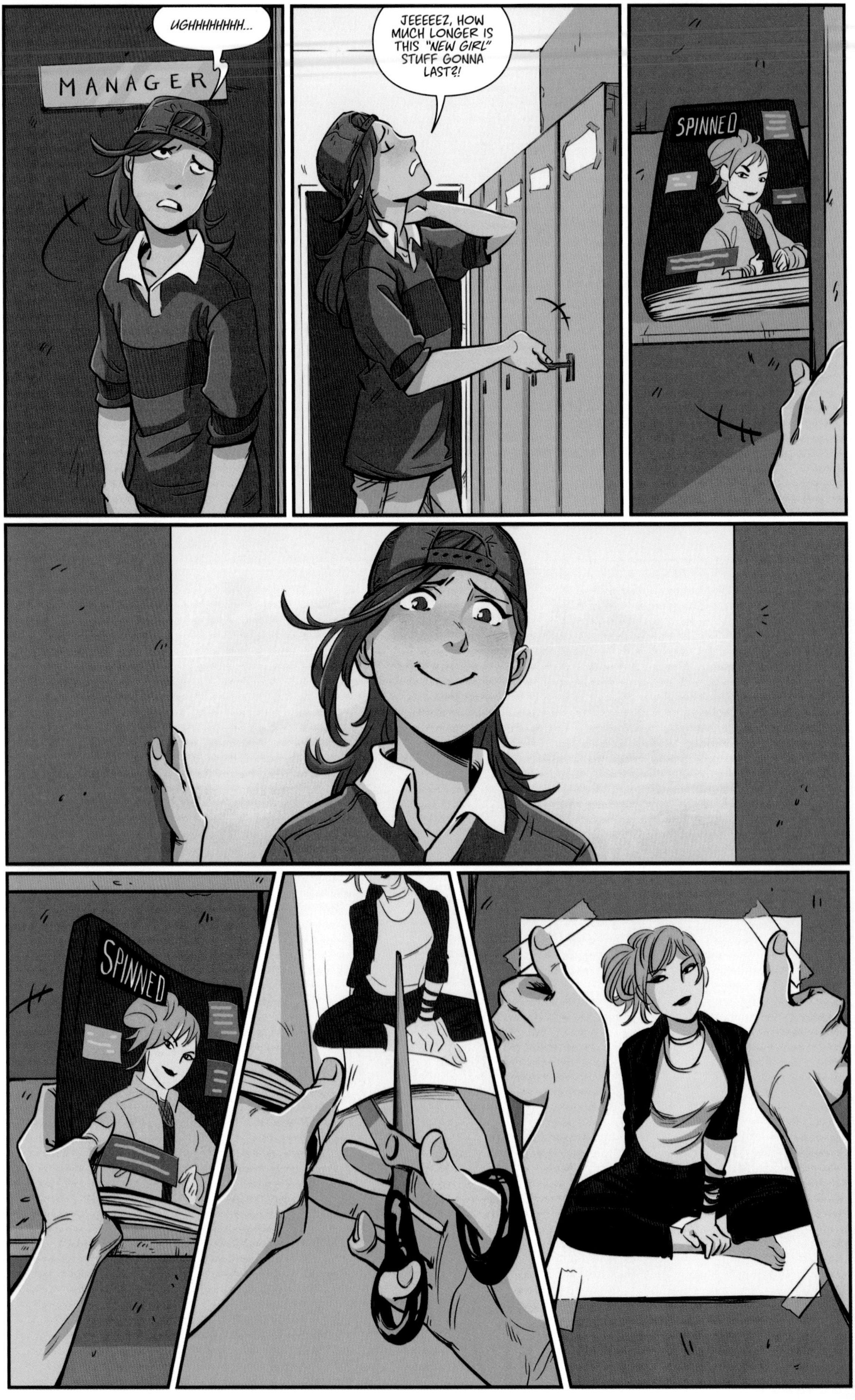
UGHHHHHHHH...
MANAGER
JEEEEEZ, HOW MUCH LONGER IS THIS "NEW GIRL" STUFF GONNA LAST?!
SPINNED
SPINNED

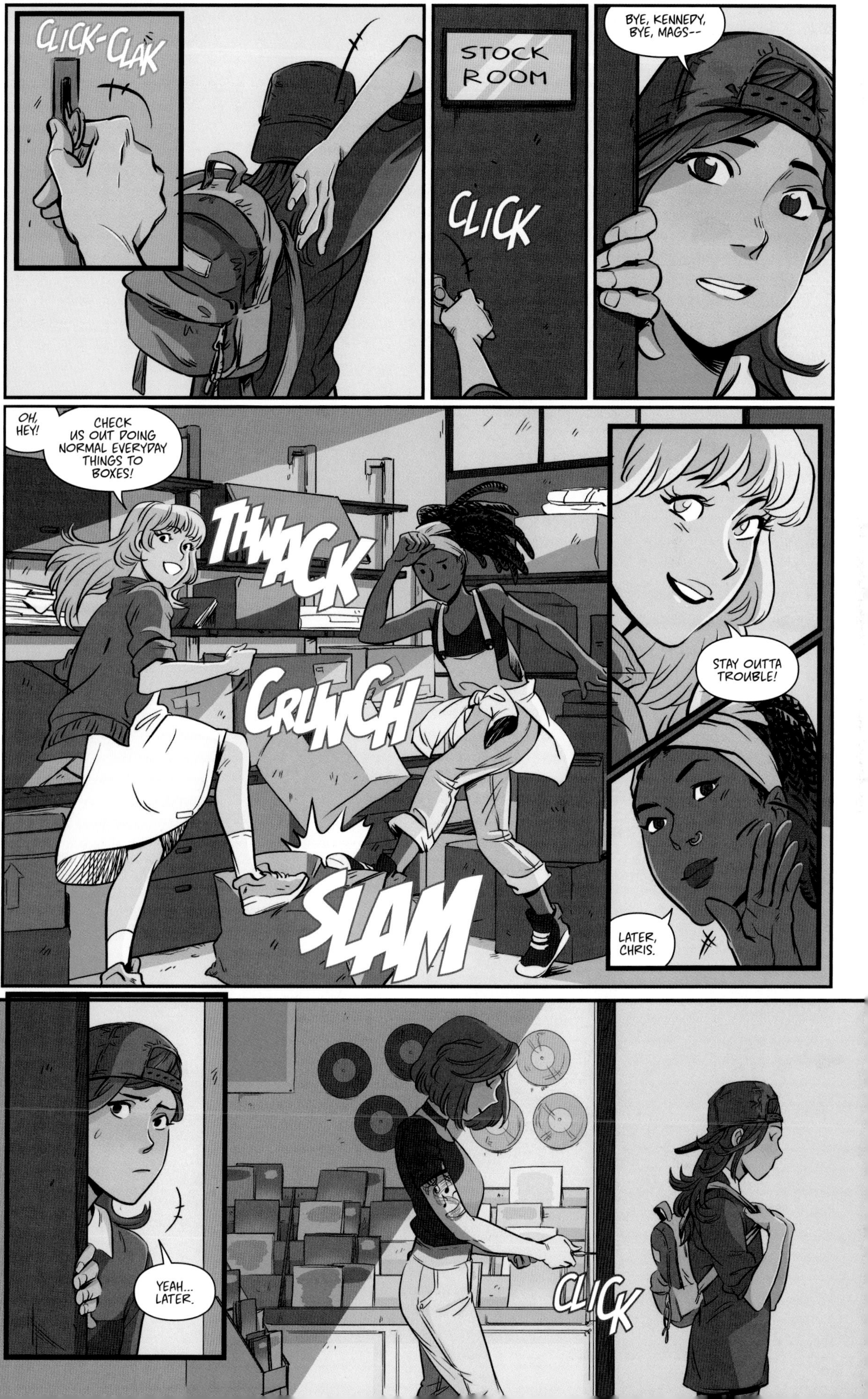
CLICK-CLAK
STOCK ROOM
CLICK
BYE, KENNEDY, BYE, MAGS--
OH, HEY!
CHECK US OUT DOING NORMAL EVERYDAY THINGS TO BOXES!
THWACK
CRUNCH
SLAM
STAY OUTTA TROUBLE!
LATER, CHRIS.
YEAH... LATER.
CLICK

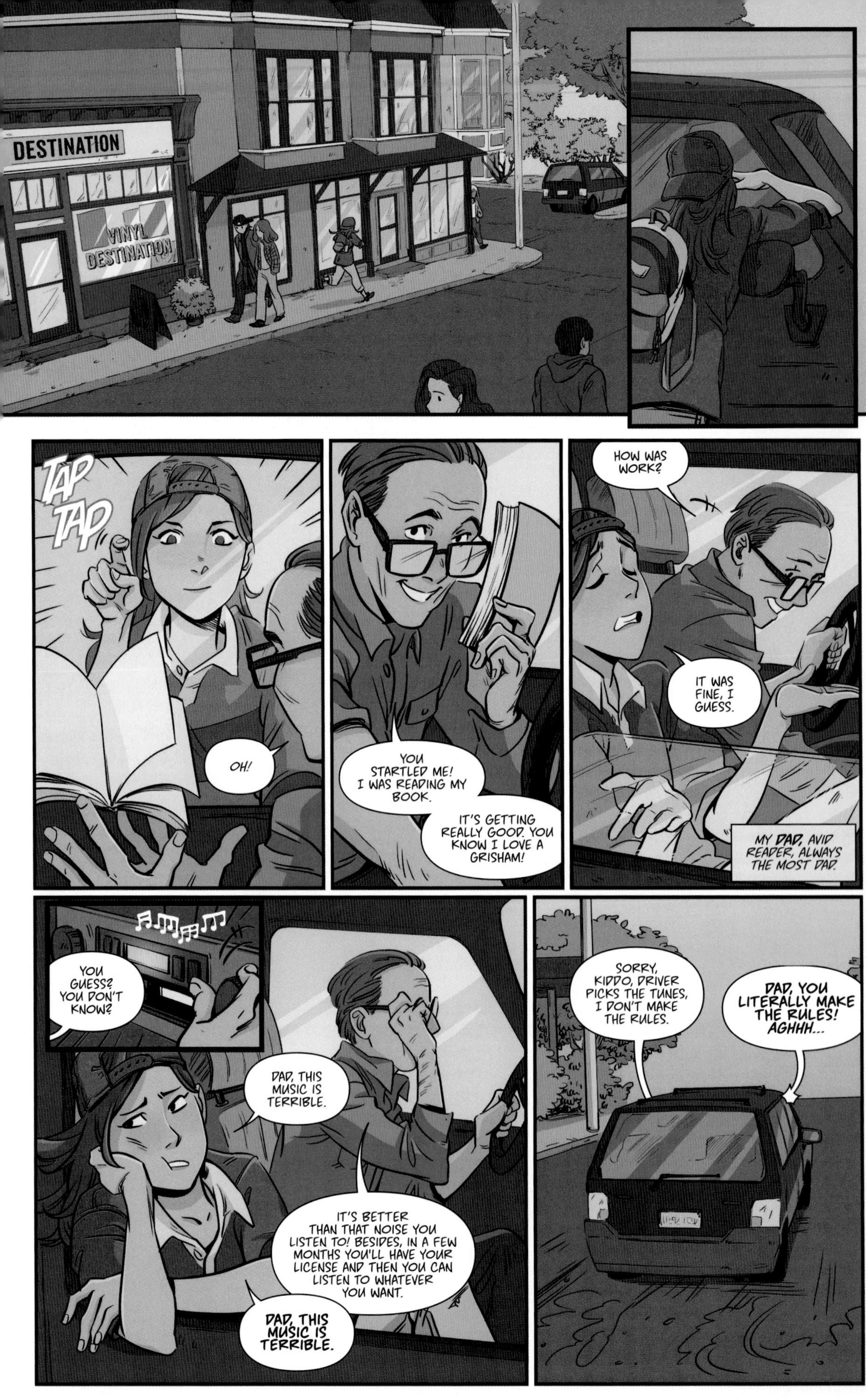
DESTINATION
VINYL DESTINATION
TAP TAP
OH!
YOU STARTLED ME! I WAS READING MY BOOK.
IT'S GETTING REALLY GOOD. YOU KNOW I LOVE A GRISHAM!
HOW WAS WORK?
IT WAS FINE, I GUESS.
MY DAD, AVID READER, ALWAYS THE MOST DAD.
YOU GUESS? YOU DON'T KNOW?
DAD, THIS MUSIC IS TERRIBLE.
IT'S BETTER THAN THAT NOISE YOU LISTEN TO! BESIDES, IN A FEW MONTHS YOU'LL HAVE YOUR LICENSE AND THEN YOU CAN LISTEN TO WHATEVER YOU WANT.
DAD, THIS MUSIC IS TERRIBLE.
SORRY, KIDDO, DRIVER PICKS THE TUNES, I DON'T MAKE THE RULES.
DAD, YOU LITERALLY MAKE THE RULES! AGHHH...

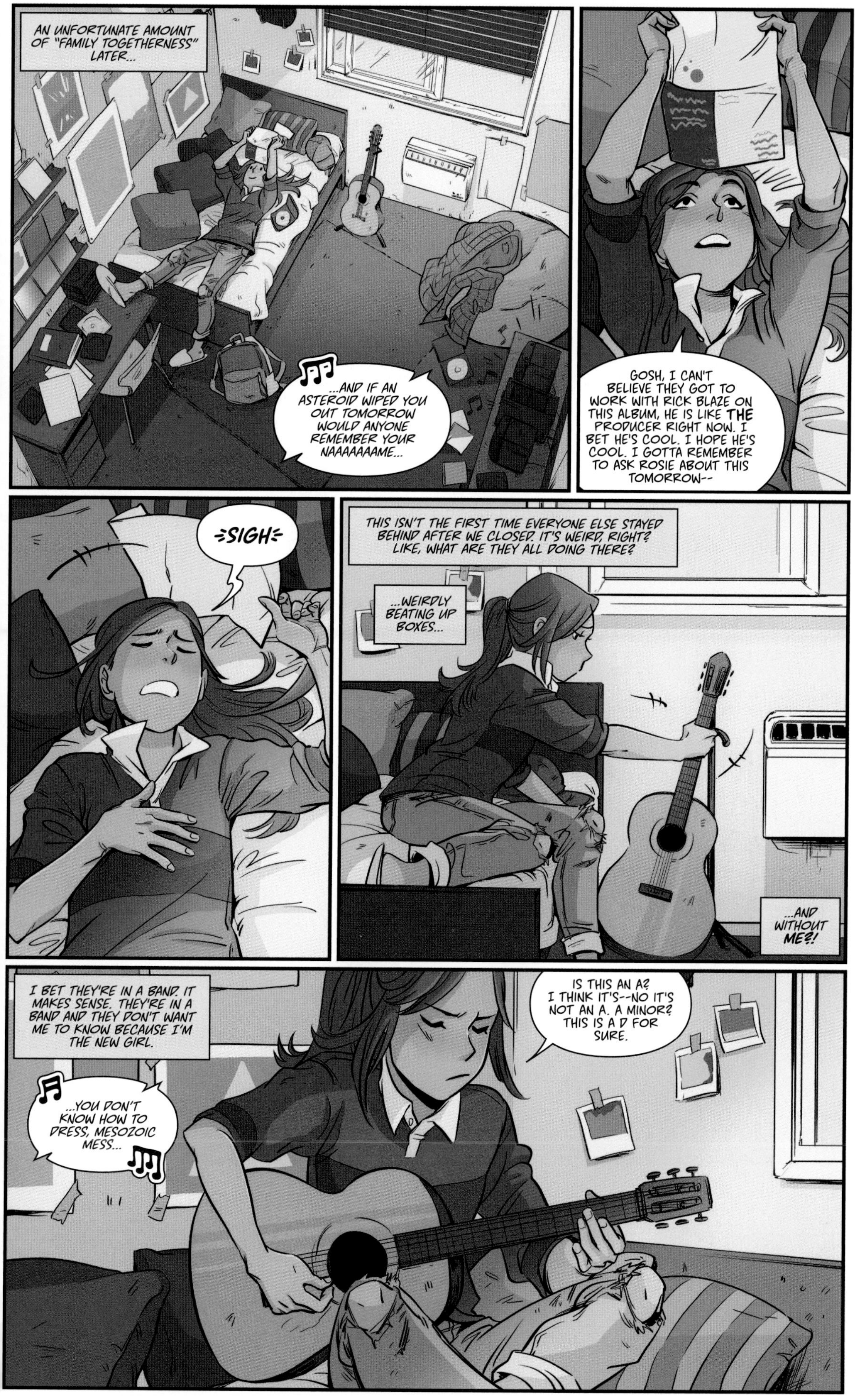
AN UNFORTUNATE AMOUNT OF "FAMILY TOGETHERNESS" LATER...
...AND IF AN ASTEROID WIPED YOU OUT TOMORROW WOULD ANYONE REMEMBER YOUR NAAAAAAAME...
GOSH, I CAN'T BELIEVE THEY GOT TO WORK WITH RICK BLAZE ON THIS ALBUM, HE IS LIKE THE PRODUCER RIGHT NOW. I BET HE'S COOL. I HOPE HE'S COOL. I GOTTA REMEMBER TO ASK ROSIE ABOUT THIS TOMORROW--
SIGH
THIS ISN'T THE FIRST TIME EVERYONE ELSE STAYED BEHIND AFTER WE CLOSED. IT'S WEIRD, RIGHT? LIKE, WHAT ARE THEY ALL DOING THERE?
...WEIRDLY BEATING UP BOXES...
...AND WITHOUT ME?!
I BET THEY'RE IN A BAND. IT MAKES SENSE. THEY'RE IN A BAND AND THEY DON'T WANT ME TO KNOW BECAUSE I'M THE NEW GIRL.
IS THIS AN A? I THINK IT'S--NO IT'S NOT AN A. A MINOR? THIS IS A D FOR SURE.
...YOU DON'T KNOW HOW TO DRESS, MESOZOIC MESS...

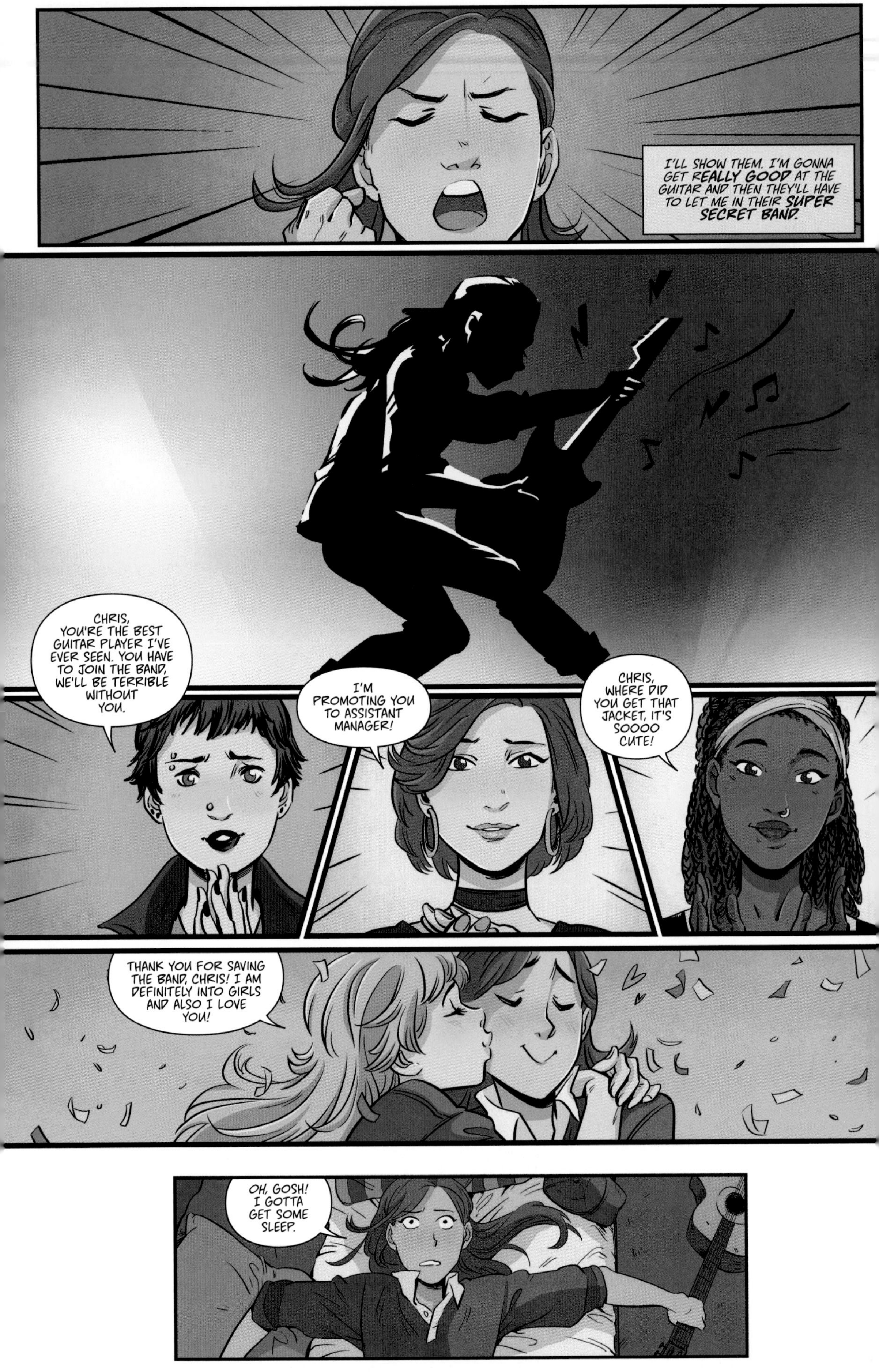
I'LL SHOW THEM. I'M GONNA GET REALLY GOOD AT THE GUITAR AND THEN THEY'LL HAVE TO LET ME IN THEIR SUPER SECRET BAND.
CHRIS, YOU'RE THE BEST GUITAR PLAYER I'VE EVER SEEN. YOU HAVE TO JOIN THE BAND, WE'LL BE TERRIBLE WITHOUT YOU.
I'M PROMOTING YOU TO ASSISTANT MANAGER!
CHRIS, WHERE DID YOU GET THAT JACKET, IT'S SOOOO CUTE!
THANK YOU FOR SAVING THE BAND, CHRIS! I AM DEFINITELY INTO GIRLS AND ALSO I LOVE YOU!
OH, GOSH! I GOTTA GET SOME SLEEP.

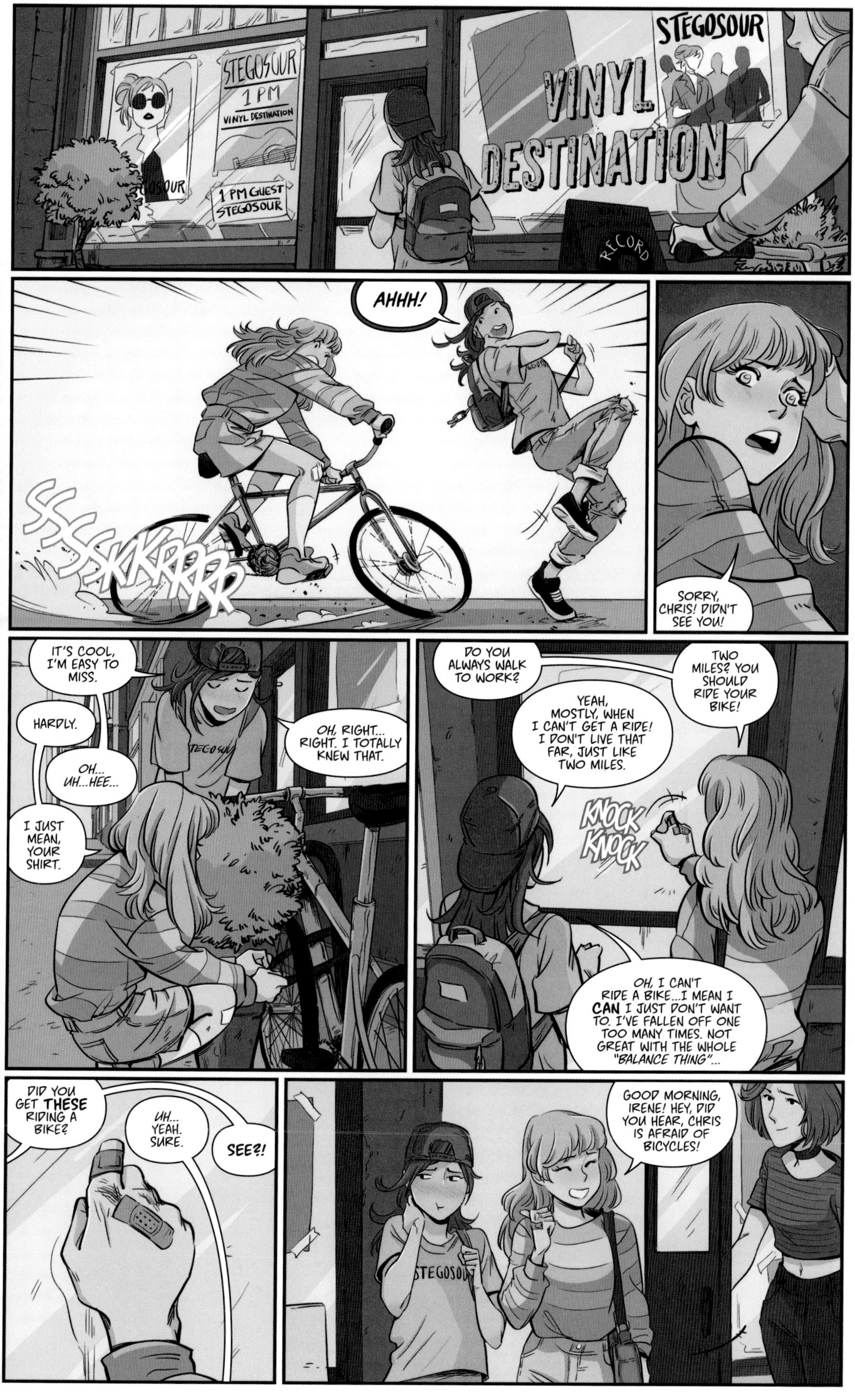

STEGOSOUR
1 PM
VINYL DESTINATION
1 PM GUEST
STEGOSOUR
VINYL DESTINATION
STEGOSOUR
RECORD
AHHH!
SSSKKRRRRR
SORRY, CHRIS! DIDN'T SEE YOU!
IT'S COOL, I'M EASY TO MISS.
HARDLY.
OH... UH...HEE...
I JUST MEAN, YOUR SHIRT.
OH, RIGHT... RIGHT. I TOTALLY KNEW THAT.
DO YOU ALWAYS WALK TO WORK?
YEAH, MOSTLY, WHEN I CAN'T GET A RIDE! I DON'T LIVE THAT FAR, JUST LIKE TWO MILES.
TWO MILES? YOU SHOULD RIDE YOUR BIKE!
KNOCK KNOCK
OH, I CAN'T RIDE A BIKE...I MEAN I CAN I JUST DON'T WANT TO. I'VE FALLEN OFF ONE TOO MANY TIMES. NOT GREAT WITH THE WHOLE "BALANCE THING"...
DID YOU GET THESE RIDING A BIKE?
UH... YEAH. SURE.
SEE?!
GOOD MORNING, IRENE! HEY, DID YOU HEAR, CHRIS IS AFRAID OF BICYCLES!
STEGOSOUR

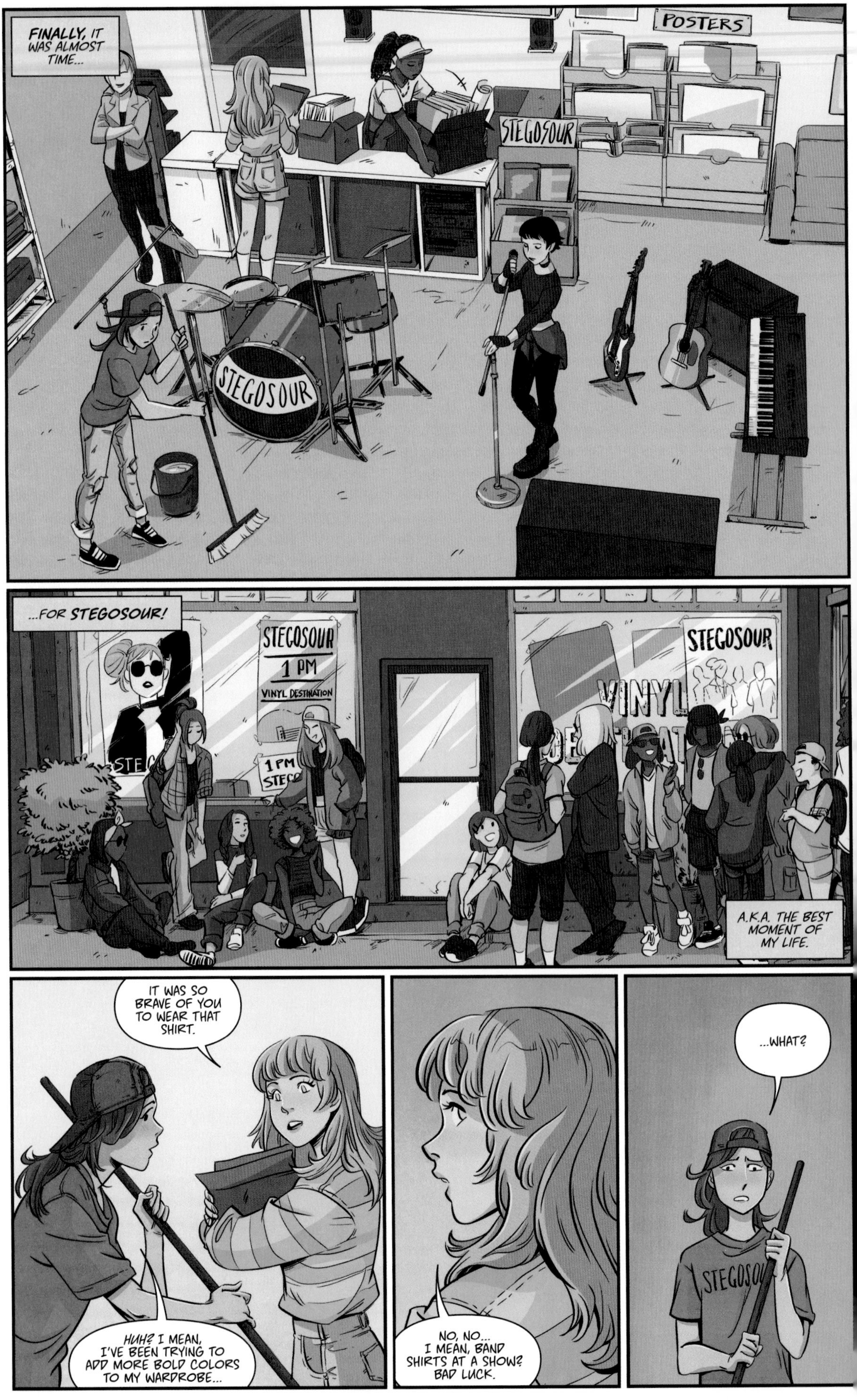
FINALLY, IT WAS ALMOST TIME...
POSTERS
STEGOSOUR
STEGOSOUR
...FOR STEGOSOUR!
STEGOSOUR
1 PM
VINYL DESTINATION
STEGOSOUR
A.K.A. THE BEST MOMENT OF MY LIFE.
IT WAS SO BRAVE OF YOU TO WEAR THAT SHIRT.
HUH? I MEAN, I'VE BEEN TRYING TO ADD MORE BOLD COLORS TO MY WARDROBE...
NO, NO... I MEAN, BAND SHIRTS AT A SHOW? BAD LUCK.
...WHAT?
STEGOSOUR

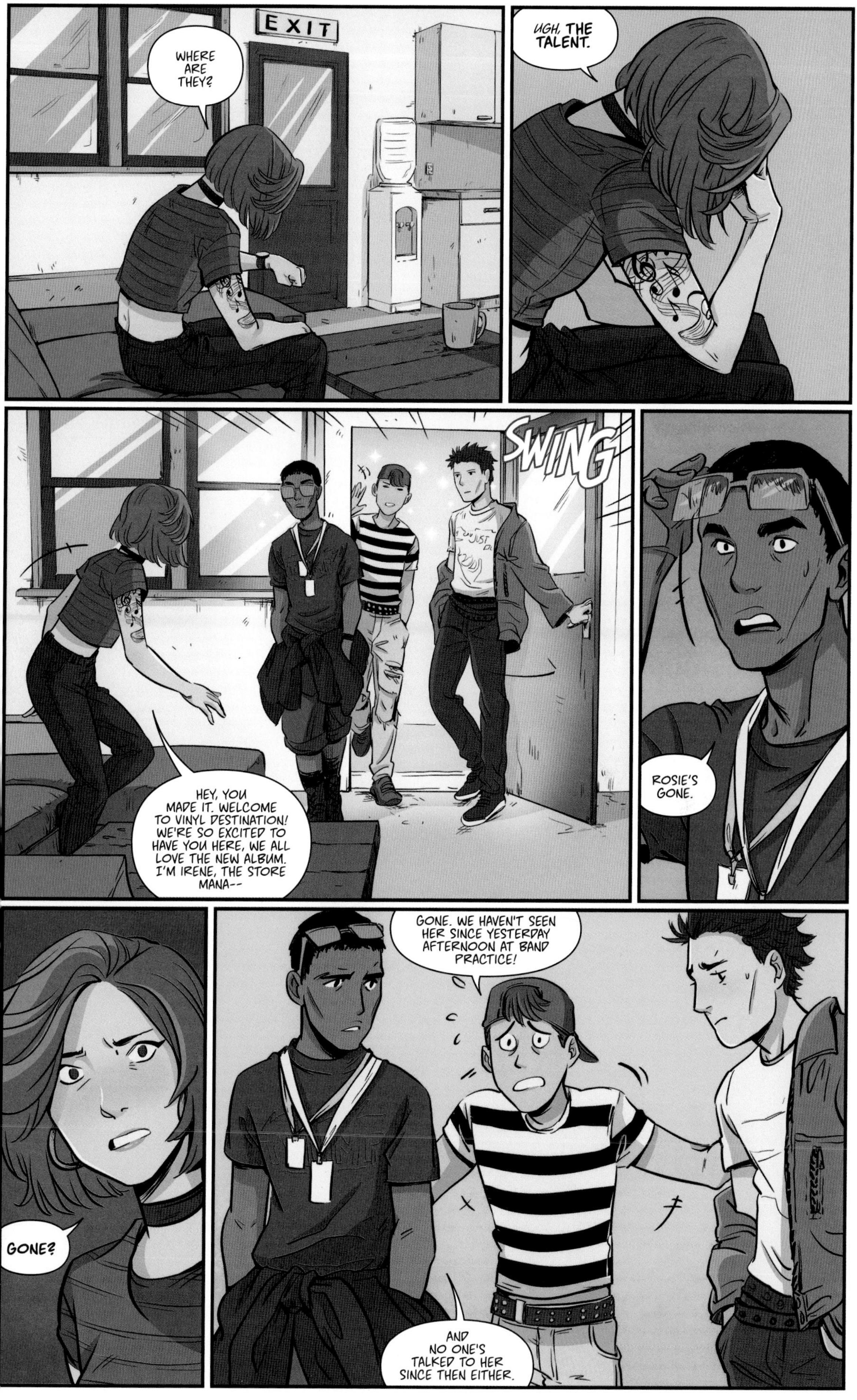
WHERE ARE THEY?
UGH, THE TALENT.
SWING
HEY, YOU MADE IT. WELCOME TO VINYL DESTINATION! WE'RE SO EXCITED TO HAVE YOU HERE, WE ALL LOVE THE NEW ALBUM. I'M IRENE, THE STORE MANA--
ROSIE'S GONE.
GONE?
GONE. WE HAVEN'T SEEN HER SINCE YESTERDAY AFTERNOON AT BAND PRACTICE!
AND NO ONE'S TALKED TO HER SINCE THEN EITHER.

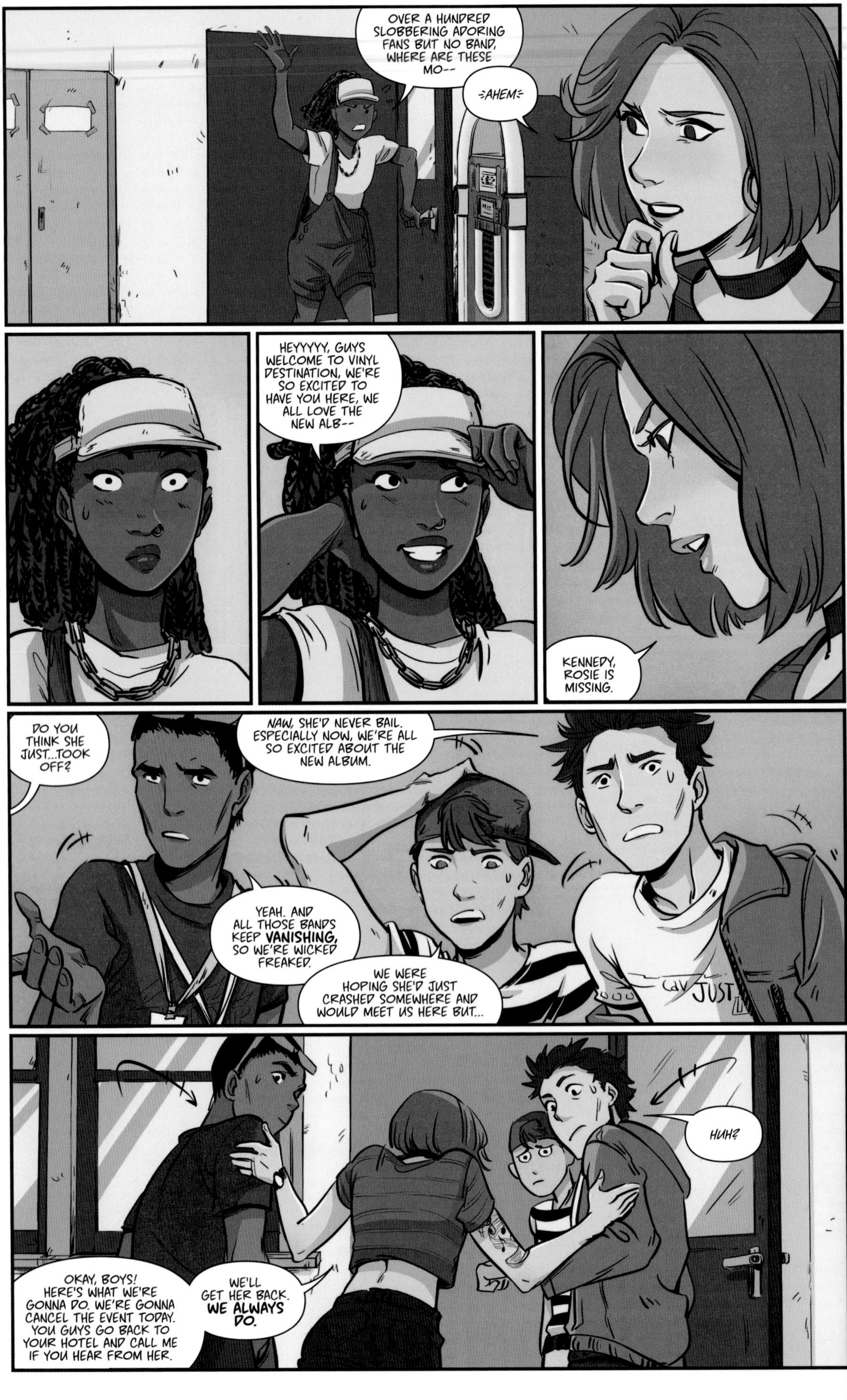
OVER A HUNDRED SLOBBERING ADORING FANS BUT NO BAND, WHERE ARE THESE MO--
AHEM
HEYYYYY, GUYS WELCOME TO VINYL DESTINATION, WE'RE SO EXCITED TO HAVE YOU HERE, WE ALL LOVE THE NEW ALB--
KENNEDY, ROSIE IS MISSING.
DO YOU THINK SHE JUST...TOOK OFF?
NAW, SHE'D NEVER BAIL. ESPECIALLY NOW, WE'RE ALL SO EXCITED ABOUT THE NEW ALBUM.
YEAH. AND ALL THOSE BANDS KEEP **VANISHING**, SO WE'RE WICKED FREAKED.
WE WERE HOPING SHE'D JUST CRASHED SOMEWHERE AND WOULD MEET US HERE BUT...
HUH?
OKAY, BOYS! HERE'S WHAT WE'RE GONNA DO. WE'RE GONNA CANCEL THE EVENT TODAY. YOU GUYS GO BACK TO YOUR HOTEL AND CALL ME IF YOU HEAR FROM HER.
WE'LL GET HER BACK. **WE ALWAYS DO.**

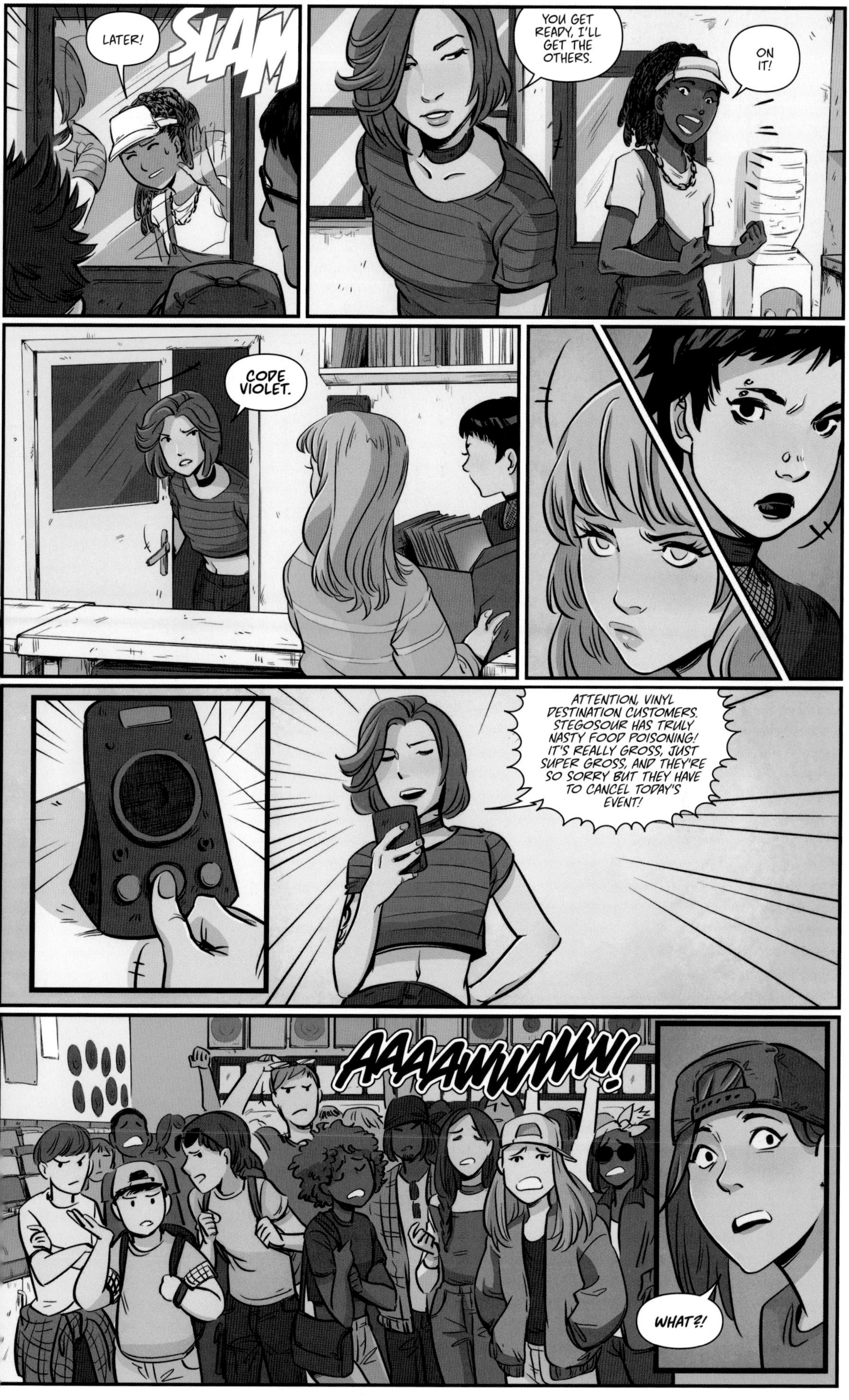
LATER!
SLAM
YOU GET READY, I'LL GET THE OTHERS.
ON IT!
CODE VIOLET.
ATTENTION, VINYL DESTINATION CUSTOMERS. STEGOSOUR HAS TRULY NASTY FOOD POISONING! IT'S REALLY GROSS, JUST SUPER GROSS, AND THEY'RE SO SORRY BUT THEY HAVE TO CANCEL TODAY'S EVENT!
AAAAWWWW!
WHAT?!

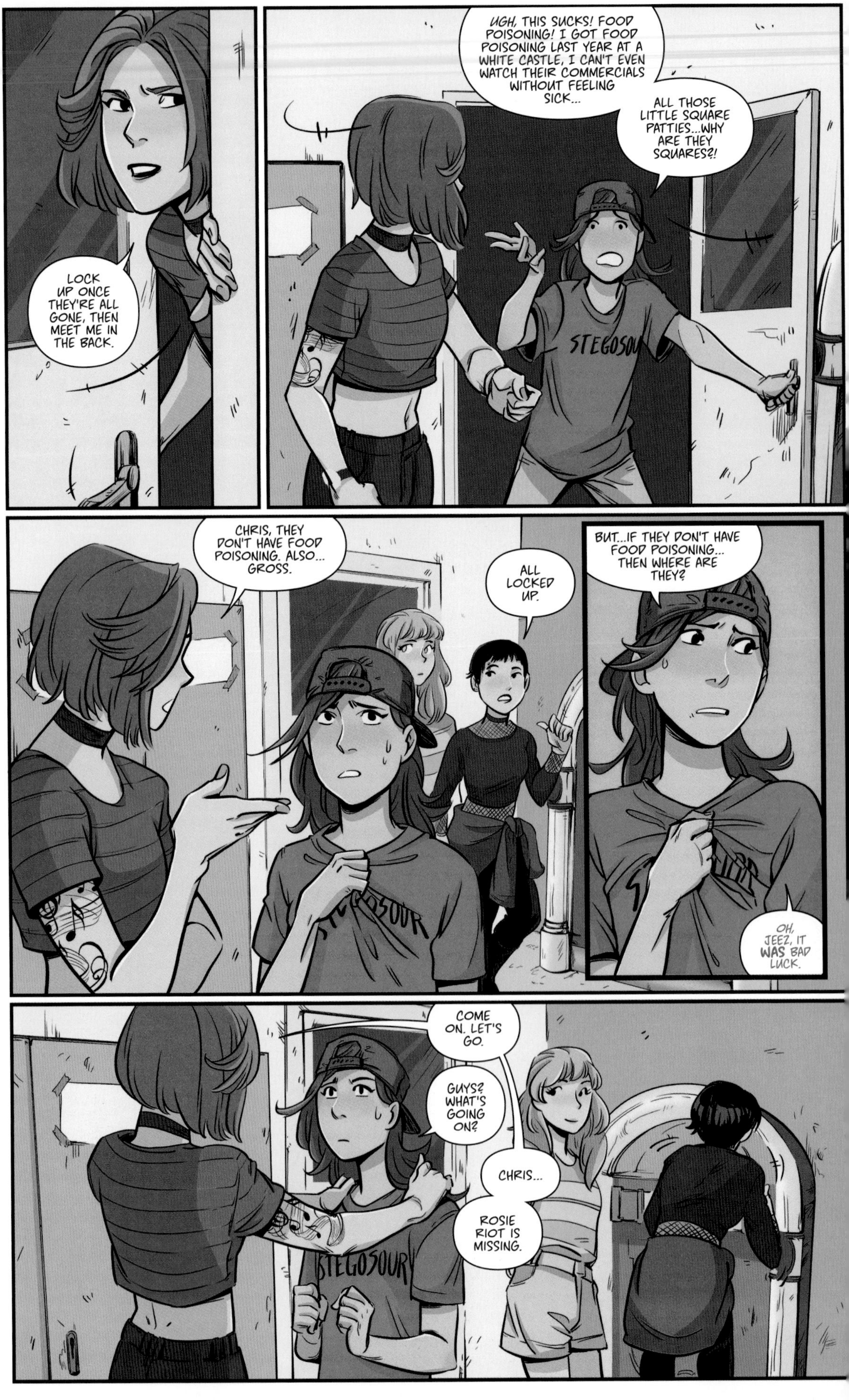
LOCK UP ONCE THEY'RE ALL GONE, THEN MEET ME IN THE BACK.
UGH, THIS SUCKS! FOOD POISONING! I GOT FOOD POISONING LAST YEAR AT A WHITE CASTLE, I CAN'T EVEN WATCH THEIR COMMERCIALS WITHOUT FEELING SICK...
ALL THOSE LITTLE SQUARE PATTIES...WHY ARE THEY SQUARES?!
STEGOSOUR
CHRIS, THEY DON'T HAVE FOOD POISONING. ALSO... GROSS.
ALL LOCKED UP.
STEGOSOUR
BUT...IF THEY DON'T HAVE FOOD POISONING... THEN WHERE ARE THEY?
OH, JEEZ, IT WAS BAD LUCK.
COME ON. LET'S GO.
GUYS? WHAT'S GOING ON?
CHRIS...
ROSIE RIOT IS MISSING.
STEGOSOUR

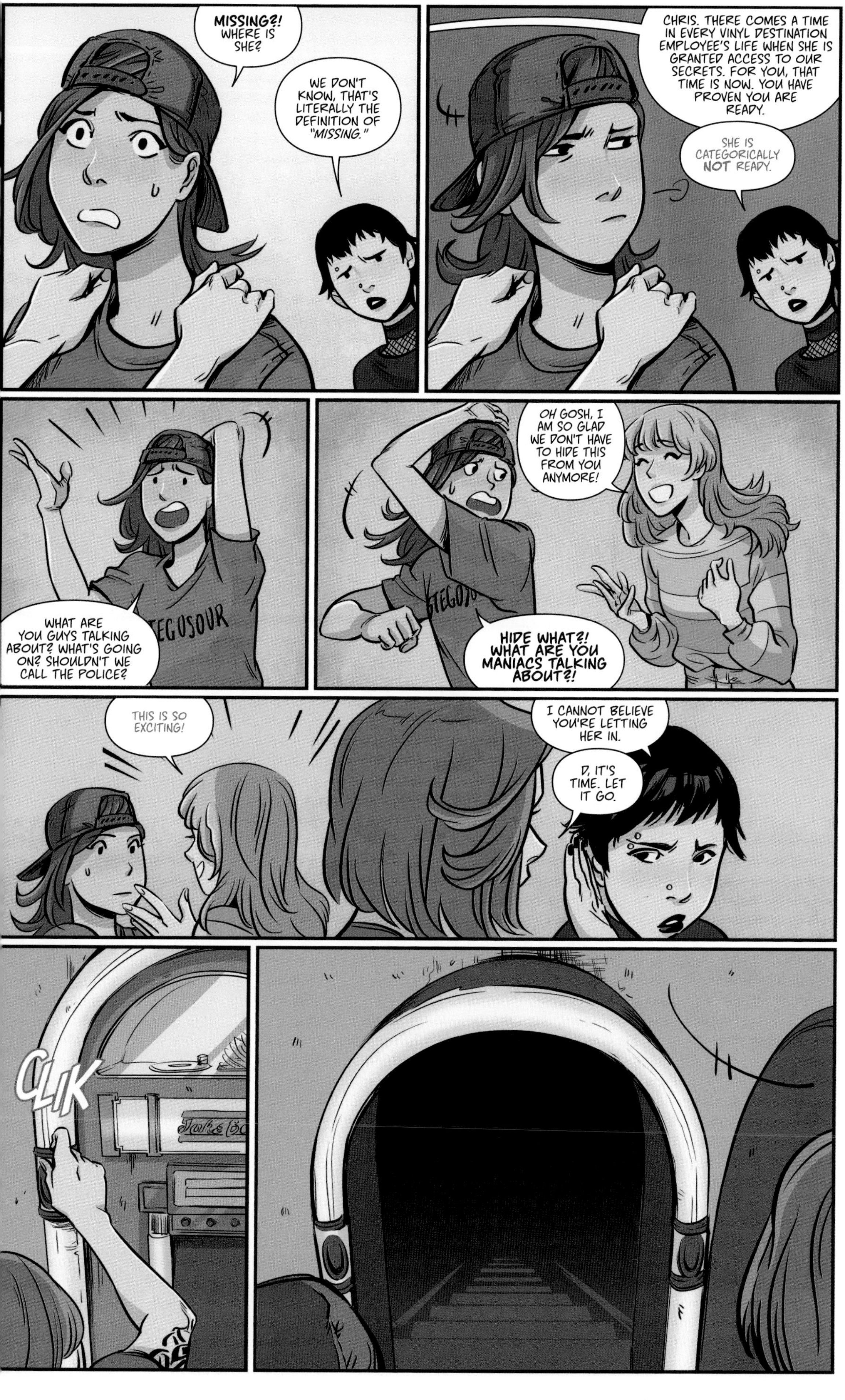
MISSING?! WHERE IS SHE?
WE DON'T KNOW, THAT'S LITERALLY THE DEFINITION OF "MISSING."
CHRIS. THERE COMES A TIME IN EVERY VINYL DESTINATION EMPLOYEE'S LIFE WHEN SHE IS GRANTED ACCESS TO OUR SECRETS. FOR YOU, THAT TIME IS NOW. YOU HAVE PROVEN YOU ARE READY.
SHE IS CATEGORICALLY NOT READY.
WHAT ARE YOU GUYS TALKING ABOUT? WHAT'S GOING ON? SHOULDN'T WE CALL THE POLICE?
STEGOSOUR
OH GOSH, I AM SO GLAD WE DON'T HAVE TO HIDE THIS FROM YOU ANYMORE!
HIDE WHAT?! WHAT ARE YOU MANIACS TALKING ABOUT?!
THIS IS SO EXCITING!
I CANNOT BELIEVE YOU'RE LETTING HER IN.
D, IT'S TIME. LET IT GO.
CLIK

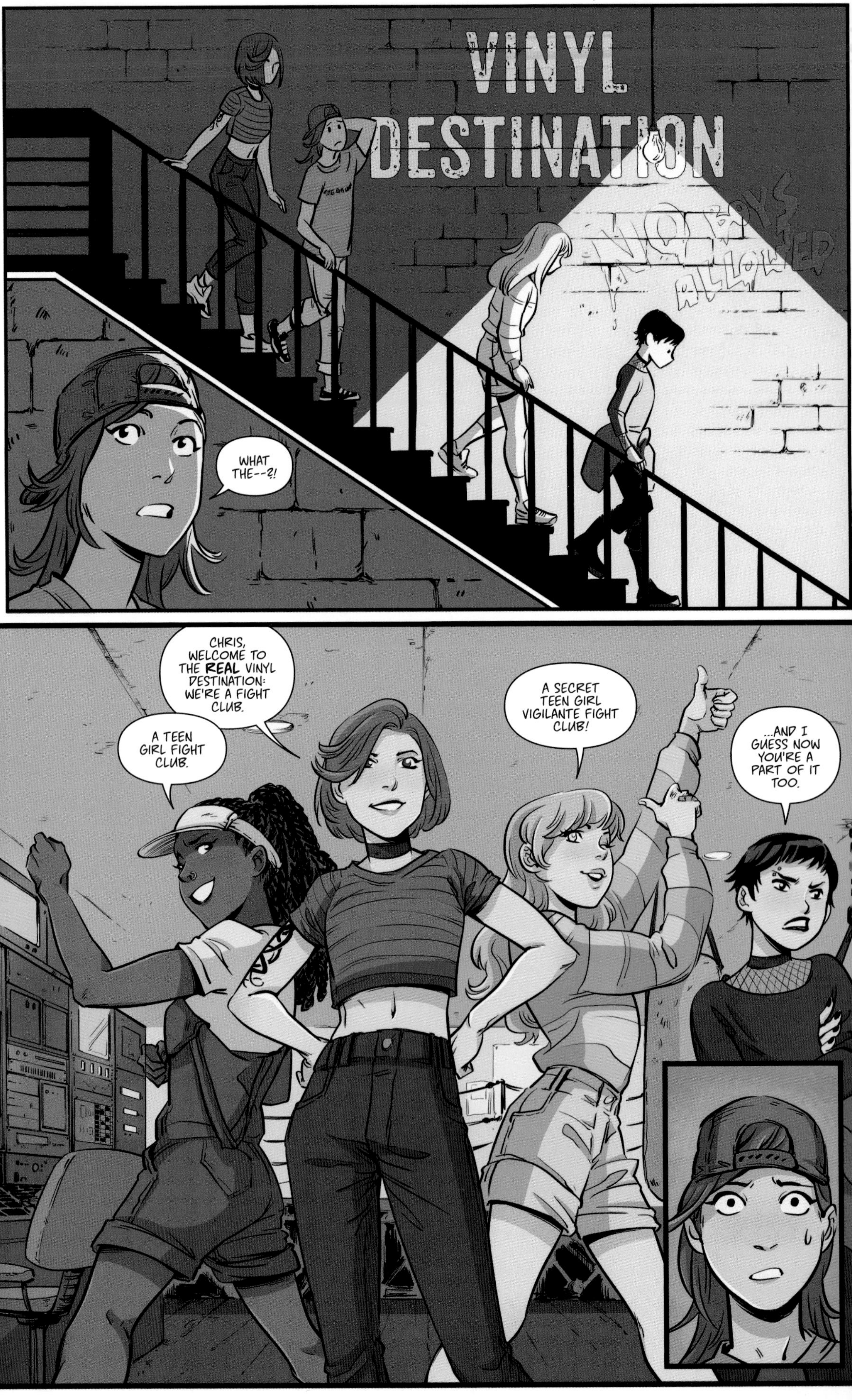
VINYL DESTINATION
NO BOYS ALLOWED
WHAT THE--?!
CHRIS, WELCOME TO THE **REAL** VINYL DESTINATION: WE'RE A FIGHT CLUB.
A TEEN GIRL FIGHT CLUB.
A SECRET TEEN GIRL VIGILANTE FIGHT CLUB!
...AND I GUESS NOW YOU'RE A PART OF IT TOO.

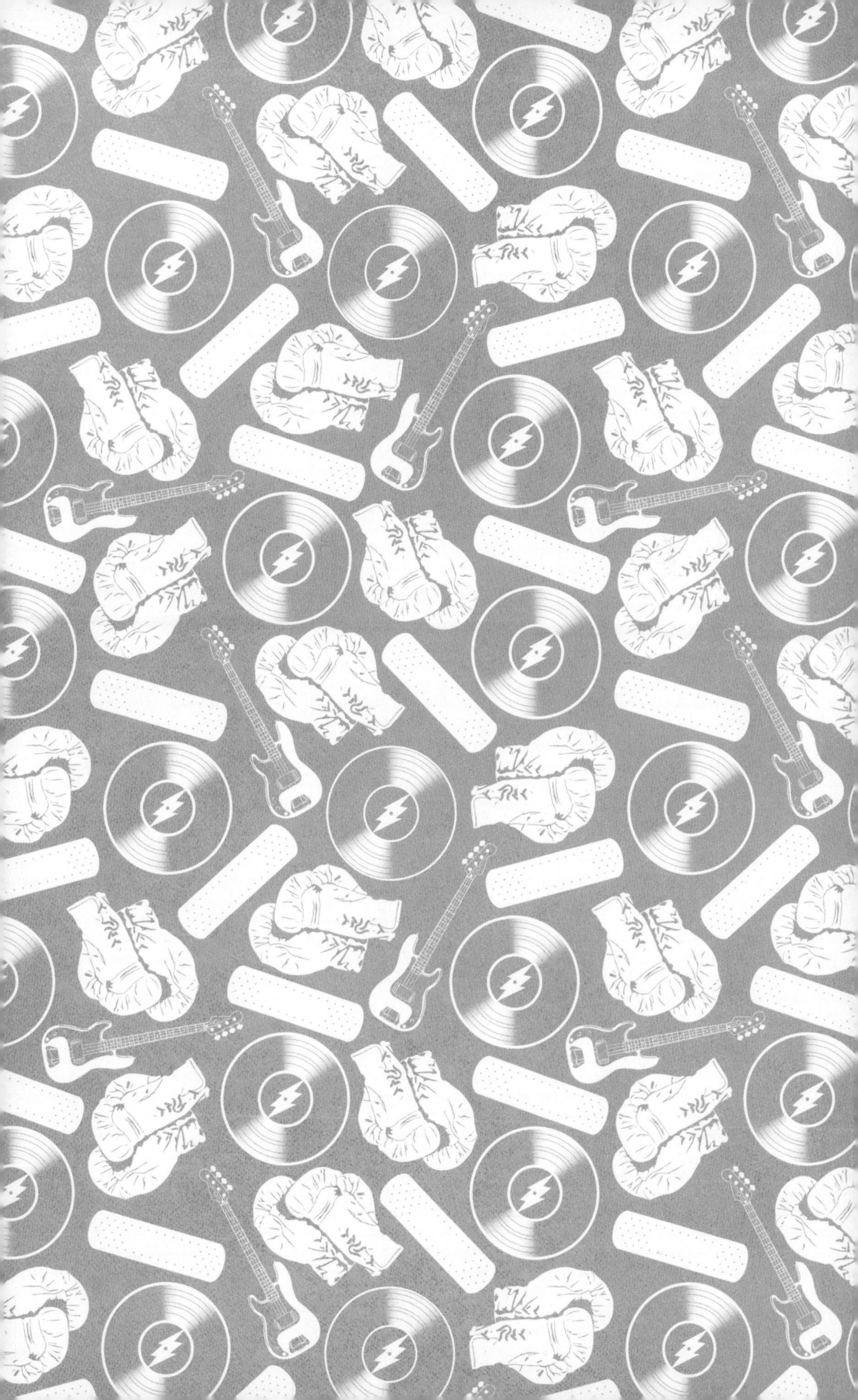

once upon a time / tHere Was nothing (yeah) /
then a big big Bang / gave Us something (yeah) /
evoluTion is our revolutioN / evolution is
oUr revolution / read between the lin
reaD between the lines / it's in Our cod
from long aGo / primordial bruise / primor
bruise / billions of years / To rule the
world (yeah) / have Brought us
volcanO girls (yeah)
revolution /
read

CHAPTER TWO

ends,
there for
volved in Jurassic
movie. A ROAR to No
and Tilt for letting us join
ped Tour! And the biggest ROAR
ve our I.S. family!!
the best label, Imaginary Selves!!
ROSIE RIOT would like to thank her idols:
Cinder, Shirley, Gwen, Poe, Joan, Kay, Skin,
Kathleen, Carrie and Corin, for showing her
the way.
CHARLIE would like to thank pizza for
always getting him through the day.

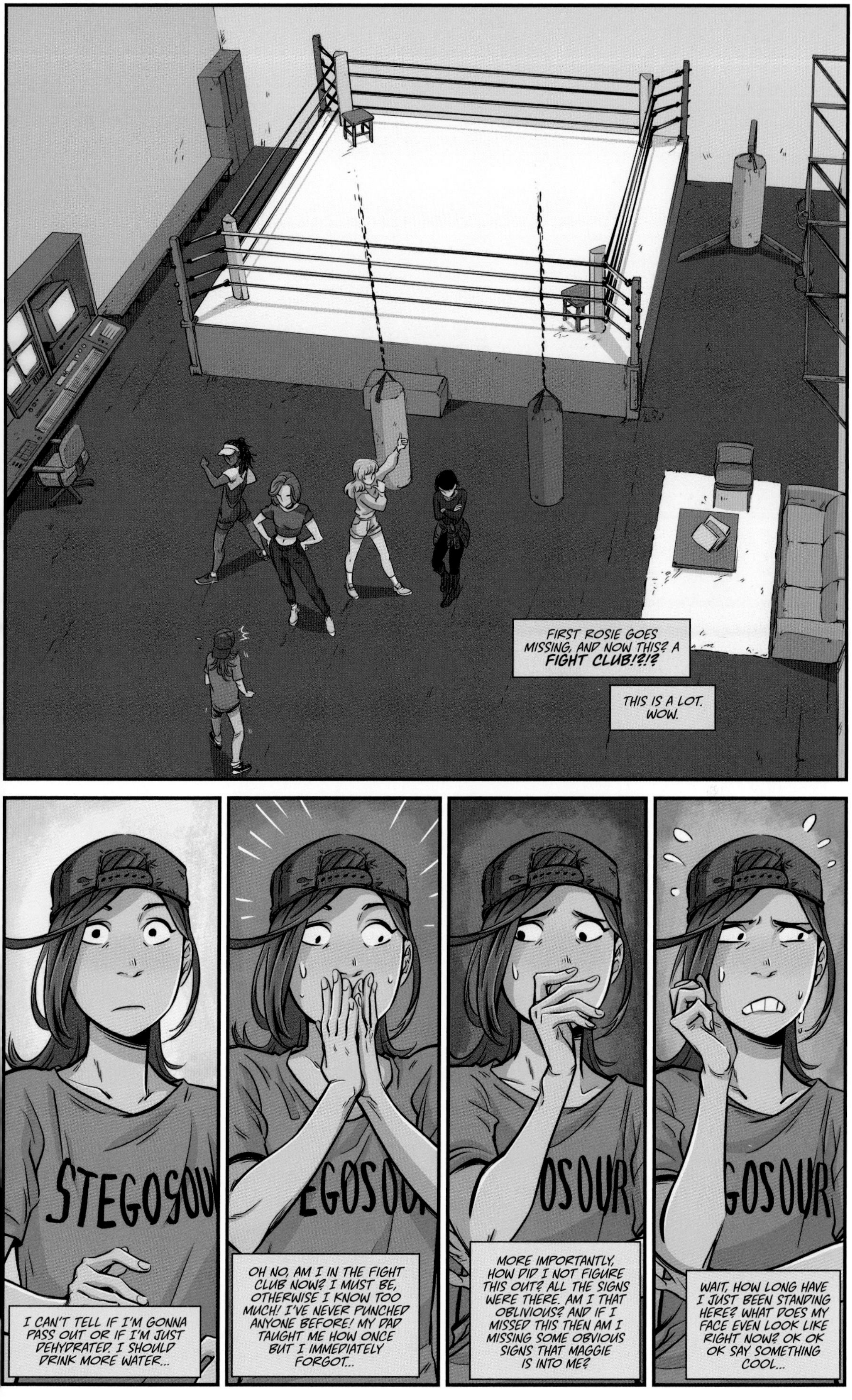
FIRST ROSIE GOES MISSING, AND NOW THIS? A **FIGHT CLUB!?!?**
THIS IS A LOT. WOW.
STEGOSOUR
I CAN'T TELL IF I'M GONNA PASS OUT OR IF I'M JUST DEHYDRATED. I SHOULD DRINK MORE WATER...
OH NO, AM I IN THE FIGHT CLUB NOW? I MUST BE, OTHERWISE I KNOW TOO MUCH! I'VE NEVER PUNCHED ANYONE BEFORE! MY DAD TAUGHT ME HOW ONCE BUT I IMMEDIATELY FORGOT...
MORE IMPORTANTLY, HOW DID I NOT FIGURE THIS OUT? ALL THE SIGNS WERE THERE. AM I THAT OBLIVIOUS? AND IF I MISSED THIS THEN AM I MISSING SOME OBVIOUS SIGNS THAT MAGGIE IS INTO ME?
WAIT, HOW LONG HAVE I JUST BEEN STANDING HERE? WHAT DOES MY FACE EVEN LOOK LIKE RIGHT NOW? OK OK OK SAY SOMETHING COOL...

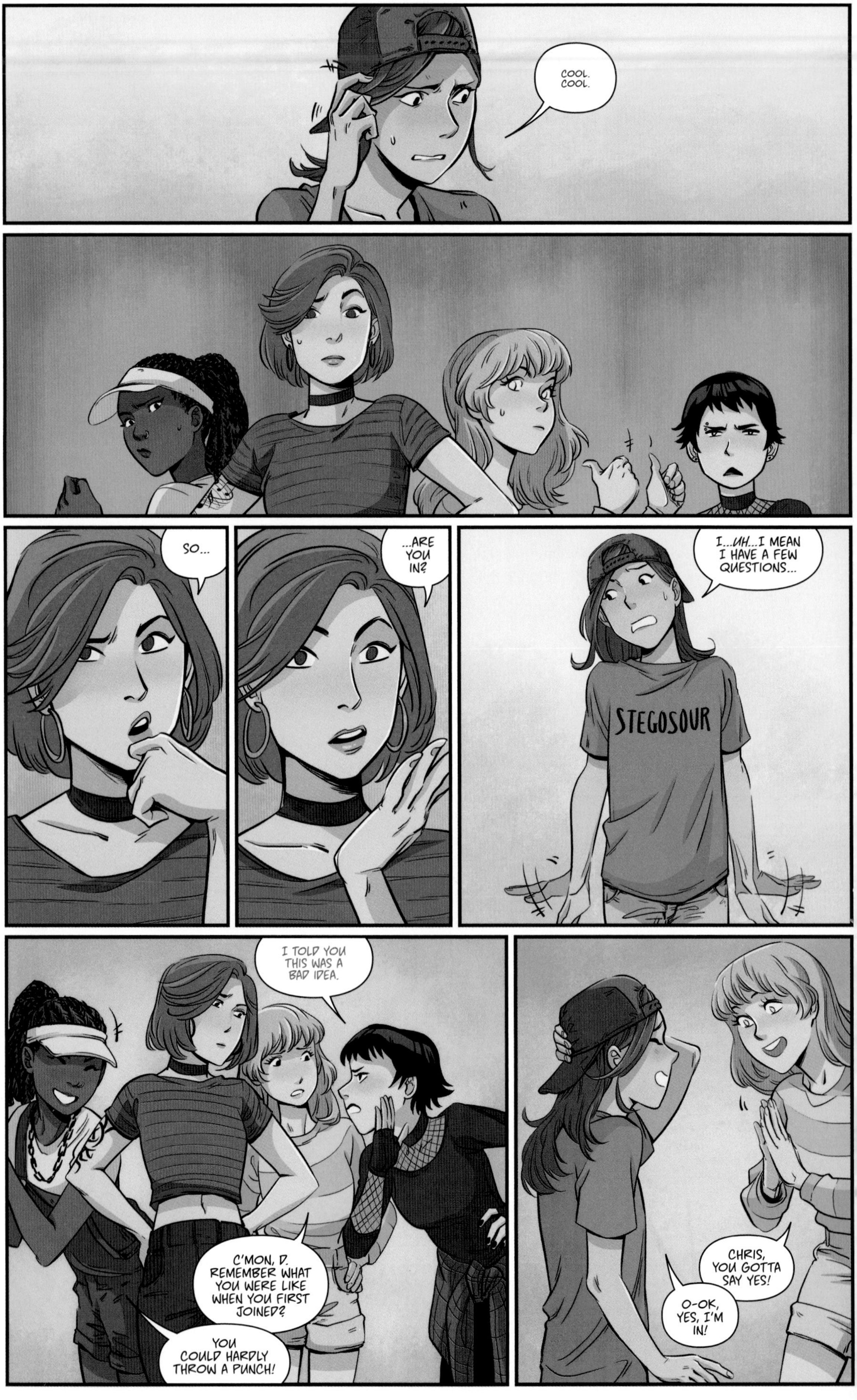
COOL. COOL.
SO...
...ARE YOU IN?
I...UH...I MEAN I HAVE A FEW QUESTIONS...
STEGOSOUR
I TOLD YOU THIS WAS A BAD IDEA.
C'MON, D. REMEMBER WHAT YOU WERE LIKE WHEN YOU FIRST JOINED?
YOU COULD HARDLY THROW A PUNCH!
CHRIS, YOU GOTTA SAY YES!
O-OK, YES, I'M IN!

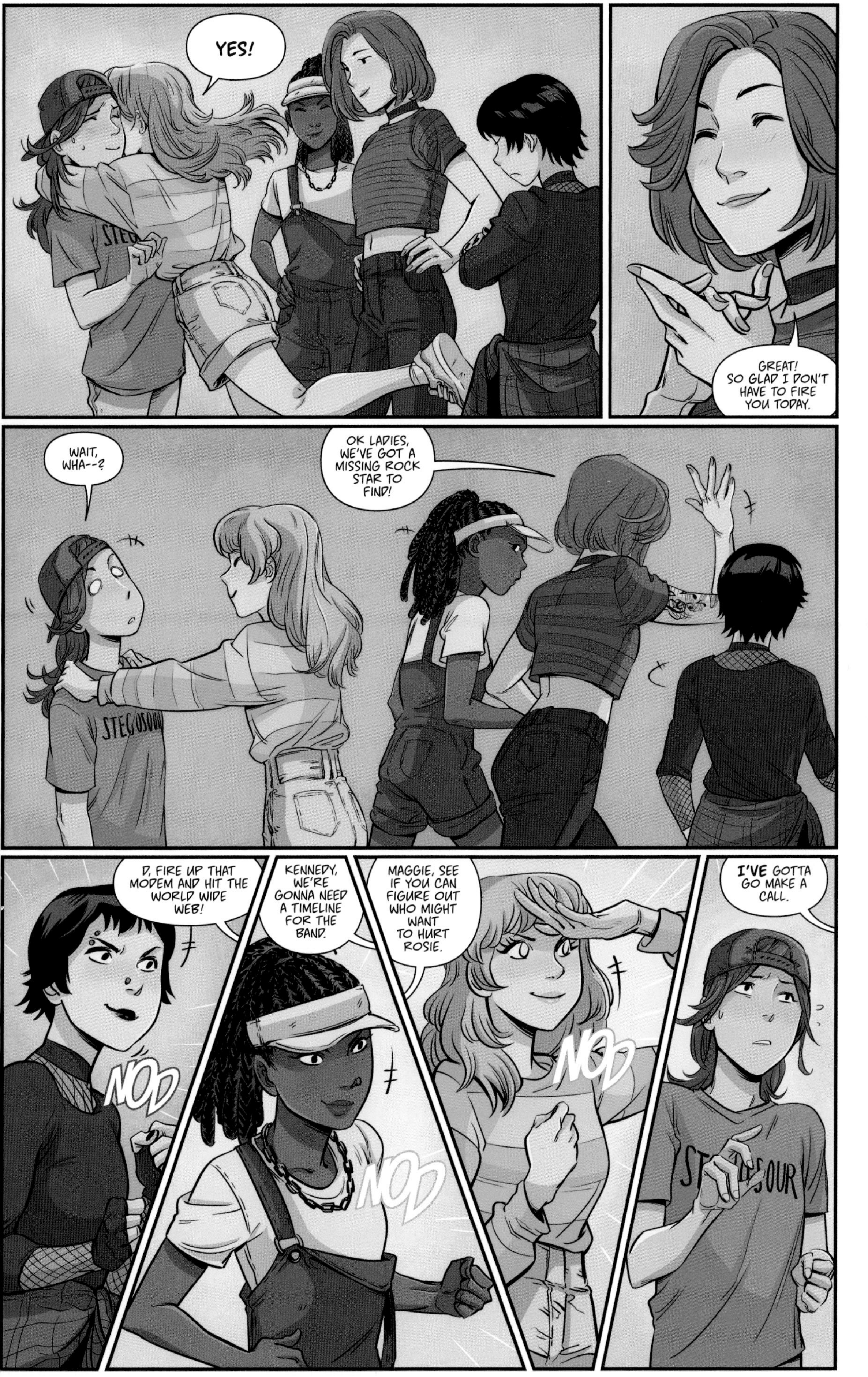
YES!
GREAT! SO GLAD I DON'T HAVE TO FIRE YOU TODAY.
WAIT, WHA--?
OK LADIES, WE'VE GOT A MISSING ROCK STAR TO FIND!
D, FIRE UP THAT MODEM AND HIT THE WORLD WIDE WEB!
NOD
KENNEDY, WE'RE GONNA NEED A TIMELINE FOR THE BAND.
NOD
MAGGIE, SEE IF YOU CAN FIGURE OUT WHO MIGHT WANT TO HURT ROSIE.
NOD
I'VE GOTTA GO MAKE A CALL.

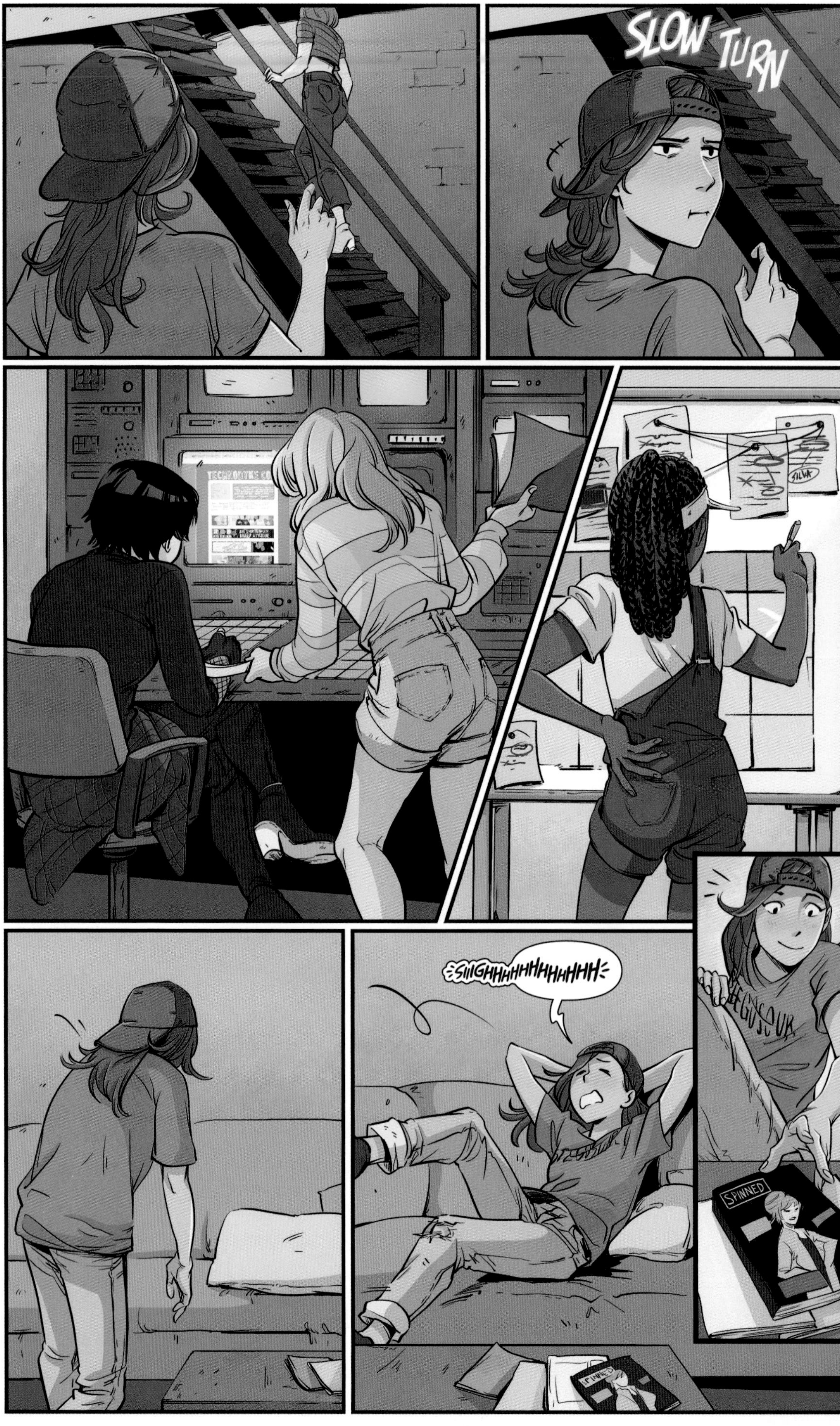
SLOW TURN
SILVA
SIIIGHHHHHHHHHHHH
SPINNED

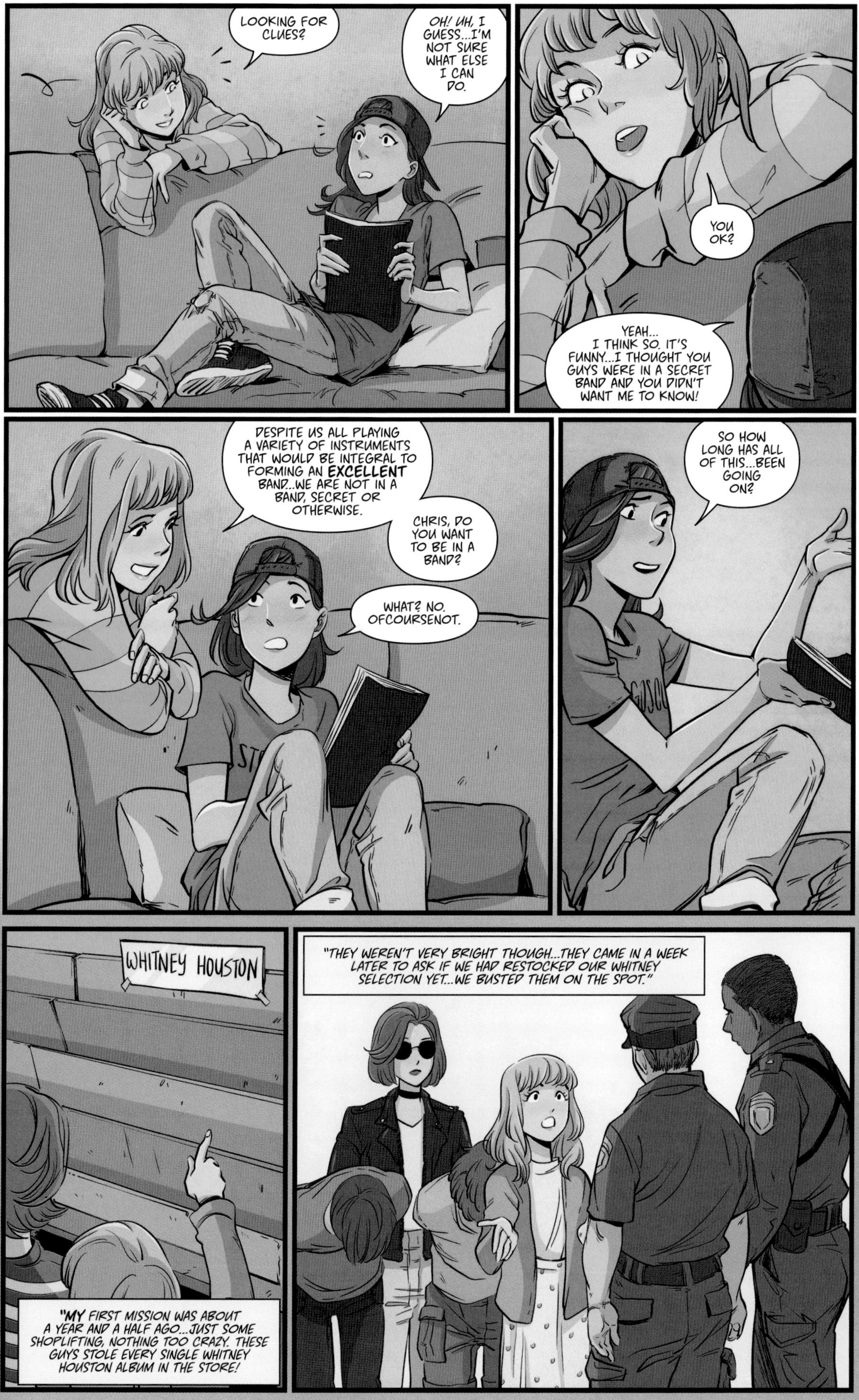

LOOKING FOR CLUES?
OH! UH, I GUESS...I'M NOT SURE WHAT ELSE I CAN DO.
YOU OK?
YEAH... I THINK SO. IT'S FUNNY...I THOUGHT YOU GUYS WERE IN A SECRET BAND AND YOU DIDN'T WANT ME TO KNOW!
DESPITE US ALL PLAYING A VARIETY OF INSTRUMENTS THAT WOULD BE INTEGRAL TO FORMING AN **EXCELLENT** BAND...WE ARE NOT IN A BAND, SECRET OR OTHERWISE.
CHRIS, DO YOU WANT TO BE IN A BAND?
WHAT? NO. OFCOURSENOT.
SO HOW LONG HAS ALL OF THIS...BEEN GOING ON?
WHITNEY HOUSTON
"**MY** FIRST MISSION WAS ABOUT A YEAR AND A HALF AGO...JUST SOME SHOPLIFTING, NOTHING TOO CRAZY. THESE GUYS STOLE EVERY SINGLE WHITNEY HOUSTON ALBUM IN THE STORE!
"THEY WEREN'T VERY BRIGHT THOUGH...THEY CAME IN A WEEK LATER TO ASK IF WE HAD RESTOCKED OUR WHITNEY SELECTION YET...WE BUSTED THEM ON THE SPOT."

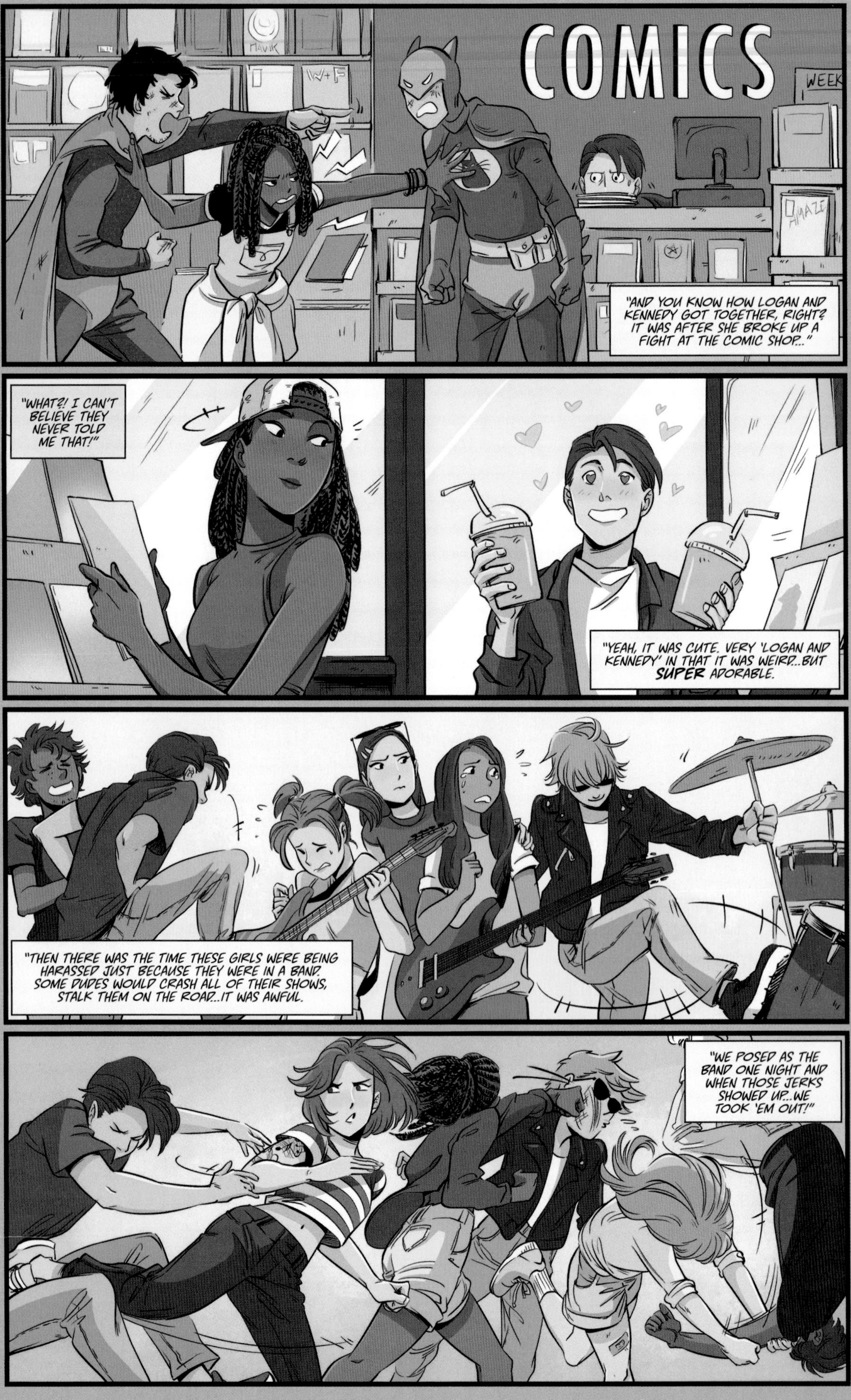
COMICS
HAVIK
W+F
WEEK
AMAZE
"AND YOU KNOW HOW LOGAN AND KENNEDY GOT TOGETHER, RIGHT? IT WAS AFTER SHE BROKE UP A FIGHT AT THE COMIC SHOP..."
"WHAT?! I CAN'T BELIEVE THEY NEVER TOLD ME THAT!"
"YEAH, IT WAS CUTE. VERY 'LOGAN AND KENNEDY' IN THAT IT WAS WEIRD...BUT SUPER ADORABLE.
"THEN THERE WAS THE TIME THESE GIRLS WERE BEING HARASSED JUST BECAUSE THEY WERE IN A BAND. SOME DUDES WOULD CRASH ALL OF THEIR SHOWS, STALK THEM ON THE ROAD...IT WAS AWFUL.
"WE POSED AS THE BAND ONE NIGHT AND WHEN THOSE JERKS SHOWED UP...WE TOOK 'EM OUT!"

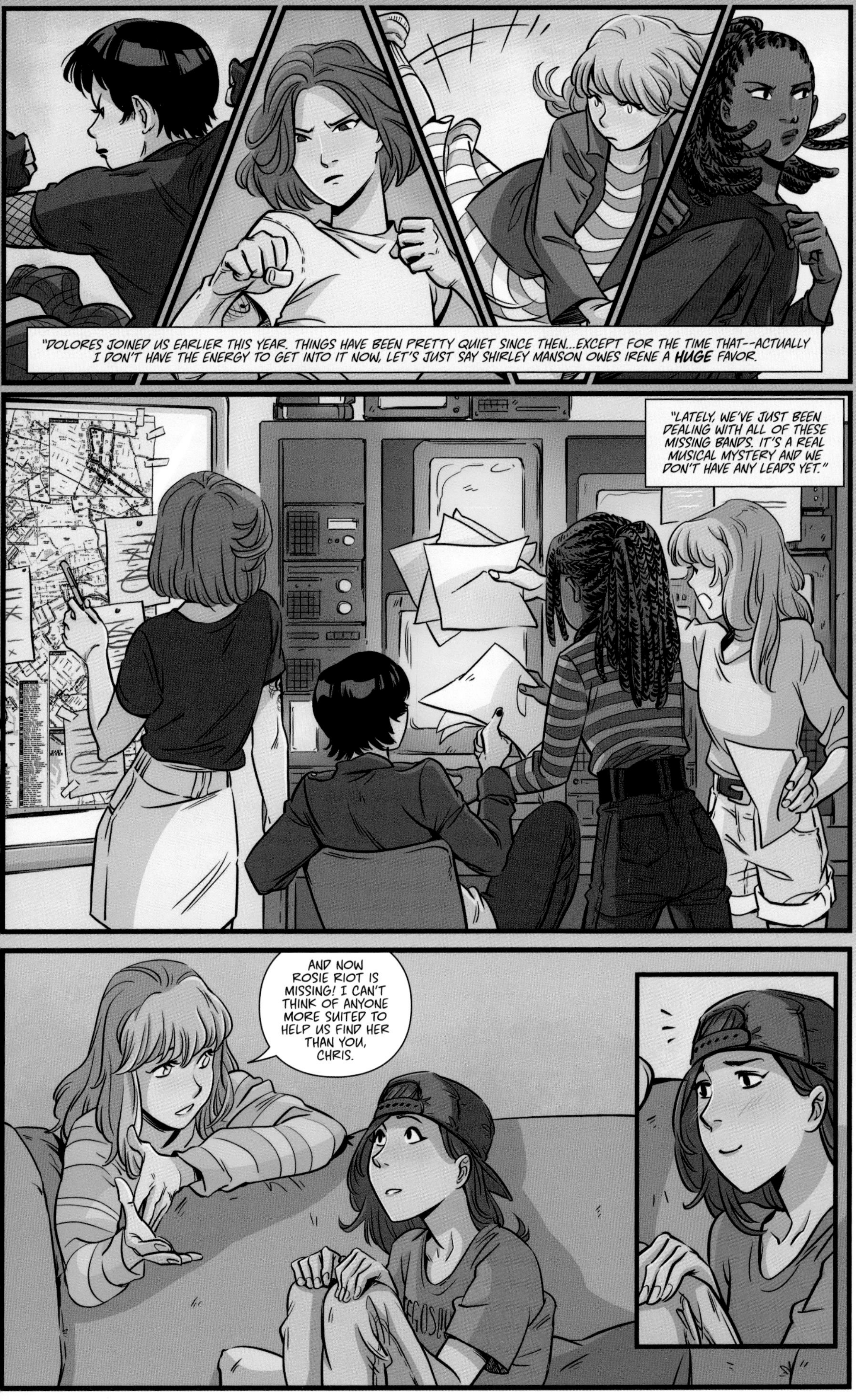
"DOLORES JOINED US EARLIER THIS YEAR. THINGS HAVE BEEN PRETTY QUIET SINCE THEN...EXCEPT FOR THE TIME THAT--ACTUALLY I DON'T HAVE THE ENERGY TO GET INTO IT NOW, LET'S JUST SAY SHIRLEY MANSON OWES IRENE A **HUGE** FAVOR.
"LATELY, WE'VE JUST BEEN DEALING WITH ALL OF THESE MISSING BANDS. IT'S A REAL MUSICAL MYSTERY AND WE DON'T HAVE ANY LEADS YET."
AND NOW ROSIE RIOT IS MISSING! I CAN'T THINK OF ANYONE MORE SUITED TO HELP US FIND HER THAN YOU, CHRIS.

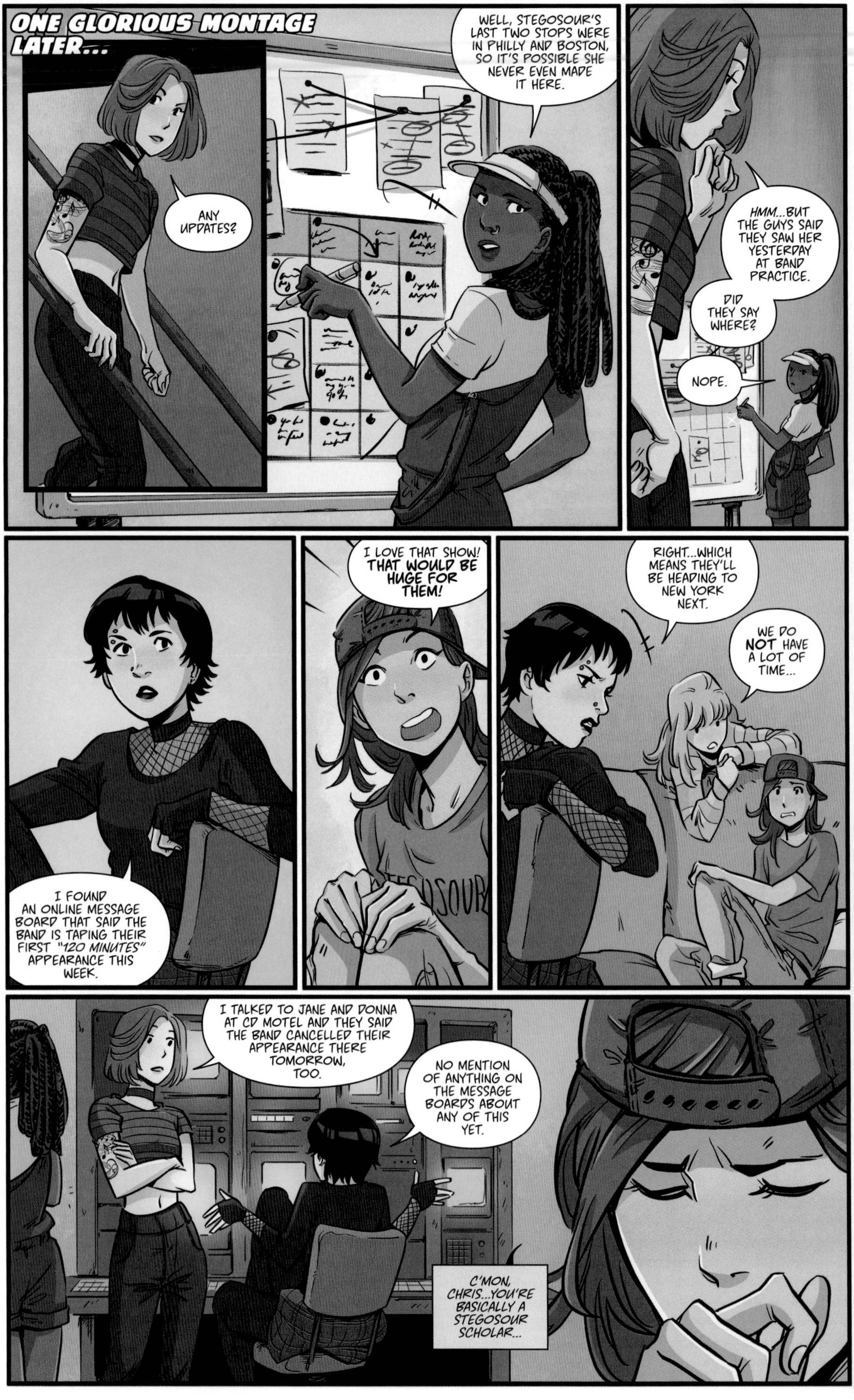
ONE GLORIOUS MONTAGE LATER...
ANY UPDATES?
WELL, STEGOSOUR'S LAST TWO STOPS WERE IN PHILLY AND BOSTON, SO IT'S POSSIBLE SHE NEVER EVEN MADE IT HERE.
HMM...BUT THE GUYS SAID THEY SAW HER YESTERDAY AT BAND PRACTICE.
DID THEY SAY WHERE?
NOPE.
I FOUND AN ONLINE MESSAGE BOARD THAT SAID THE BAND IS TAPING THEIR FIRST "120 MINUTES" APPEARANCE THIS WEEK.
I LOVE THAT SHOW! THAT WOULD BE HUGE FOR THEM!
RIGHT...WHICH MEANS THEY'LL BE HEADING TO NEW YORK NEXT.
WE DO NOT HAVE A LOT OF TIME...
I TALKED TO JANE AND DONNA AT CD MOTEL AND THEY SAID THE BAND CANCELLED THEIR APPEARANCE THERE TOMORROW, TOO.
NO MENTION OF ANYTHING ON THE MESSAGE BOARDS ABOUT ANY OF THIS YET.
C'MON, CHRIS...YOU'RE BASICALLY A STEGOSOUR SCHOLAR...

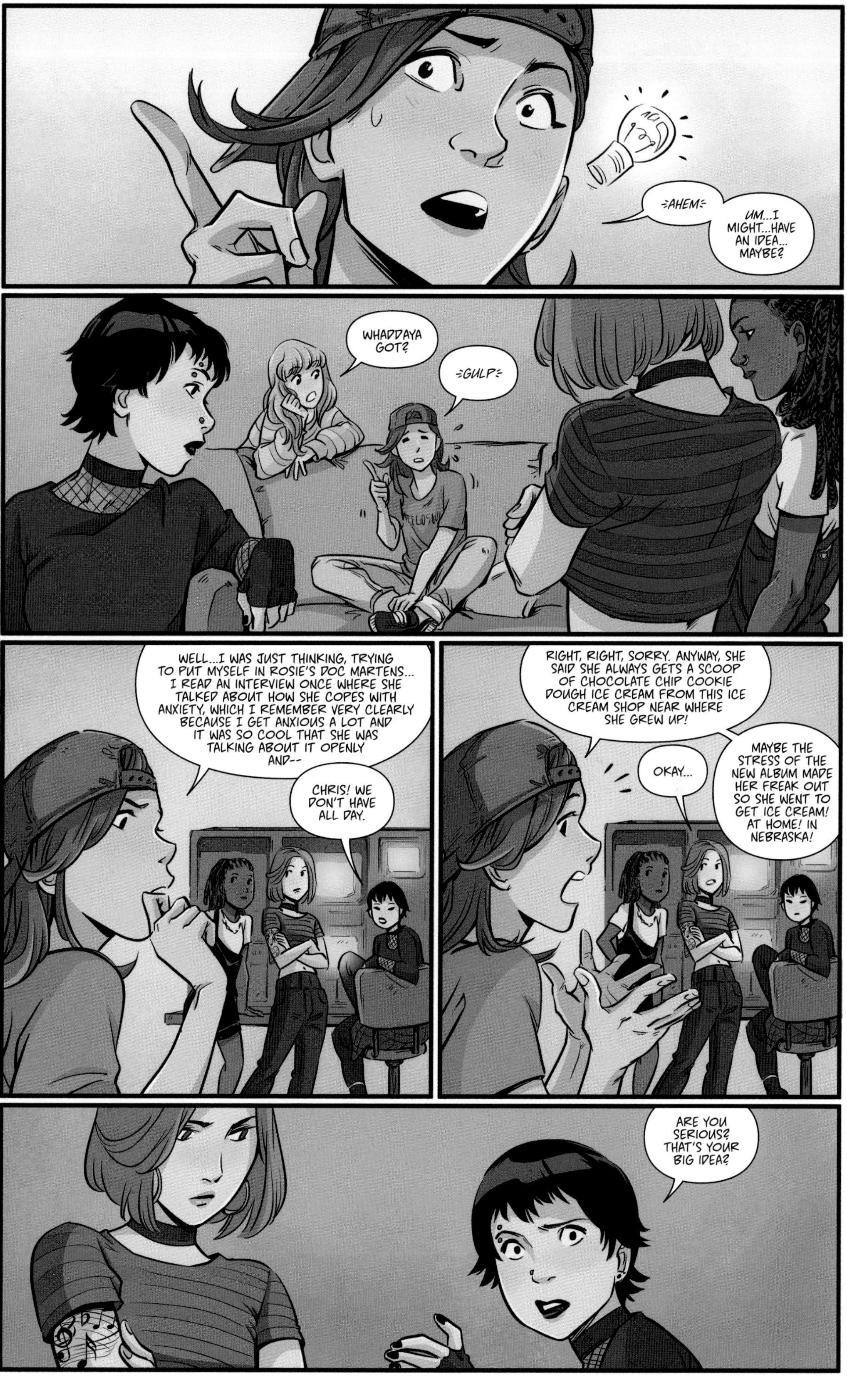

=AHEM=
UM...I MIGHT...HAVE AN IDEA... MAYBE?
WHADDAYA GOT?
=GULP=
WELL...I WAS JUST THINKING, TRYING TO PUT MYSELF IN ROSIE'S DOC MARTENS... I READ AN INTERVIEW ONCE WHERE SHE TALKED ABOUT HOW SHE COPES WITH ANXIETY, WHICH I REMEMBER VERY CLEARLY BECAUSE I GET ANXIOUS A LOT AND IT WAS SO COOL THAT SHE WAS TALKING ABOUT IT OPENLY AND--
CHRIS! WE DON'T HAVE ALL DAY.
RIGHT, RIGHT, SORRY. ANYWAY, SHE SAID SHE ALWAYS GETS A SCOOP OF CHOCOLATE CHIP COOKIE DOUGH ICE CREAM FROM THIS ICE CREAM SHOP NEAR WHERE SHE GREW UP!
OKAY...
MAYBE THE STRESS OF THE NEW ALBUM MADE HER FREAK OUT SO SHE WENT TO GET ICE CREAM! AT HOME! IN NEBRASKA!
ARE YOU SERIOUS? THAT'S YOUR BIG IDEA?

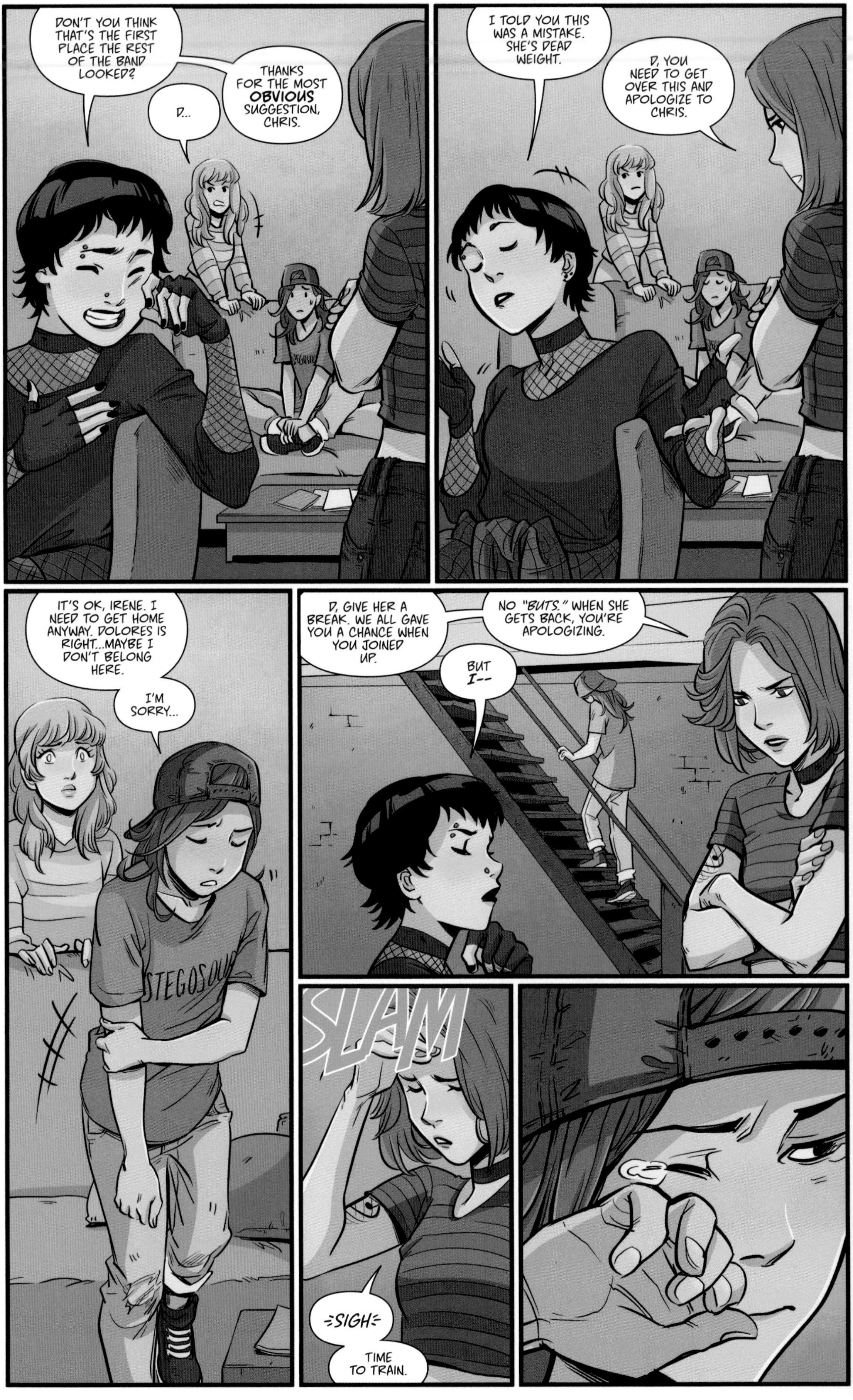
DON'T YOU THINK THAT'S THE FIRST PLACE THE REST OF THE BAND LOOKED?
D...
THANKS FOR THE MOST OBVIOUS SUGGESTION, CHRIS.
I TOLD YOU THIS WAS A MISTAKE. SHE'S DEAD WEIGHT.
D, YOU NEED TO GET OVER THIS AND APOLOGIZE TO CHRIS.
IT'S OK, IRENE. I NEED TO GET HOME ANYWAY. DOLORES IS RIGHT...MAYBE I DON'T BELONG HERE.
I'M SORRY...
D, GIVE HER A BREAK. WE ALL GAVE YOU A CHANCE WHEN YOU JOINED UP.
BUT I--
NO "BUTS." WHEN SHE GETS BACK, YOU'RE APOLOGIZING.
SLAM
=SIGH=
TIME TO TRAIN.

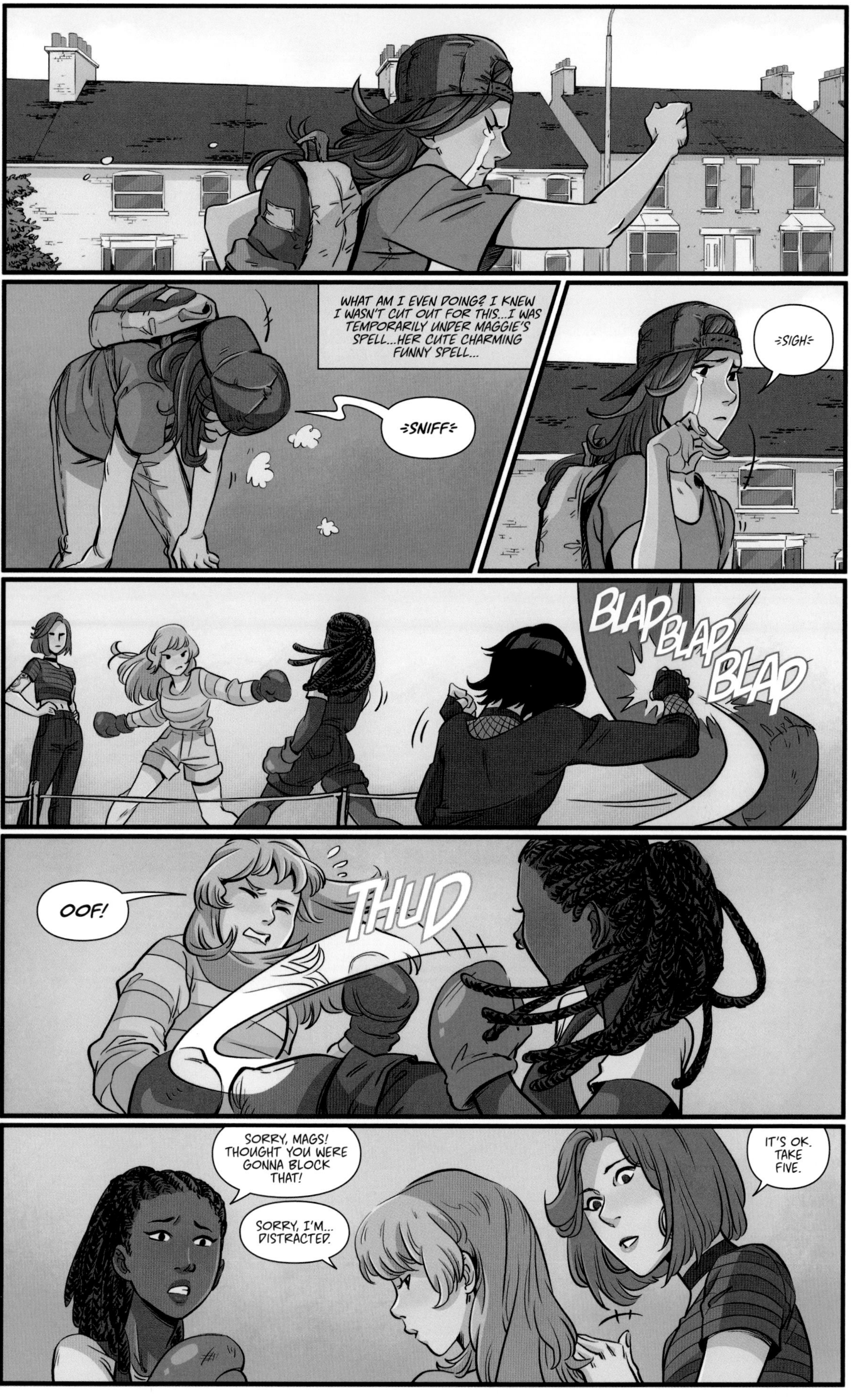
WHAT AM I EVEN DOING? I KNEW I WASN'T CUT OUT FOR THIS...I WAS TEMPORARILY UNDER MAGGIE'S SPELL...HER CUTE CHARMING FUNNY SPELL...
SNIFF
SIGH
BLAP BLAP BLAP
OOF!
THUD
SORRY, MAGS! THOUGHT YOU WERE GONNA BLOCK THAT!
SORRY, I'M... DISTRACTED.
IT'S OK. TAKE FIVE.

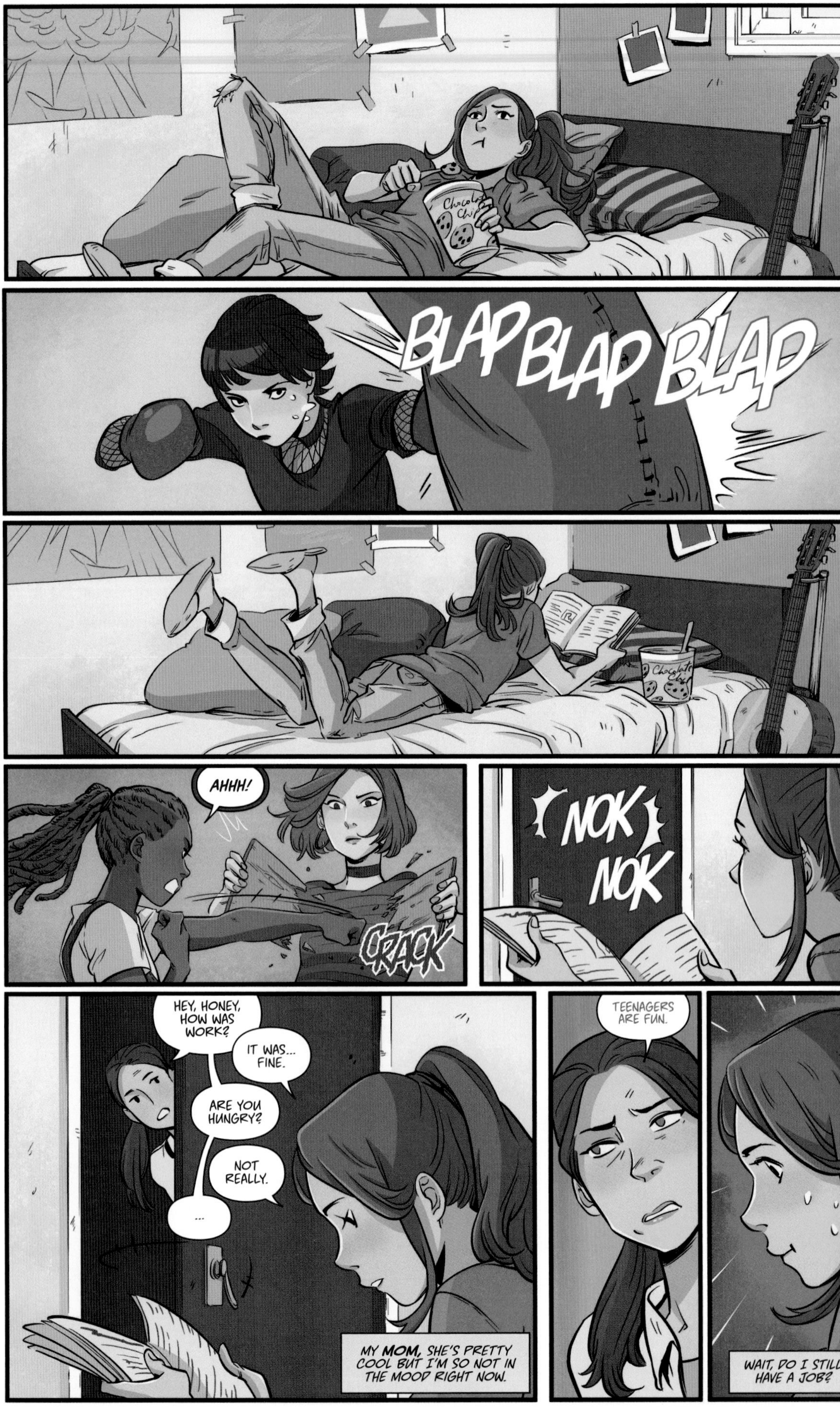

BLAP BLAP BLAP
AHHH!
CRACK
NOK NOK
HEY, HONEY, HOW WAS WORK?
IT WAS... FINE.
ARE YOU HUNGRY?
NOT REALLY.
...
MY MOM, SHE'S PRETTY COOL BUT I'M SO NOT IN THE MOOD RIGHT NOW.
TEENAGERS ARE FUN.
WAIT, DO I STILL HAVE A JOB?

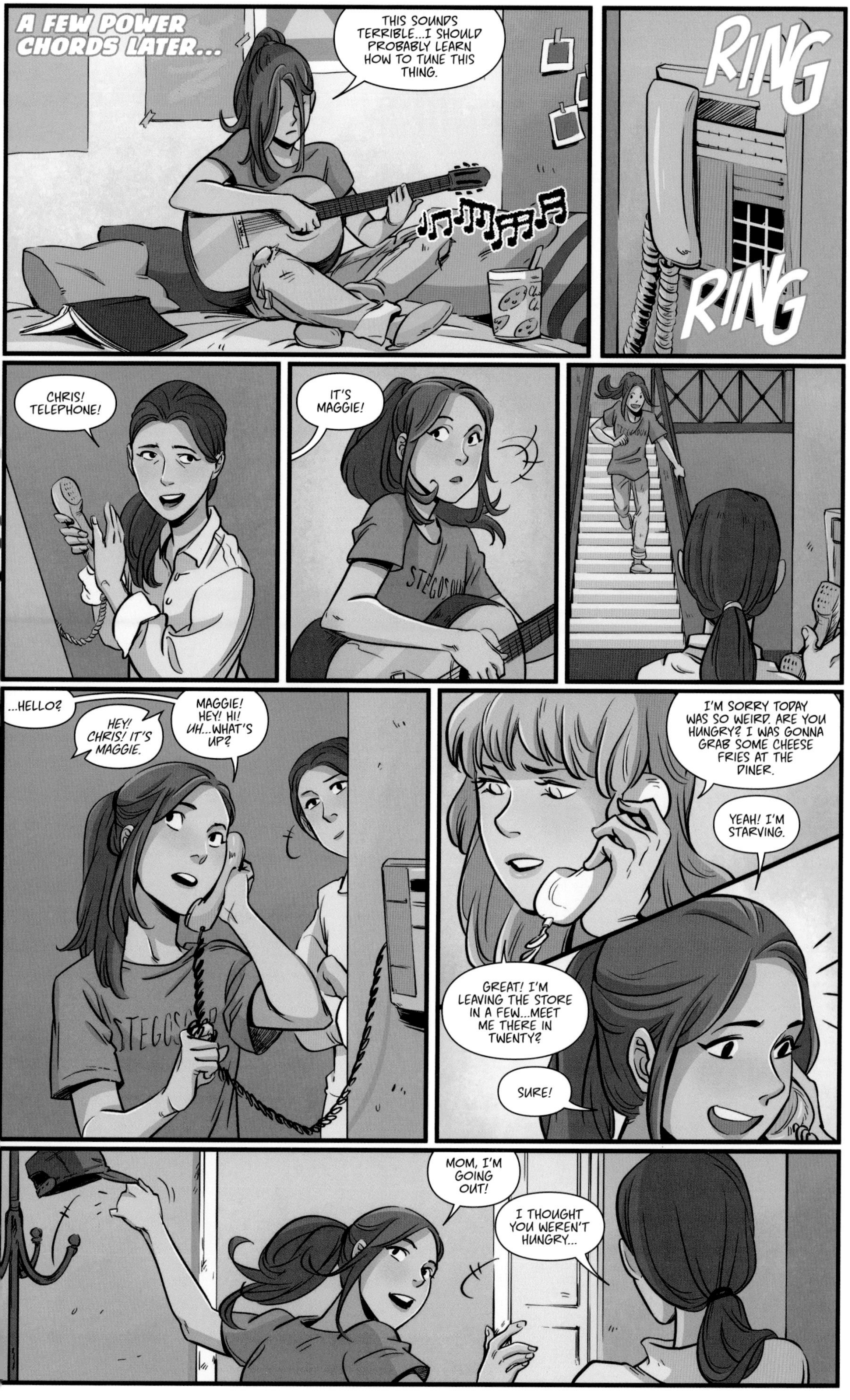
A FEW POWER CHORDS LATER...
THIS SOUNDS TERRIBLE...I SHOULD PROBABLY LEARN HOW TO TUNE THIS THING.
RING
RING
CHRIS! TELEPHONE!
IT'S MAGGIE!
...HELLO?
HEY! CHRIS! IT'S MAGGIE.
MAGGIE! HEY! HI! UH...WHAT'S UP?
I'M SORRY TODAY WAS SO WEIRD. ARE YOU HUNGRY? I WAS GONNA GRAB SOME CHEESE FRIES AT THE DINER.
YEAH! I'M STARVING.
GREAT! I'M LEAVING THE STORE IN A FEW...MEET ME THERE IN TWENTY?
SURE!
MOM, I'M GOING OUT!
I THOUGHT YOU WEREN'T HUNGRY...

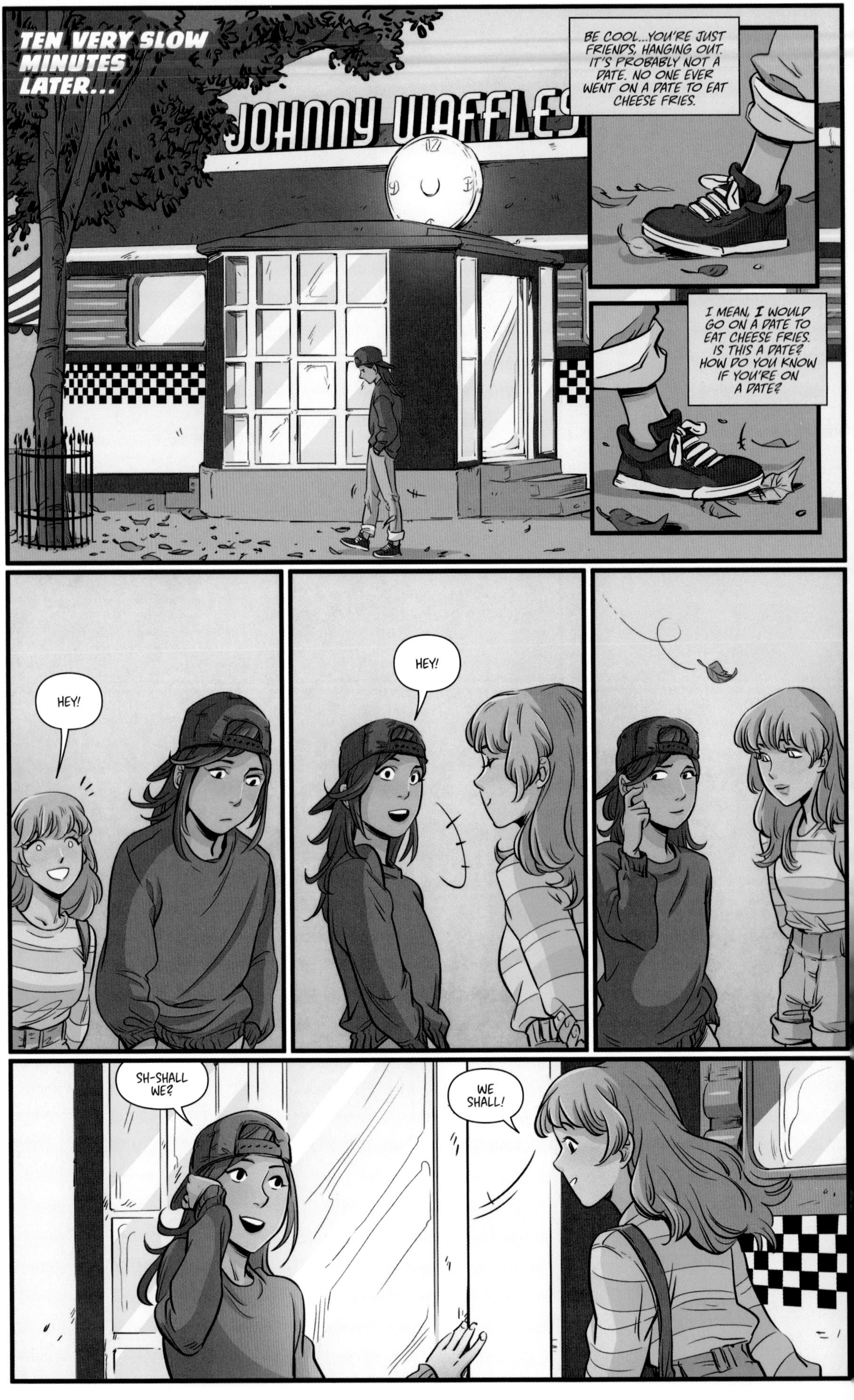
TEN VERY SLOW MINUTES LATER...
JOHNNY WAFFLES
BE COOL...YOU'RE JUST FRIENDS, HANGING OUT. IT'S PROBABLY NOT A DATE. NO ONE EVER WENT ON A DATE TO EAT CHEESE FRIES.
I MEAN, I WOULD GO ON A DATE TO EAT CHEESE FRIES. IS THIS A DATE? HOW DO YOU KNOW IF YOU'RE ON A DATE?
HEY!
HEY!
SH-SHALL WE?
WE SHALL!

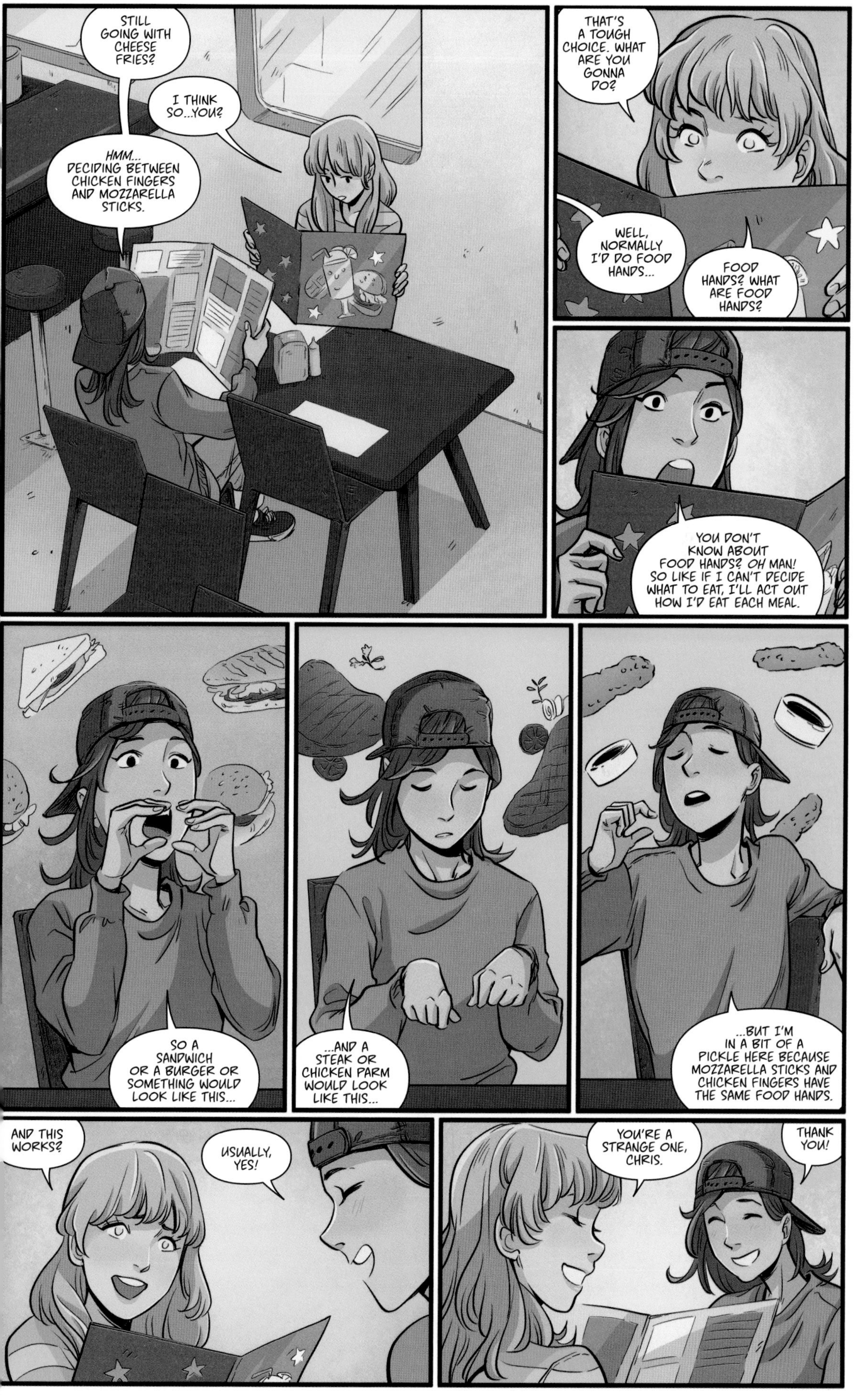

STILL GOING WITH CHEESE FRIES?
I THINK SO...YOU?
HMM... DECIDING BETWEEN CHICKEN FINGERS AND MOZZARELLA STICKS.
THAT'S A TOUGH CHOICE. WHAT ARE YOU GONNA DO?
WELL, NORMALLY I'D DO FOOD HANDS...
FOOD HANDS? WHAT ARE FOOD HANDS?
YOU DON'T KNOW ABOUT FOOD HANDS? OH MAN! SO LIKE IF I CAN'T DECIDE WHAT TO EAT, I'LL ACT OUT HOW I'D EAT EACH MEAL.
SO A SANDWICH OR A BURGER OR SOMETHING WOULD LOOK LIKE THIS...
...AND A STEAK OR CHICKEN PARM WOULD LOOK LIKE THIS...
...BUT I'M IN A BIT OF A PICKLE HERE BECAUSE MOZZARELLA STICKS AND CHICKEN FINGERS HAVE THE SAME FOOD HANDS.
AND THIS WORKS?
USUALLY, YES!
YOU'RE A STRANGE ONE, CHRIS.
THANK YOU!

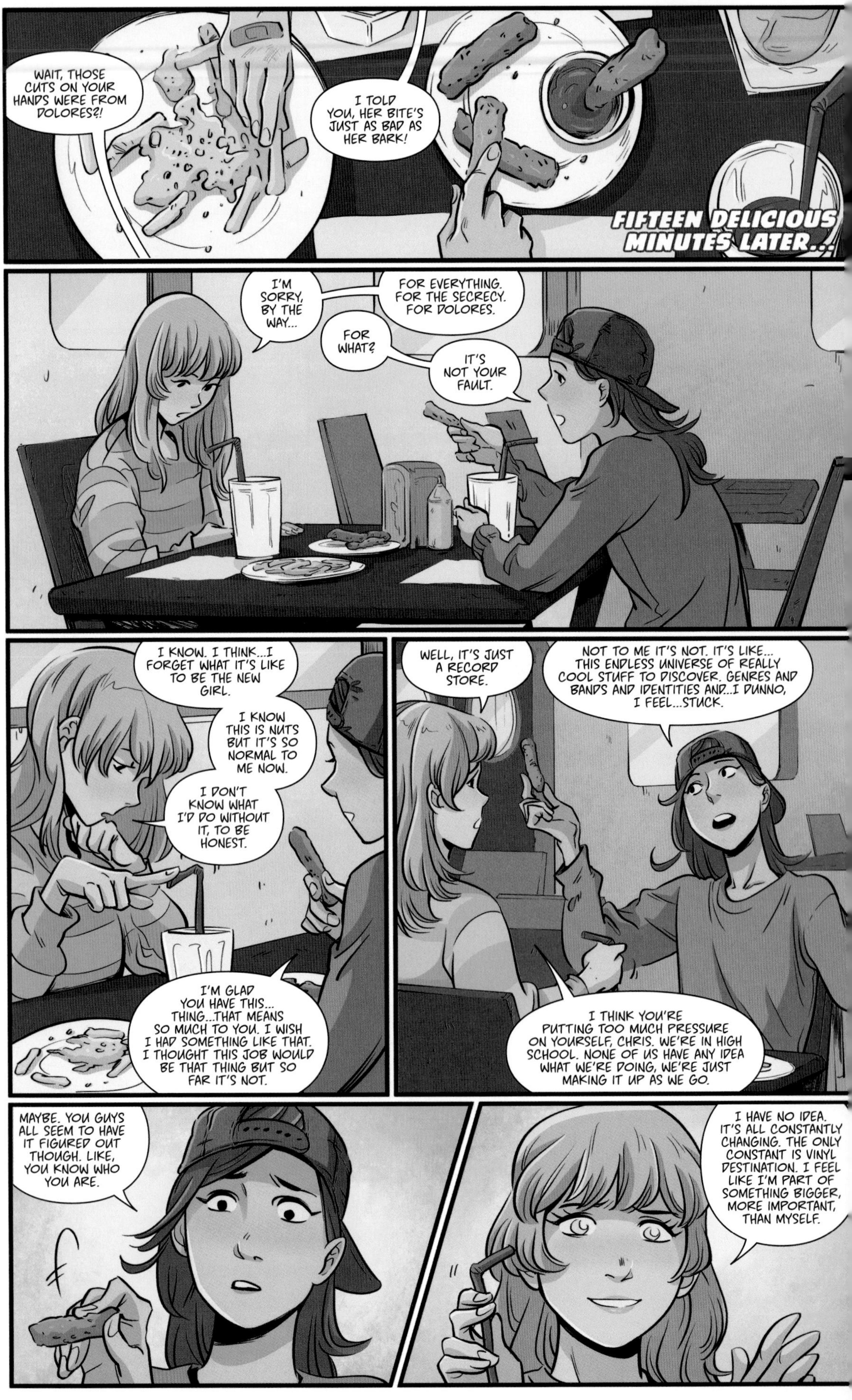
WAIT, THOSE CUTS ON YOUR HANDS WERE FROM DOLORES?!
I TOLD YOU, HER BITE'S JUST AS BAD AS HER BARK!
FIFTEEN DELICIOUS MINUTES LATER...
I'M SORRY, BY THE WAY...
FOR WHAT?
FOR EVERYTHING. FOR THE SECRECY. FOR DOLORES.
IT'S NOT YOUR FAULT.
I KNOW. I THINK...I FORGET WHAT IT'S LIKE TO BE THE NEW GIRL.
I KNOW THIS IS NUTS BUT IT'S SO NORMAL TO ME NOW.
I DON'T KNOW WHAT I'D DO WITHOUT IT, TO BE HONEST.
I'M GLAD YOU HAVE THIS... THING...THAT MEANS SO MUCH TO YOU. I WISH I HAD SOMETHING LIKE THAT. I THOUGHT THIS JOB WOULD BE THAT THING BUT SO FAR IT'S NOT.
WELL, IT'S JUST A RECORD STORE.
NOT TO ME IT'S NOT. IT'S LIKE... THIS ENDLESS UNIVERSE OF REALLY COOL STUFF TO DISCOVER. GENRES AND BANDS AND IDENTITIES AND...I DUNNO, I FEEL...STUCK.
I THINK YOU'RE PUTTING TOO MUCH PRESSURE ON YOURSELF, CHRIS. WE'RE IN HIGH SCHOOL. NONE OF US HAVE ANY IDEA WHAT WE'RE DOING, WE'RE JUST MAKING IT UP AS WE GO.
MAYBE. YOU GUYS ALL SEEM TO HAVE IT FIGURED OUT THOUGH. LIKE, YOU KNOW WHO YOU ARE.
I HAVE NO IDEA. IT'S ALL CONSTANTLY CHANGING. THE ONLY CONSTANT IS VINYL DESTINATION. I FEEL LIKE I'M PART OF SOMETHING BIGGER, MORE IMPORTANT, THAN MYSELF.

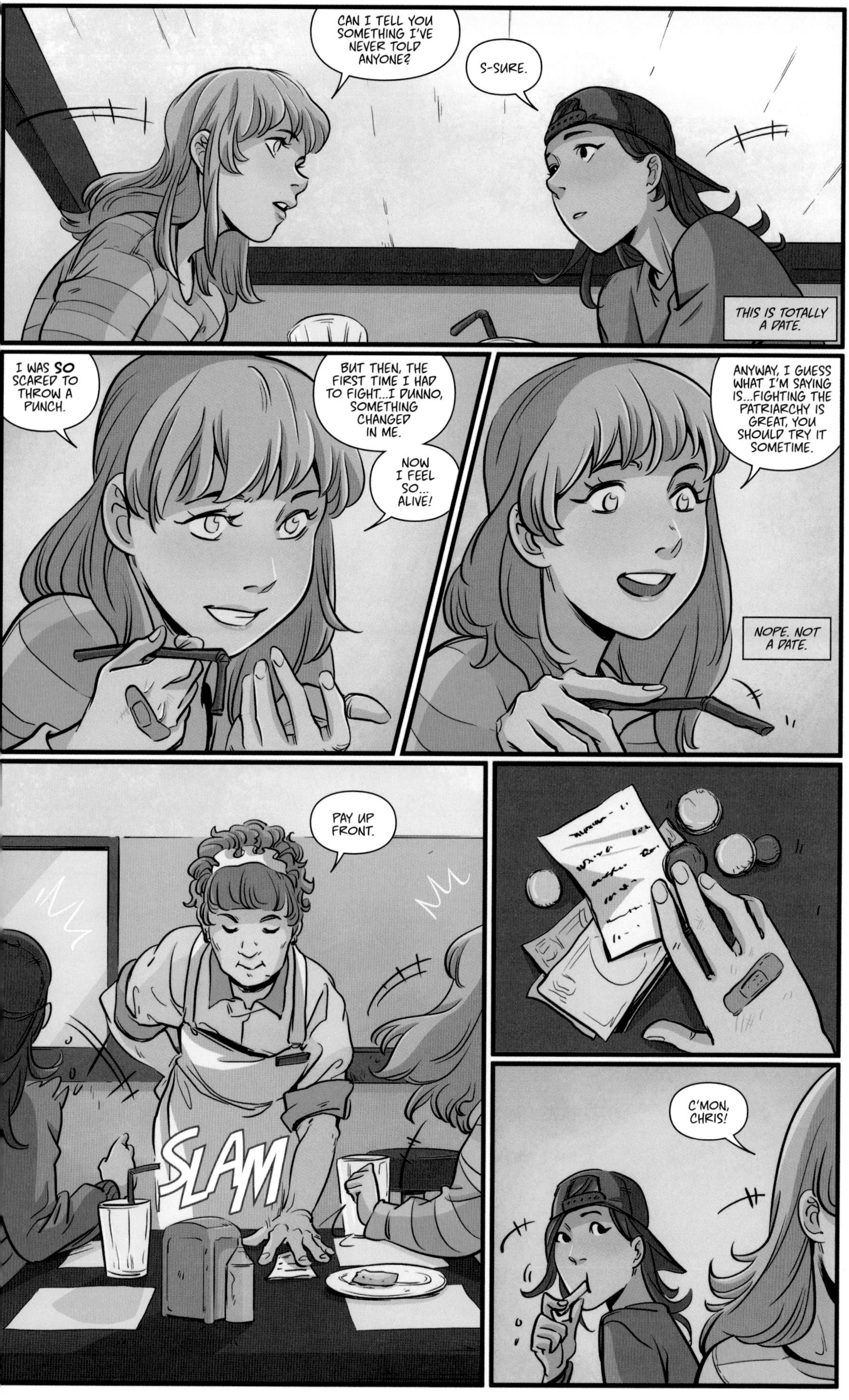
CAN I TELL YOU SOMETHING I'VE NEVER TOLD ANYONE?
S-SURE.
THIS IS TOTALLY A DATE.
I WAS **SO** SCARED TO THROW A PUNCH.
BUT THEN, THE FIRST TIME I HAD TO FIGHT...I DUNNO, SOMETHING CHANGED IN ME.
NOW I FEEL SO... ALIVE!
ANYWAY, I GUESS WHAT I'M SAYING IS...FIGHTING THE PATRIARCHY IS GREAT, YOU SHOULD TRY IT SOMETIME.
NOPE. NOT A DATE.
PAY UP FRONT.
SLAM
C'MON, CHRIS!

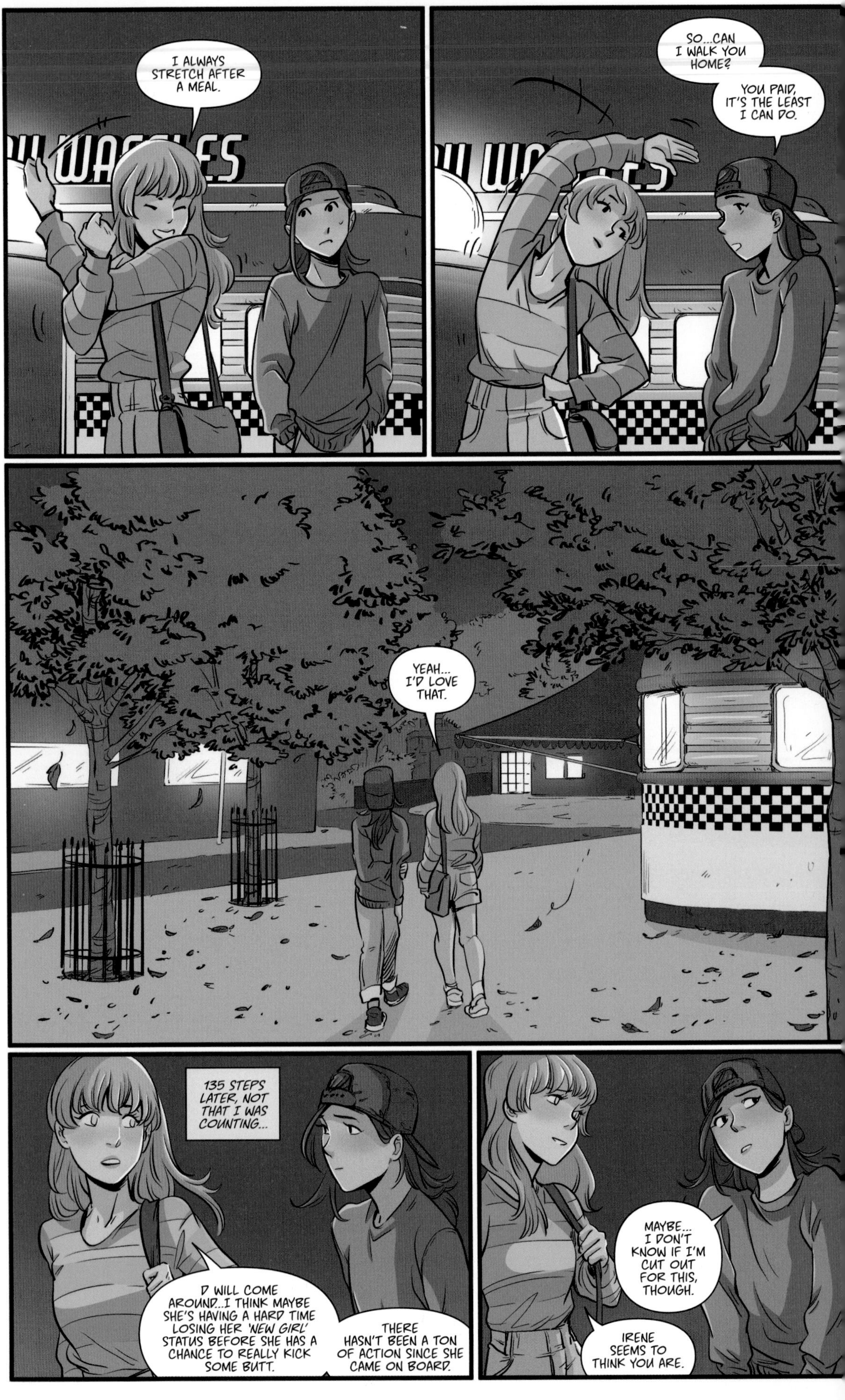
I ALWAYS STRETCH AFTER A MEAL.
SO...CAN I WALK YOU HOME?
YOU PAID, IT'S THE LEAST I CAN DO.
YEAH... I'D LOVE THAT.
135 STEPS LATER, NOT THAT I WAS COUNTING...
D WILL COME AROUND...I THINK MAYBE SHE'S HAVING A HARD TIME LOSING HER 'NEW GIRL' STATUS BEFORE SHE HAS A CHANCE TO REALLY KICK SOME BUTT.
THERE HASN'T BEEN A TON OF ACTION SINCE SHE CAME ON BOARD.
MAYBE... I DON'T KNOW IF I'M CUT OUT FOR THIS, THOUGH.
IRENE SEEMS TO THINK YOU ARE.

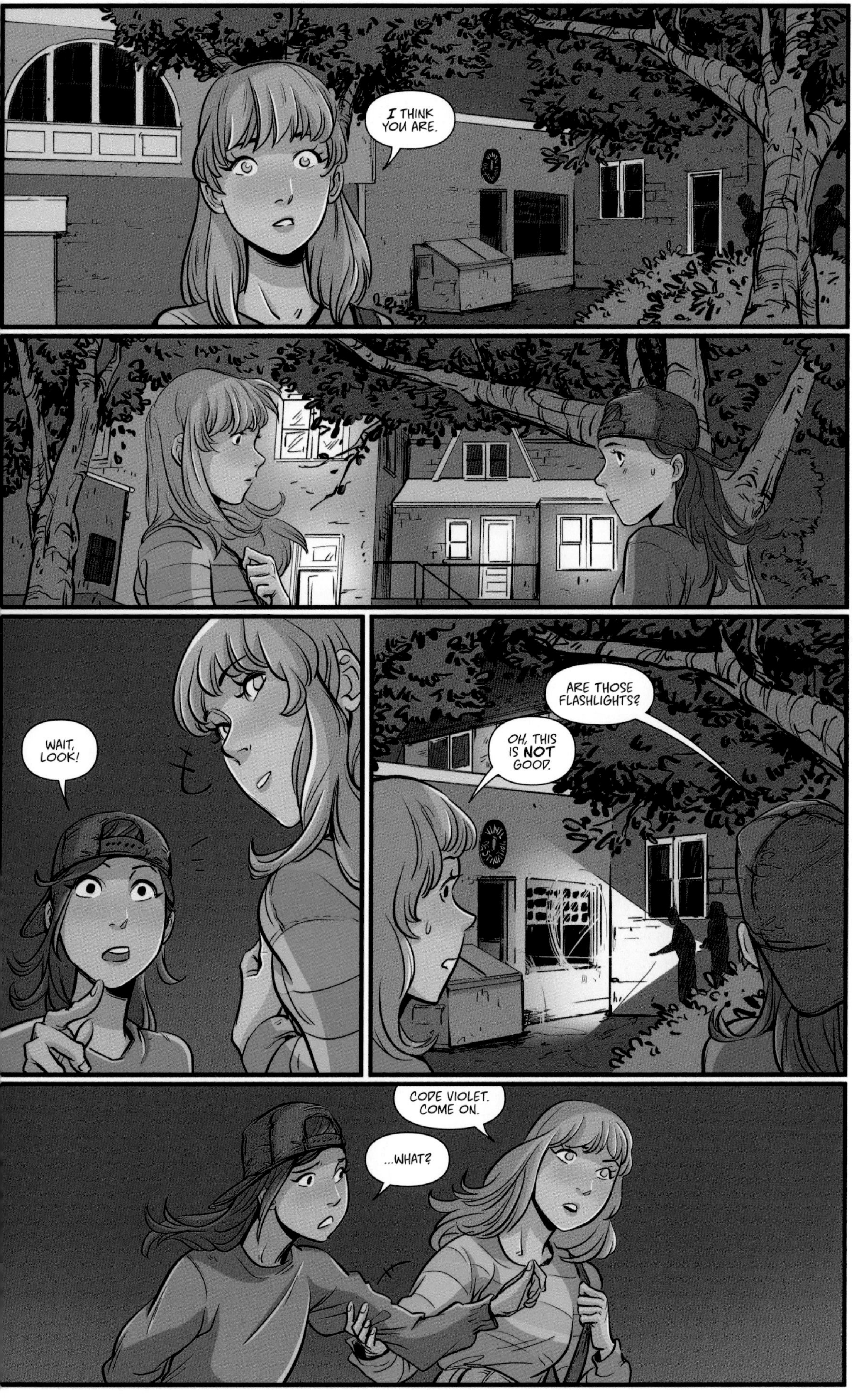
I THINK YOU ARE.
WAIT, LOOK!
ARE THOSE FLASHLIGHTS?
OH, THIS IS NOT GOOD.
CODE VIOLET. COME ON.
...WHAT?

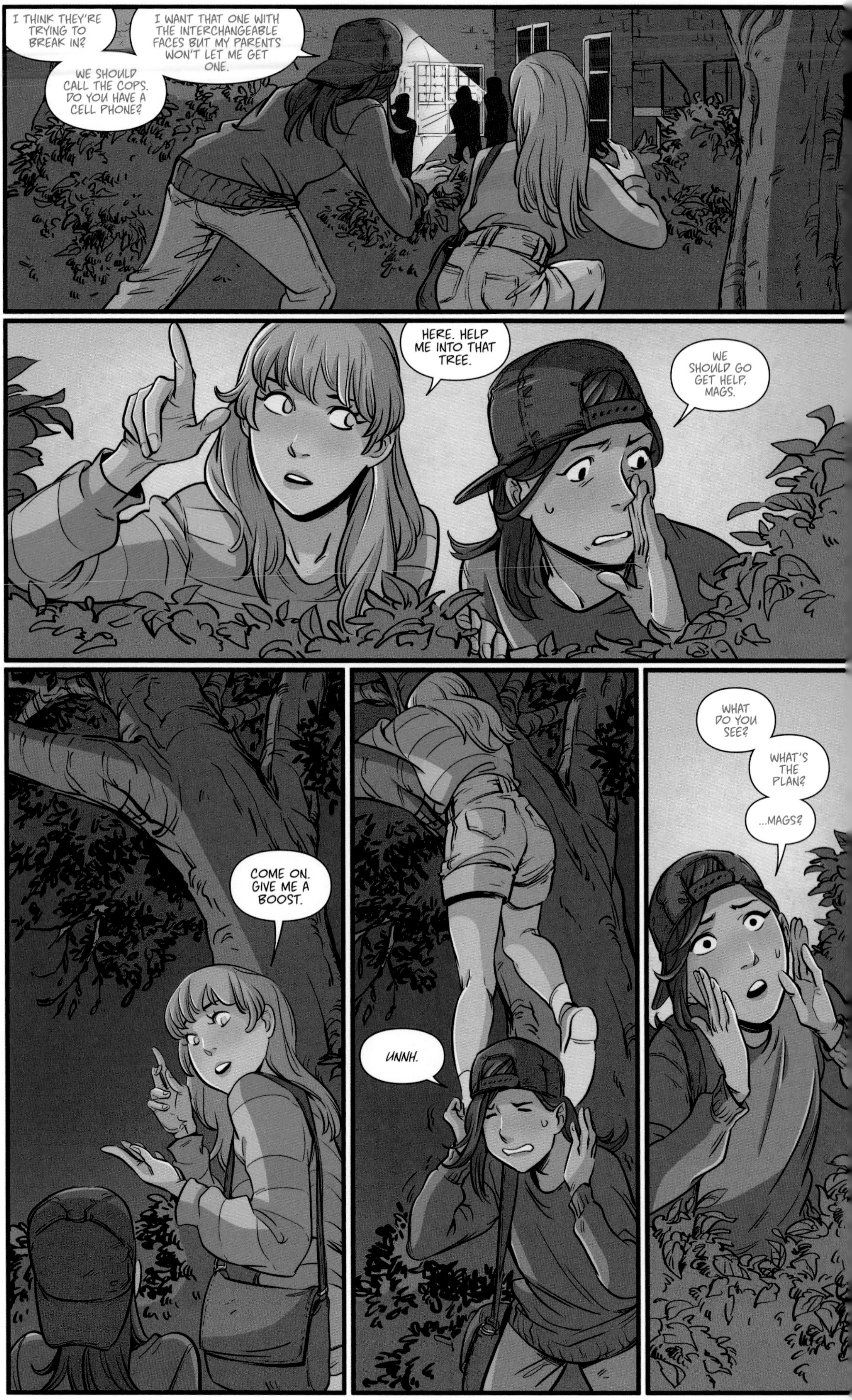
I THINK THEY'RE TRYING TO BREAK IN?
WE SHOULD CALL THE COPS. DO YOU HAVE A CELL PHONE?
I WANT THAT ONE WITH THE INTERCHANGEABLE FACES BUT MY PARENTS WON'T LET ME GET ONE.
HERE. HELP ME INTO THAT TREE.
WE SHOULD GO GET HELP, MAGS.
COME ON. GIVE ME A BOOST.
UNNH.
WHAT DO YOU SEE?
WHAT'S THE PLAN?
...MAGS?

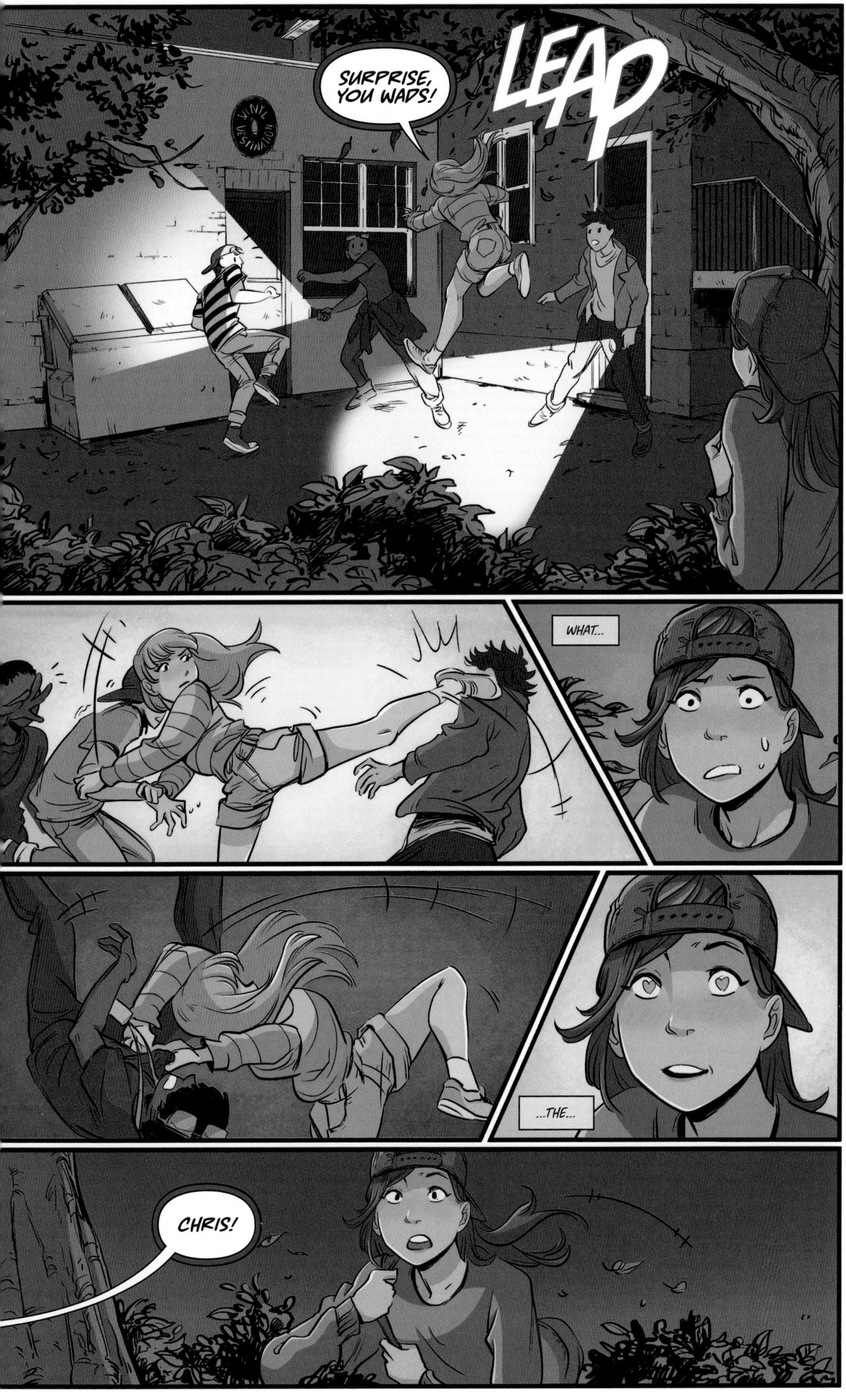
SURPRISE, YOU WADS!
LEAP
VINYL DESTINATION
WHAT...
...THE...
CHRIS!

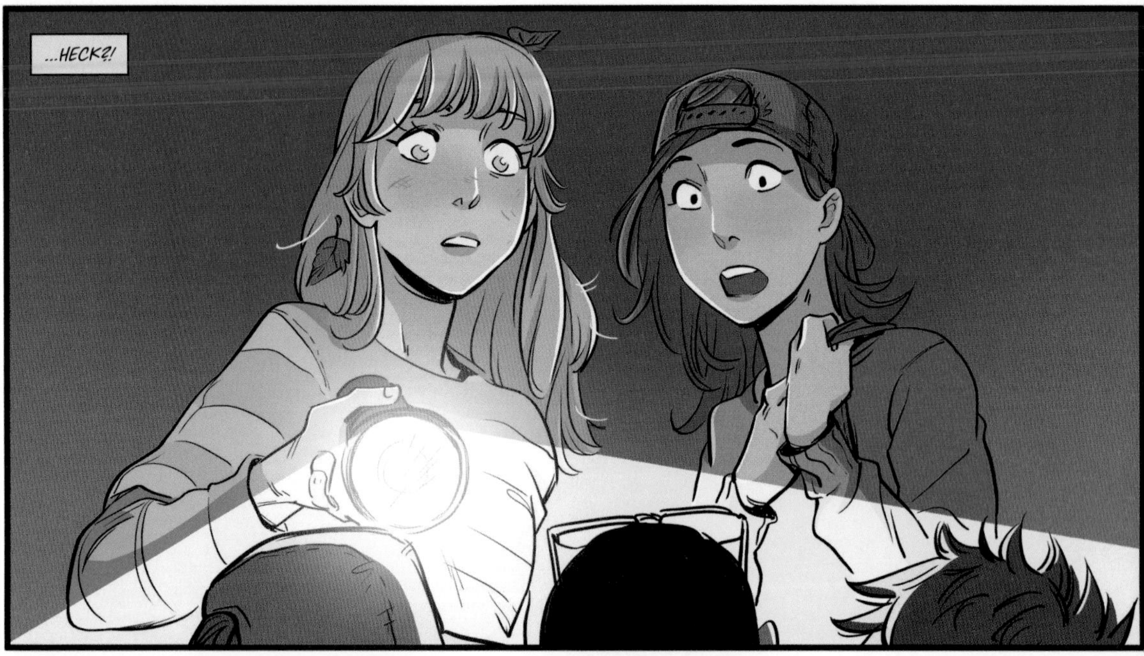
...HECK?!

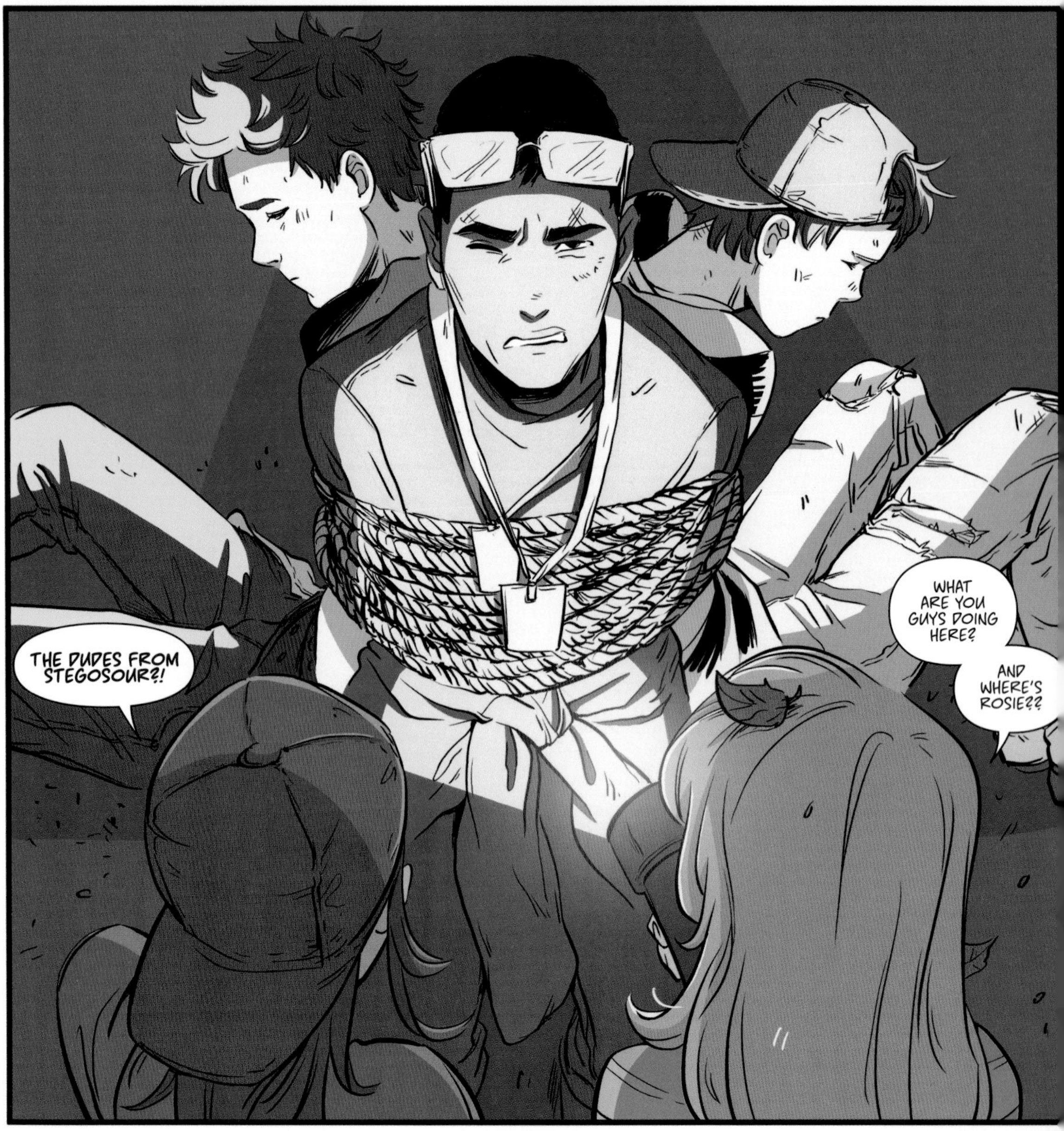
THE DUDES FROM STEGOSOUR?!
WHAT ARE YOU GUYS DOING HERE?
AND WHERE'S ROSIE??

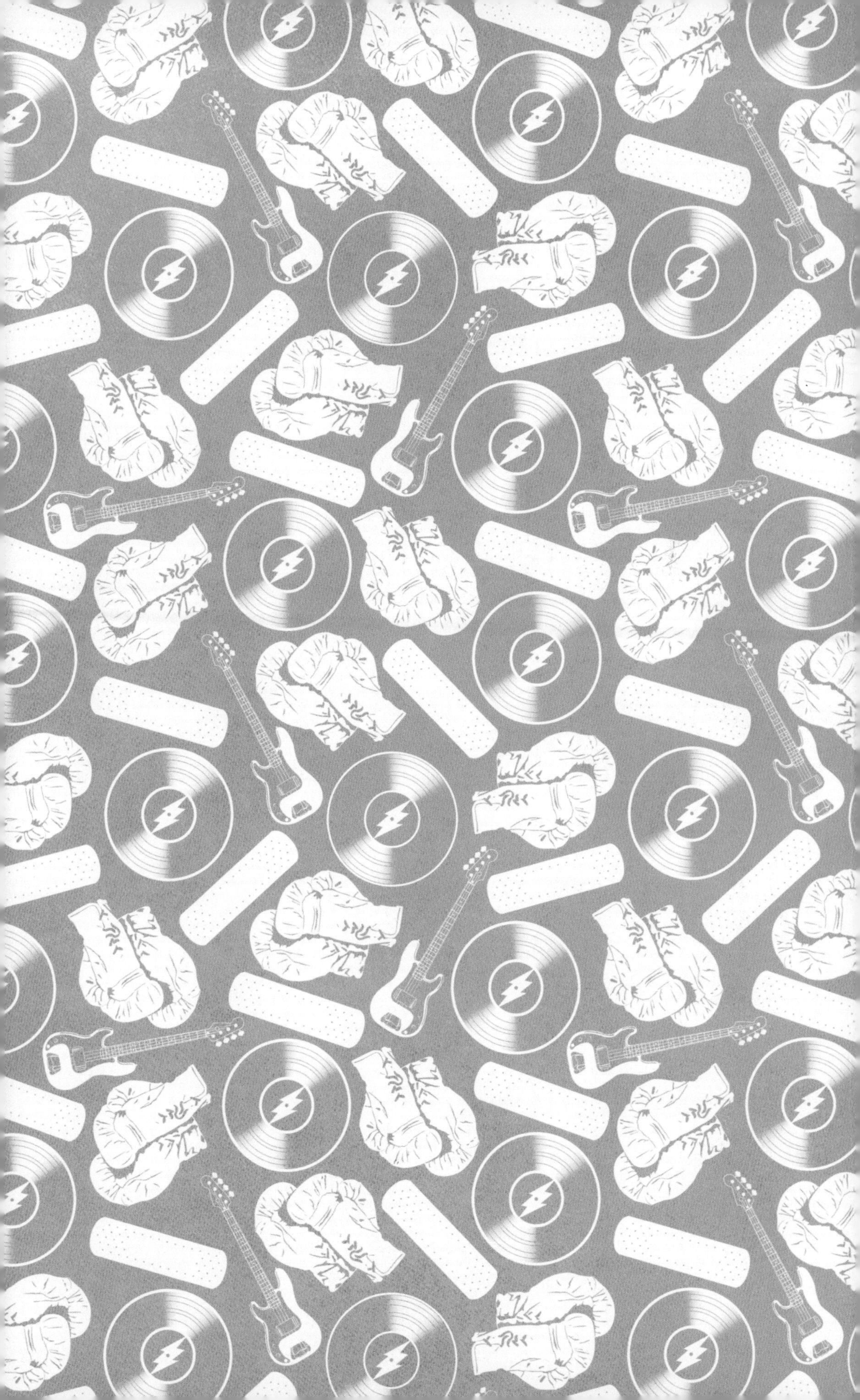

once upon a time / tHere Was nothing (yeah) /
then a big big Bang / gave Us something (yeah) /
evoluTion is our revolutioN / evolution is
oUr revolution / read between the lin___
reaD between the lines / it's in Our cod___
from long aGo / primordial bruise / primor___
bruise / billions of years / To rule the
world (yeah) / have Brought us ___
volcanO girls (yeah) / ___
revolution / ___
read ___

CHAPTER THREE

___nds,
___ there for
___ our guidance.
___olved in Jurassic
___novie. A ROAR to No
___ and Tilt for letting us join
___ped Tour! And the biggest ROAR
___ the best label, Imaginary Selves!!
___ve our I.S. family!!
ROSIE RIOT would like to thank her idols:
Cinder, Shirley, Gwen, Poe, Joan, Kay, Skin,
Kathleen, Carrie and Corin, for showing her
the way.
CHARLIE would like to thank pizza for
always getting him through the day.

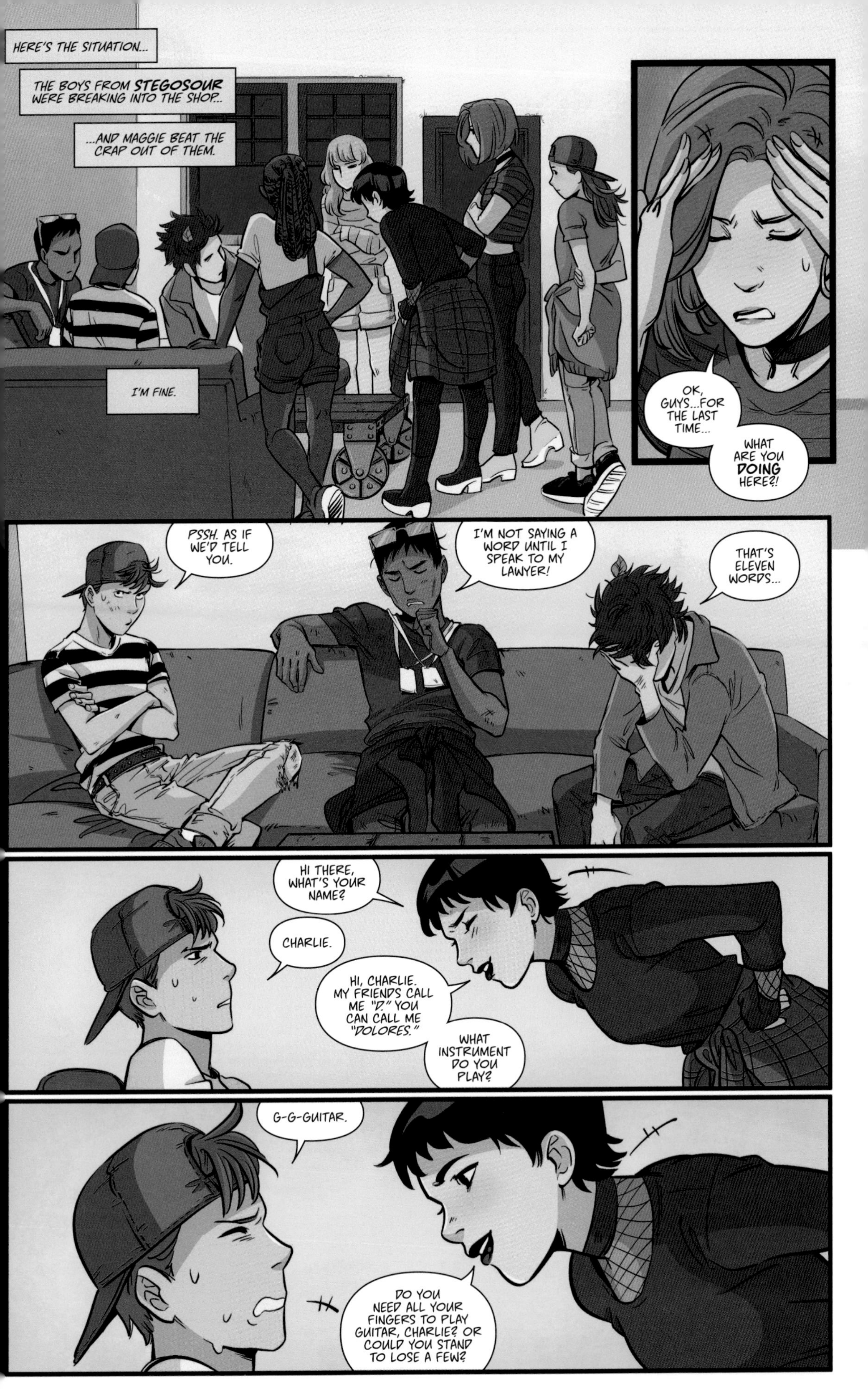
HERE'S THE SITUATION...
THE BOYS FROM STEGOSOUR WERE BREAKING INTO THE SHOP...
...AND MAGGIE BEAT THE CRAP OUT OF THEM.
I'M FINE.
OK, GUYS...FOR THE LAST TIME...
WHAT ARE YOU DOING HERE?!
PSSH. AS IF WE'D TELL YOU.
I'M NOT SAYING A WORD UNTIL I SPEAK TO MY LAWYER!
THAT'S ELEVEN WORDS...
HI THERE, WHAT'S YOUR NAME?
CHARLIE.
HI, CHARLIE. MY FRIENDS CALL ME "D." YOU CAN CALL ME "DOLORES."
WHAT INSTRUMENT DO YOU PLAY?
G-G-GUITAR.
DO YOU NEED ALL YOUR FINGERS TO PLAY GUITAR, CHARLIE? OR COULD YOU STAND TO LOSE A FEW?

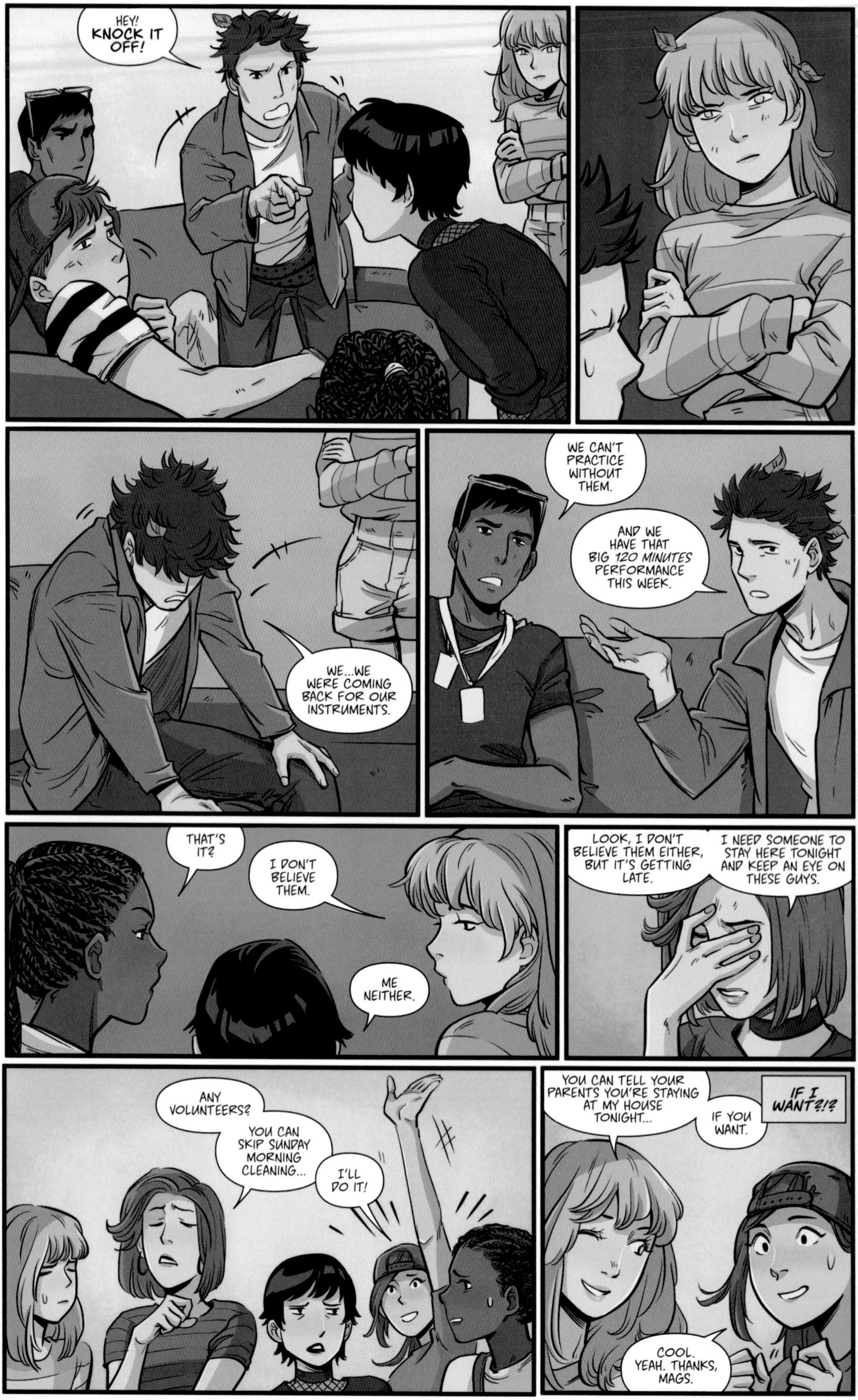
HEY! KNOCK IT OFF!
WE...WE WERE COMING BACK FOR OUR INSTRUMENTS.
WE CAN'T PRACTICE WITHOUT THEM.
AND WE HAVE THAT BIG 120 MINUTES PERFORMANCE THIS WEEK.
THAT'S IT?
I DON'T BELIEVE THEM.
ME NEITHER.
LOOK, I DON'T BELIEVE THEM EITHER, BUT IT'S GETTING LATE.
I NEED SOMEONE TO STAY HERE TONIGHT AND KEEP AN EYE ON THESE GUYS.
ANY VOLUNTEERS?
YOU CAN SKIP SUNDAY MORNING CLEANING...
I'LL DO IT!
YOU CAN TELL YOUR PARENTS YOU'RE STAYING AT MY HOUSE TONIGHT...
IF YOU WANT.
IF I WANT?!?
COOL. YEAH. THANKS, MAGS.

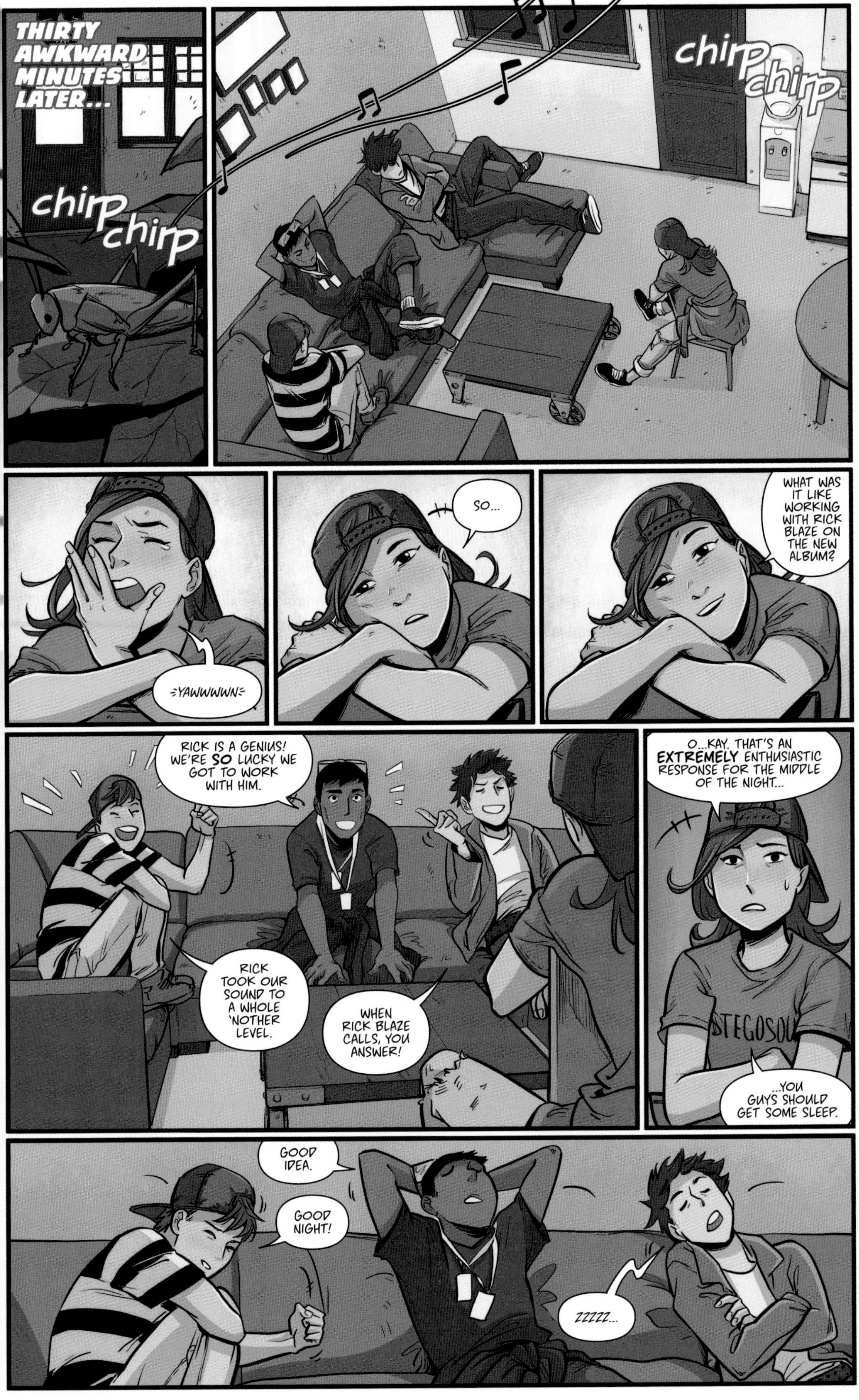
THIRTY AWKWARD MINUTES LATER...
chirp chirp
chirp chirp
=YAWWWWN=
SO...
WHAT WAS IT LIKE WORKING WITH RICK BLAZE ON THE NEW ALBUM?
RICK IS A GENIUS! WE'RE SO LUCKY WE GOT TO WORK WITH HIM.
RICK TOOK OUR SOUND TO A WHOLE 'NOTHER LEVEL.
WHEN RICK BLAZE CALLS, YOU ANSWER!
O...KAY. THAT'S AN EXTREMELY ENTHUSIASTIC RESPONSE FOR THE MIDDLE OF THE NIGHT...
...YOU GUYS SHOULD GET SOME SLEEP.
GOOD IDEA.
GOOD NIGHT!
ZZZZZ...

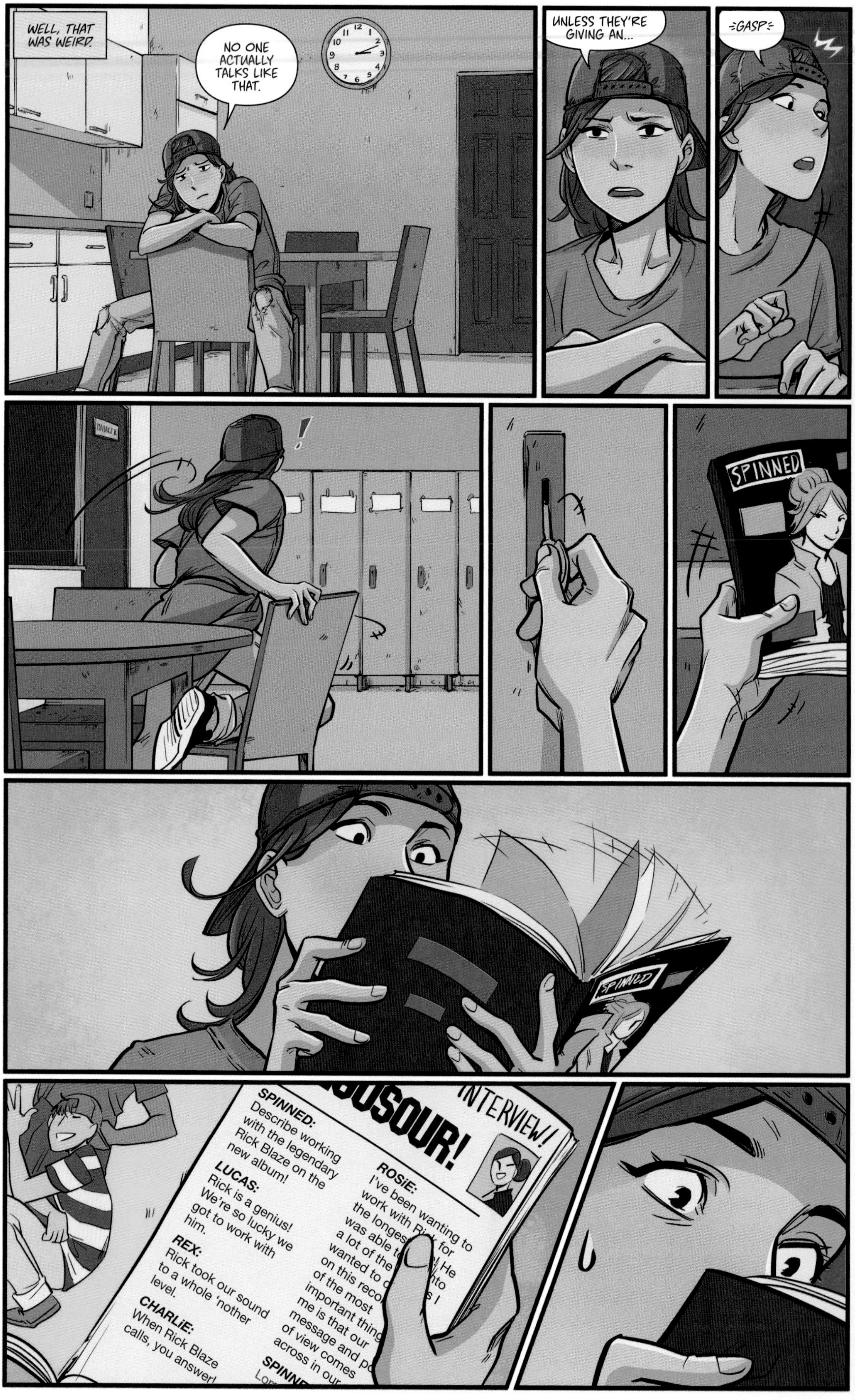
WELL, THAT WAS WEIRD.
NO ONE ACTUALLY TALKS LIKE THAT.
UNLESS THEY'RE GIVING AN...
GASP
SPINNED
INTERVIEW!
SPINNED:
Describe working with the legendary Rick Blaze on the new album!
LUCAS:
Rick is a genius! We're so lucky we got to work with him.
REX:
Rick took our sound to a whole 'nother level.
CHARLiE:
When Rick Blaze calls, you answer!
ROSiE:
I've been wanting to work with
the longes
was able t
a lot of the
wanted to
on this reco
of the most
important thing
me is that our
message and p
of view comes
across in our

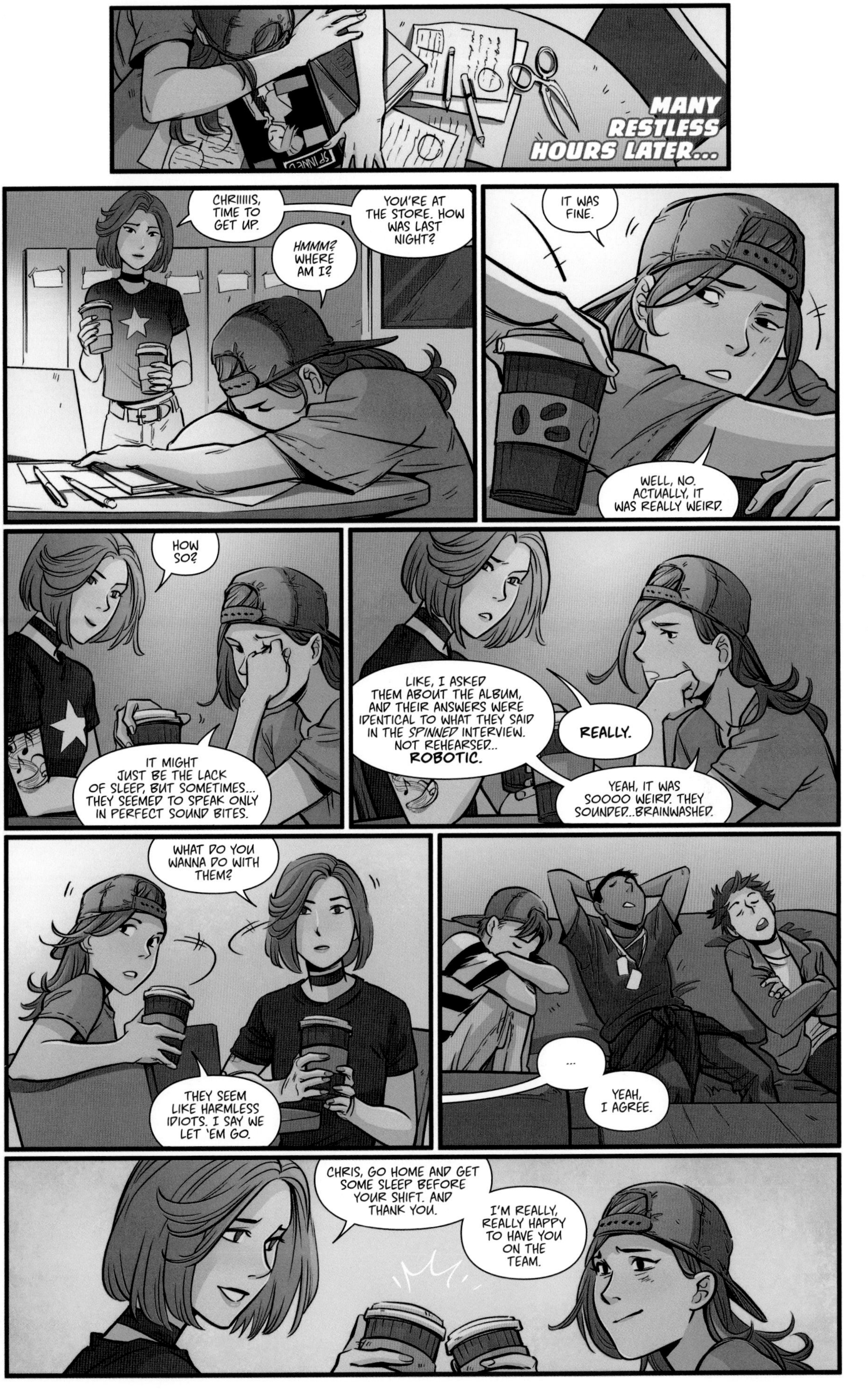
MANY RESTLESS HOURS LATER...
SPINNED
CHRIIIIS, TIME TO GET UP.
HMMM? WHERE AM I?
YOU'RE AT THE STORE. HOW WAS LAST NIGHT?
IT WAS FINE.
WELL, NO. ACTUALLY, IT WAS REALLY WEIRD.
HOW SO?
IT MIGHT JUST BE THE LACK OF SLEEP, BUT SOMETIMES... THEY SEEMED TO SPEAK ONLY IN PERFECT SOUND BITES.
LIKE, I ASKED THEM ABOUT THE ALBUM, AND THEIR ANSWERS WERE IDENTICAL TO WHAT THEY SAID IN THE *SPINNED* INTERVIEW. NOT REHEARSED... **ROBOTIC.**
REALLY.
YEAH, IT WAS SOOOO WEIRD. THEY SOUNDED...BRAINWASHED.
WHAT DO YOU WANNA DO WITH THEM?
THEY SEEM LIKE HARMLESS IDIOTS. I SAY WE LET 'EM GO.
...
YEAH, I AGREE.
CHRIS, GO HOME AND GET SOME SLEEP BEFORE YOUR SHIFT. AND THANK YOU.
I'M REALLY, REALLY HAPPY TO HAVE YOU ON THE TEAM.

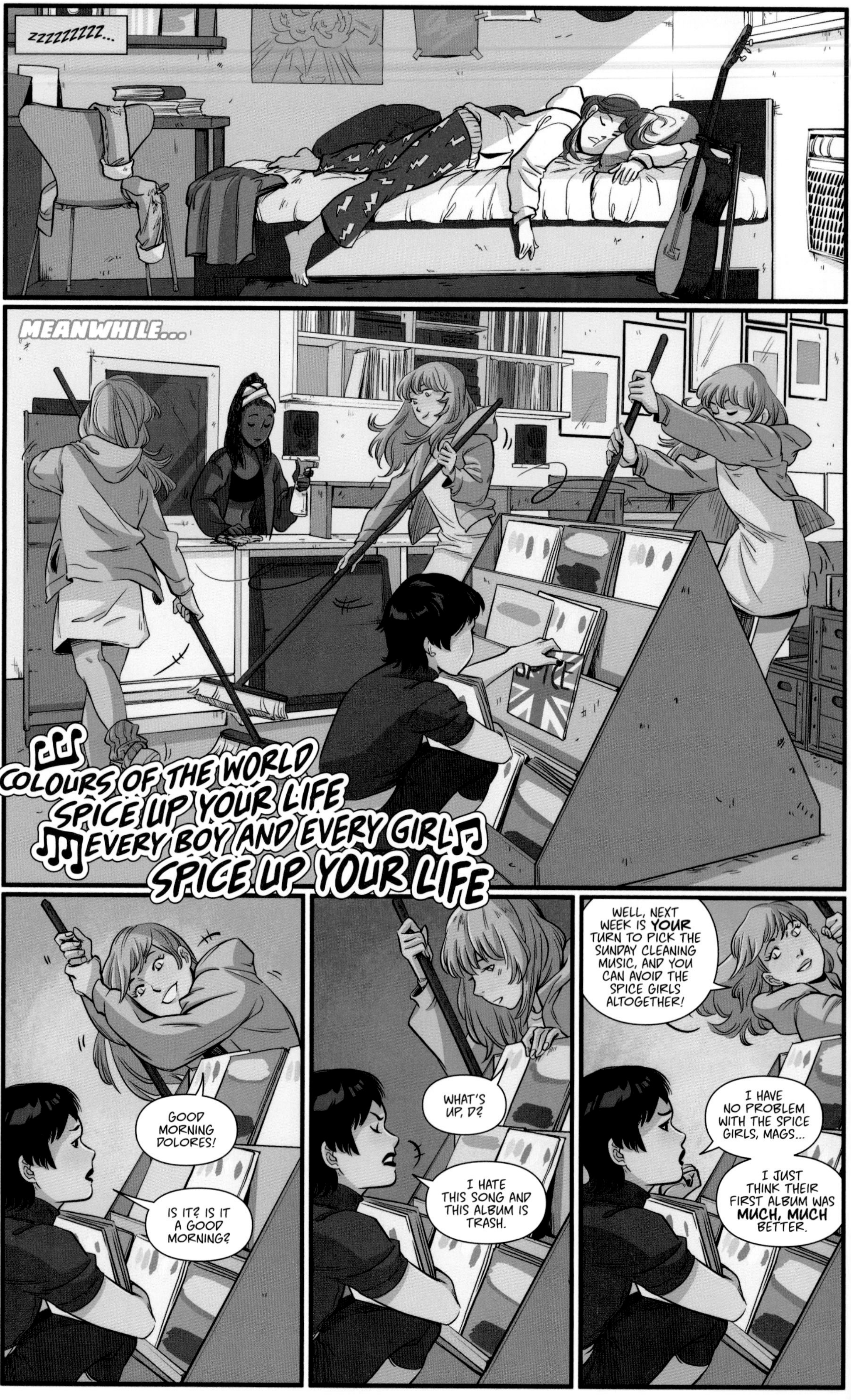

ZZZZZZZZZ...
MEANWHILE...
COLOURS OF THE WORLD
SPICE UP YOUR LIFE
EVERY BOY AND EVERY GIRL
SPICE UP YOUR LIFE
GOOD MORNING DOLORES!
IS IT? IS IT A GOOD MORNING?
WHAT'S UP, D?
I HATE THIS SONG AND THIS ALBUM IS TRASH.
WELL, NEXT WEEK IS **YOUR** TURN TO PICK THE SUNDAY CLEANING MUSIC, AND YOU CAN AVOID THE SPICE GIRLS ALTOGETHER!
I HAVE NO PROBLEM WITH THE SPICE GIRLS, MAGS...
I JUST THINK THEIR FIRST ALBUM WAS **MUCH, MUCH** BETTER.

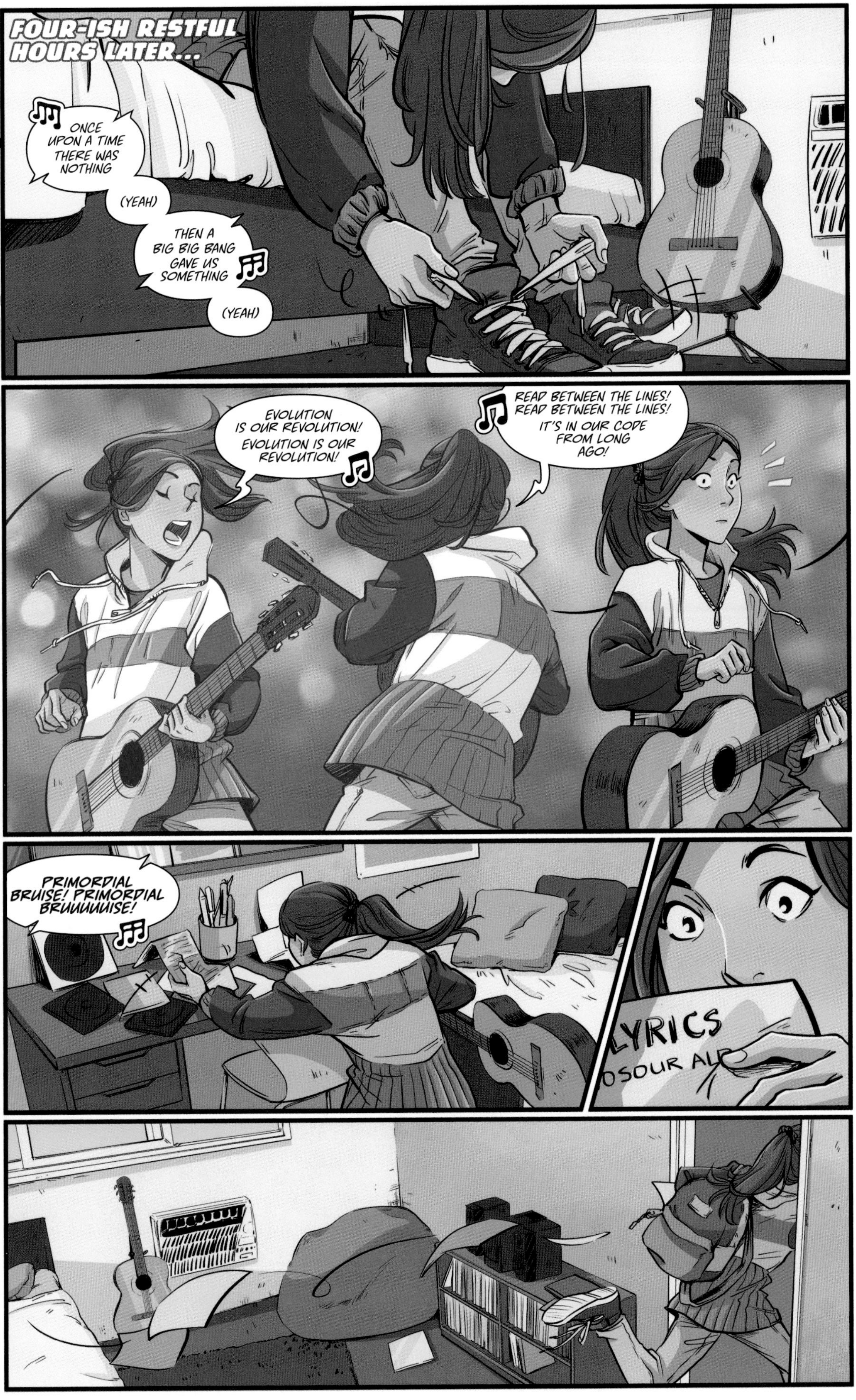
FOUR-ISH RESTFUL HOURS LATER...
ONCE UPON A TIME THERE WAS NOTHING
(YEAH)
THEN A BIG BIG BANG GAVE US SOMETHING
(YEAH)
EVOLUTION IS OUR REVOLUTION! EVOLUTION IS OUR REVOLUTION!
READ BETWEEN THE LINES! READ BETWEEN THE LINES! IT'S IN OUR CODE FROM LONG AGO!
PRIMORDIAL BRUISE! PRIMORDIAL BRUUUUUISE!
LYRICS

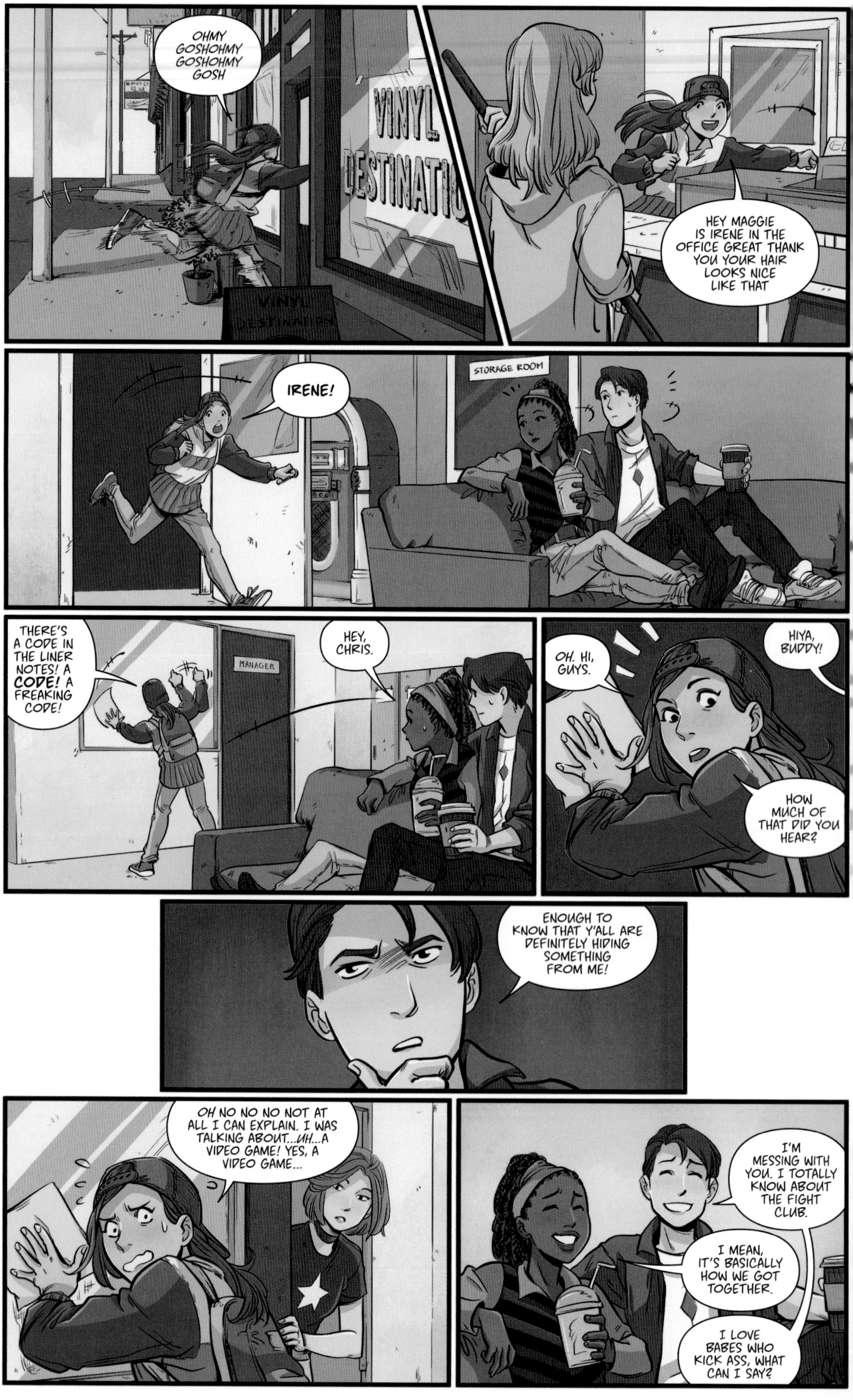

OHMY GOSHOHMY GOSHOHMY GOSH
VINYL DESTINATIO
VINYL DESTINATION
HEY MAGGIE IS IRENE IN THE OFFICE GREAT THANK YOU YOUR HAIR LOOKS NICE LIKE THAT
STORAGE ROOM
IRENE!
THERE'S A CODE IN THE LINER NOTES! A CODE! A FREAKING CODE!
MANAGER
HEY, CHRIS.
OH. HI, GUYS.
HIYA, BUDDY!
HOW MUCH OF THAT DID YOU HEAR?
ENOUGH TO KNOW THAT Y'ALL ARE DEFINITELY HIDING SOMETHING FROM ME!
OH NO NO NO NOT AT ALL I CAN EXPLAIN. I WAS TALKING ABOUT...UH...A VIDEO GAME! YES, A VIDEO GAME...
I'M MESSING WITH YOU. I TOTALLY KNOW ABOUT THE FIGHT CLUB.
I MEAN, IT'S BASICALLY HOW WE GOT TOGETHER.
I LOVE BABES WHO KICK ASS, WHAT CAN I SAY?

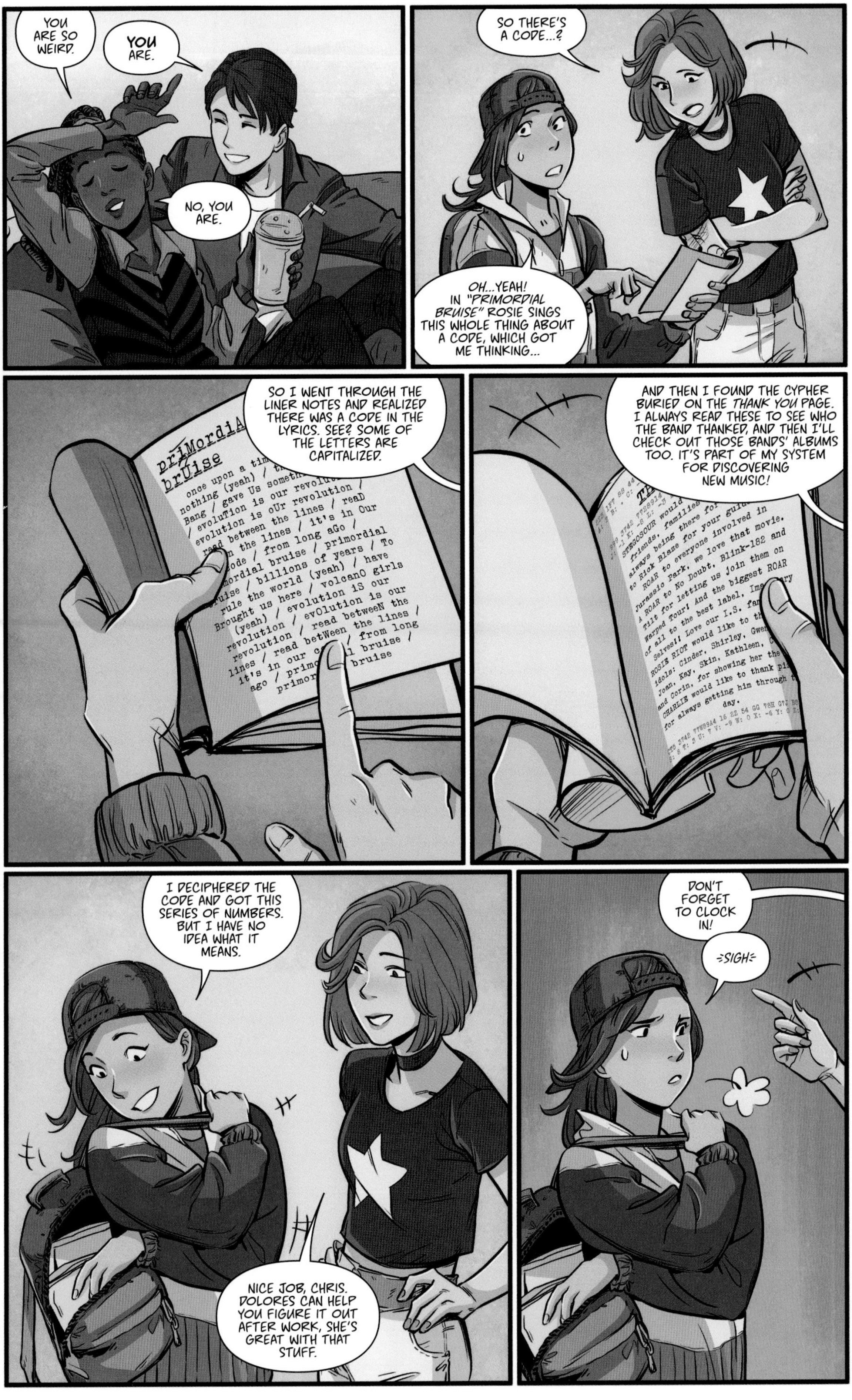
YOU ARE SO WEIRD.
YOU ARE.
NO, YOU ARE.
SO THERE'S A CODE...?
OH...YEAH! IN "PRIMORDIAL BRUISE" ROSIE SINGS THIS WHOLE THING ABOUT A CODE, WHICH GOT ME THINKING...
SO I WENT THROUGH THE LINER NOTES AND REALIZED THERE WAS A CODE IN THE LYRICS. SEE? SOME OF THE LETTERS ARE CAPITALIZED.
AND THEN I FOUND THE CYPHER BURIED ON THE THANK YOU PAGE. I ALWAYS READ THESE TO SEE WHO THE BAND THANKED, AND THEN I'LL CHECK OUT THOSE BANDS' ALBUMS TOO. IT'S PART OF MY SYSTEM FOR DISCOVERING NEW MUSIC!
I DECIPHERED THE CODE AND GOT THIS SERIES OF NUMBERS. BUT I HAVE NO IDEA WHAT IT MEANS.
NICE JOB, CHRIS. DOLORES CAN HELP YOU FIGURE IT OUT AFTER WORK, SHE'S GREAT WITH THAT STUFF.
DON'T FORGET TO CLOCK IN!
SIGH

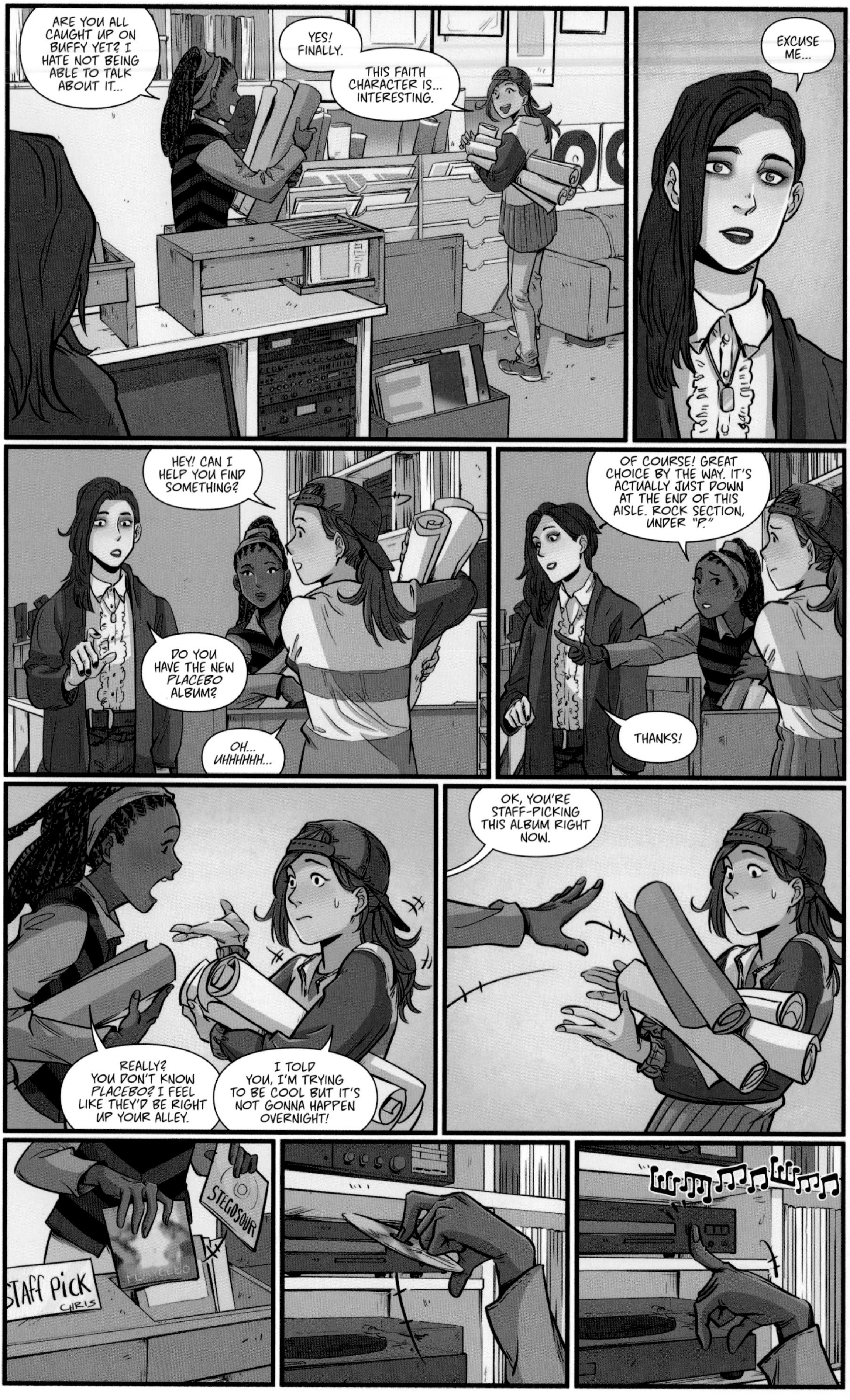
ARE YOU ALL CAUGHT UP ON BUFFY YET? I HATE NOT BEING ABLE TO TALK ABOUT IT...
YES! FINALLY.
THIS FAITH CHARACTER IS... INTERESTING.
EXCUSE ME...
HEY! CAN I HELP YOU FIND SOMETHING?
DO YOU HAVE THE NEW PLACEBO ALBUM?
OH... UHHHHHH...
OF COURSE! GREAT CHOICE BY THE WAY. IT'S ACTUALLY JUST DOWN AT THE END OF THIS AISLE. ROCK SECTION, UNDER "P."
THANKS!
REALLY? YOU DON'T KNOW PLACEBO? I FEEL LIKE THEY'D BE RIGHT UP YOUR ALLEY.
I TOLD YOU, I'M TRYING TO BE COOL BUT IT'S NOT GONNA HAPPEN OVERNIGHT!
OK, YOU'RE STAFF-PICKING THIS ALBUM RIGHT NOW.
STEGOSOUR
STAFF PICK
CHRIS

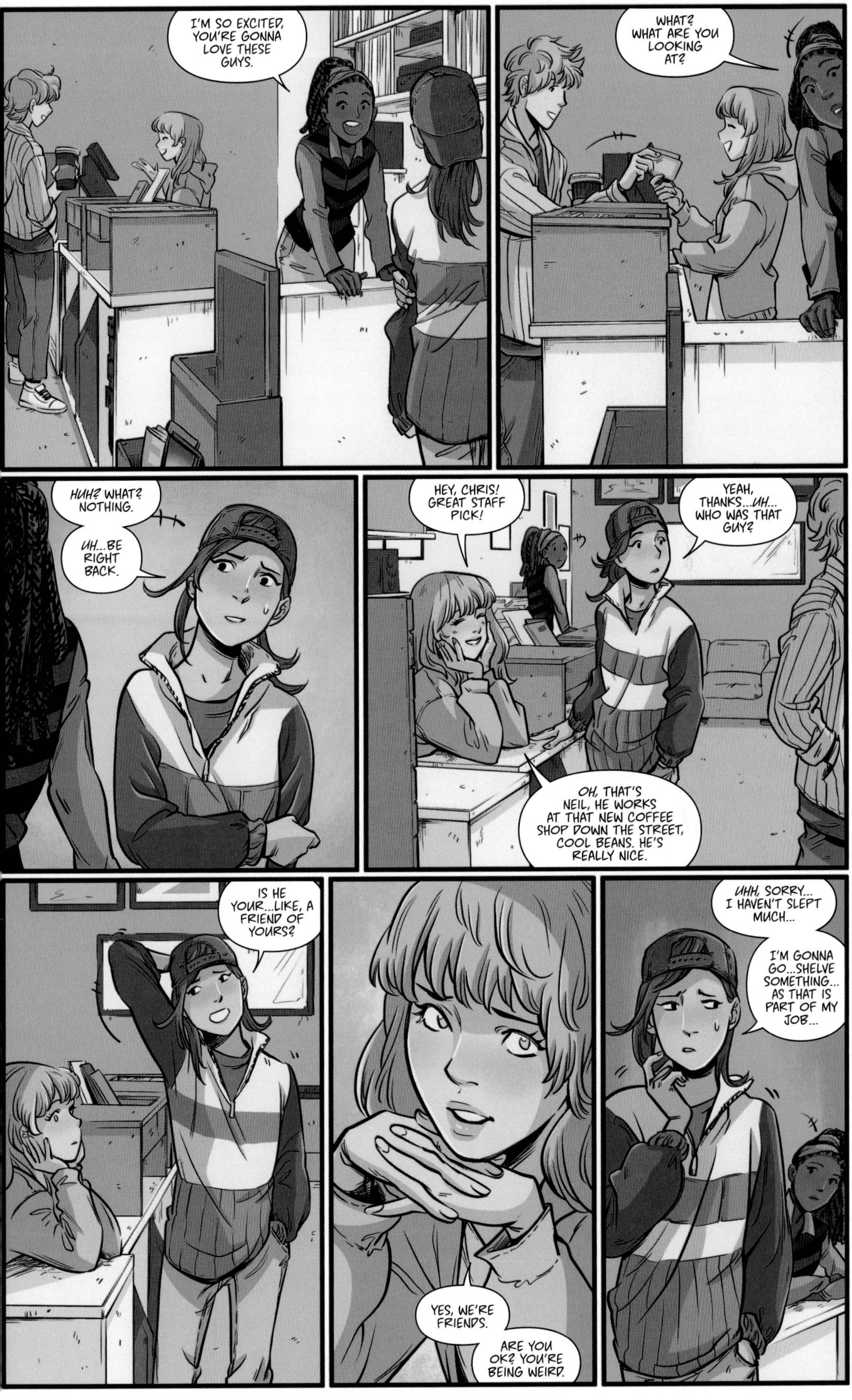
I'M SO EXCITED, YOU'RE GONNA LOVE THESE GUYS.
WHAT? WHAT ARE YOU LOOKING AT?
HUH? WHAT? NOTHING.
UH...BE RIGHT BACK.
HEY, CHRIS! GREAT STAFF PICK!
YEAH, THANKS...UH... WHO WAS THAT GUY?
OH, THAT'S NEIL, HE WORKS AT THAT NEW COFFEE SHOP DOWN THE STREET, COOL BEANS. HE'S REALLY NICE.
IS HE YOUR...LIKE, A FRIEND OF YOURS?
YES, WE'RE FRIENDS.
ARE YOU OK? YOU'RE BEING WEIRD.
UHH, SORRY... I HAVEN'T SLEPT MUCH...
I'M GONNA GO...SHELVE SOMETHING... AS THAT IS PART OF MY JOB...

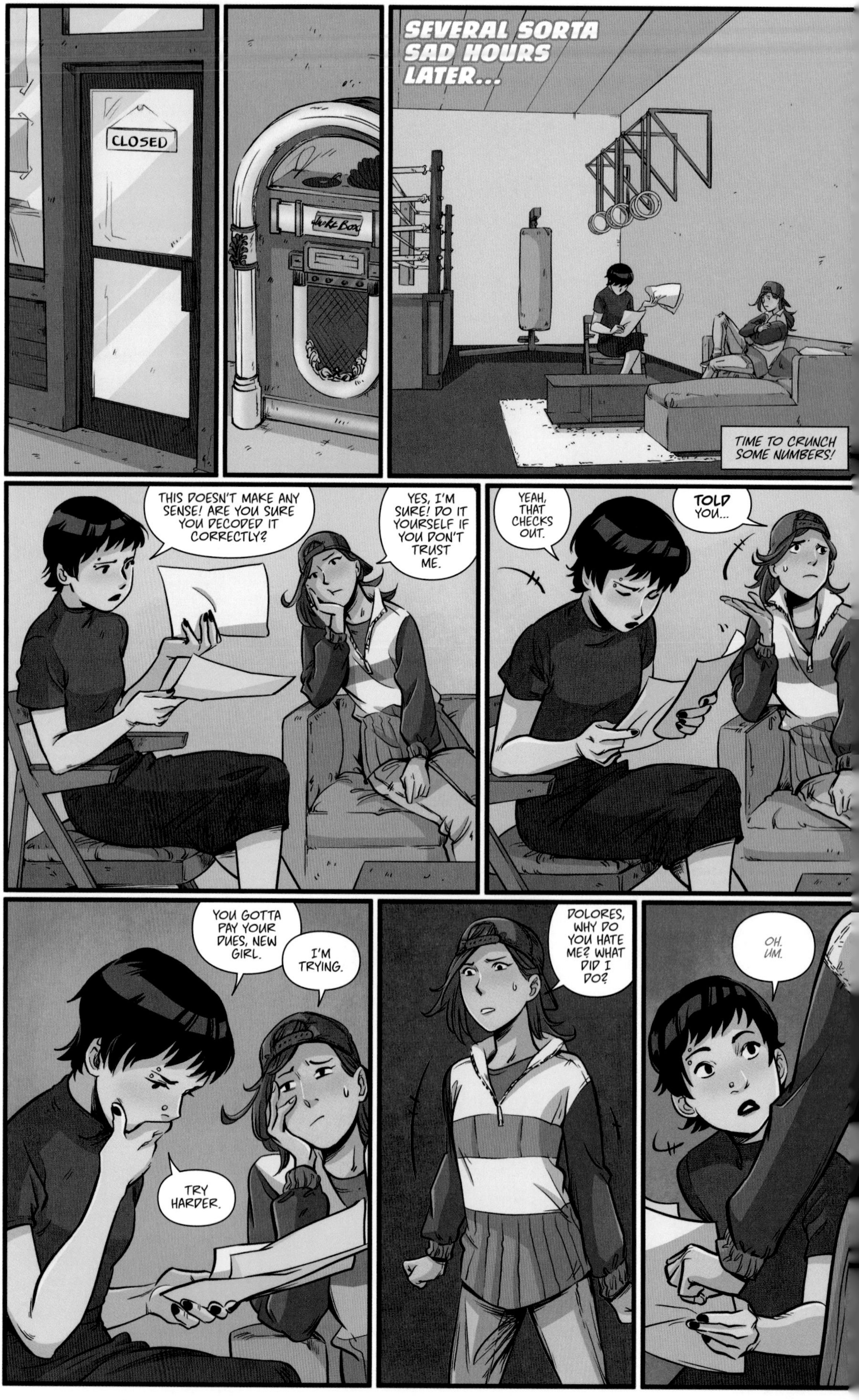

CLOSED
Juke Box
SEVERAL SORTA SAD HOURS LATER...
TIME TO CRUNCH SOME NUMBERS!
THIS DOESN'T MAKE ANY SENSE! ARE YOU SURE YOU DECODED IT CORRECTLY?
YES, I'M SURE! DO IT YOURSELF IF YOU DON'T TRUST ME.
YEAH, THAT CHECKS OUT.
TOLD YOU...
YOU GOTTA PAY YOUR DUES, NEW GIRL.
I'M TRYING.
TRY HARDER.
DOLORES, WHY DO YOU HATE ME? WHAT DID I DO?
OH. UM.

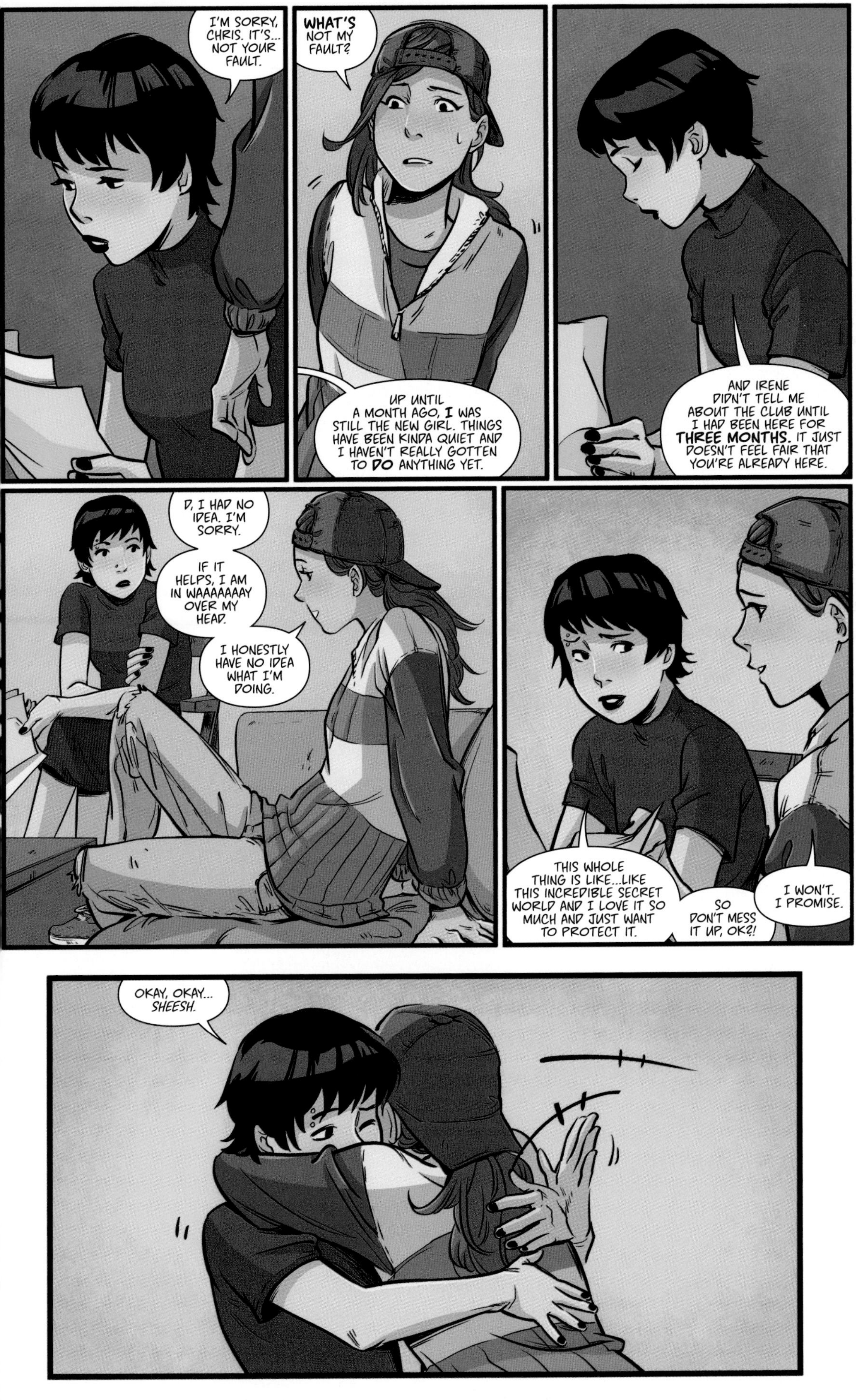
I'M SORRY, CHRIS. IT'S... NOT YOUR FAULT.
WHAT'S NOT MY FAULT?
UP UNTIL A MONTH AGO, I WAS STILL THE NEW GIRL. THINGS HAVE BEEN KINDA QUIET AND I HAVEN'T REALLY GOTTEN TO DO ANYTHING YET.
AND IRENE DIDN'T TELL ME ABOUT THE CLUB UNTIL I HAD BEEN HERE FOR THREE MONTHS. IT JUST DOESN'T FEEL FAIR THAT YOU'RE ALREADY HERE.
D, I HAD NO IDEA. I'M SORRY.
IF IT HELPS, I AM IN WAAAAAAAY OVER MY HEAD.
I HONESTLY HAVE NO IDEA WHAT I'M DOING.
THIS WHOLE THING IS LIKE...LIKE THIS INCREDIBLE SECRET WORLD AND I LOVE IT SO MUCH AND JUST WANT TO PROTECT IT.
SO DON'T MESS IT UP, OK?!
I WON'T. I PROMISE.
OKAY, OKAY... SHEESH.

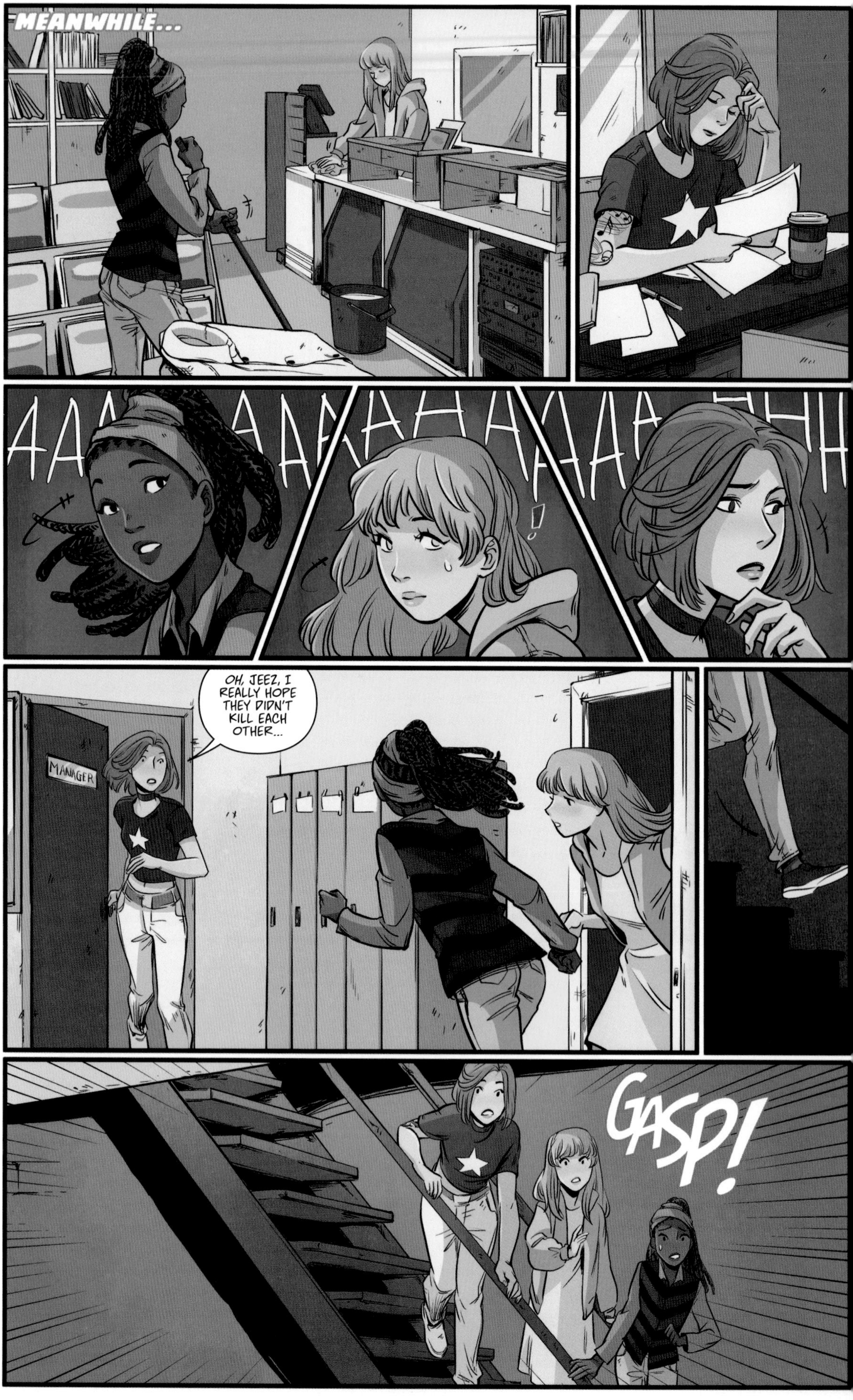
MEANWHILE...
AAAAAAAAAAAAAAAAHHH
OH, JEEZ, I REALLY HOPE THEY DIDN'T KILL EACH OTHER...
MANAGER
GASP!

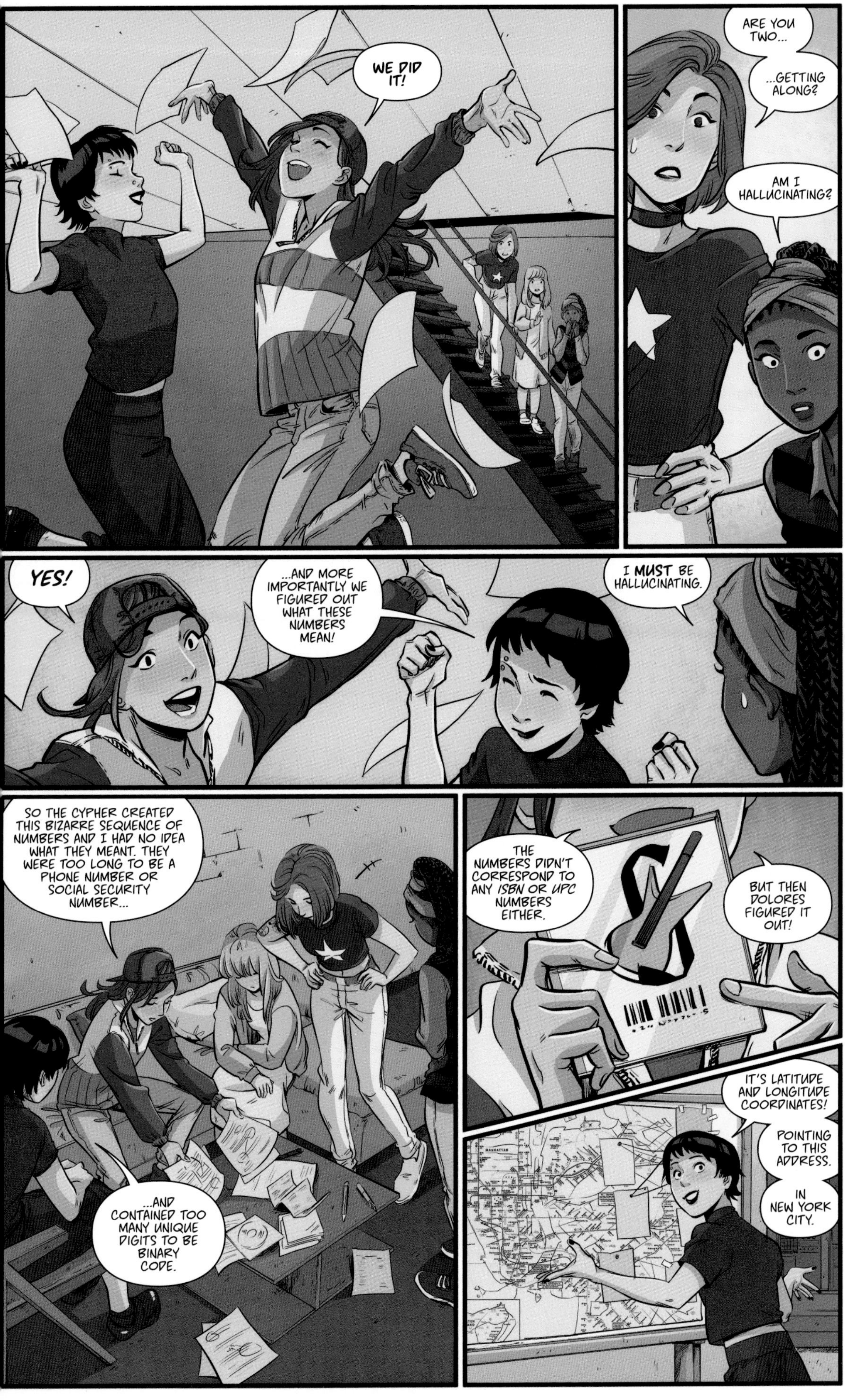
WE DID IT!
ARE YOU TWO...
...GETTING ALONG?
AM I HALLUCINATING?
YES!
...AND MORE IMPORTANTLY WE FIGURED OUT WHAT THESE NUMBERS MEAN!
I MUST BE HALLUCINATING.
SO THE CYPHER CREATED THIS BIZARRE SEQUENCE OF NUMBERS AND I HAD NO IDEA WHAT THEY MEANT. THEY WERE TOO LONG TO BE A PHONE NUMBER OR SOCIAL SECURITY NUMBER...
...AND CONTAINED TOO MANY UNIQUE DIGITS TO BE BINARY CODE.
THE NUMBERS DIDN'T CORRESPOND TO ANY ISBN OR UPC NUMBERS EITHER.
BUT THEN DOLORES FIGURED IT OUT!
IT'S LATITUDE AND LONGITUDE COORDINATES!
POINTING TO THIS ADDRESS.
IN NEW YORK CITY.

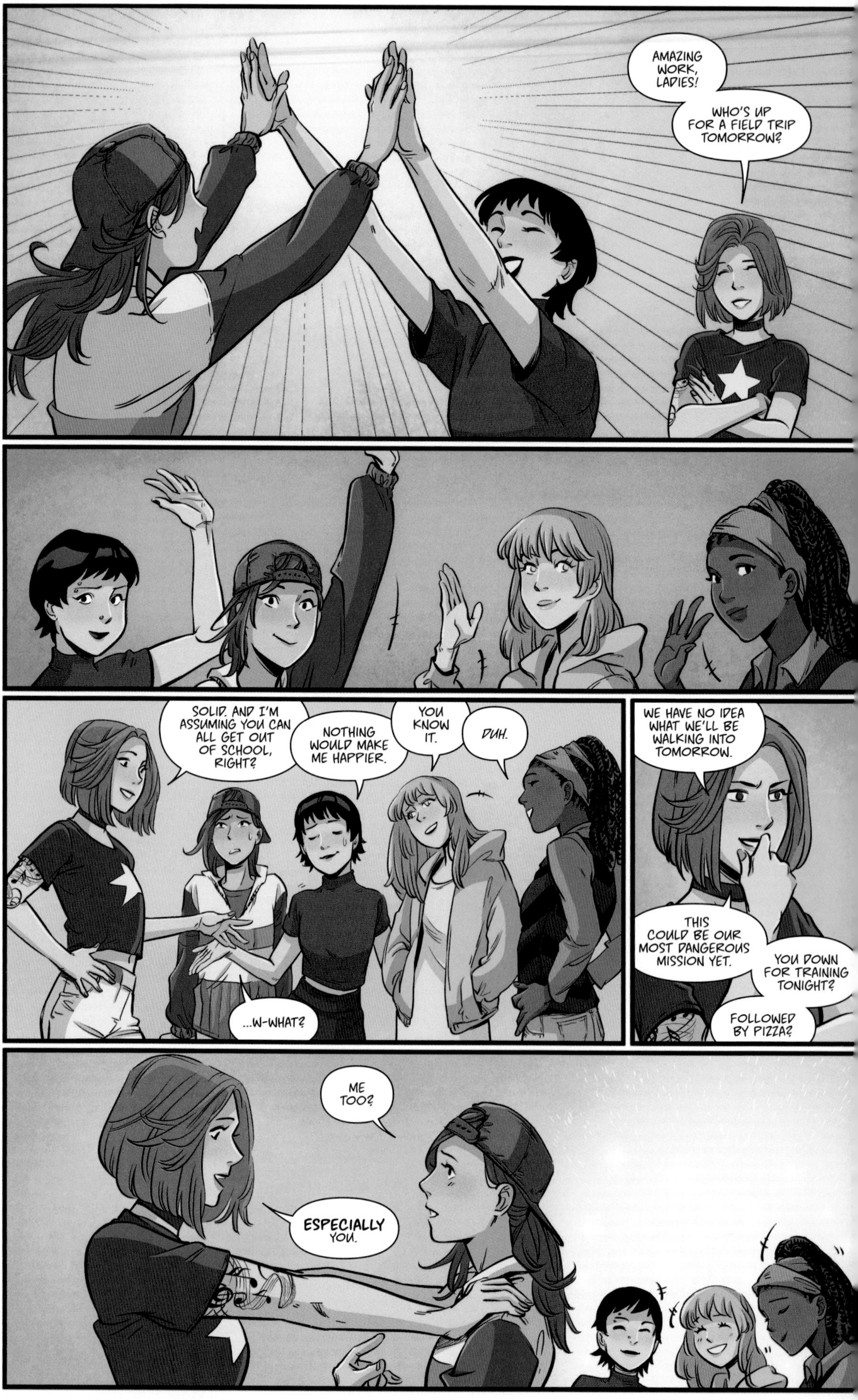
AMAZING WORK, LADIES!
WHO'S UP FOR A FIELD TRIP TOMORROW?
SOLID. AND I'M ASSUMING YOU CAN ALL GET OUT OF SCHOOL, RIGHT?
NOTHING WOULD MAKE ME HAPPIER.
YOU KNOW IT.
DUH.
...W-WHAT?
WE HAVE NO IDEA WHAT WE'LL BE WALKING INTO TOMORROW.
THIS COULD BE OUR MOST DANGEROUS MISSION YET.
YOU DOWN FOR TRAINING TONIGHT?
FOLLOWED BY PIZZA?
ME TOO?
ESPECIALLY YOU.

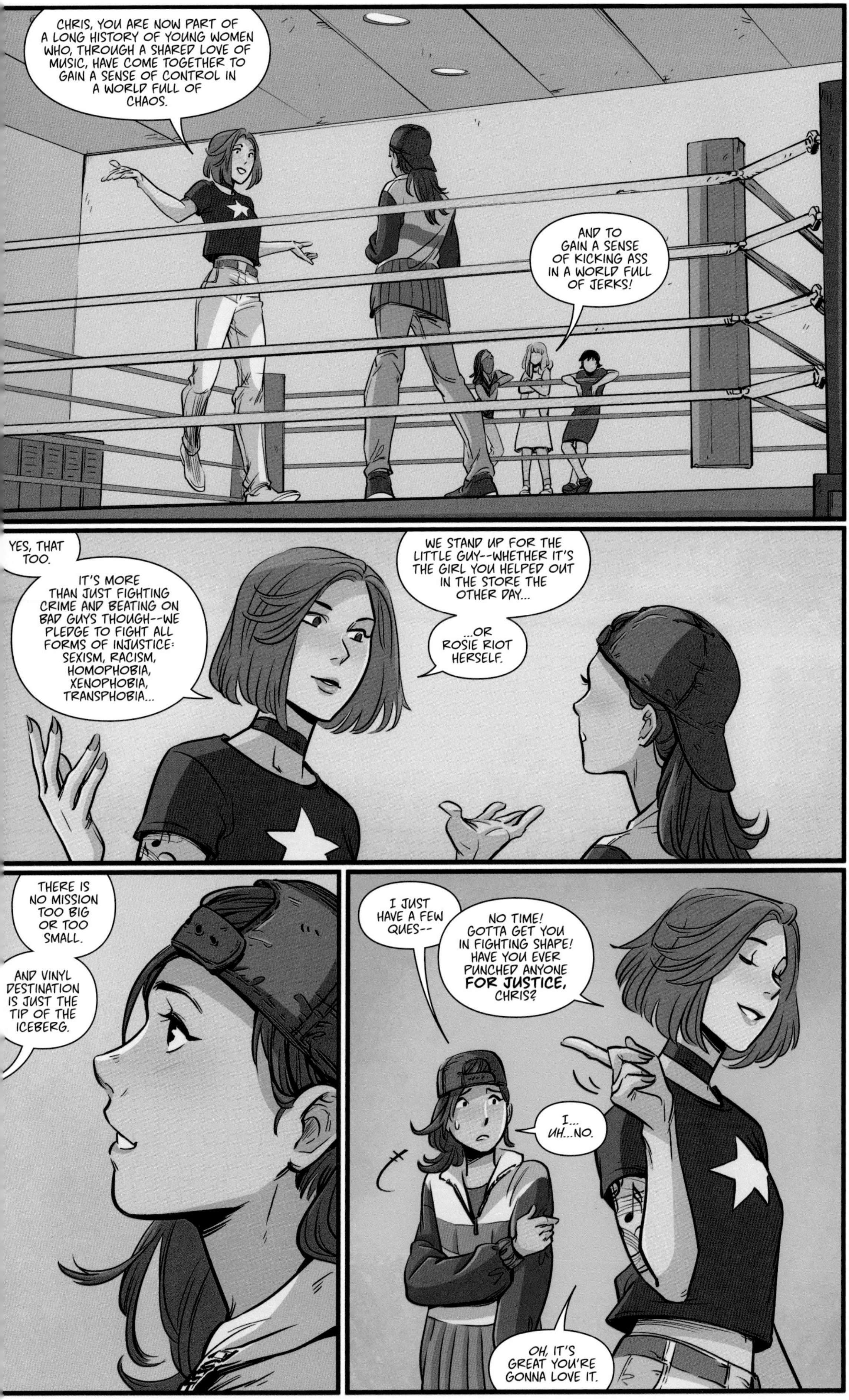
CHRIS, YOU ARE NOW PART OF A LONG HISTORY OF YOUNG WOMEN WHO, THROUGH A SHARED LOVE OF MUSIC, HAVE COME TOGETHER TO GAIN A SENSE OF CONTROL IN A WORLD FULL OF CHAOS.
AND TO GAIN A SENSE OF KICKING ASS IN A WORLD FULL OF JERKS!
YES, THAT TOO.
IT'S MORE THAN JUST FIGHTING CRIME AND BEATING ON BAD GUYS THOUGH--WE PLEDGE TO FIGHT ALL FORMS OF INJUSTICE: SEXISM, RACISM, HOMOPHOBIA, XENOPHOBIA, TRANSPHOBIA...
WE STAND UP FOR THE LITTLE GUY--WHETHER IT'S THE GIRL YOU HELPED OUT IN THE STORE THE OTHER DAY...
...OR ROSIE RIOT HERSELF.
THERE IS NO MISSION TOO BIG OR TOO SMALL.
AND VINYL DESTINATION IS JUST THE TIP OF THE ICEBERG.
I JUST HAVE A FEW QUES--
NO TIME! GOTTA GET YOU IN FIGHTING SHAPE! HAVE YOU EVER PUNCHED ANYONE **FOR JUSTICE,** CHRIS?
I... UH...NO.
OH, IT'S GREAT YOU'RE GONNA LOVE IT.

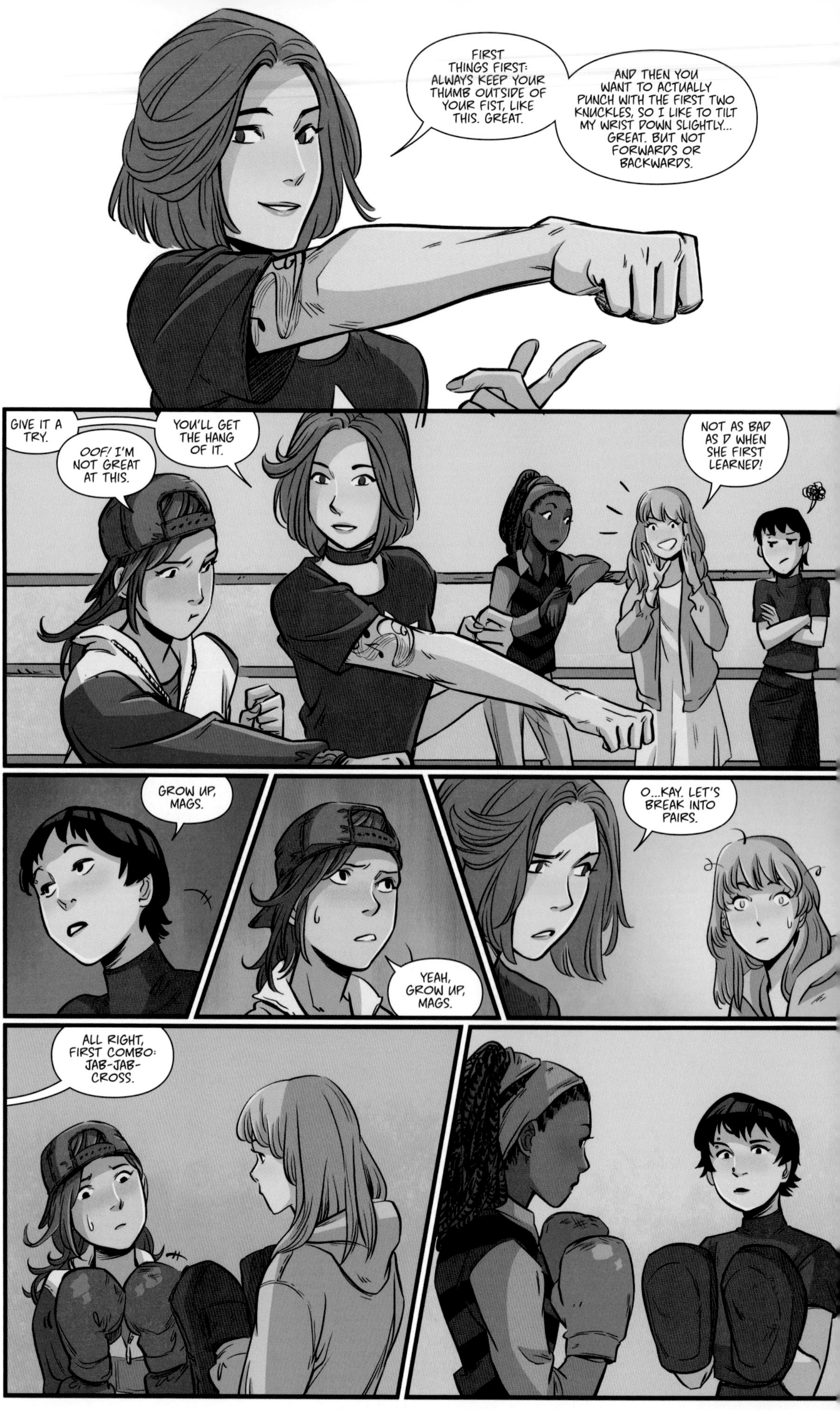

FIRST THINGS FIRST: ALWAYS KEEP YOUR THUMB OUTSIDE OF YOUR FIST, LIKE THIS. GREAT.
AND THEN YOU WANT TO ACTUALLY PUNCH WITH THE FIRST TWO KNUCKLES, SO I LIKE TO TILT MY WRIST DOWN SLIGHTLY... GREAT. BUT NOT FORWARDS OR BACKWARDS.
GIVE IT A TRY.
OOF! I'M NOT GREAT AT THIS.
YOU'LL GET THE HANG OF IT.
NOT AS BAD AS D WHEN SHE FIRST LEARNED!
GROW UP, MAGS.
YEAH, GROW UP, MAGS.
O...KAY. LET'S BREAK INTO PAIRS.
ALL RIGHT, FIRST COMBO: JAB-JAB-CROSS.

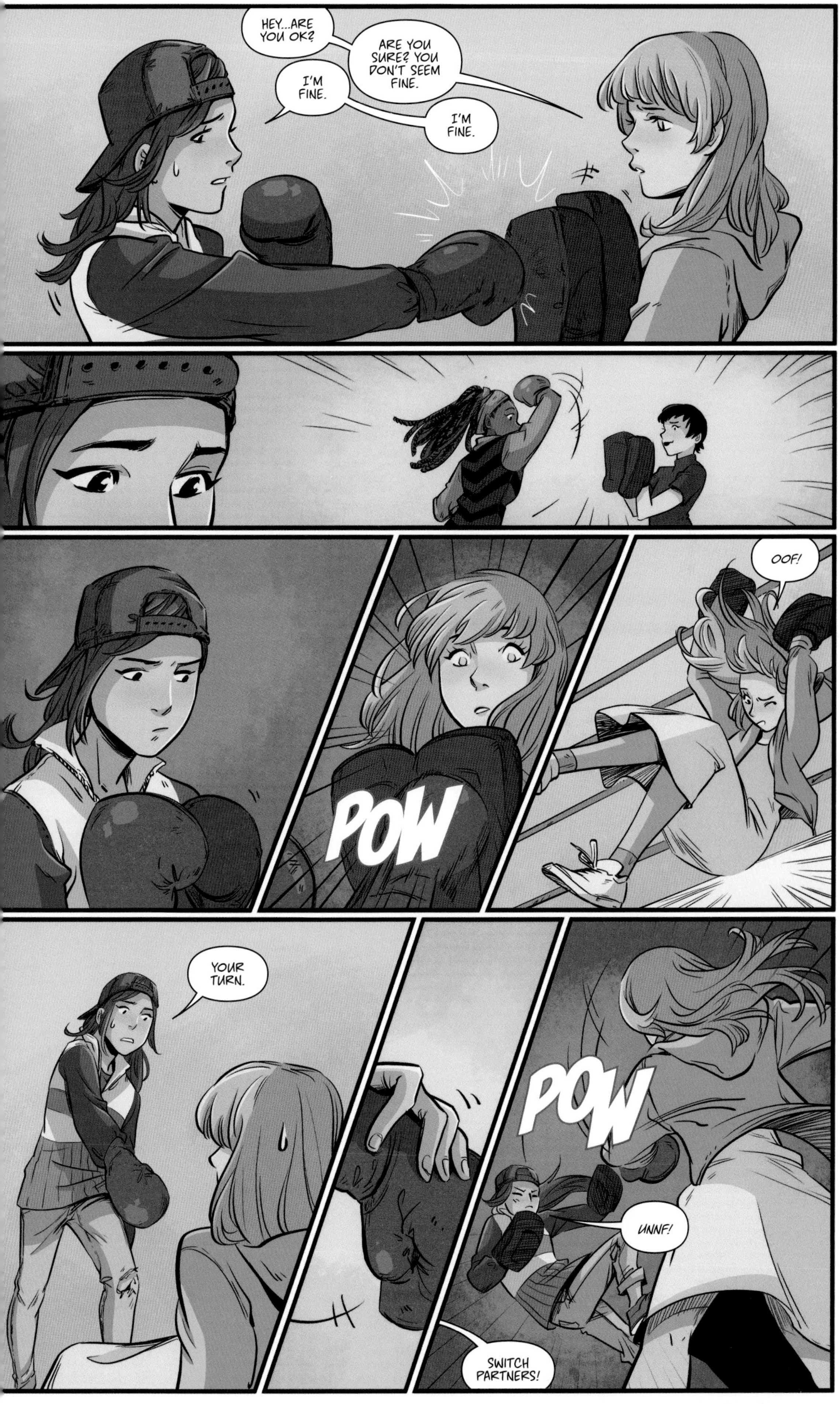
HEY...ARE YOU OK?
I'M FINE.
ARE YOU SURE? YOU DON'T SEEM FINE.
I'M FINE.
OOF!
POW
YOUR TURN.
POW
UNNF!
SWITCH PARTNERS!

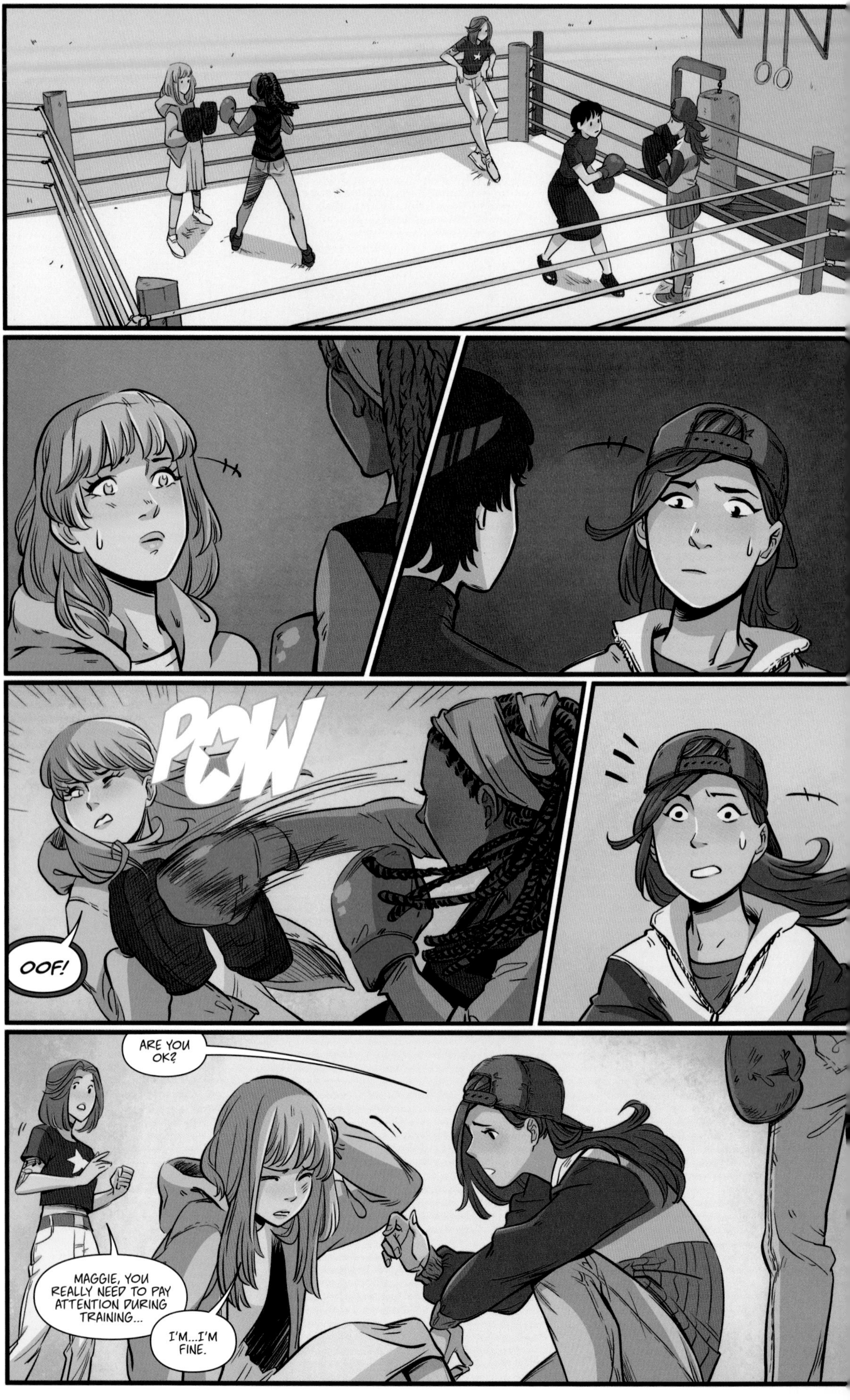
POW
OOF!
ARE YOU OK?
MAGGIE, YOU REALLY NEED TO PAY ATTENTION DURING TRAINING...
I'M...I'M FINE.

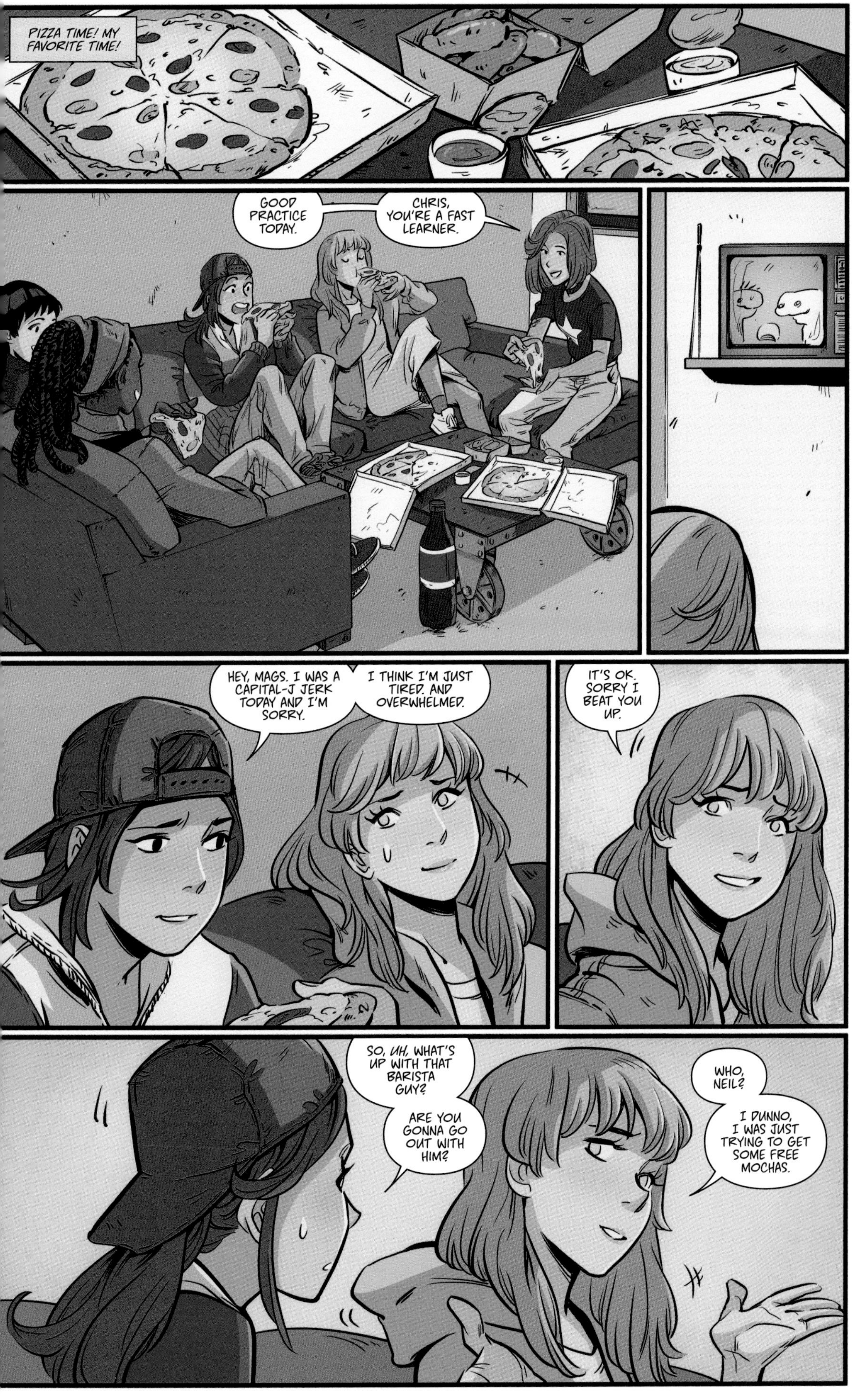
PIZZA TIME! MY FAVORITE TIME!
GOOD PRACTICE TODAY.
CHRIS, YOU'RE A FAST LEARNER.
HEY, MAGS. I WAS A CAPITAL-J JERK TODAY AND I'M SORRY.
I THINK I'M JUST TIRED. AND OVERWHELMED.
IT'S OK. SORRY I BEAT YOU UP.
SO, UH, WHAT'S UP WITH THAT BARISTA GUY?
ARE YOU GONNA GO OUT WITH HIM?
WHO, NEIL?
I DUNNO, I WAS JUST TRYING TO GET SOME FREE MOCHAS.

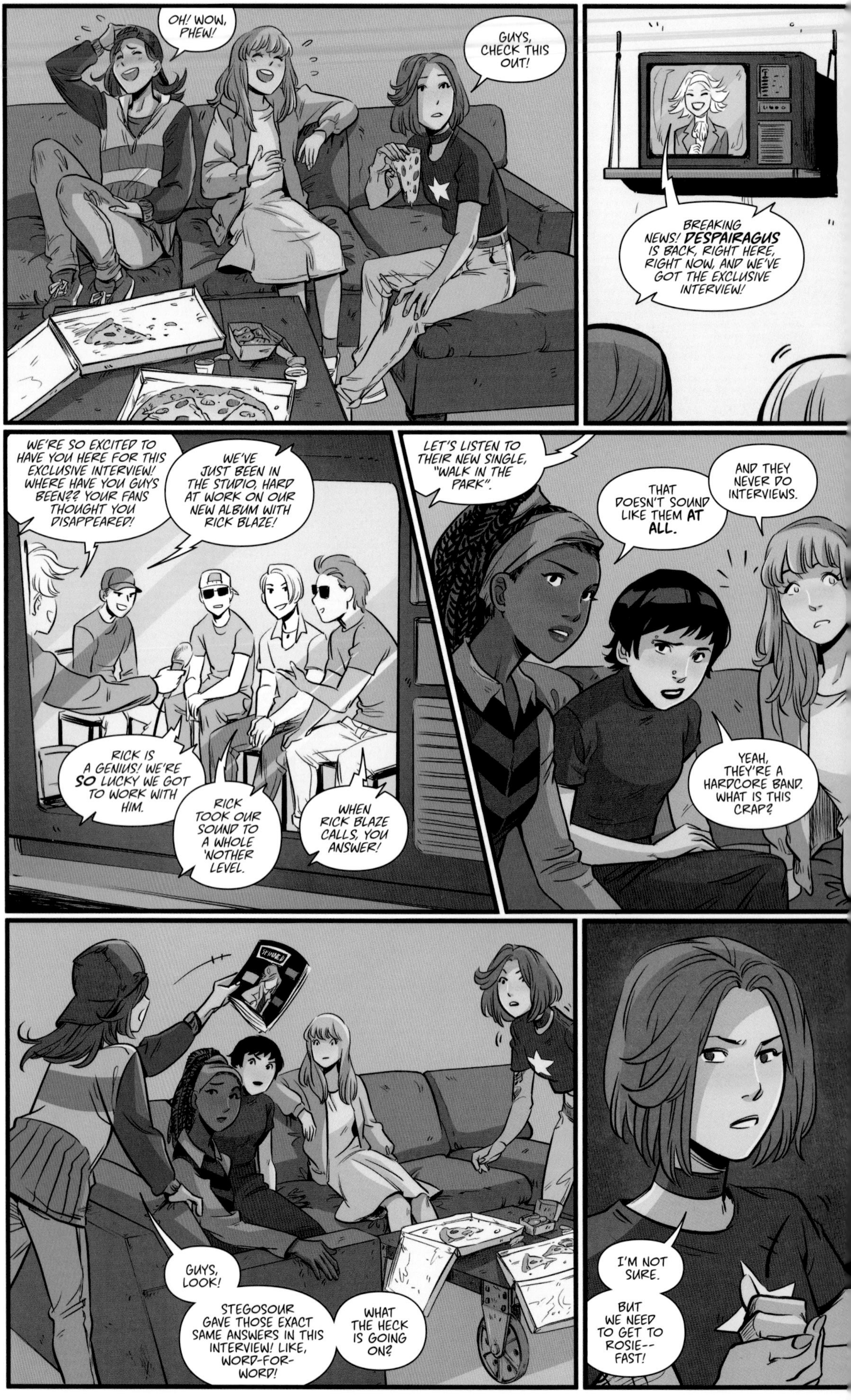
OH! WOW, PHEW!
GUYS, CHECK THIS OUT!
BREAKING NEWS! DESPAIRAGUS IS BACK, RIGHT HERE, RIGHT NOW, AND WE'VE GOT THE EXCLUSIVE INTERVIEW!
WE'RE SO EXCITED TO HAVE YOU HERE FOR THIS EXCLUSIVE INTERVIEW! WHERE HAVE YOU GUYS BEEN?? YOUR FANS THOUGHT YOU DISAPPEARED!
WE'VE JUST BEEN IN THE STUDIO, HARD AT WORK ON OUR NEW ALBUM WITH RICK BLAZE!
RICK IS A GENIUS! WE'RE SO LUCKY WE GOT TO WORK WITH HIM.
RICK TOOK OUR SOUND TO A WHOLE 'NOTHER LEVEL.
WHEN RICK BLAZE CALLS, YOU ANSWER!
LET'S LISTEN TO THEIR NEW SINGLE, "WALK IN THE PARK".
THAT DOESN'T SOUND LIKE THEM AT ALL.
AND THEY NEVER DO INTERVIEWS.
YEAH, THEY'RE A HARDCORE BAND. WHAT IS THIS CRAP?
SPINNED
GUYS, LOOK!
STEGOSOUR GAVE THOSE EXACT SAME ANSWERS IN THIS INTERVIEW! LIKE, WORD-FOR-WORD!
WHAT THE HECK IS GOING ON?
I'M NOT SURE.
BUT WE NEED TO GET TO ROSIE-- FAST!

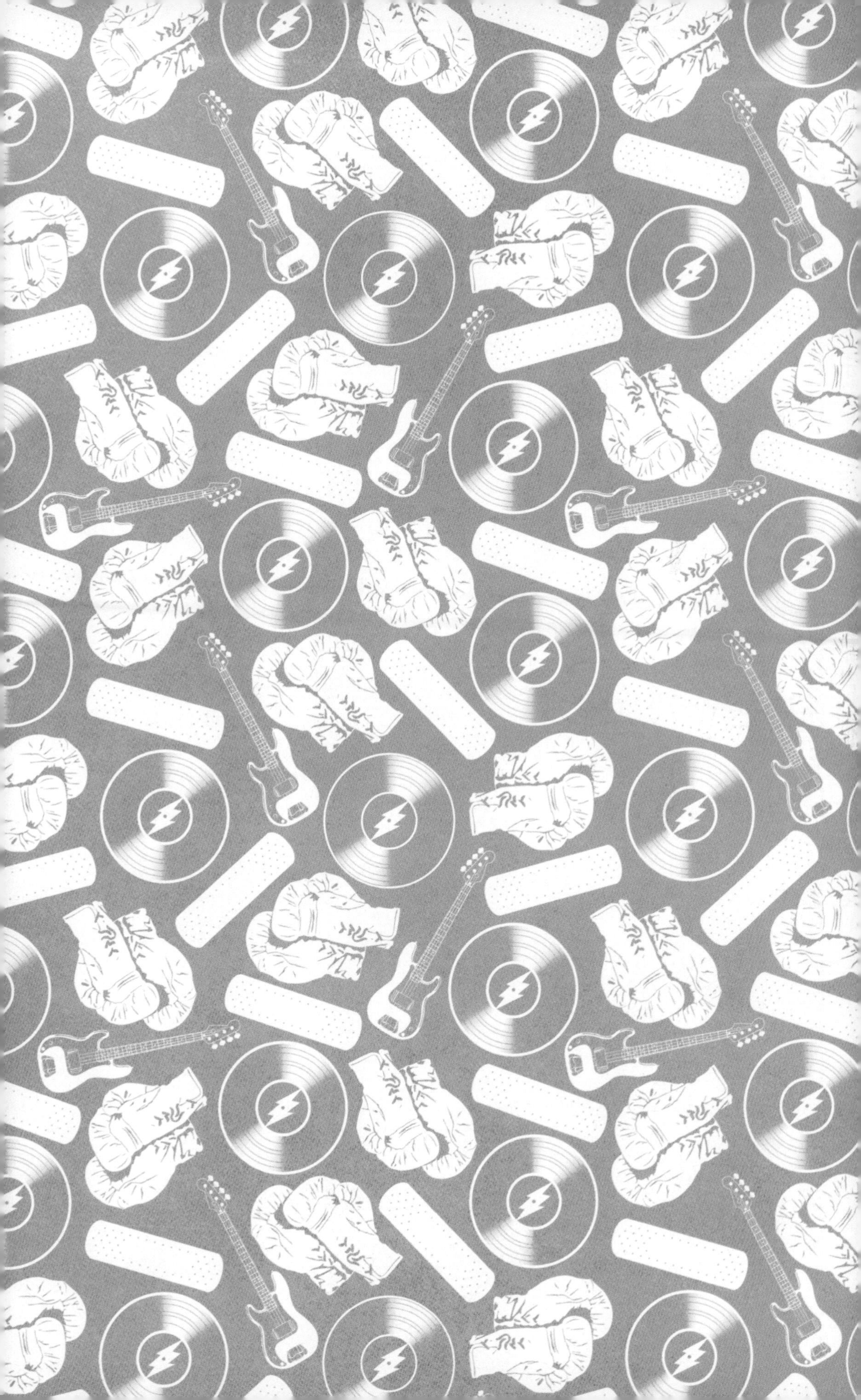

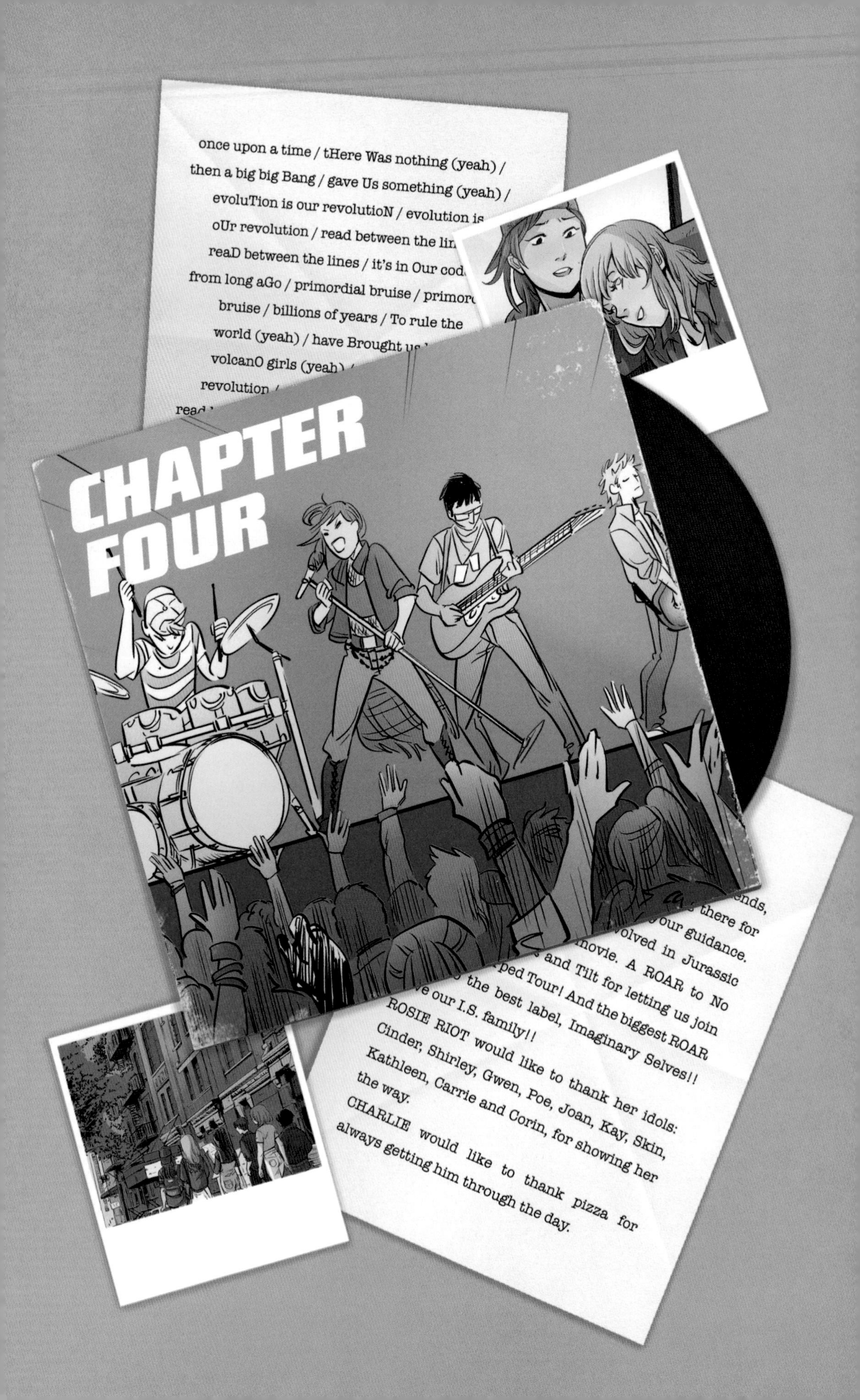
once upon a time / tHere Was nothing (yeah) /
then a big big Bang / gave Us something (yeah) /
evoluTion is our revolutioN / evolution is
oUr revolution / read between the
reaD between the lines / it's in Our
from long aGo / primordial bruise /
bruise / billions of years / To rule the
world (yeah) / have Brought
volcanO girls (yeah) /
revolution /
CHAPTER FOUR
ends,
there for
our guidance.
volved in Jurassic
movie. A ROAR to No
and Tilt for letting us join
ped Tour! And the biggest ROAR
the best label, Imaginary Selves!!
our I.S. family!!
ROSIE RIOT would like to thank her idols:
Cinder, Shirley, Gwen, Poe, Joan, Kay, Skin,
Kathleen, Carrie and Corin, for showing her
the way.
CHARLIE would like to thank pizza for
always getting him through the day.

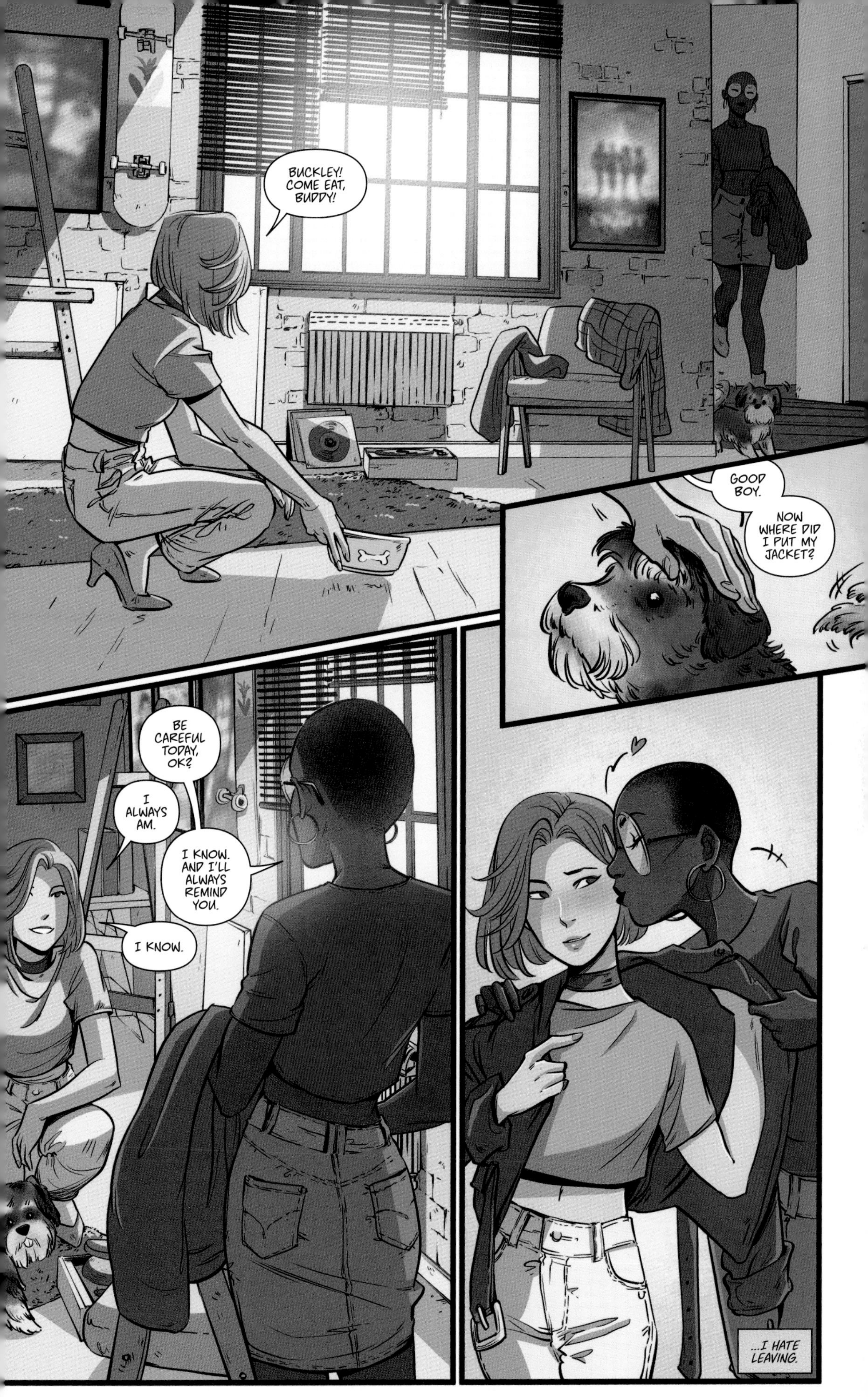
BUCKLEY! COME EAT, BUDDY!
GOOD BOY.
NOW WHERE DID I PUT MY JACKET?
BE CAREFUL TODAY, OK?
I ALWAYS AM.
I KNOW. AND I'LL ALWAYS REMIND YOU.
I KNOW.
...I HATE LEAVING.

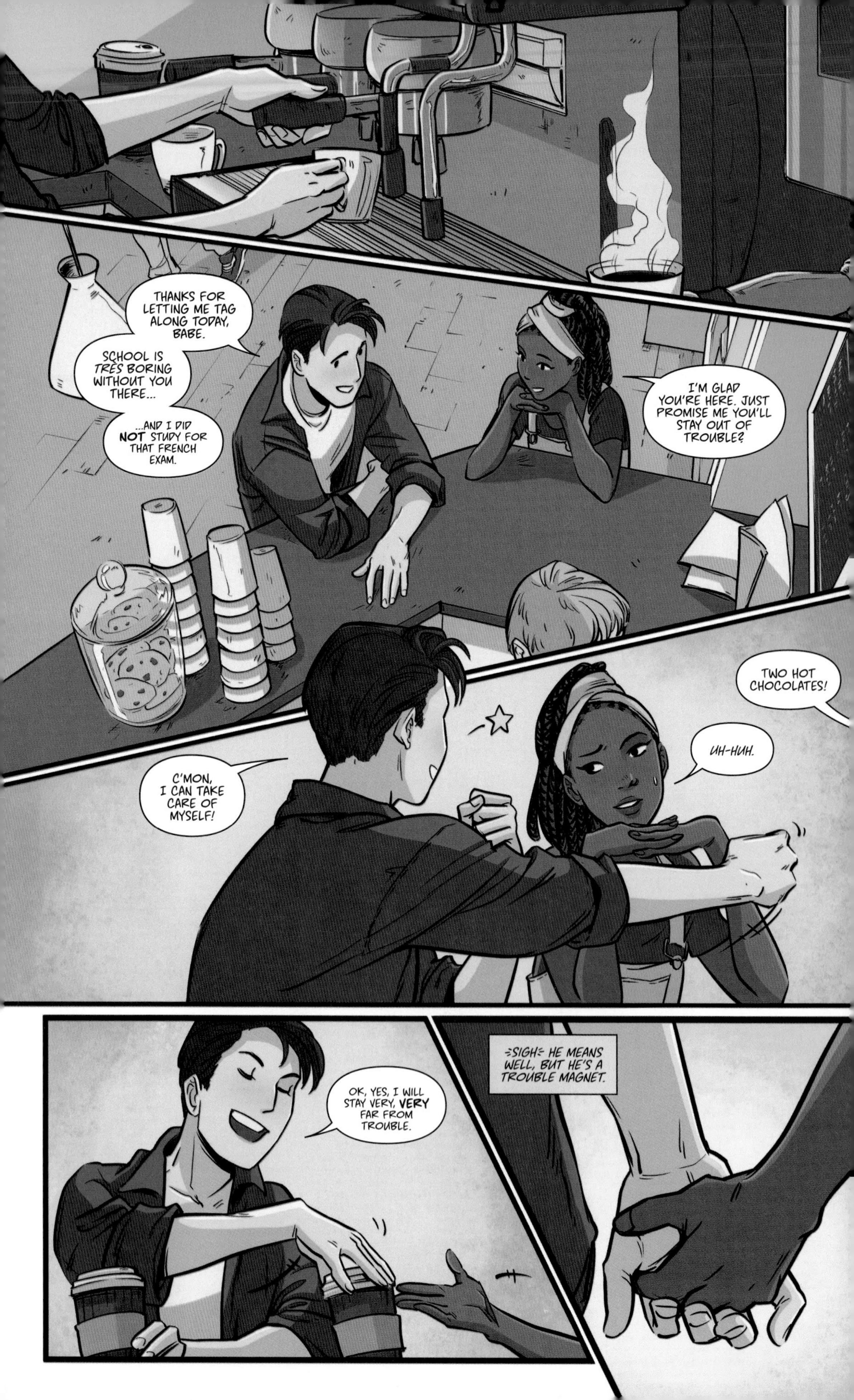
THANKS FOR LETTING ME TAG ALONG TODAY, BABE.
SCHOOL IS TRÈS BORING WITHOUT YOU THERE...
...AND I DID NOT STUDY FOR THAT FRENCH EXAM.
I'M GLAD YOU'RE HERE. JUST PROMISE ME YOU'LL STAY OUT OF TROUBLE?
TWO HOT CHOCOLATES!
UH-HUH.
C'MON, I CAN TAKE CARE OF MYSELF!
OK, YES, I WILL STAY VERY, VERY FAR FROM TROUBLE.
=SIGH= HE MEANS WELL, BUT HE'S A TROUBLE MAGNET.

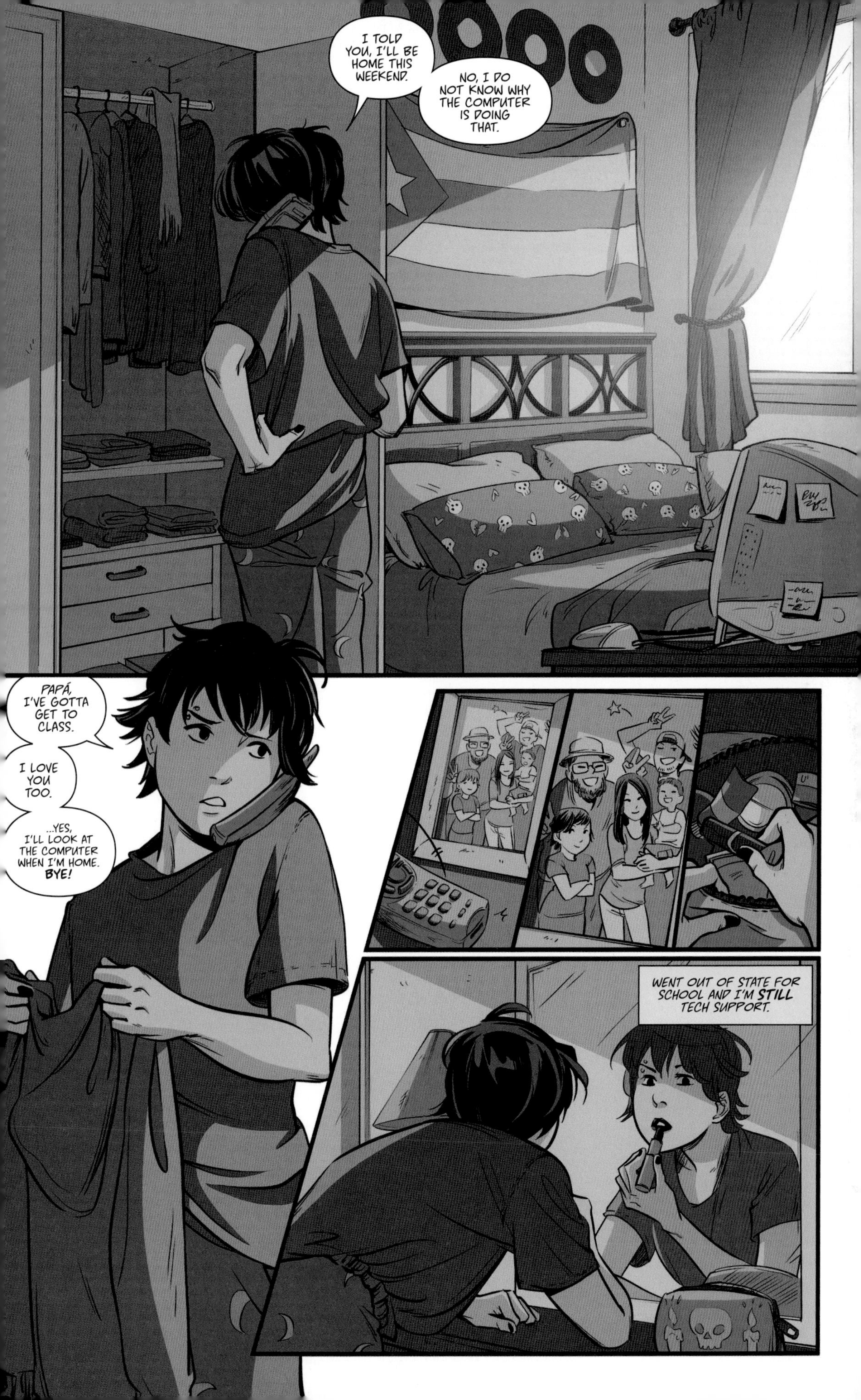
I TOLD YOU, I'LL BE HOME THIS WEEKEND.
NO, I DO NOT KNOW WHY THE COMPUTER IS DOING THAT.
PAPÁ, I'VE GOTTA GET TO CLASS.
I LOVE YOU TOO.
...YES, I'LL LOOK AT THE COMPUTER WHEN I'M HOME. **BYE!**
WENT OUT OF STATE FOR SCHOOL AND I'M **STILL** TECH SUPPORT.

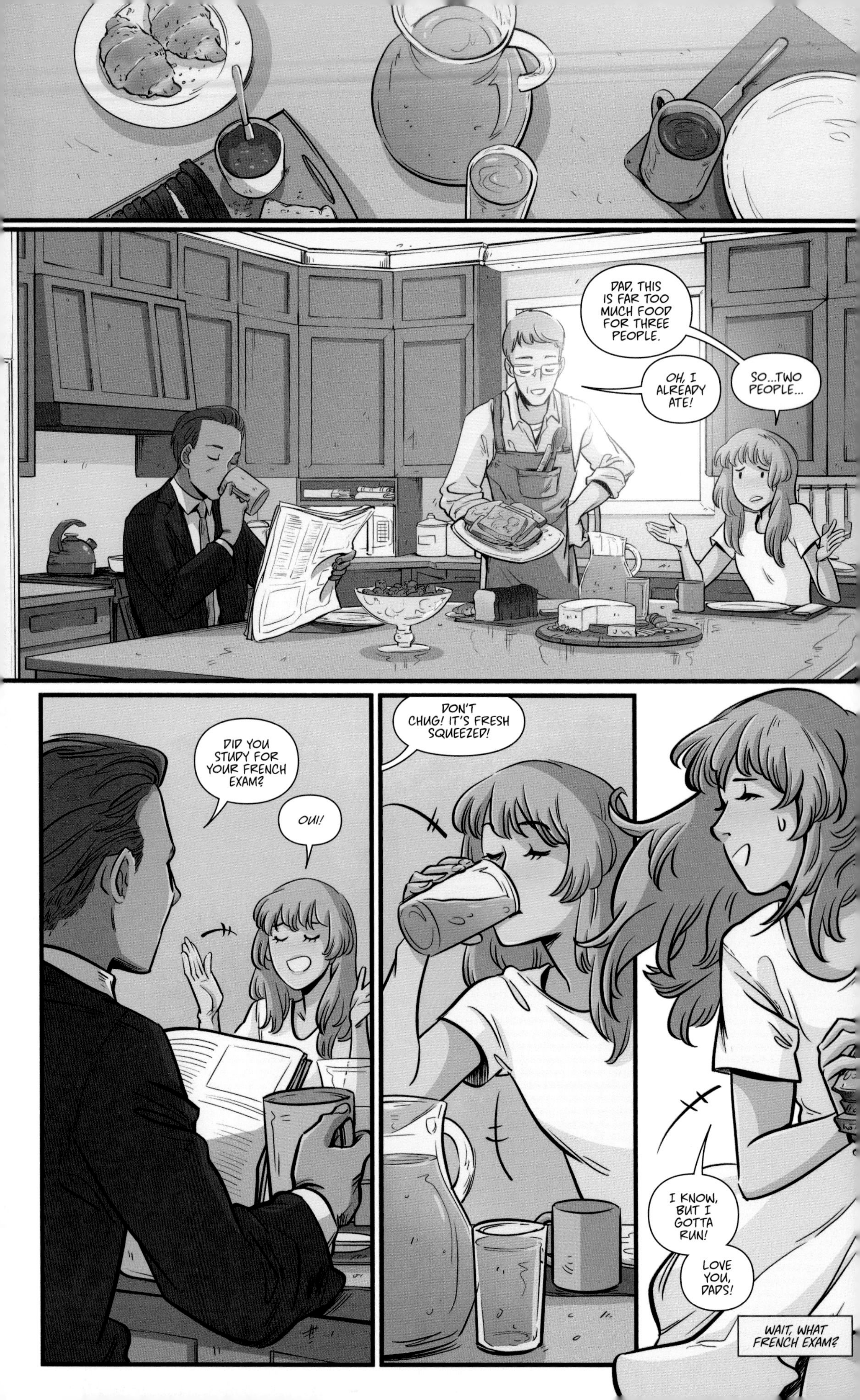
DAD, THIS IS FAR TOO MUCH FOOD FOR THREE PEOPLE.
OH, I ALREADY ATE!
SO...TWO PEOPLE...
DID YOU STUDY FOR YOUR FRENCH EXAM?
OUI!
DON'T CHUG! IT'S FRESH SQUEEZED!
I KNOW, BUT I GOTTA RUN!
LOVE YOU, DADS!
WAIT, WHAT FRENCH EXAM?

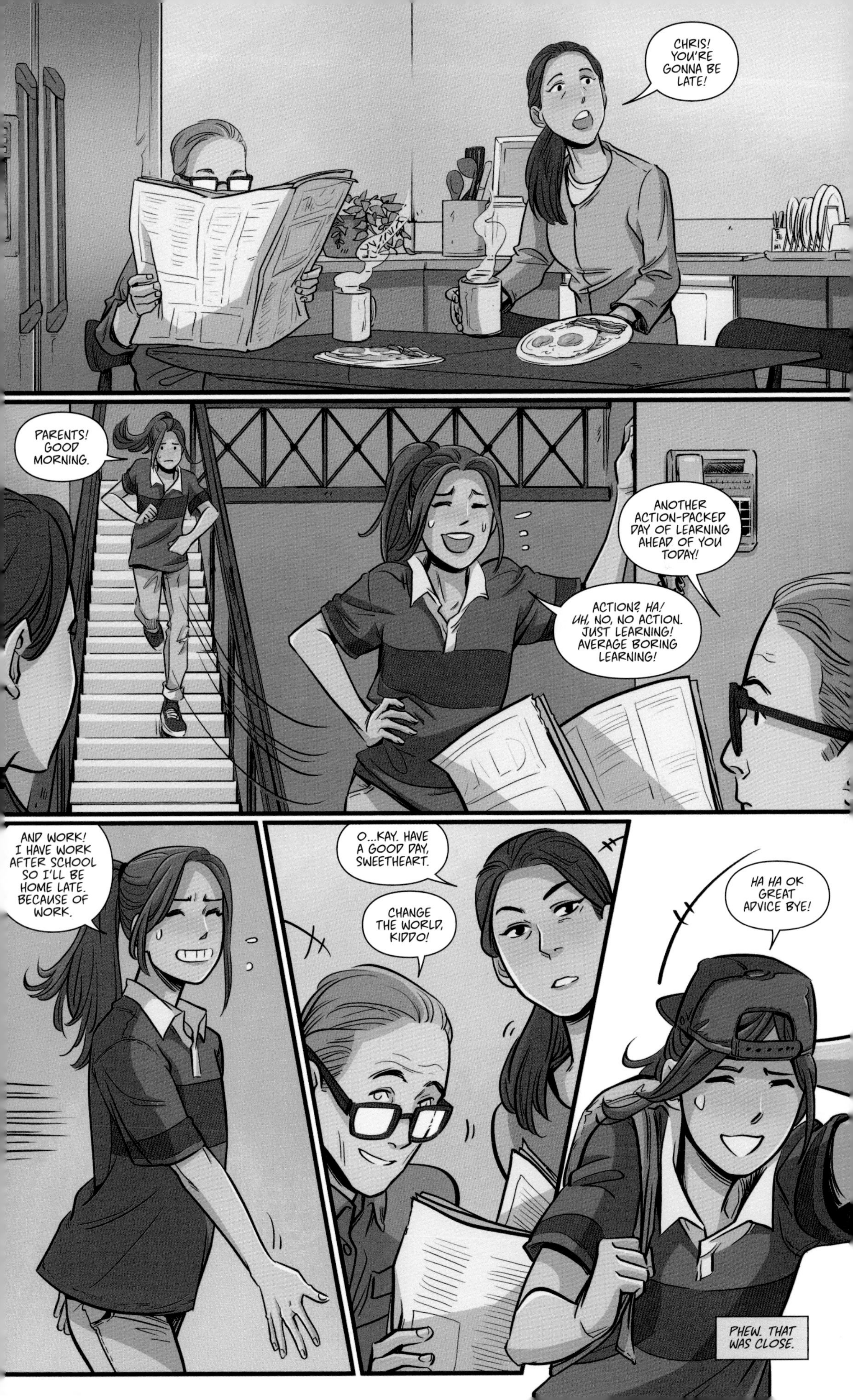
CHRIS! YOU'RE GONNA BE LATE!
PARENTS! GOOD MORNING.
ANOTHER ACTION-PACKED DAY OF LEARNING AHEAD OF YOU TODAY!
ACTION? HA! UH, NO, NO ACTION. JUST LEARNING! AVERAGE BORING LEARNING!
AND WORK! I HAVE WORK AFTER SCHOOL SO I'LL BE HOME LATE. BECAUSE OF WORK.
O...KAY. HAVE A GOOD DAY, SWEETHEART.
CHANGE THE WORLD, KIDDO!
HA HA OK GREAT ADVICE BYE!
PHEW. THAT WAS CLOSE.

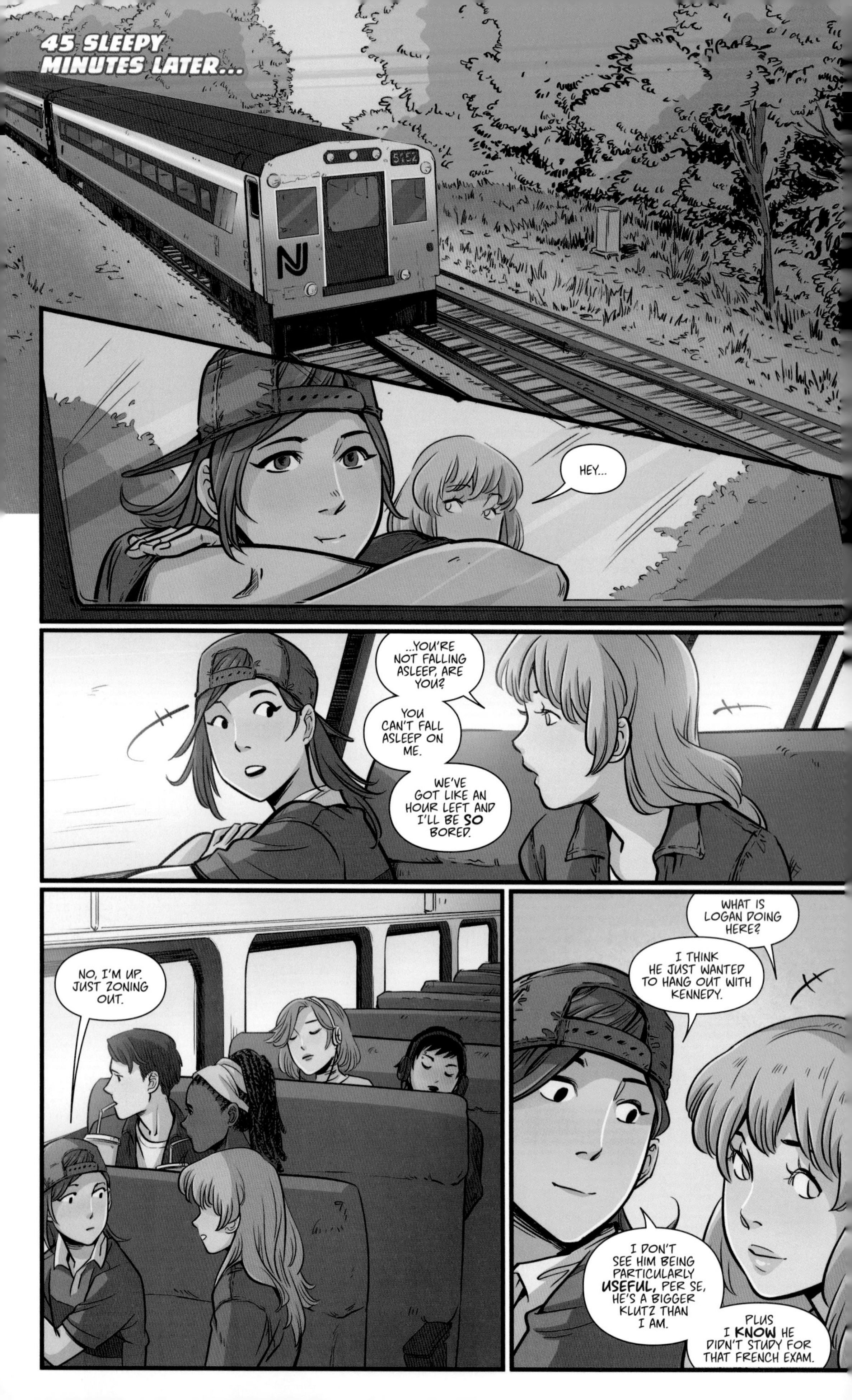
45 SLEEPY MINUTES LATER...
5152
HEY...
...YOU'RE NOT FALLING ASLEEP, ARE YOU?
YOU CAN'T FALL ASLEEP ON ME.
WE'VE GOT LIKE AN HOUR LEFT AND I'LL BE **SO** BORED.
NO, I'M UP. JUST ZONING OUT.
WHAT IS LOGAN DOING HERE?
I THINK HE JUST WANTED TO HANG OUT WITH KENNEDY.
I DON'T SEE HIM BEING PARTICULARLY **USEFUL,** PER SE, HE'S A BIGGER KLUTZ THAN I AM.
PLUS I **KNOW** HE DIDN'T STUDY FOR THAT FRENCH EXAM.

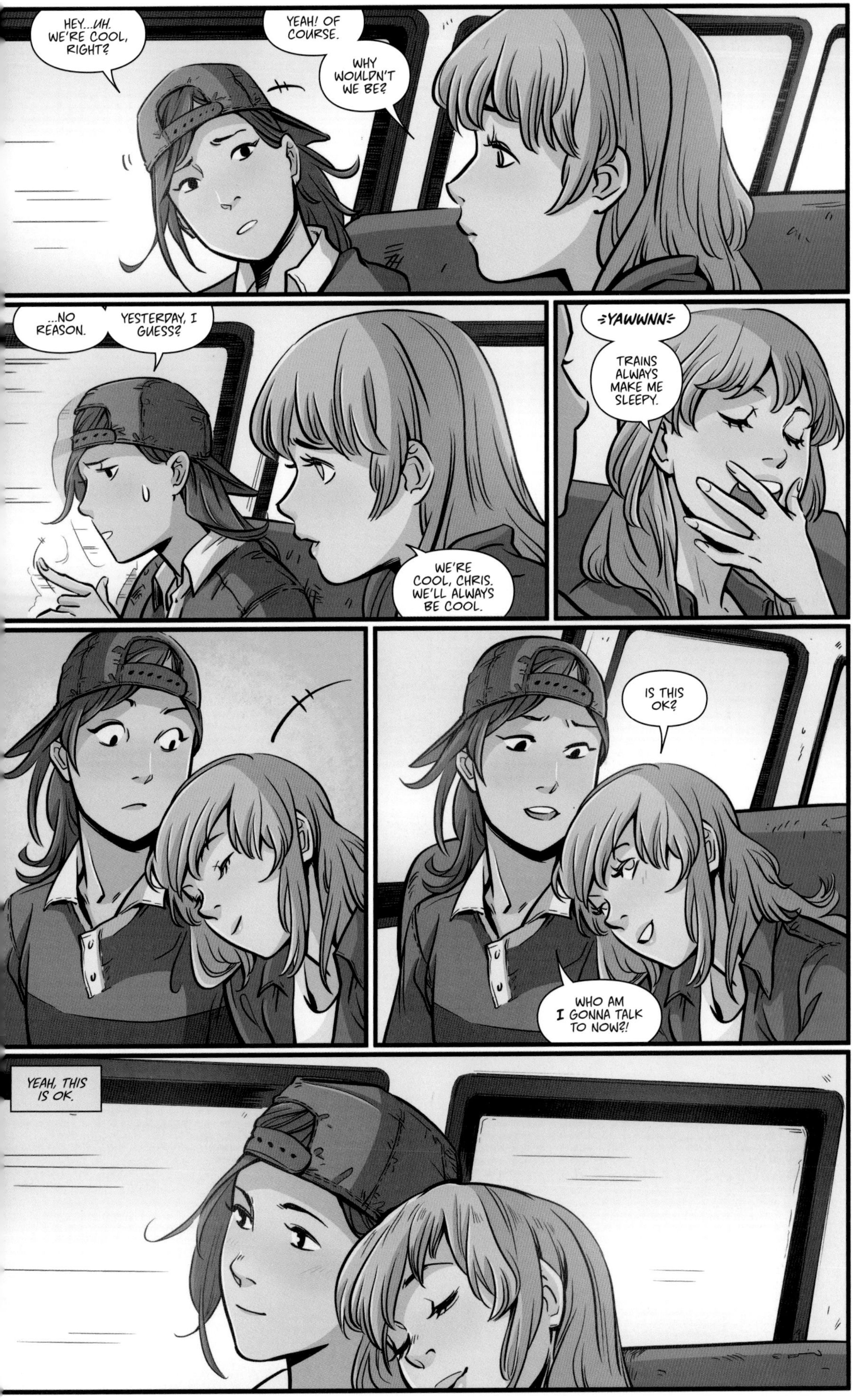
HEY...UH. WE'RE COOL, RIGHT?
YEAH! OF COURSE.
WHY WOULDN'T WE BE?
...NO REASON.
YESTERDAY, I GUESS?
WE'RE COOL, CHRIS. WE'LL ALWAYS BE COOL.
YAWWNN
TRAINS ALWAYS MAKE ME SLEEPY.
IS THIS OK?
WHO AM I GONNA TALK TO NOW?!
YEAH, THIS IS OK.

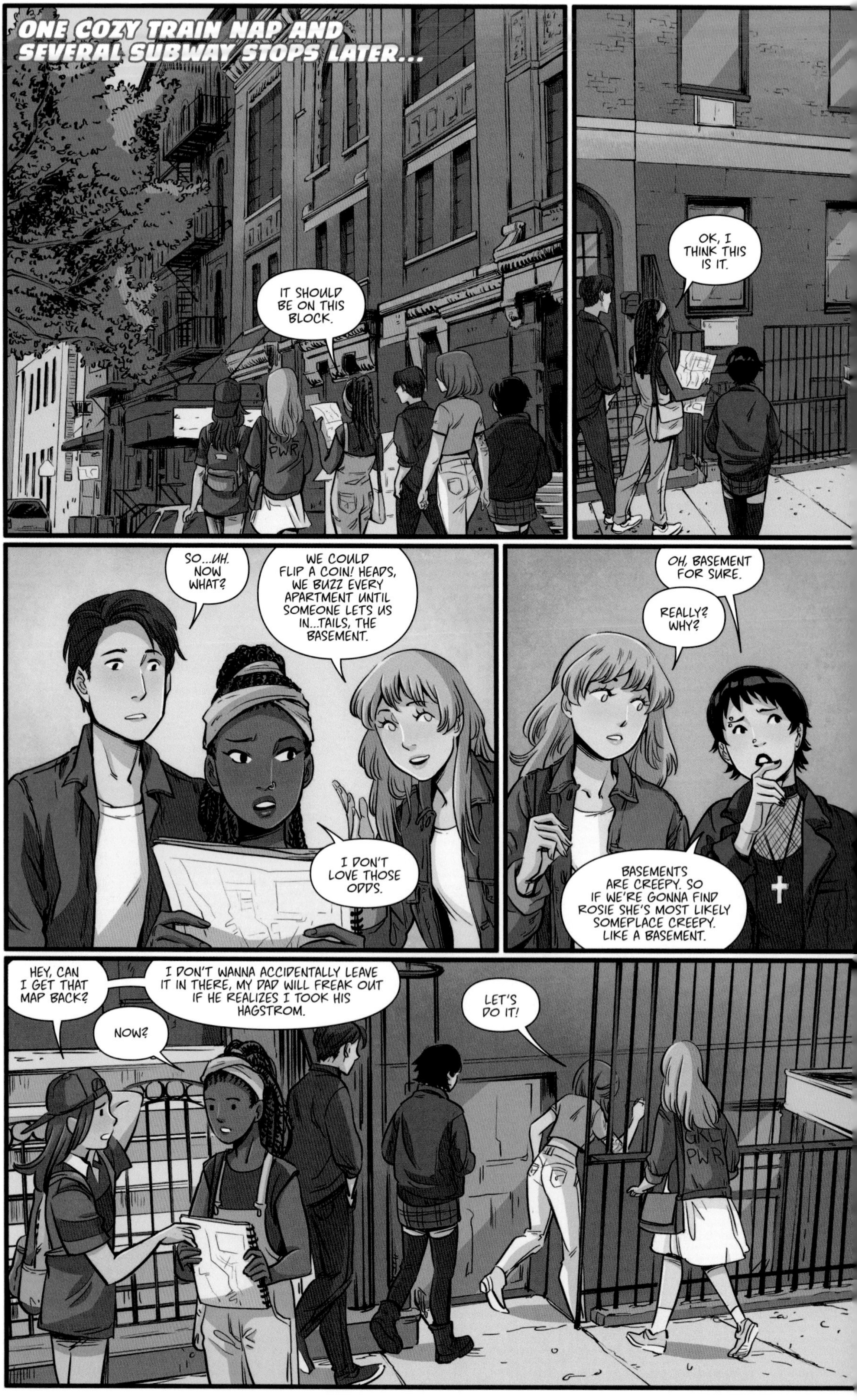
ONE COZY TRAIN NAP AND SEVERAL SUBWAY STOPS LATER...
IT SHOULD BE ON THIS BLOCK.
OK, I THINK THIS IS IT.
SO...UH. NOW WHAT?
WE COULD FLIP A COIN! HEADS, WE BUZZ EVERY APARTMENT UNTIL SOMEONE LETS US IN...TAILS, THE BASEMENT.
I DON'T LOVE THOSE ODDS.
OH, BASEMENT FOR SURE.
REALLY? WHY?
BASEMENTS ARE CREEPY. SO IF WE'RE GONNA FIND ROSIE SHE'S MOST LIKELY SOMEPLACE CREEPY. LIKE A BASEMENT.
HEY, CAN I GET THAT MAP BACK?
I DON'T WANNA ACCIDENTALLY LEAVE IT IN THERE, MY DAD WILL FREAK OUT IF HE REALIZES I TOOK HIS HAGSTROM.
NOW?
LET'S DO IT!

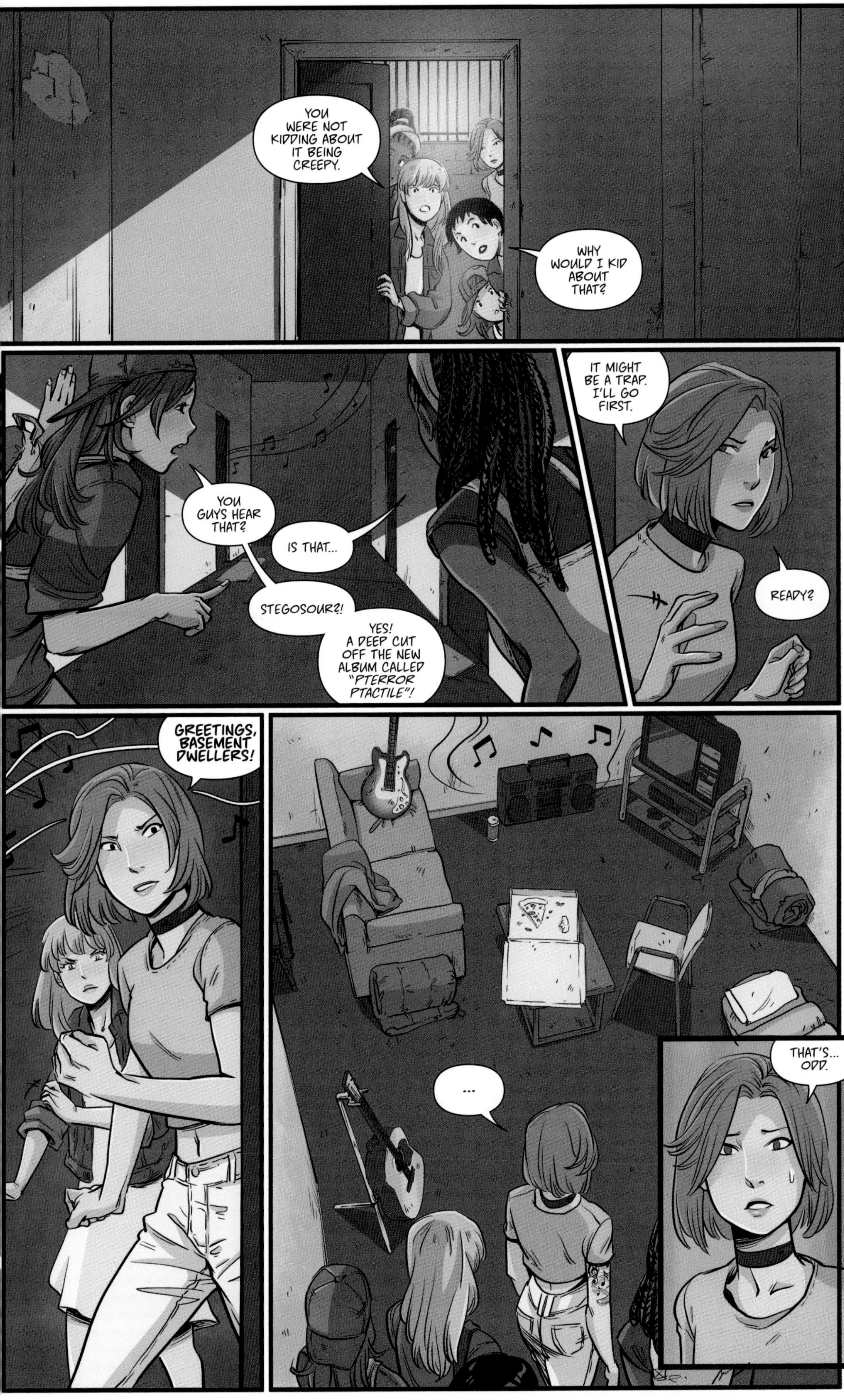

YOU WERE NOT KIDDING ABOUT IT BEING CREEPY.
WHY WOULD I KID ABOUT THAT?
YOU GUYS HEAR THAT?
IS THAT...
STEGOSOUR?!
YES! A DEEP CUT OFF THE NEW ALBUM CALLED "PTERROR PTACTILE"!
IT MIGHT BE A TRAP. I'LL GO FIRST.
READY?
GREETINGS, BASEMENT DWELLERS!
...
THAT'S... ODD.

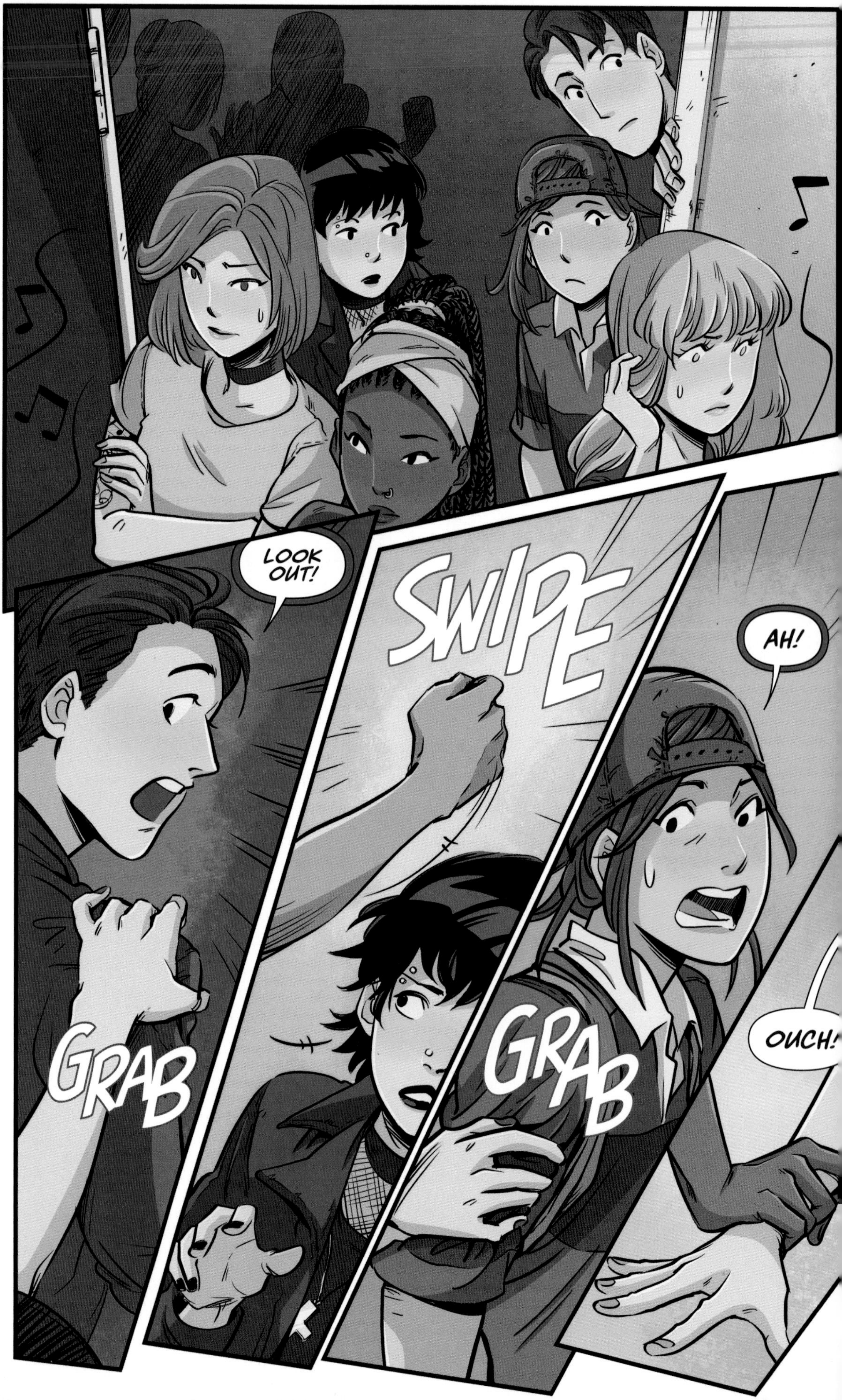

LOOK OUT!
GRAB
SWIPE
GRAB
AH!
OUCH!

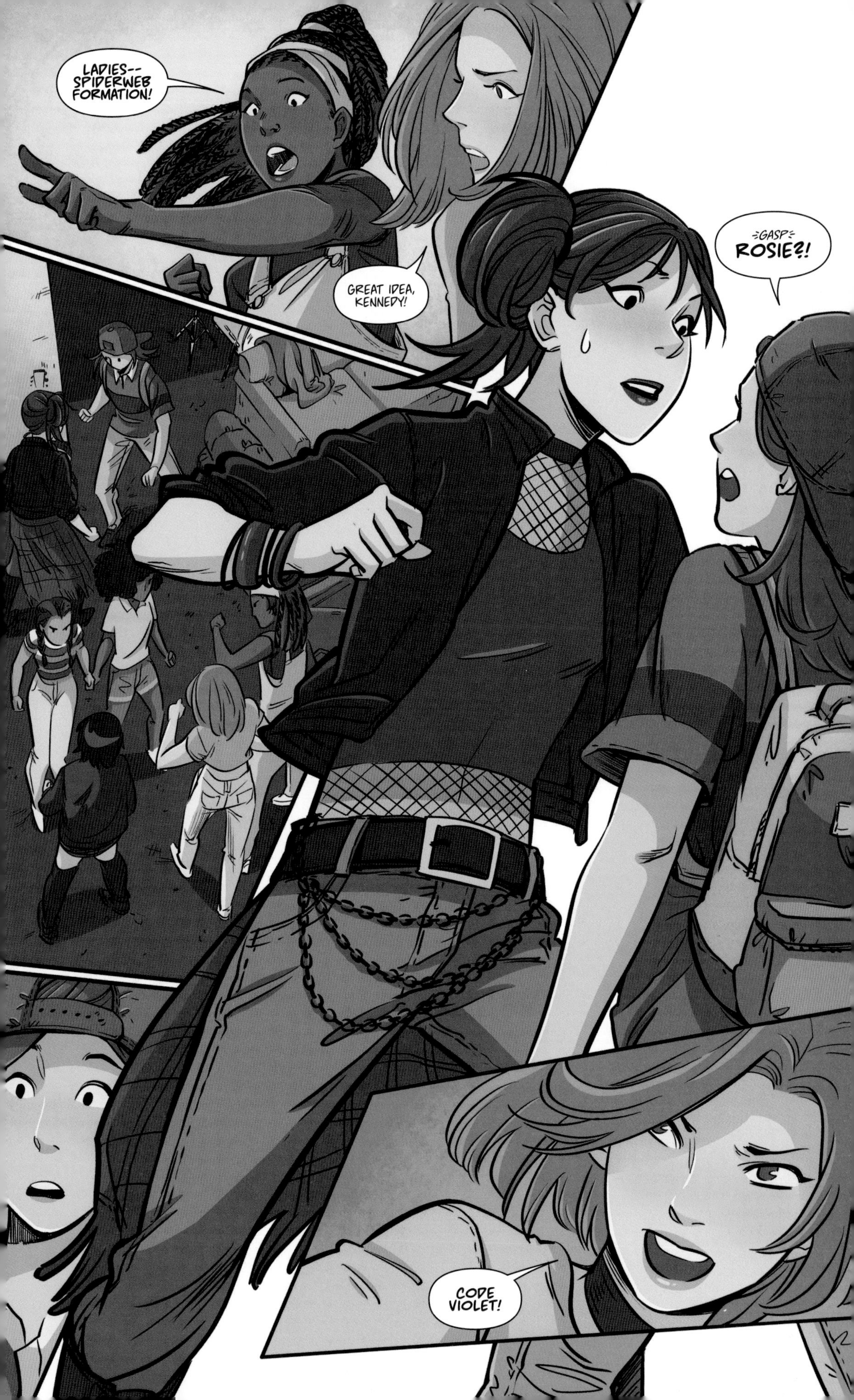
LADIES--
SPIDERWEB
FORMATION!
GREAT IDEA,
KENNEDY!
GASP
ROSIE?!
CODE
VIOLET!

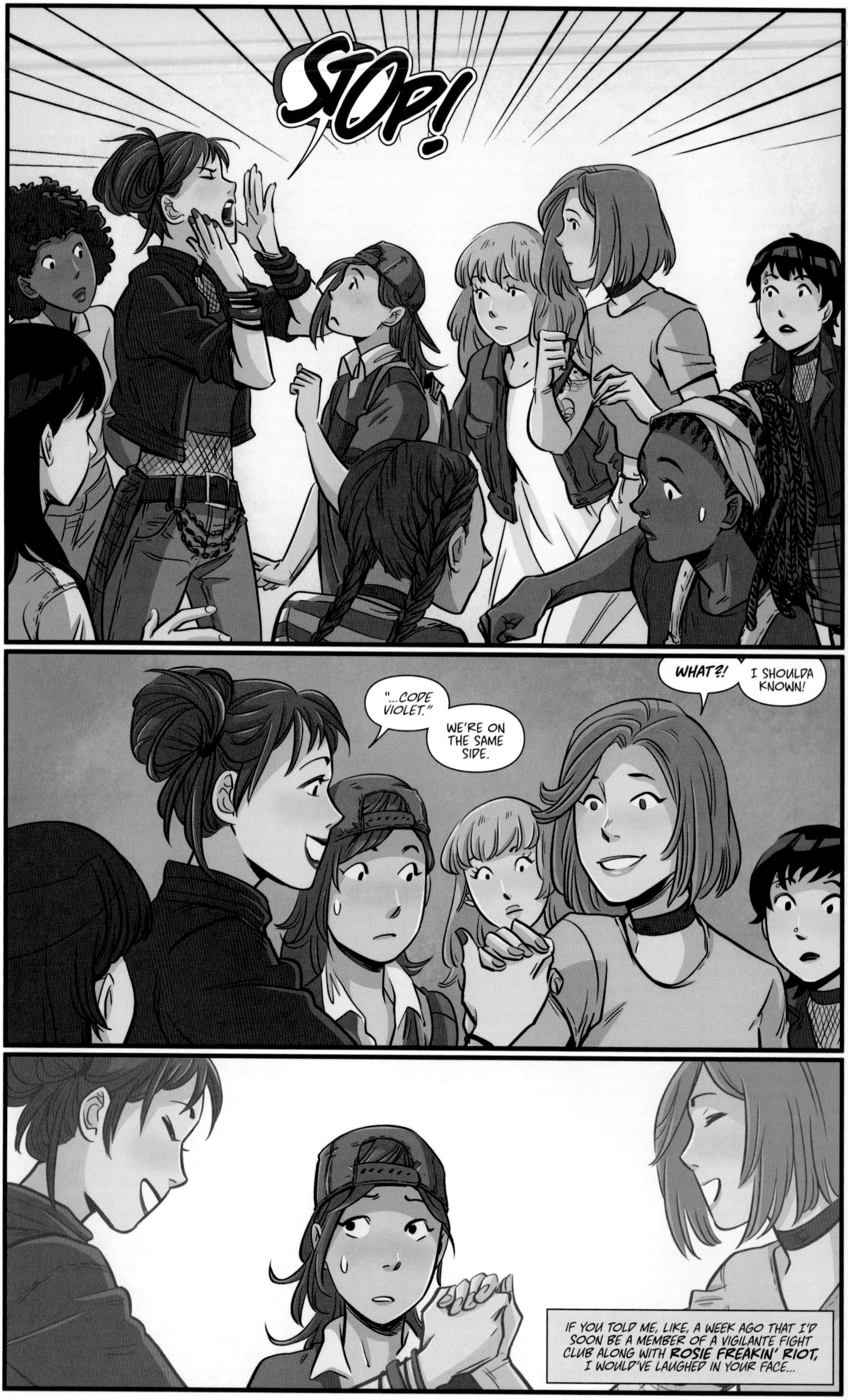
STOP!
"...CODE VIOLET."
WE'RE ON THE SAME SIDE.
WHAT?!
I SHOULDA KNOWN!
IF YOU TOLD ME, LIKE, A WEEK AGO THAT I'D SOON BE A MEMBER OF A VIGILANTE FIGHT CLUB ALONG WITH ROSIE FREAKIN' RIOT, I WOULD'VE LAUGHED IN YOUR FACE...

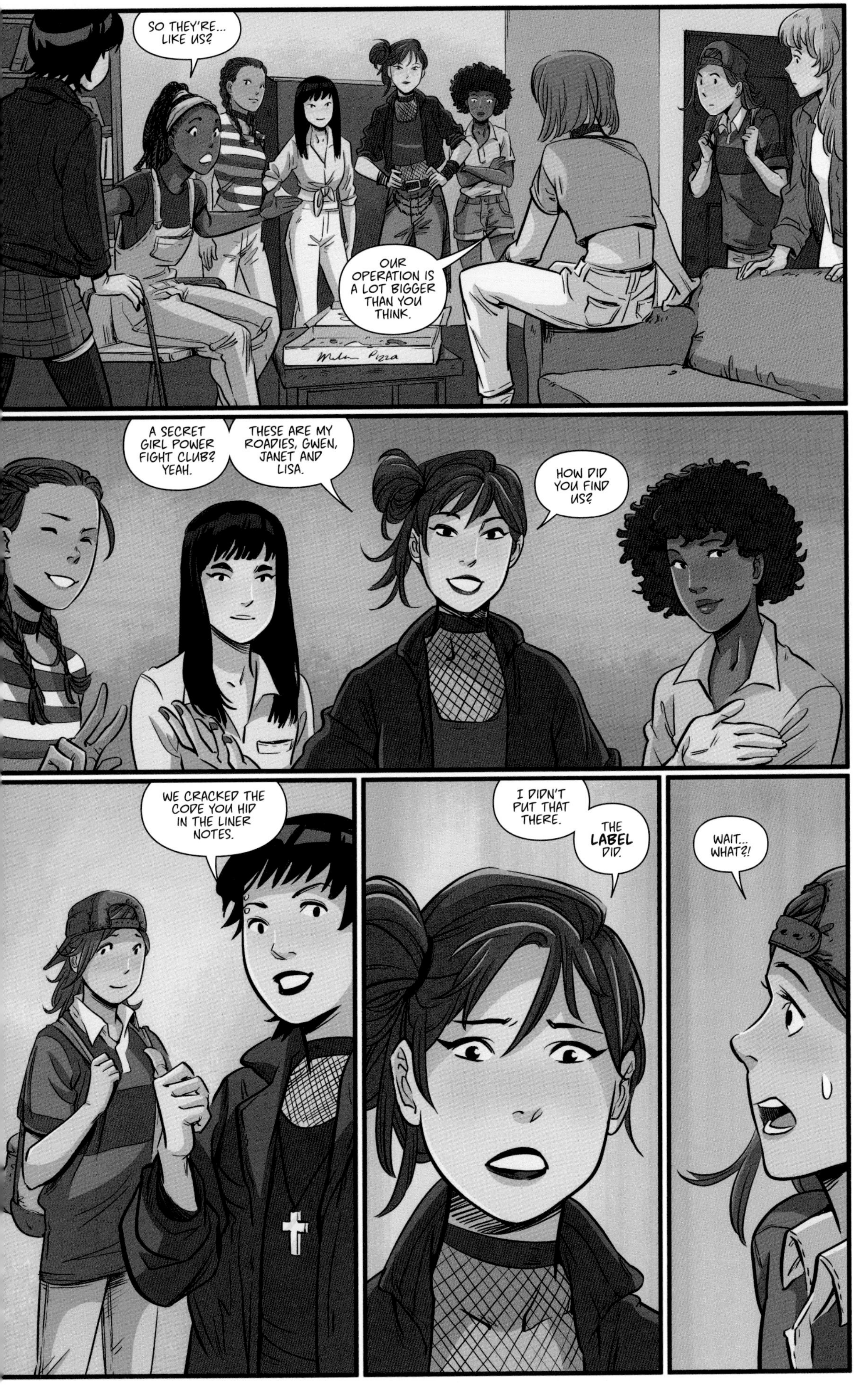
SO THEY'RE... LIKE US?
OUR OPERATION IS A LOT BIGGER THAN YOU THINK.
A SECRET GIRL POWER FIGHT CLUB? YEAH.
THESE ARE MY ROADIES, GWEN, JANET AND LISA.
HOW DID YOU FIND US?
WE CRACKED THE CODE YOU HID IN THE LINER NOTES.
I DIDN'T PUT THAT THERE.
THE **LABEL** DID.
WAIT... WHAT?!

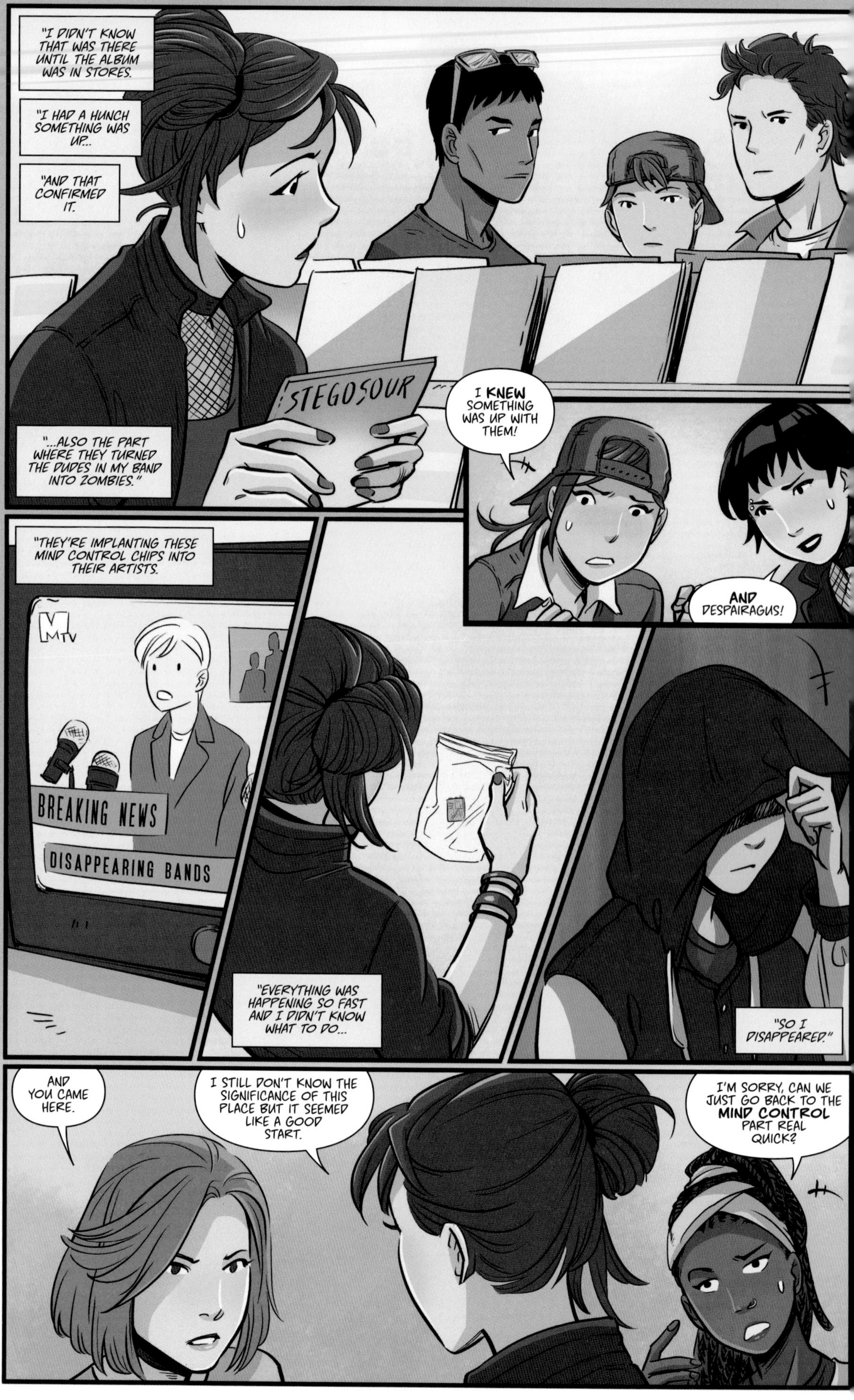
"I DIDN'T KNOW THAT WAS THERE UNTIL THE ALBUM WAS IN STORES.
"I HAD A HUNCH SOMETHING WAS UP...
"AND THAT CONFIRMED IT.
STEGOSOUR
"...ALSO THE PART WHERE THEY TURNED THE DUDES IN MY BAND INTO ZOMBIES."
I KNEW SOMETHING WAS UP WITH THEM!
AND DESPAIRAGUS!
"THEY'RE IMPLANTING THESE MIND CONTROL CHIPS INTO THEIR ARTISTS.
MTV
BREAKING NEWS
DISAPPEARING BANDS
"EVERYTHING WAS HAPPENING SO FAST AND I DIDN'T KNOW WHAT TO DO...
"SO I DISAPPEARED."
AND YOU CAME HERE.
I STILL DON'T KNOW THE SIGNIFICANCE OF THIS PLACE BUT IT SEEMED LIKE A GOOD START.
I'M SORRY, CAN WE JUST GO BACK TO THE MIND CONTROL PART REAL QUICK?

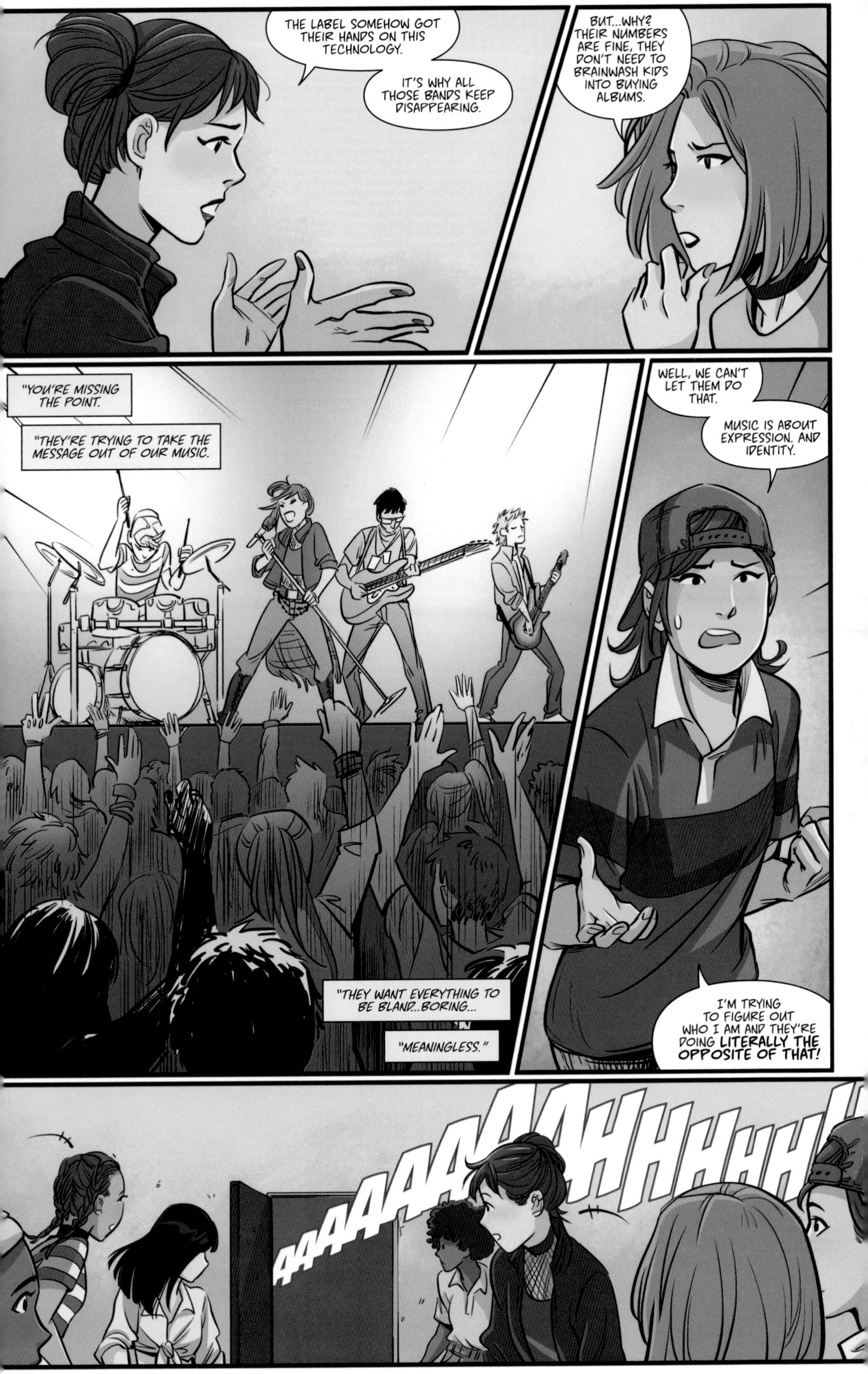
THE LABEL SOMEHOW GOT THEIR HANDS ON THIS TECHNOLOGY.
IT'S WHY ALL THOSE BANDS KEEP DISAPPEARING.
BUT...WHY? THEIR NUMBERS ARE FINE, THEY DON'T NEED TO BRAINWASH KIDS INTO BUYING ALBUMS.
"YOU'RE MISSING THE POINT.
"THEY'RE TRYING TO TAKE THE MESSAGE OUT OF OUR MUSIC.
"THEY WANT EVERYTHING TO BE BLAND...BORING...
"MEANINGLESS."
WELL, WE CAN'T LET THEM DO THAT.
MUSIC IS ABOUT EXPRESSION. AND IDENTITY.
I'M TRYING TO FIGURE OUT WHO I AM AND THEY'RE DOING **LITERALLY THE OPPOSITE OF THAT!**
AAAAAAAAAHHHHHHH!!

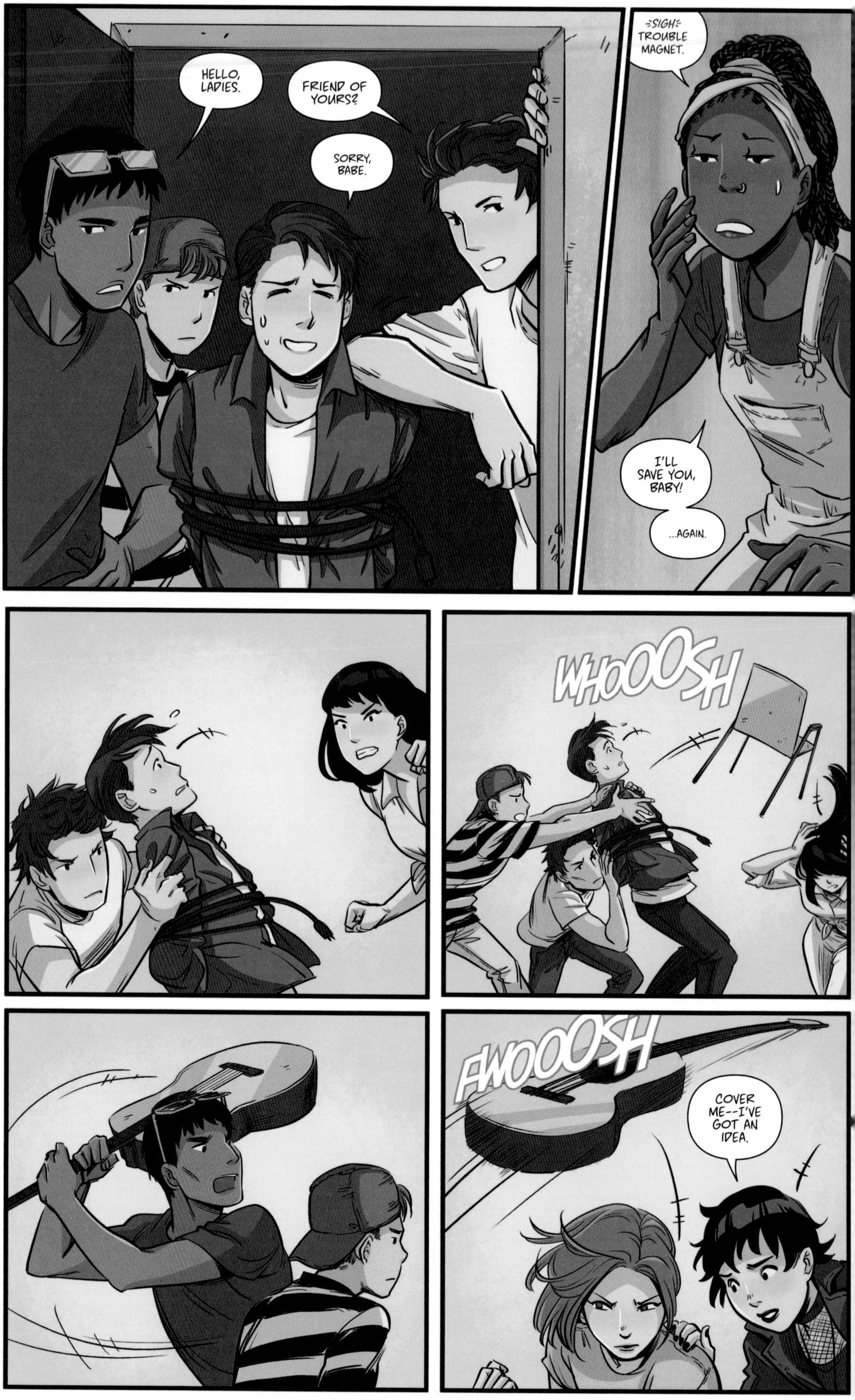
HELLO, LADIES.
FRIEND OF YOURS?
SORRY, BABE.
SIGH TROUBLE MAGNET.
I'LL SAVE YOU, BABY!
...AGAIN.
WHOOOOSH
FWOOOOSH
COVER ME--I'VE GOT AN IDEA.

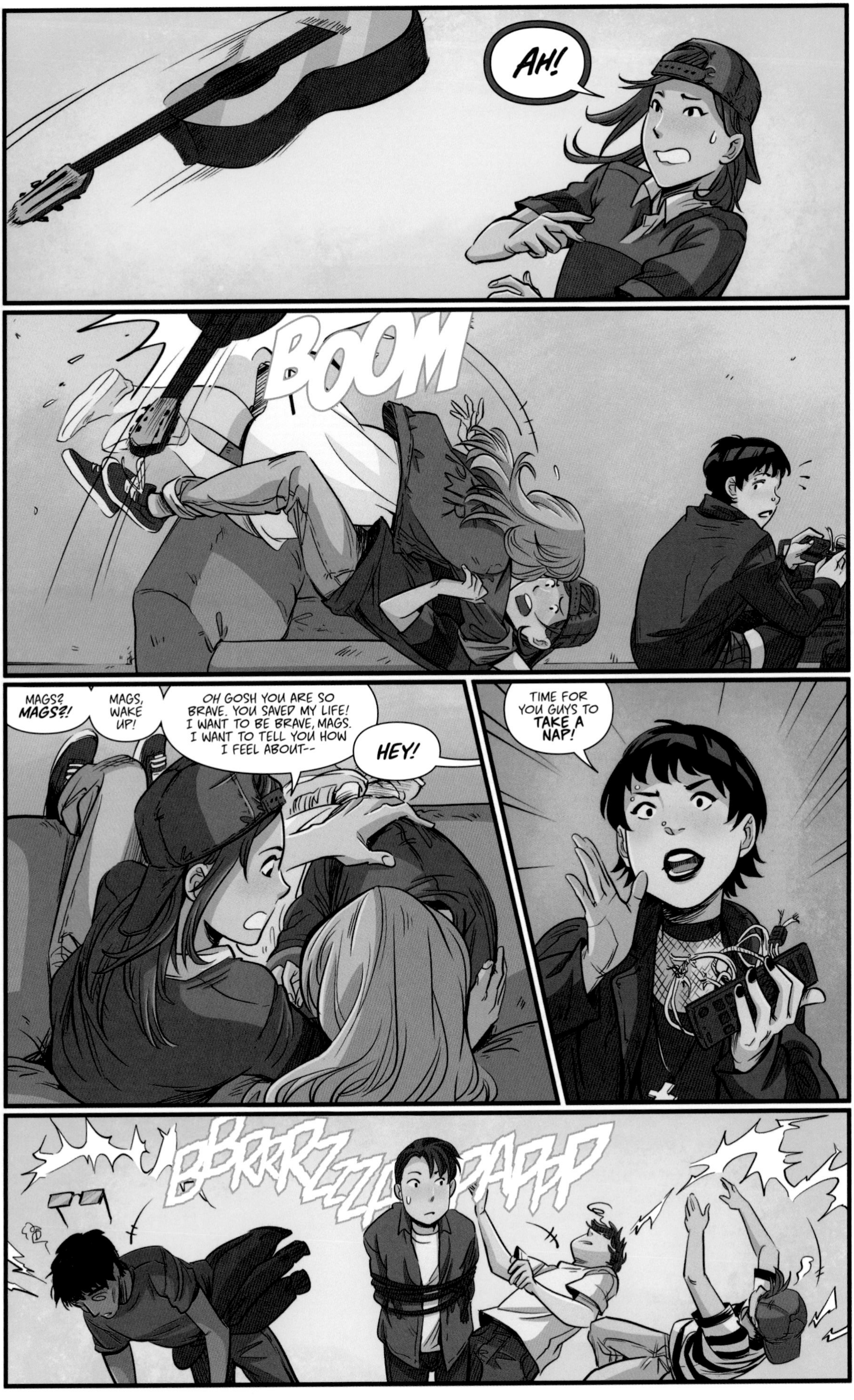
AH!
BOOM
MAGS? MAGS?!
MAGS, WAKE UP!
OH GOSH YOU ARE SO BRAVE. YOU SAVED MY LIFE! I WANT TO BE BRAVE, MAGS. I WANT TO TELL YOU HOW I FEEL ABOUT--
HEY!
TIME FOR YOU GUYS TO TAKE A NAP!
BBRRRZZZZAPPP

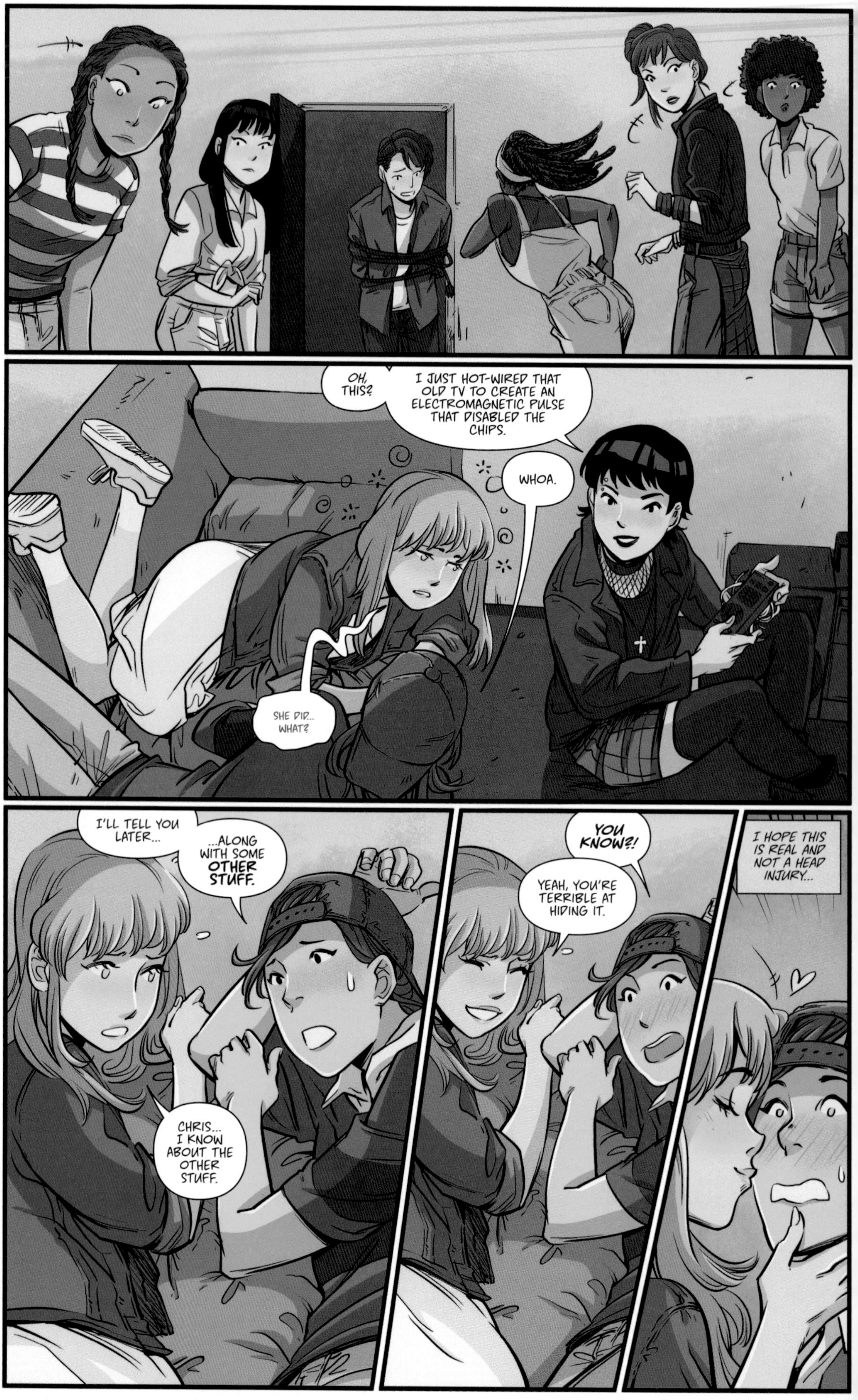
OH, THIS?
I JUST HOT-WIRED THAT OLD TV TO CREATE AN ELECTROMAGNETIC PULSE THAT DISABLED THE CHIPS.
WHOA.
SHE DID... WHAT?
I'LL TELL YOU LATER...
...ALONG WITH SOME OTHER STUFF.
CHRIS... I KNOW ABOUT THE OTHER STUFF.
YOU KNOW?!
YEAH, YOU'RE TERRIBLE AT HIDING IT.
I HOPE THIS IS REAL AND NOT A HEAD INJURY...

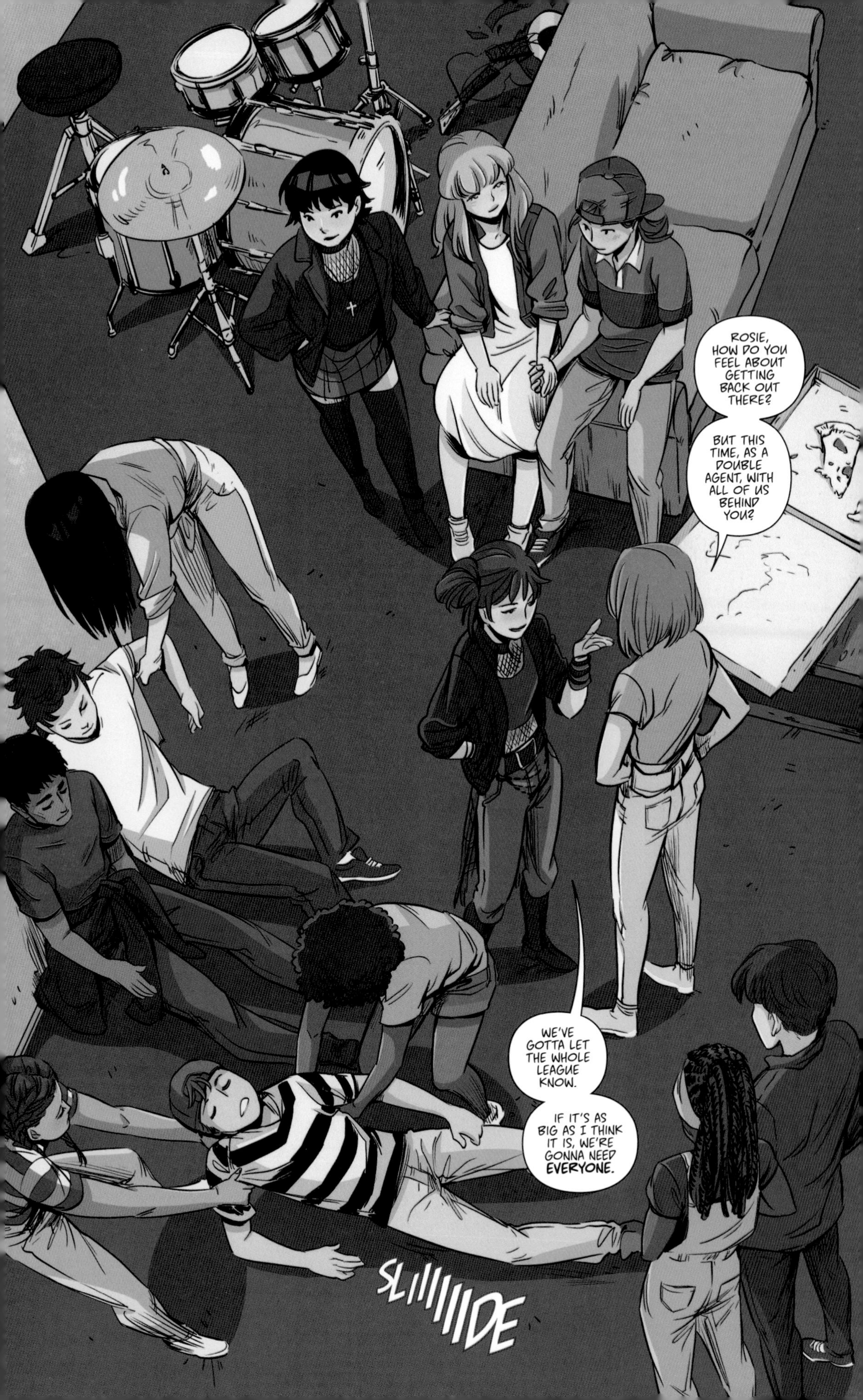
ROSIE, HOW DO YOU FEEL ABOUT GETTING BACK OUT THERE?
BUT THIS TIME, AS A DOUBLE AGENT, WITH ALL OF US BEHIND YOU?
WE'VE GOTTA LET THE WHOLE LEAGUE KNOW.
IF IT'S AS BIG AS I THINK IT IS, WE'RE GONNA NEED **EVERYONE**.
SLIIIIIDE

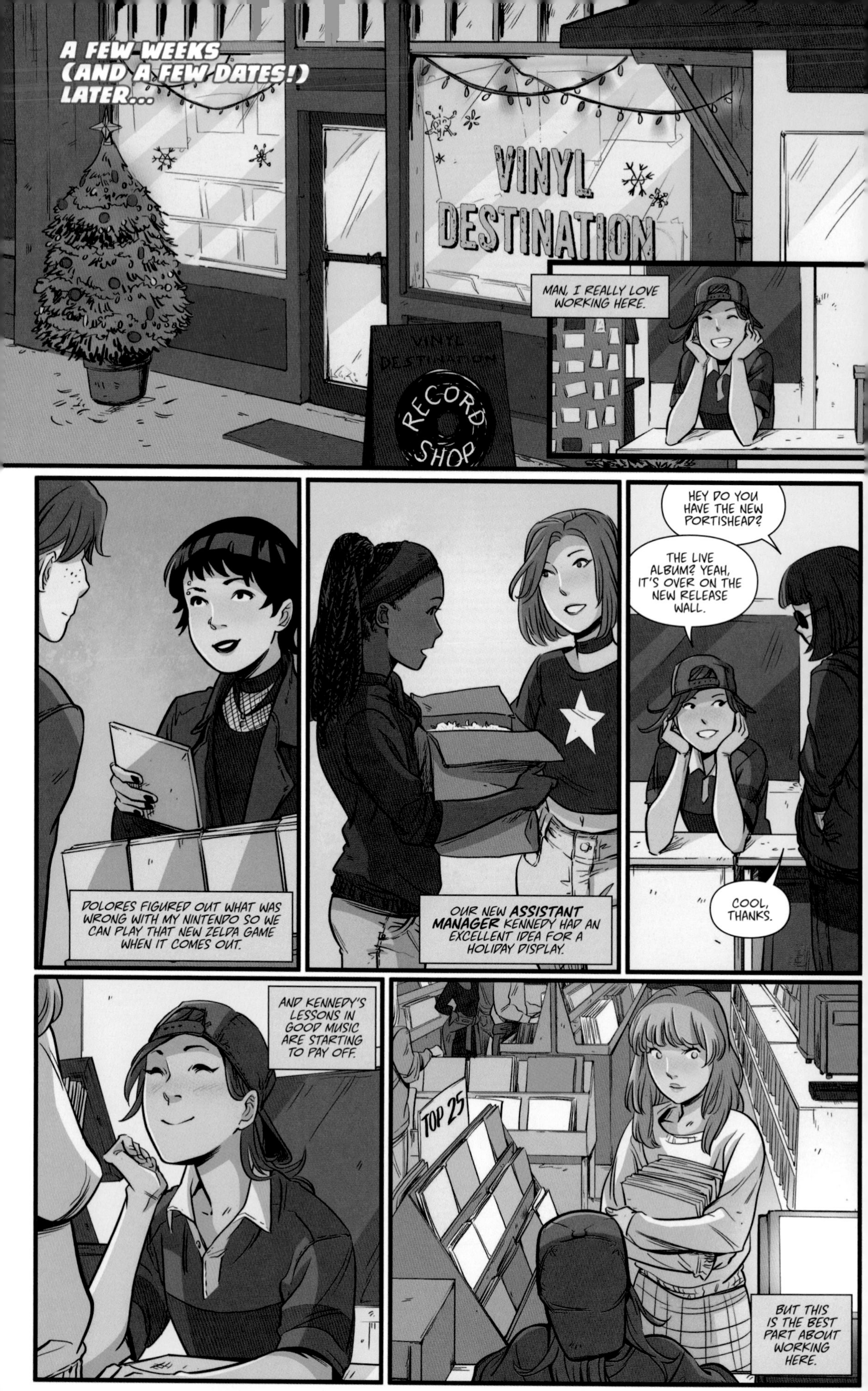

A FEW WEEKS (AND A FEW DATES!) LATER...
VINYL DESTINATION
VINYL DESTINATION
RECORD SHOP
MAN, I REALLY LOVE WORKING HERE.
DOLORES FIGURED OUT WHAT WAS WRONG WITH MY NINTENDO SO WE CAN PLAY THAT NEW ZELDA GAME WHEN IT COMES OUT.
OUR NEW **ASSISTANT MANAGER** KENNEDY HAD AN EXCELLENT IDEA FOR A HOLIDAY DISPLAY.
HEY DO YOU HAVE THE NEW PORTISHEAD?
THE LIVE ALBUM? YEAH, IT'S OVER ON THE NEW RELEASE WALL.
COOL, THANKS.
AND KENNEDY'S LESSONS IN GOOD MUSIC ARE STARTING TO PAY OFF.
TOP 25
BUT THIS IS THE BEST PART ABOUT WORKING HERE.

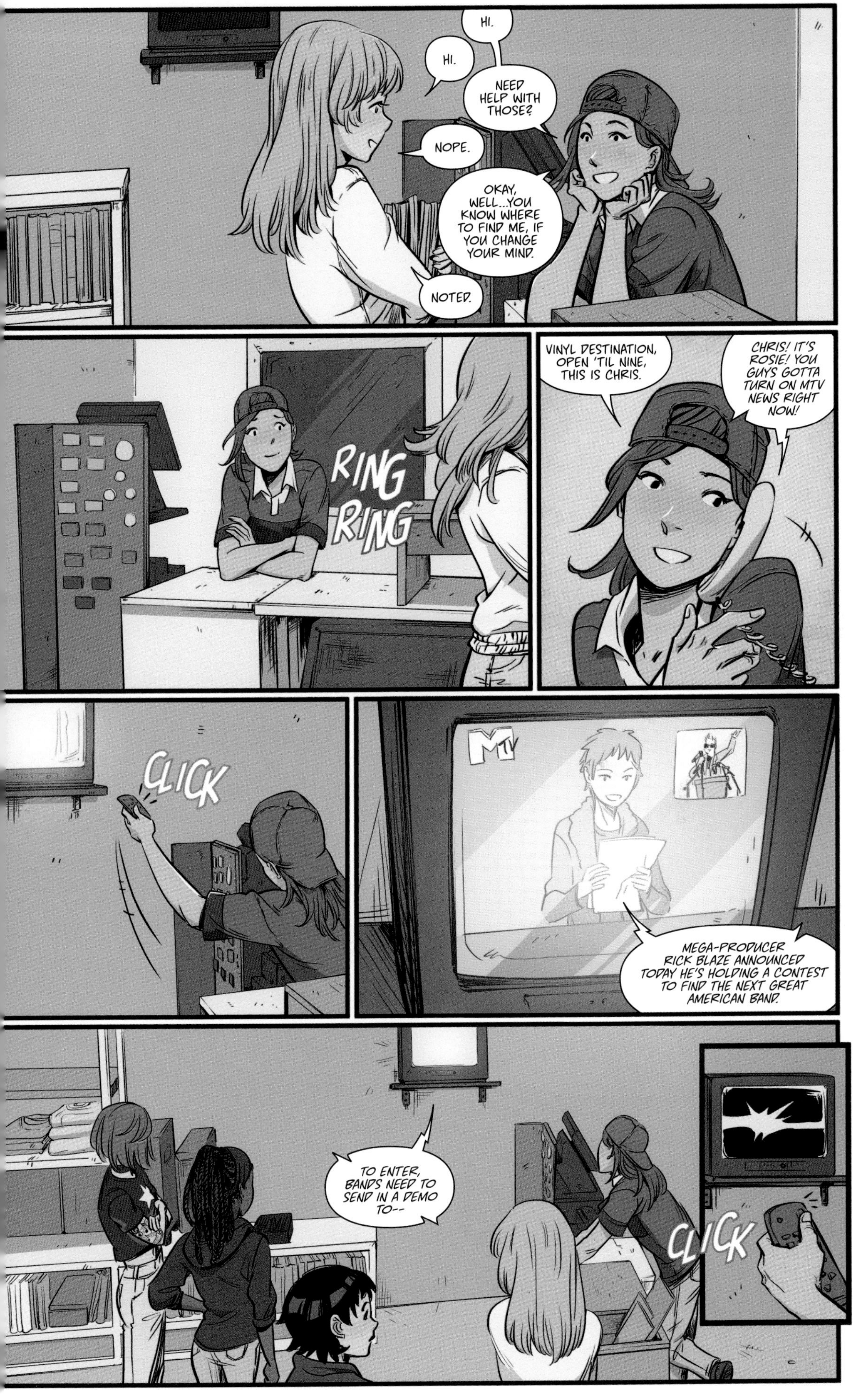
HI.
HI.
NEED HELP WITH THOSE?
NOPE.
OKAY, WELL...YOU KNOW WHERE TO FIND ME, IF YOU CHANGE YOUR MIND.
NOTED.
RING RING
VINYL DESTINATION, OPEN 'TIL NINE, THIS IS CHRIS.
CHRIS! IT'S ROSIE! YOU GUYS GOTTA TURN ON MTV NEWS RIGHT NOW!
CLICK
MTV
MEGA-PRODUCER RICK BLAZE ANNOUNCED TODAY HE'S HOLDING A CONTEST TO FIND THE NEXT GREAT AMERICAN BAND.
TO ENTER, BANDS NEED TO SEND IN A DEMO TO--
CLICK

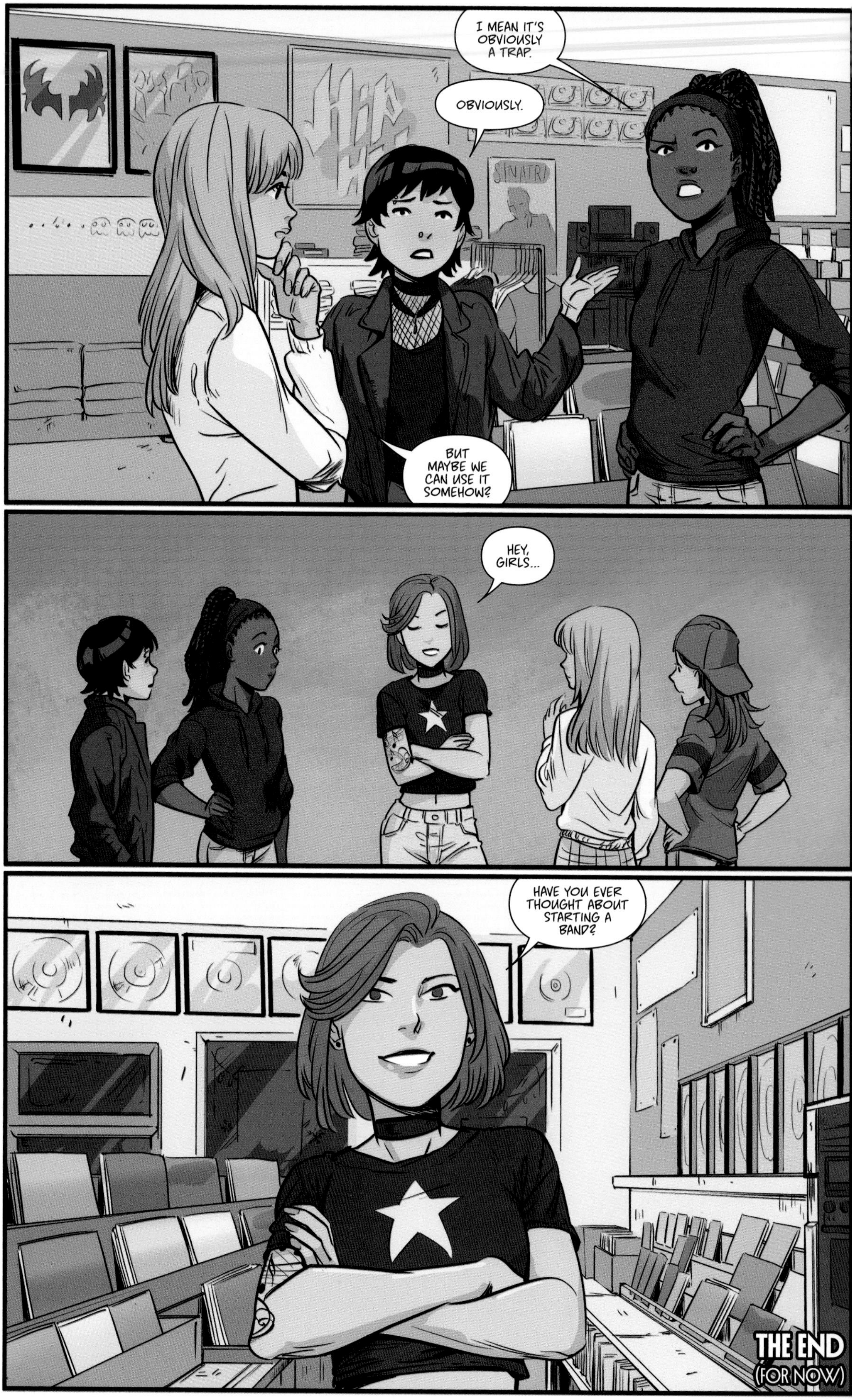
I MEAN IT'S OBVIOUSLY A TRAP.
OBVIOUSLY.
BUT MAYBE WE CAN USE IT SOMEHOW?
HEY, GIRLS...
HAVE YOU EVER THOUGHT ABOUT STARTING A BAND?
THE END (FOR NOW)

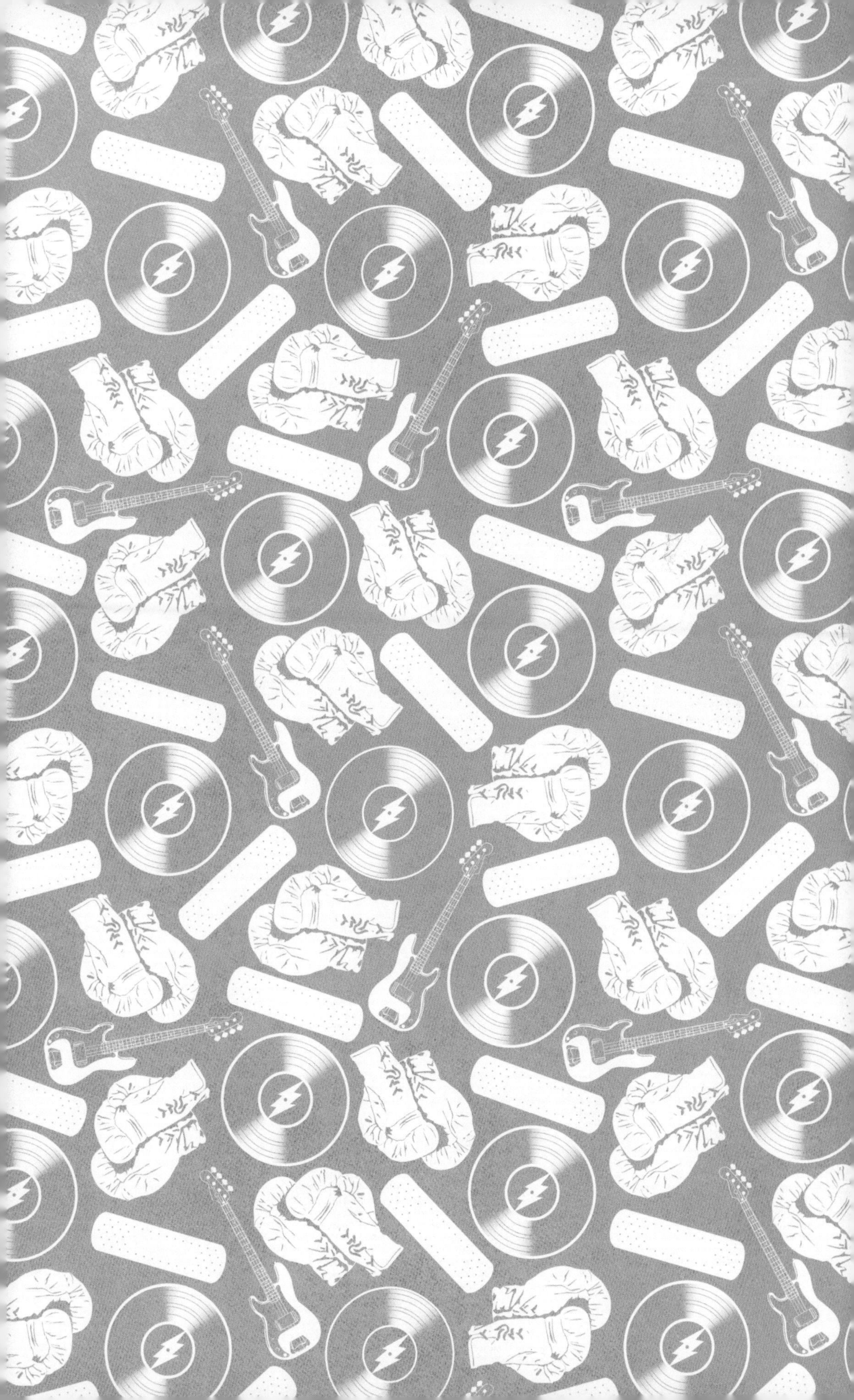

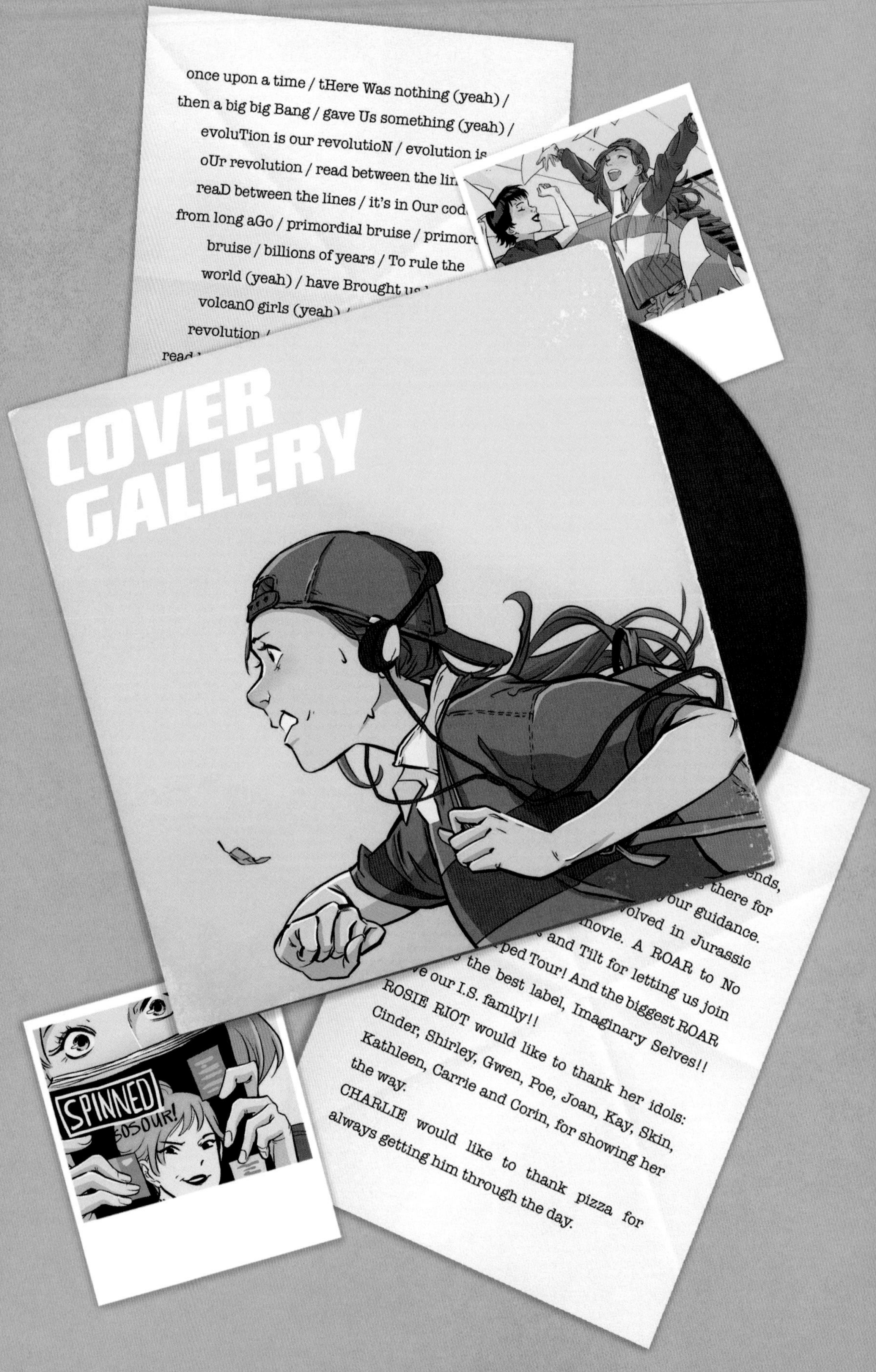

once upon a time / tHere Was nothing (yeah) /
then a big big Bang / gave Us something (yeah) /
evoluTion is our revolutioN / evolution is
oUr revolution / read between the lin
reaD between the lines / it's in Our cod
from long aGo / primordial bruise / primor
bruise / billions of years / To rule the
world (yeah) / have Brought us
volcanO girls (yeah)
revolution
COVER
GALLERY
ends,
there for
our guidance.
volved in Jurassic
movie. A ROAR to No
and Tilt for letting us join
ped Tour! And the biggest ROAR
the best label, Imaginary Selves!!
e our I.S. family!!
ROSIE RIOT would like to thank her idols:
Cinder, Shirley, Gwen, Poe, Joan, Kay, Skin,
Kathleen, Carrie and Corin, for showing her
the way.
CHARLIE would like to thank pizza for
always getting him through the day.
SPINNED
SOSOUR!

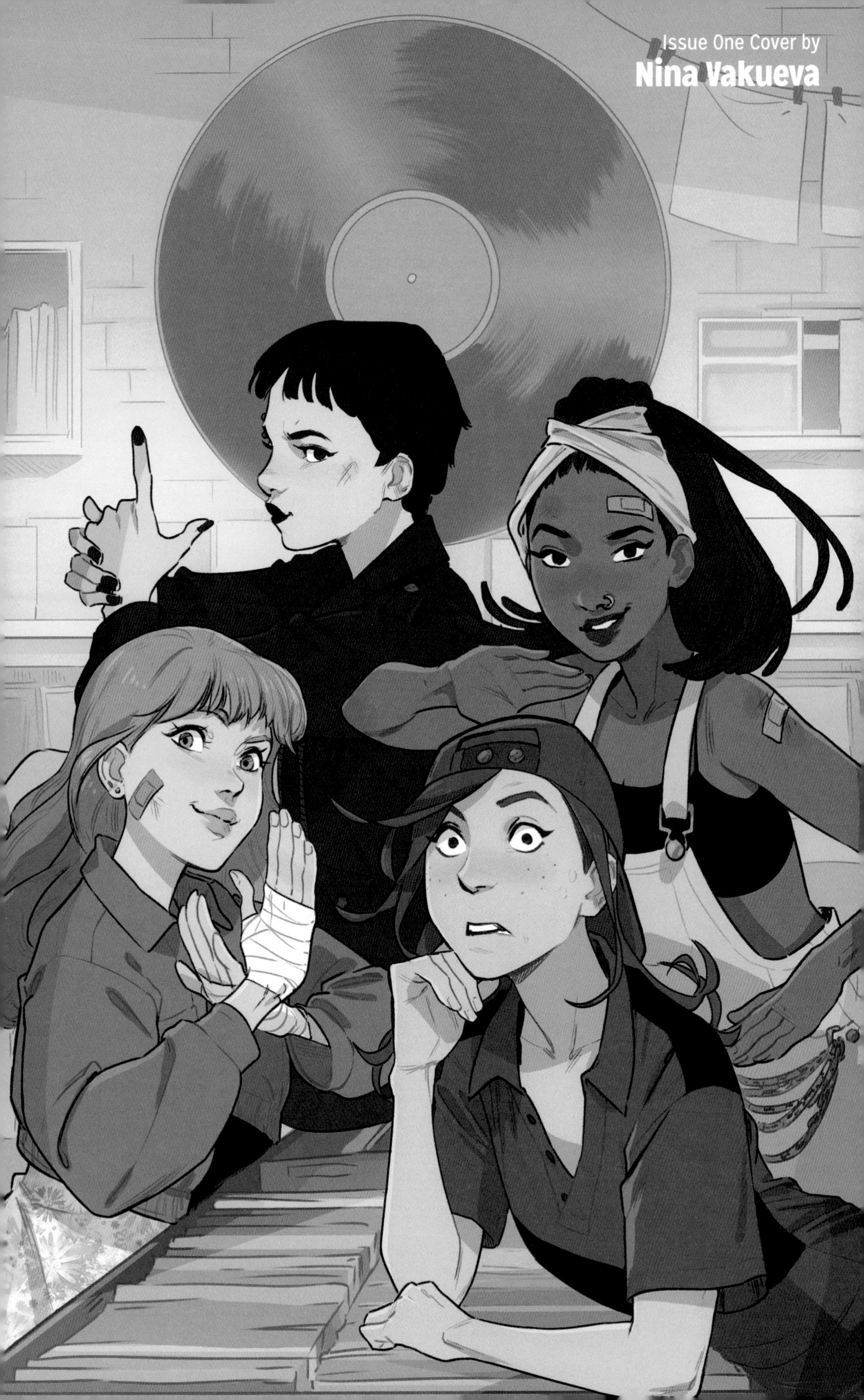
Issue One Cover by
Nina Vakueva

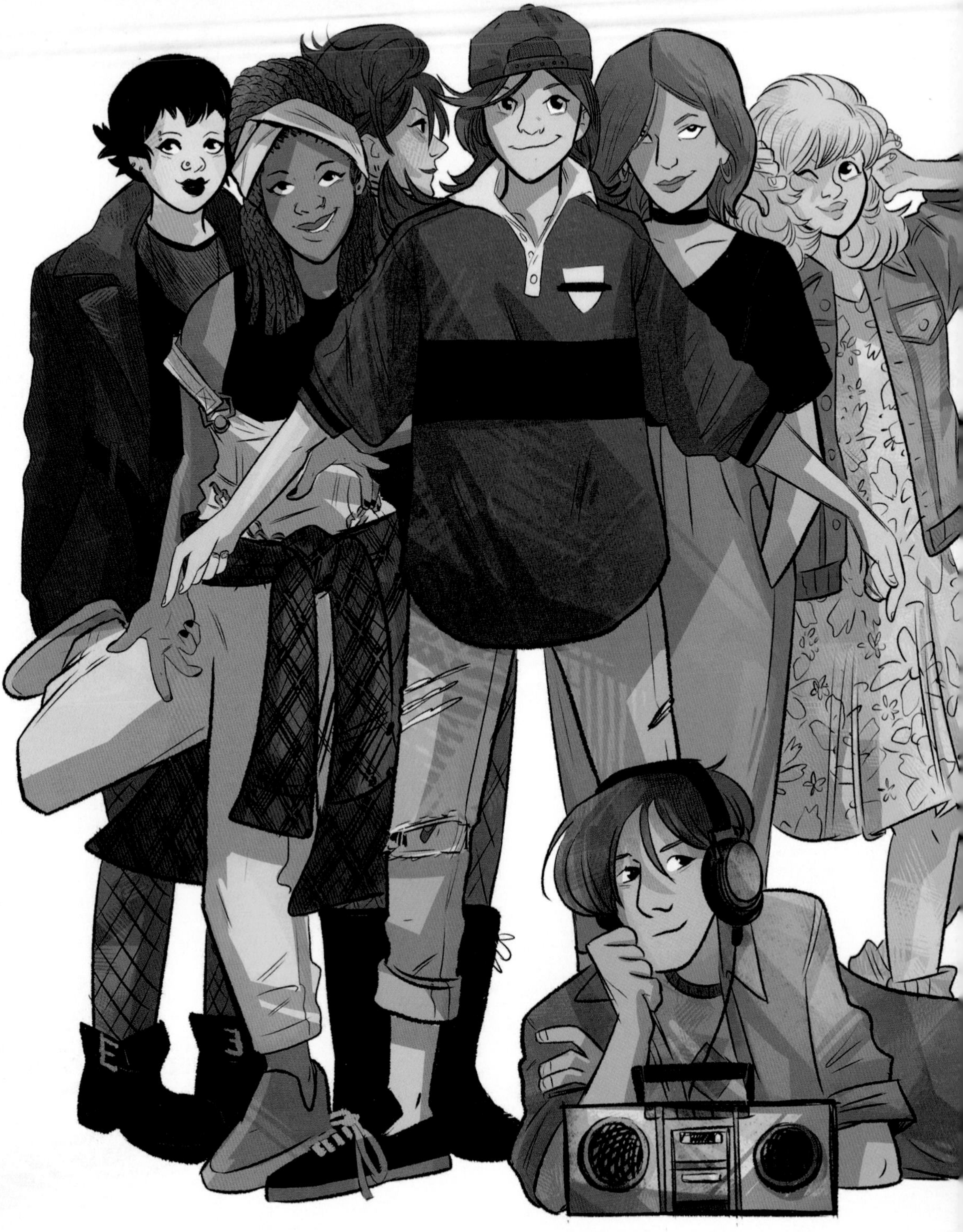

Issue One Teen Movie Homage Variant Cover by
Brooklyn Allen
colors by **Marie Enger**

Issue One Unlocked Retailer Variant Cover by
Veronica Fish

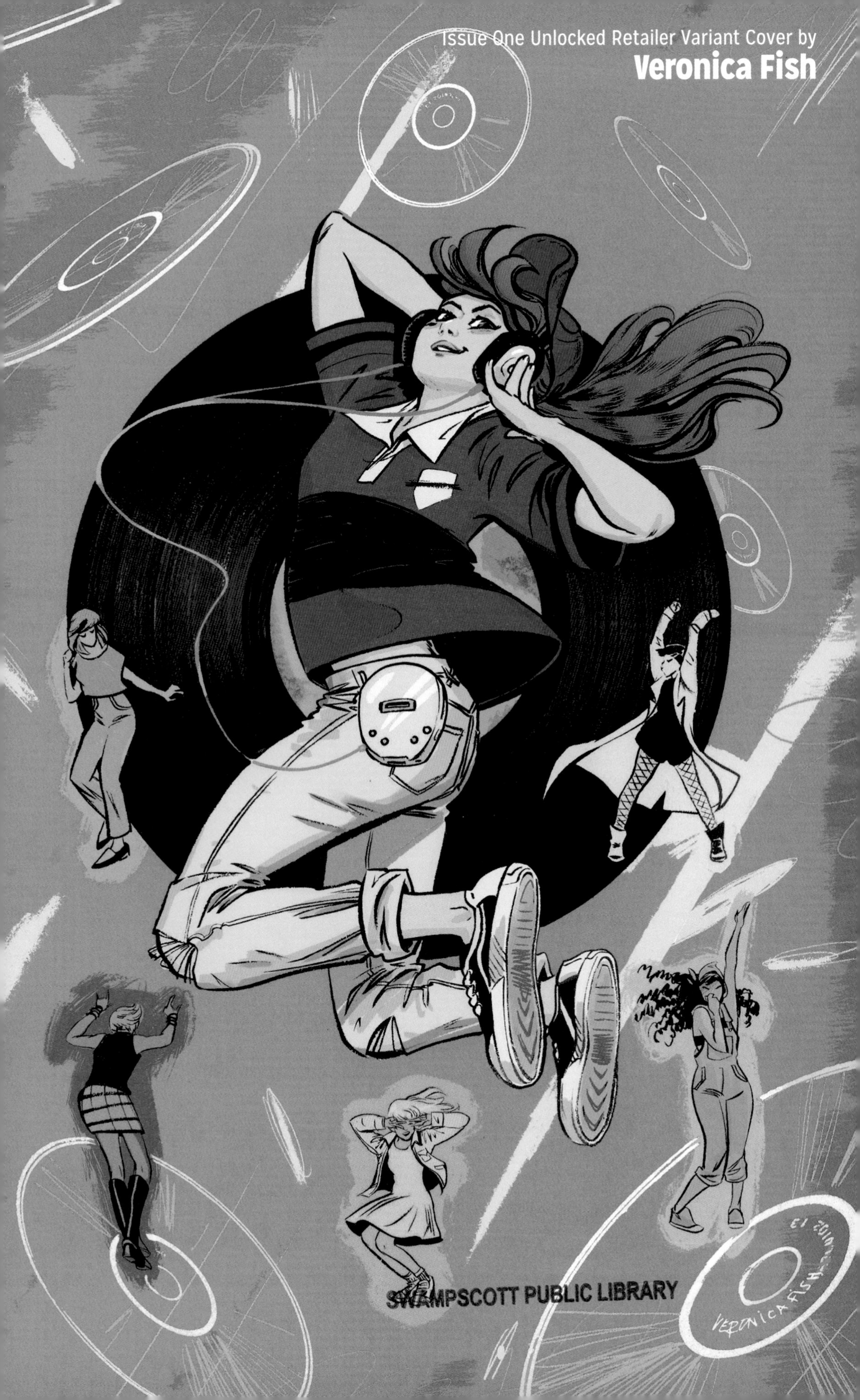
VERONICA FISH

Issue Two Cover by

Nina Vakueva

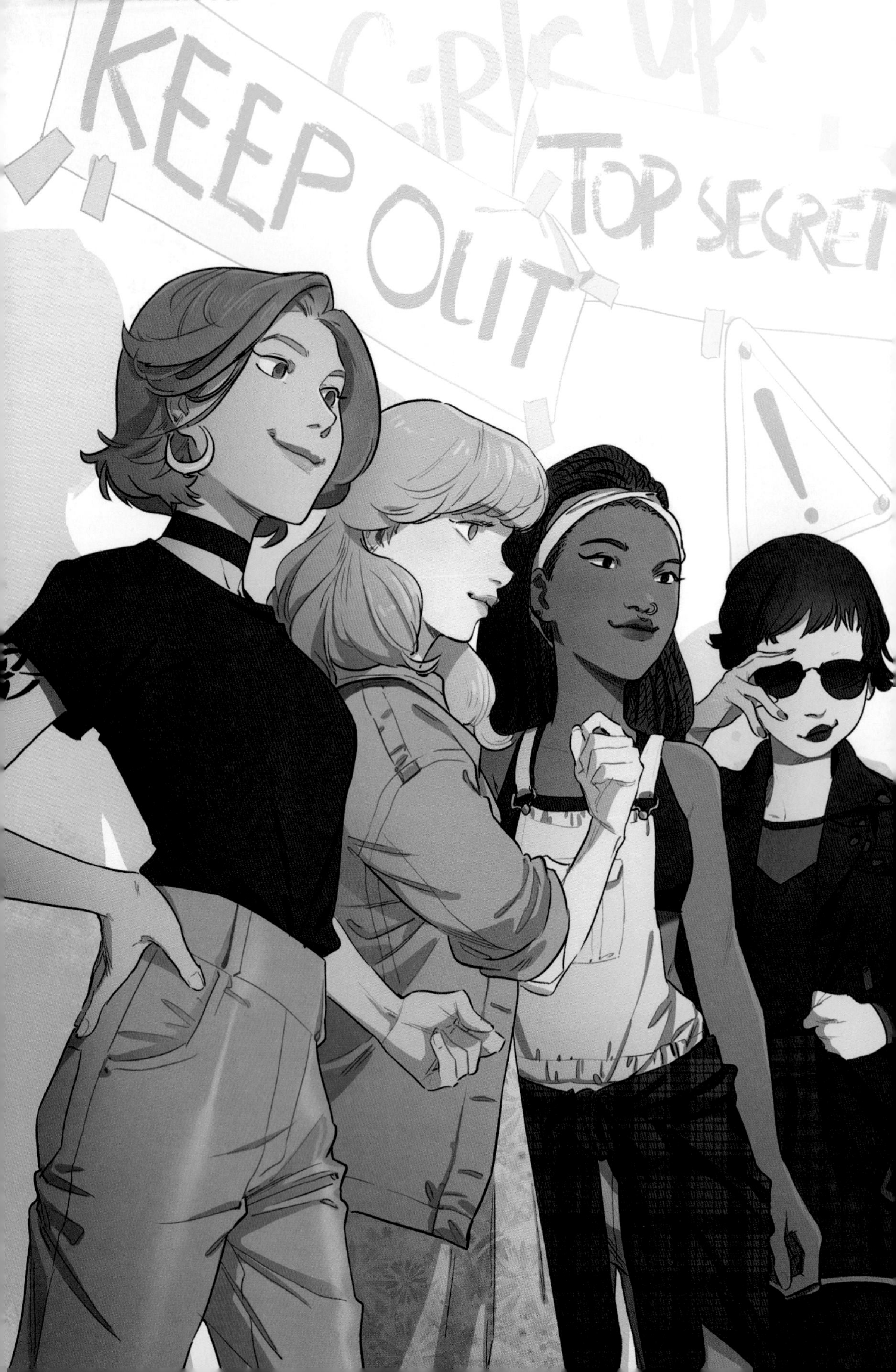

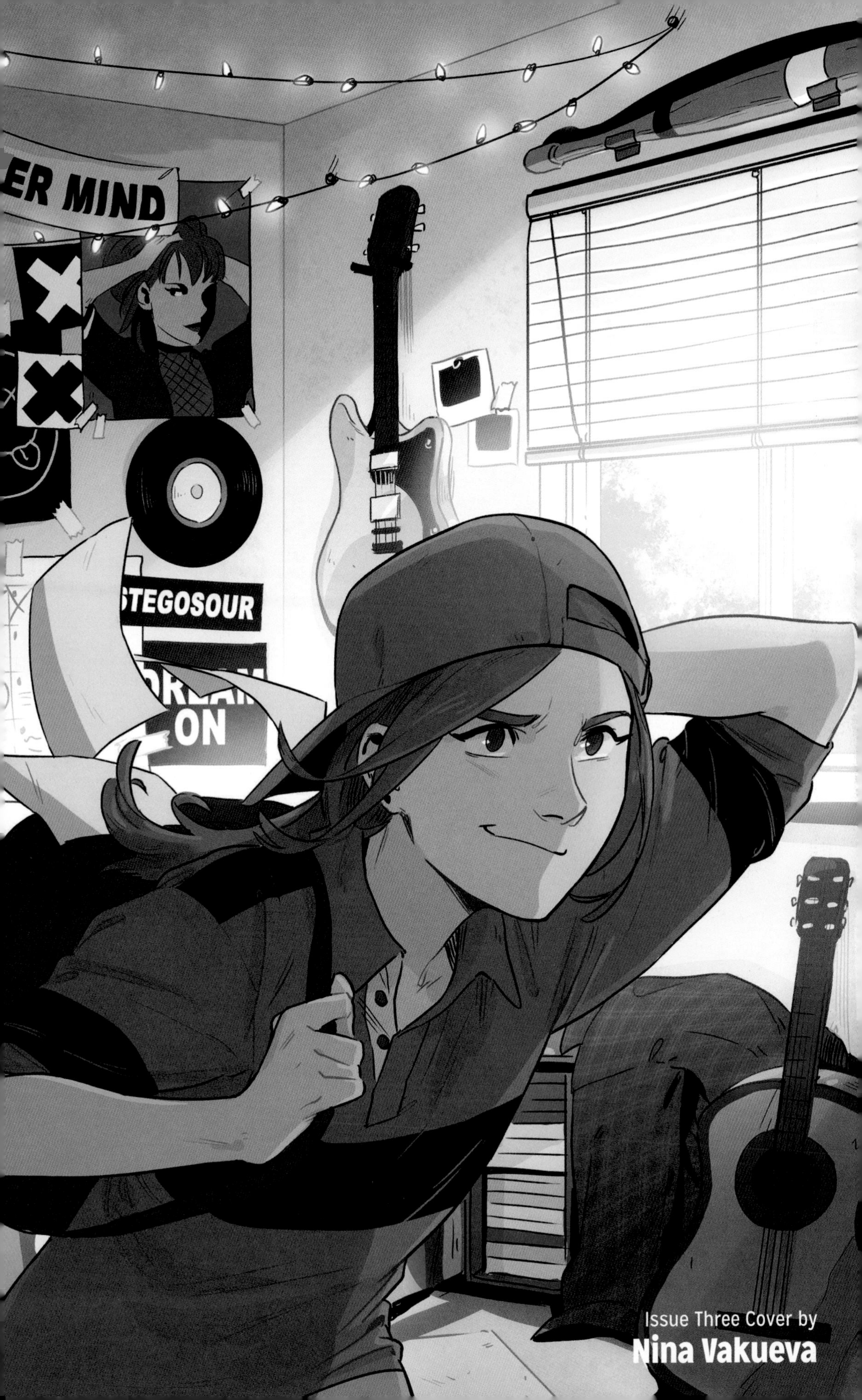
ER MIND
STEGOSOUR
ON

Issue Three Cover by
Nina Vakueva

Issue Four Cover by

Nina Vakueva

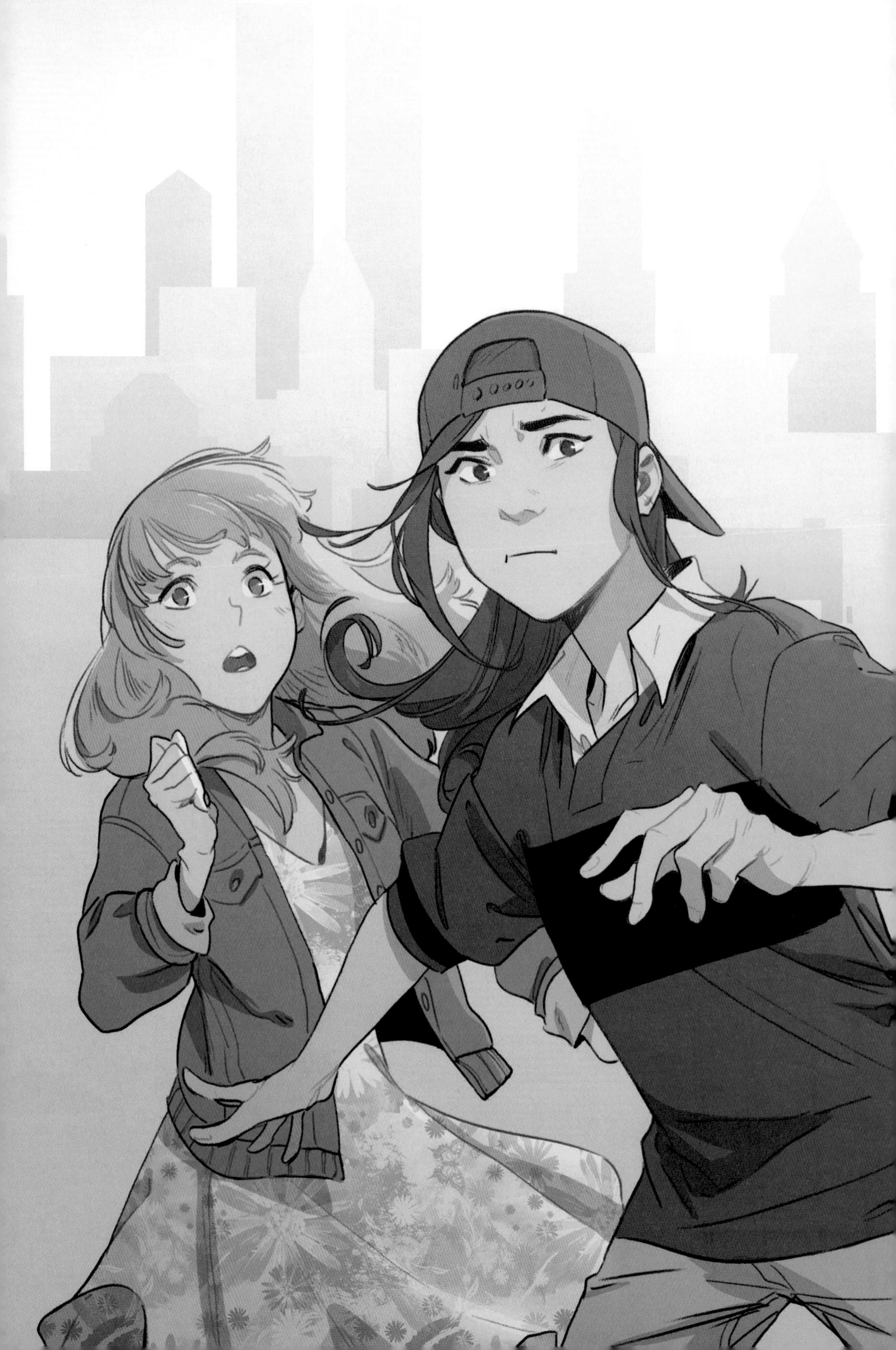

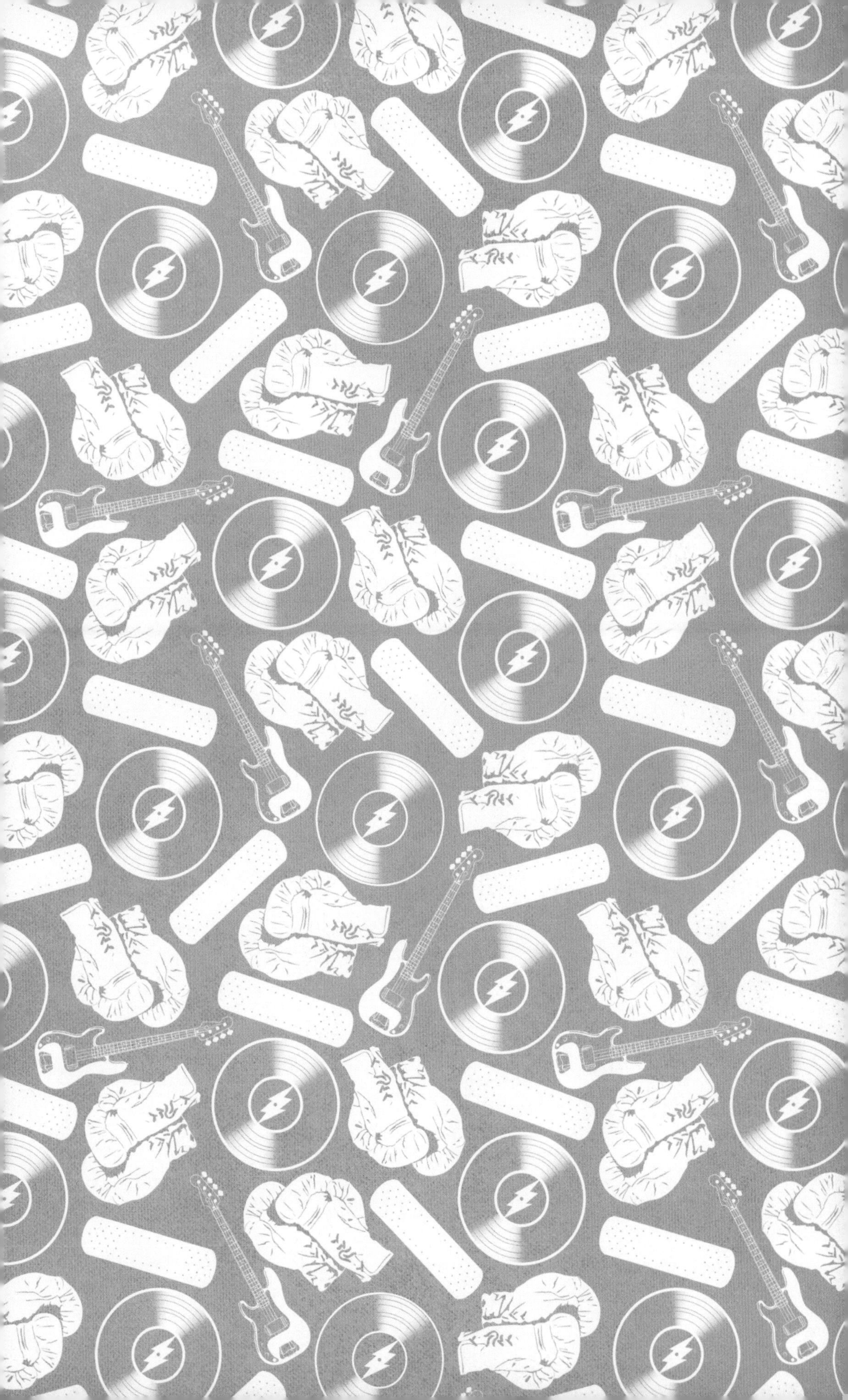

Character Designs by

Nina Vakueva

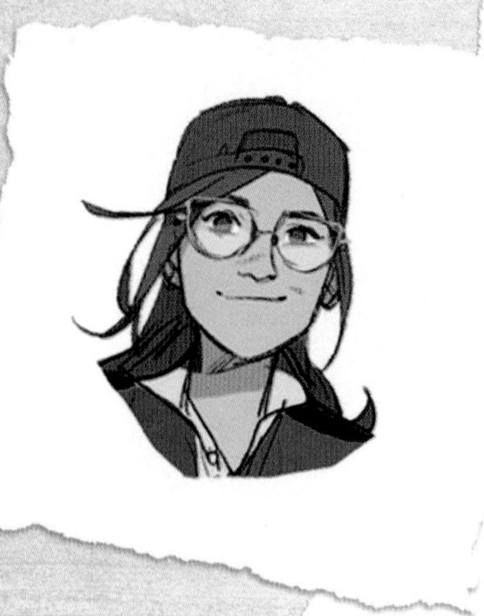

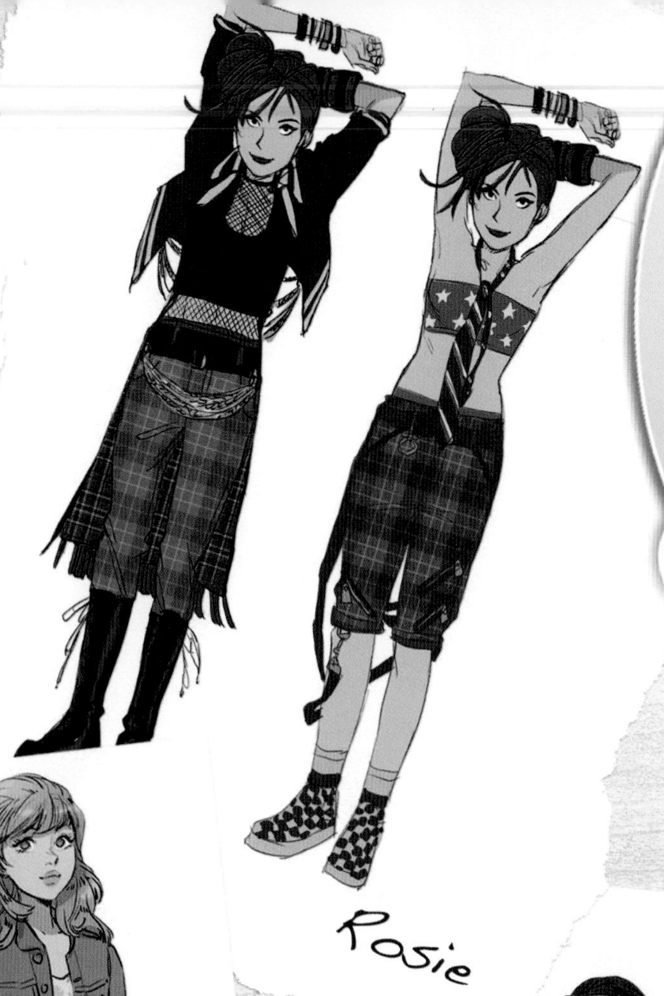
Rosie

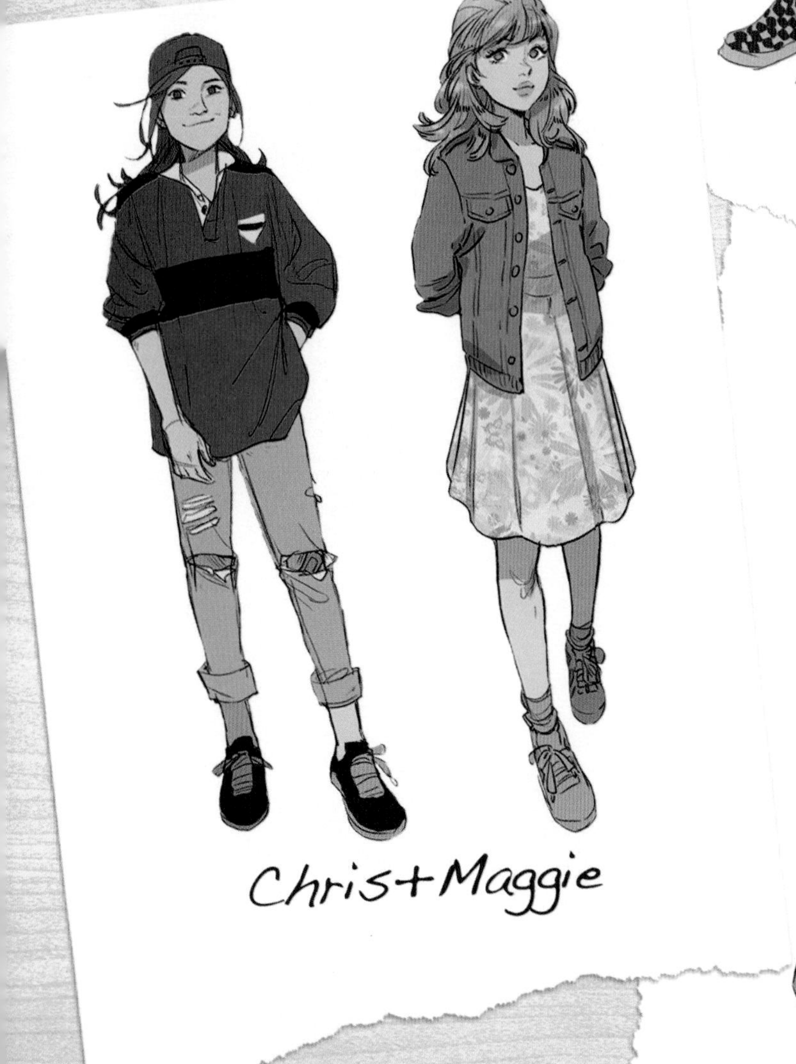
Chris+Maggie

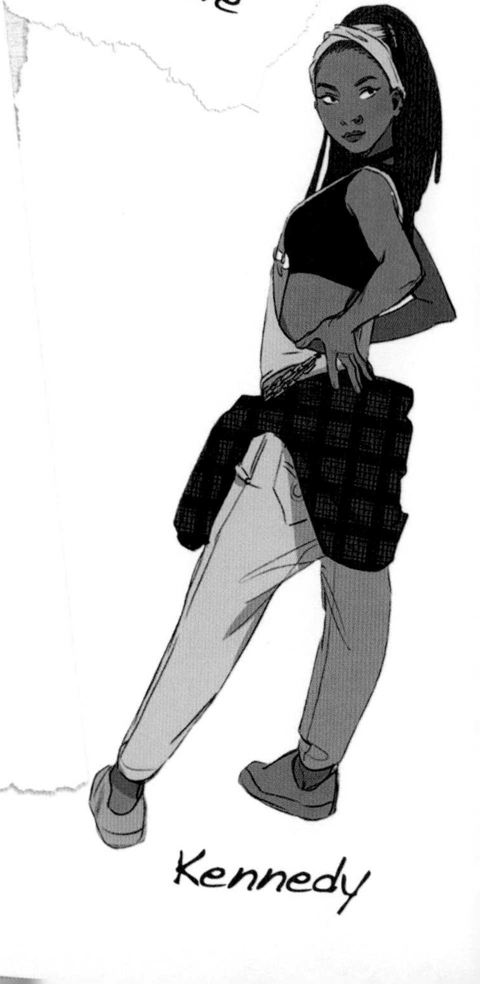
Kennedy

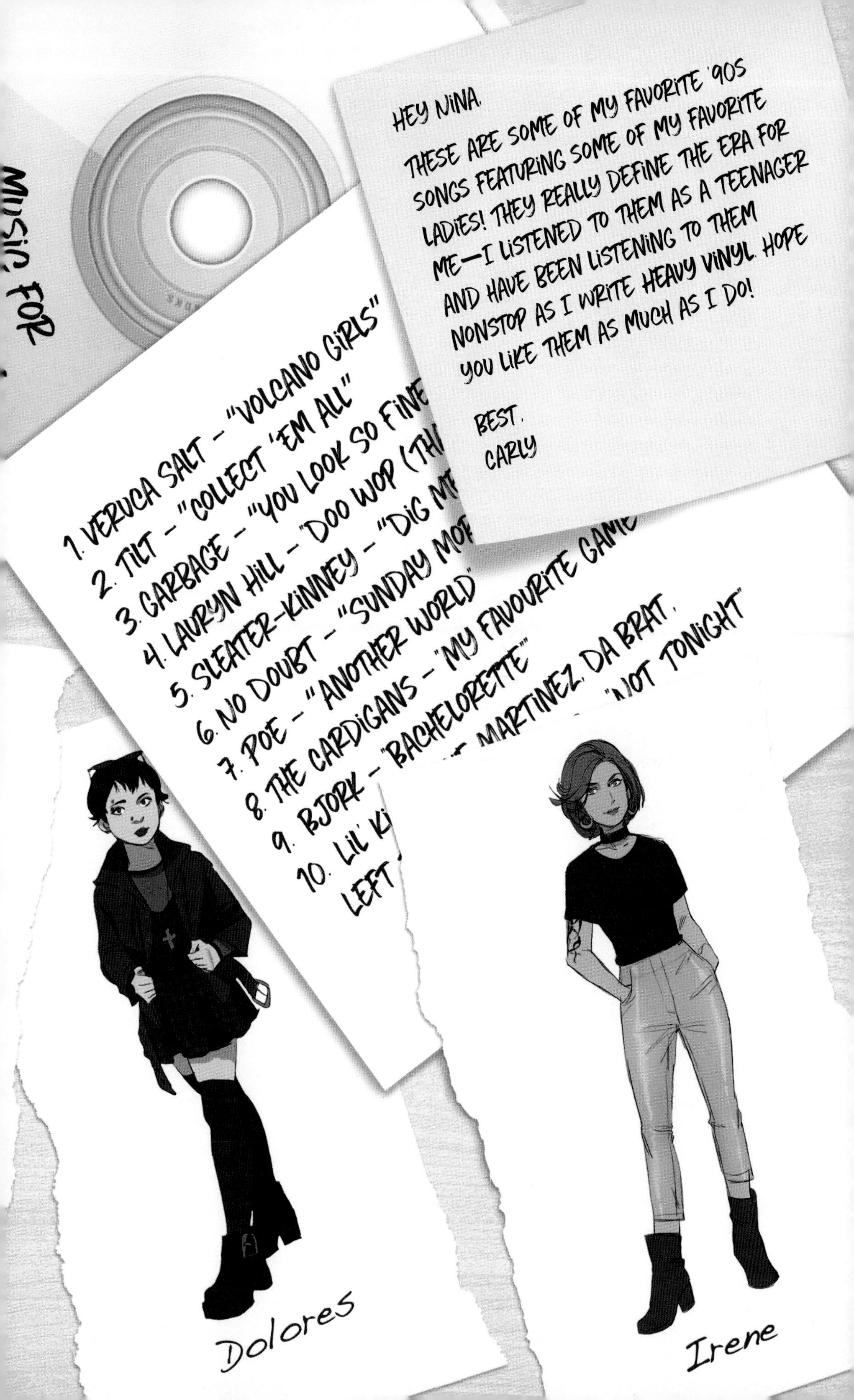
MUSIC FOR
HEY NINA,
THESE ARE SOME OF MY FAVORITE '90S SONGS FEATURING SOME OF MY FAVORITE LADIES! THEY REALLY DEFINE THE ERA FOR ME—I LISTENED TO THEM AS A TEENAGER AND HAVE BEEN LISTENING TO THEM NONSTOP AS I WRITE HEAVY VINYL. HOPE YOU LIKE THEM AS MUCH AS I DO!
BEST,
CARLY
1. VERUCA SALT – "VOLCANO GIRLS"
2. TILT – "COLLECT 'EM ALL"
3. GARBAGE – "YOU LOOK SO FINE
4. LAURYN HILL – "DOO WOP (TH
5. SLEATER-KINNEY – "DIG M
6. NO DOUBT – "SUNDAY MO
7. POE – "ANOTHER WORLD"
8. THE CARDIGANS – "MY FAVOURITE GAME"
9. BJORK – "BACHELORETTE"
10. LIL' K MARTINEZ, DA BRAT,
LEFT "NOT TONIGHT"
Dolores
Irene

DISCOVER
ALL THE HITS

STEVENSON • ELLIS • WATTERS • ALLEN
LUMBERJANES
BEWARE THE KITTEN HOLY
NEW YORK TIMES BESTSELLING SERIES

Allison + Treiman + Cogar
GIANT DAYS
VOLUME ONE

RIBON • FISH • PEER
SLAM!
VOLUME ONE

Hope Larson • Brittney Williams • Sarah Stern
GOLDIE VANCE
Volume One

THE BACKSTAGERS

TYSON HESSE'S
DIESEL
IGNITION

BOOM! BOX

AVAILABLE AT YOUR LOCAL COMICS SHOP AND BOOKSTORE

To find a comics shop in your area, call 1-888-266-4226

WWW.**BOOM-STUDIOS**.COM

Lumberjanes
Noelle Stevenson, Shannon Watters, Grace Ellis, Brooklyn Allen, and Others
Volume 1: Beware the Kitten Holy
ISBN: 978-1-60886-687-8 | $14.99 US
Volume 2: Friendship to the Max
ISBN: 978-1-60886-737-0 | $14.99 US
Volume 3: A Terrible Plan
ISBN: 978-1-60886-803-2 | $14.99 US
Volume 4: Out of Time
ISBN: 978-1-60886-860-5 | $14.99 US
Volume 5: Band Together
ISBN: 978-1-60886-919-0 | $14.99 US

Giant Days
John Allison, Lissa Treiman, Max Sarin
Volume 1
ISBN: 978-1-60886-789-9 | $9.99 US
Volume 2
ISBN: 978-1-60886-804-9 | $14.99 US
Volume 3
ISBN: 978-1-60886-851-3 | $14.99 US

Jonesy
Sam Humphries, Caitlin Rose Boyle
Volume 1
ISBN: 978-1-60886-883-4 | $9.99 US
Volume 2
ISBN: 978-1-60886-999-2 | $14.99 US

Slam!
Pamela Ribon, Veronica Fish, Brittany Peer
Volume 1
ISBN: 978-1-68415-004-5 | $14.99 US

Goldie Vance
Hope Larson, Brittney Williams
Volume 1
ISBN: 978-1-60886-898-8 | $9.99 US
Volume 2
ISBN: 978-1-60886-974-9 | $14.99 US

The Backstagers
James Tynion IV, Rian Sygh
Volume 1
ISBN: 978-1-60886-993-0 | $14.99 US

Tyson Hesse's Diesel: Ignition
Tyson Hesse
ISBN: 978-1-60886-907-7 | $14.99 US

Coady & The Creepies
Liz Prince, Amanda Kirk, Hannah Fisher
ISBN: 978-1-68415-029-8 | $14.99 US

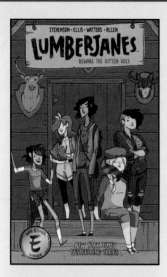

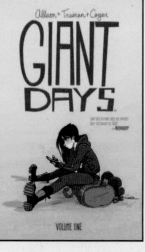

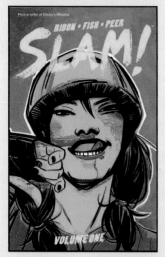

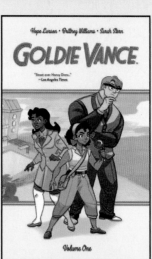

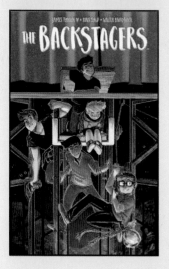

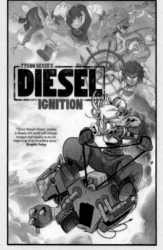